CHRAONOS CHRONICLES

EIDOLON OF FATE

THE PREQUEL NOVEL

JOSHUA EVANS

Copyright © 2022 Joshua Evans.

All rights reserved. No part of this book may be reproduced, stored, or transmitted by any means—whether auditory, graphic, mechanical, or electronic—without written permission of both publisher and author, except in the case of brief excerpts used in critical articles and reviews. Unauthorized reproduction of any part of this work is illegal and is punishable by law.

ISBN: 979-8-88640-109-7 (sc)
ISBN: 979-8-88640-110-3 (hc)
ISBN: 979-8-88640-111-0 (e)

Because of the dynamic nature of the Internet, any web addresses or links contained in this book may have changed since publication and may no longer be valid. The views expressed in this work are solely those of the author and do not necessarily reflect the views of the publisher, and the publisher hereby disclaims any responsibility for them.

One Galleria Blvd., Suite 1900, Metairie, LA 70001
1-888-421-2397

I dedicate this book to all of my children, but especially to my son Josiah and his battle against cancer. This is his second battle against the disease and he is only four years old; he is showing me what true strength really is and how fragile life can be. As I sit here and type this book, he is showing me the true definition of perseverance. Battle on, my son, battle on. And I will be at your side every step of the way.

CONTENTS

Chapter 1   Fate's Vale 1
Chapter 2   Buried Truth 9
Chapter 3   Sparks and Smoke 25
Chapter 4   From Fist to Claw 33
Chapter 5   Lurking Amidst the Snowdrift 52
Chapter 6   Blood of the Resolved 68
Chapter 7   Heart of the Skull 76
Chapter 8   Spider Eye Canyon 85
Chapter 9   Kul'sadar 95
Chapter 10 Crystalline Sun 104
Chapter 11 Scars and Embers 110
Chapter 12 Ca'or 120
Chapter 13 Prowess 127
Chapter 14 Upheaval 135
Chapter 15 Puzzles 145
Chapter 16 Cherry Blossoms 158
Chapter 17 Unlikely Savior 172
Chapter 18 Questions and Quandaries 183
Chapter 19 Anomaly 197

Chapter 20 Wavering Reflections 206

Chapter 21 Mercenaries Divurge... 215

Chapter 22 Toil of the Tundra...226

Chapter 23 Pieces of the Past...244

Chapter 24 An Invitation 252

Chapter 25 Disgraced..258

Chapter 26 Fugitive...265

Chapter 27 Deception 279

CHAPTER ONE

Fate's Vale

The center of the planet was cold and lonely by Aelora Aegus' estimate, cold and not the place that she would choose to die. If it was, in fact, her choice at all, which she was sure it was not. Finding the single entrance to the center of the planet had been rough, the path that snaked through the planet's crust and into the most unbearable of terrain a secret that only a single soul had known about. Lots of money had been the exchange for that piece of knowledge; that and a menacing letter from the King himself. The team that Aelora Aegus had assembled over the countless years had strained under the pressure of the three-month journey. The constant battles of nameless creatures, the dozens of paths and chasms they were forced to navigate in the darkest of darks, and even the rigors of journeying to the core of a planet that was smoldering hot had each of her crew on the edge of complete madness. And now before them stood a giant, grimy marble temple that had somehow been carved into a colossal stone crevice that marked this as, in fact, the center of the very planet that supported so many twisted life forms.

The temple had been built on a stout, rugged plane of stone, with dozens of stone pillars surrounding the temple as the only means of obtaining entrance to the sacred structure. Floating above the sickly-looking sanctuary was hundreds of wispy lights; lights that pulsed to a single rhythm; a rhythm much akin to a beating heart. Despite the flickering lights, the center of the planet was dark enough to hide what lay just beyond the temple, a site that her team had scouted out only minutes before. The core of the planet, a place where time, memories, and energy collided to create and reincarnate what lives on the surface above. The silence was looming and deafening, and gravity only seemed a ghost of what it was on the surface. Her comrades, Jocksen and Mkaile, stood gaping on one side of Aelora, while Boldrem and Tichiko stood with arms crossed on the other; each of them cast in a blue bath of light. The last of Aelora's team, Kordethion, Szuke, and Jjairel were already breaching the great broken temple door, their shadows long and thin and stretching to the scuff marks on Aelora's boots. All her team had to do now was beg the Father of Elders for the only sky'un'grael ever created, a relic of power that was created by the very planet itself. To hold this artifact is rumored to be holding the heart of the planet. Hoisting her soiled knapsack over her shoulder, Aelora found the closest plateau and started her long ascent to the most sacred building ever created. She was Aelora Aegus, and if she couldn't bargain with the Father of Elders, then perhaps this age was never meant to be.

Time. Fate. For some, time and fate are one and the same; for others, they are completely separate entities. For K'vosser Illasa, the meaning of time and fate was blurred to the point where he couldn't distinguish where one started and the other stopped. That was just as well though because he couldn't even tell where he himself was any different from those other two entities. Inside of the phenomenon known as Julian's Fortress, fate, time, and K'vosser were one and the same. All three seemed to exist as individual pieces that created a surreal whole. You see, Julian's Fortress was something of a rarity, a castle that was caught in a stray rift of time that devoured the castle akin to a black hole devouring a star. Some believed that the occurrence happened due to an abnormal accident, their meager brains unable to grasp the severity of a colossal castle just disappearing from the mountains in which it rested upon. K'vosser knew better however. The whole incident had happened because of an artifact called the Azure Rose, a fragment of time that was created out of pieces of sapphire and electumite, constructed to resemble a crystalline rose.

It was K'vosser's deepest secret; he loathed himself for it. No, he *hated himself* for being the one to whisper in the king's ear about glorious treasures to be had at the Gates of Keiadanis. But K'vosser just had to know. He needed to understand what the gates led to, what was residing so close to the realm of Pry'ama. They had eventually found treasures, but they had come at a steep price. In short, the rose had been stolen from the center of the planet to be experimented on. When the Azure Rose had first been discovered, some had taken to calling it the Father of Elder's heart; the Father of Elders was supposedly the keeper of the planet. It was K'vosser that had suggested that Aelora and her team be the ones to travel beneath the planet's crust, to enter the gates. The king himself should have known better than to bargain with the Father of Elder himself just to acquire an artifact that none knew how to activate, or even use. But the king was full of temptation. K'vosser remembered seeing the Azure Rose for the first time, clasped in the hands of Aelora Aegus, her spirit broken from losing her entire team to the wrath of the Father of Elders. Her clothes and armor had been decimated to mere rags of what they once had been, and the only treasure that she'd escaped with, besides the rose, was a knapsack full of colorful orbs that were each pockmarked with dozens of holes, each hole emitting a creeping mist that overflowed from the bag and onto the tiled flooring. K'vosser had seen an orb like them before, in fact, that very orb was within his lab, powering prototype technology that was supposed to be keeping Pry'ama in check. He called the prototype 'THORN', and the one sky'un'grael that he had was the power source. Now that there were several of them in existence? Whose to say what will happen. Curious, that. An anomaly that would disrupt the very fabrics of time if left unchecked, for their could only be one sky'un'grael.

Alas, none had known the repercussions for stealing such a sacred artifact, and K'vosser was the one that ultimately paid for it; the cost was just his mere existence. K'vosser remembered that his team had just finished setting up nine individual evolution stations for nine very special babies, babies that had been created via a very unique experiment. K'vosser remembered the lead scientist of his team bursting into the simple chamber excited, his hands clutching the fabled azure rose. The man rambled on for minutes on end, but eventually K'vosser got the gist of it. The azure rose was theirs now. For weeks they experimented on the fragile artifact, tentatively using various methods and energies on it as if it was capable of demolishing everything within its vicinity.

Despite all manners of experimentation, the artifact refused to respond to any type of tampering. Scientists became baffled after months of experimentation and eventually the Father of Elder's Heart was left resting in the very room where the special babies were residing. It was K'vosser's fault, really. He had been awake for almost two days straight, trying to prepare the last baby of the nine for its evolution process in its special incubator when K'vosser noticed that the entire room was suddenly cast in a violent blue light. It was the azure rose, finally reacting to *something* within its vicinity. Picking the rose up, K'vosser brought it close to his face and gasped at what he saw; he was of course staring at himself in its reflective surface, but his face transformed before his very eyes. His head tilted back and he screamed, his face warping and changing into a twisted mess of what it had been before. It was now furry, his eyes beady, and his nose elongated. He looked nothing so much like an enormous ferret! K'vosser dropped the Azure Rose in surprise, its plummet to the rough floor just enough for the rose to break off one of its sapphire petals.The artifact hit the floor, and time itself seemed to pause and then burst as if a thousand cannons had been fired at once.

It was deep into the night, the only person awake inside of his chambers being himself and this last baby boy. K'vosser and the boy were the only ones that witnessed the very fabrics of time start to shift and shatter all around the room as the azure rose finally awoke from its restful sleep. As time itself seemed to snap and tear all around him, he knew what he needed to do before all of Sparodin broke loose. K'vosser remembered grasping the broken piece of sapphire in his clumsy ferret like hands and setting it down on the stone table beside the screaming baby. K'vosser was dead certain that the baby had been the reason that the azure rose had surged, and now both himself and the baby were invariably tied together in the fingers of fate as the relic exploded with algorithms and inconsistencies of time that K'vosser couldn't even begin to fathom. Memories surged all around K'vosser and the baby as he tried to quickly work, his mind able to function vastly faster than his clawed hands were able to. Moments of time seemed to flicker in and out of existence as fate relinquished its internal secrets. A cooling breeze carrying the fragrance of maple leaves gently rolled across K'vosser's nose, the breeze originating from some unknown age. A miserable pair of blonde women wearing white draping hats flickered for just a few moments beside the stone table, their quivering mouths and tear-stained eyes gazing down at something at the base of their white slippered feet. Acting as one, the pair of women raised their arms and before them appeared a crooked doorway that looked as if it had manifested from the galaxy itself. One woman held a tome while the other possessed a wooden harp; the pair both gazed over their shoulders at something unknown. Both women shook their heads in fear and before K'vosser could make heads or tails of the situation, they flickered back out of existence.

Just a few feet from where the women had stood were a handful of rugged looking warriors, all wearing different manners of weapons and armor as if they had been assembled from all corners of Pry'ama. Their hair and garments billowed against a ferocious wind, each warrior's face painted with the most brilliant of paints. As one, the gang of warriors tipped their heads back and roared a mighty roar, each soldier bathed in some type of brilliant gray light. Just as quickly as they had appeared, they were gone. K'vosser ignored it all; his very existence hung in the balance now and he couldn't let any type of distraction get in his way of living. Grasping the last item in the room that would aid him in surviving, a palm-sized stone cube that rested on one of the many wooden shelves that lined the cellar, K'vosser went to work on his plan. This stone cube was unique, something that he himself had been tinkering with for the better part of five years now. It had been found in an abandoned room in this fortress, and none that K'vosser had spoken to had even an inkling of where it could have originated from. K'vosser had tentatively started calling it the fusion cube because of the artifact's amazing capabilities.

Finding his belt knife, K'vosser sliced open the tip of one of his hairy claws and let the blood dribble onto the center of one side of the cube. The blood seemed to withdraw into the stone cube. Next, K'vosser did the same procedure to the screaming baby, nicking the tip of one of the child's fingers and allowing the few drops of blood to spatter onto another face of the cube. Unlatching the top face of the cube, K'vosser lifted the stone plate up and gently placed within the hollow cube the fragment of the azure rose. This is the part of the process that always astounded people; lowering the stone face of the cube and latching it in place, K'vosser immediately felt as if his very soul slithered inside of himself from both excruciating pain and immeasurable pleasure. K'vosser could almost feel the piece of his soul leave his body and, in turn, K'vosser could feel a new, energetic piece of soul replace what he had just lost. *Now, myself and the baby are one and the same! He is as much a part of me as I am a part of him now,* K'vosser thought to himself desperately. K'vosser's body seemed to shake with spasms as the essence of the azure rose embedded itself within K'vosser. His very mind seemed to expand and contract from random moments and memories that intruded and then settled into his soul, K'vosser screaming as his bones felt as if they were being crushed, snapped, and then remade from second to second, and from the look in the baby's eyes and the screams emitting from him, the baby was experiencing the same pain. K'vosser blacked out.

K'vosser remembered waking up and finding that his experiment had been a complete success. The baby had survived and was now sleeping soundly atop the stone table, and better yet, on both faces of the cube where his and the baby's blood had touched—was now a very detailed picture of himself on one side of the cube, himself still looking like a humanoid ferret, and on the other side of the cube was a picture of the baby. K'vosser did not know yet what these stone pictures represented but, in any case, he broke the cube down by a series of hidden latches and proceeded to pocket the two stone cards. On one card was a detailed picture of himself screaming into the heavens, on the other was an intricate picture of the child resting soundly. He could only shake his head at what that could possibly mean. Retrieving two new stone cards from his stash, K'vosser let his misshapen claws work of their own accord as he reassembled the Cube of Fusion. For the rest of the following day and night, K'vosser busied himself by trapping this last baby within the remaining incubator, the same type of incubator that housed the other eight babies. These incubators and babies had been transported from the headquarters of the Goldenfist Corp. itself after some type of cataclysmic catastrophe had happened, and the duty of installing the incubators here in Julian's Fortress and seeing to the babies being properly incubated had fallen on K'vosser's shoulders. If the evolution process was going to succeed, then this had to be done just right. Even if fate was crushing them in its mighty maw.

K'vosser might be trapped in this bloody humanoid ferret's body and melded into both time and fate, but these babies would leave eventually, and once this specific baby evolves and leaves this fortress, that was when K'vosser had an inkling of a chance of seeing the outside world ever again. All that baby had to do was tap into the power of the azure rose fragment and everything else would be taken care of. K'vosser's soul would replace the child's soul in its body and, in return, the baby's soul would then inhabit K'vosser's body. It was as simple as that, as long as he possessed these stone cards, that is. K'vosser was almost finished with his plan, he just had one more final task to complete. Hobbling over to where the azure rose rested, K'vosser grabbed it with both of his gnarled claws and stared at it once more. Images flashed before his eyes, images of destruction, of stars, of the ocean, and of gargantuan creatures. K'vosser shook his head and snarled at the artifact. He had to do this before he completely lost his free will; it was for the best. Whipping both of his claws behind his head, K'vosser heaved the azure rose through the open window and into the mercy of the broken fabric of time. Almost instantaneously the artifact seemed to... unravel... and where it reappeared was not K'vosser's problem. He just wanted that damn artifact out of his sight.

—⚜—

Nytoria Breannache stood on the edge of the rock face, his eyes disbelieving as he watched an entire fortress unravel into nothing. Sitting at his feet was the chest that he'd been entrusted with by high chancellor Aelthin, a silver chest that was filled with majestic orbs that seeped colored mist from their pores. Aelthin had told him that these relics were too sacred to stay in the confines of a castle. A castle that had somehow disappeared into nothing. Nytoria rubbed at his eyes, his mind in shock. Aelthin told him that he needed to take these artifacts to Cathedral Laondrein, the priests there would know what to do with them. These orbs were very much akin to ones that were written about in the Scripture of Astarial, Aelthin had told him. These orbs *needed* to be at the monastery. And that was precisely what he was going to do. Depression settled in as Nytoria realized that all of his friends and comrades that he'd grown to love had just perished into nothing. Tears fell from his eyes in waves as his cries of despair intermingled with the harsh howling of the wind. Hanging his head, he stoically tucked the chest into the crook of his arm and continued onwards into the cold vale, his eyes glancing back one last time at a phenomenon that only he'd been able to witness. At one of the greatest grave sites that none could see.

CHAPTER TWO

Buried Truth

The Chronicles of Chraonos is a series of tomes that depict what some would call a perfect rendition of history, while others would deem them biased and false. A secret was discovered in a tome known as the 'Eoghan Chronicles'. A secret that told of artifacts and origins. From this secret, murmurings started to occur, murmurings that told of devious endings and perilous beginnings. Events that none could have predicted. Floating amidst the cold winds of change was a dream that a young man had been chasing for several years, an ambition that floated just outside of his reach; you see, it was not just an ambition to help alter a false era, nor was it an ambition to harness older ideology. But it *was* an ambition to help and change this era into something that all could live and thrive in. Resting in front of a young man named Aeven Kvalheim, this ambition established itself in the form of a book, a book that lay forgotten on the grainy sands of an abandoned beach. This young man found himself humbly opening the cover of the book, thus opening the beginning of an age that was not foreseen by even the most tenacious of scholars.

Velara 18th, 1301 - Life, as a book, has a beginning, and an end. Books, just as people, have judgments and words that cannot be understood unless the time is taken to unfold the pages and read what words are scribed.

Words provoke thoughts, thoughts provoke action, and action creates the paths we tread. In short, books—or more importantly, the words that make up the book—are not created out of planning nor out of certainty. Quite the contrary. Both are fashioned out of the thoughts we deem are important enough in the here and now, important enough to repudiate all other thoughts that we might have at the time. Our hearts create the will to pick up the quill and write what we feel is so important that it bursts from our soul, through our fingers and onto the blank paper. I leave this first passage as a memoir for my journey to come, a journey that will take me through the very depths of sparodin and into the domain of this very planet. I shutter at what I might encounter, and yet I must admit that my heart is excited at the thought of finally obtaining one of the fabled artifacts of Laedrea. I leave this passage with a final, passing word: action. Yours truly, Aelora Aegus

Slamming the scarred hardbound cover shut, Aeven Kvalheim had to admit that the crashing waves against the rough, salty rocks held him in a thoughtful peace. It had been days since a moment of rest had found him, and truth be told Aeven was starting to think that the very gods were placing bets against him. Danger seemed to hound him at every corner and yet he still found himself at a dead-end. Truthfully, it wasn't as if he was going out of his way to avoid trouble either; being a mercenary was about the action, the money, and a bloody good start for initiating his career as a bounty hunter. Being hired for someone's dirty work isn't exactly the ideal job, yet if you could kick your boots up on the table at the end of the day beside the crackling fire and have an enthralling story to tell, then that's a day well-earned in Aeven's book. Aeven was sure that Aelora had had the same thoughts about her adventure, at least in the beginning, she did. He'd heard rumors of her and her exploits, and they weren't good. How her diary had washed up on this obscure beach intact was something that confounded him fiercely.

Clasping his gloved fingers around the second item he'd found that morning, an item that was roped together with the scarred book he'd discovered, Aeven lost himself in a warm blanket of contemplation. This item, like the book, was intriguing; it seemed to hold more questions than answers. It was an orb that looked much like a hand-blown glass ball. It was an alluring, dazzling colored blue with layers of depth that Aeven could sit and stare at for hours. Several pearl sized holes pockmarked this orb; each hole producing a colored, misty substance that dissipated when it reached the ground.

Aeven took a literal as well as a metaphorical meaning to the book and orb being tied together; he knew that they had a purpose. A puzzle that would have to come together later. Using the ropes that bound the sphere and book together, Aeven created a small net that the orb could rest within, and then hooked it to his belt. His mind regained focus. The mission he'd undertaken was to find and eliminate a thief named Keyamir Abernathy, a sleek, cunning man that outsmarted even himself and allowed his ambitions get the better of him. Aeven knew that being a mercenary meant that his head hunter never had to explain the reasoning behind his target's demise. All that Aeven needed to know was that Keyamir now possessed an item that held very significant value. The item had been described as some type of artifact of power. That was reason enough for a hit to be put out on a renowned thief, and Aeven was more than justified in fulfilling the job. Stealing property from a lord was an incredibly foolhardy thing to do, but that went without saying.

Aeven was fairly young for being in the mercenary business, was slightly chunky, and not overly tall. He was by no means fat, he had some good muscles on him from years of tracking various criminals across the country side, yet when it came to roughing it, Aeven vastly preferred an inn with spacious room instead of a ragged campsite with a spitting fire. Aeven Kvalheim's hair was dirty dishwater brown, short, and held a slight tint of red, his eyes hazel, and could even be described as powerfully attentive. Adjusting himself atop the fractured boulder, Aeven heard his buckskin tunic groan as he hoisted himself to his sore feet, the blatant view of the brilliant blue ocean grasping Aeven's desire to quit the mercenaries life altogether and just enjoy life for what it was. There was no money to be had in that, though.

Aeven found his thoughts drifting to a time when men such as Keyamir had no room to exist. A time when justice drove people's hearts, not harnessed their wallets; a time when knights were honored and not rebuked in common society. It was a different era now, however. People sold whatever information you needed from them, for a price. That's how he'd tracked the thief this far along the coast. Aeven had spent the last fortnight camping around the outskirts of the small city of Koronin, dead certain that the estranged thief would have found refuge amidst one of the dozens of caverns surrounding this isolated beach. Instead, Aeven found himself with nothing but a wandering mind and a battered tome.

Involuntarily, his eyes wandered to the book's cover, the author's name scribed neatly in the lower left corner. Aelora Aegus. Long dead, Aelora Aegus was a conqueror that tore enemies asunder. She was a passionate soldier who walked the country when society produced warriors of epic hearts, of colossal spirits, and of ghastly deeds. A time when men tampered with the soul of the galaxy to create an abomination so abhorrent and disgusting that fighters such as Aelora had to intervene with bravery and guile to defeat an entity that goes unnamed to this day. Using a combination of artifacts and divine energy, the men of that age tried to create what was not meant to be, and ultimately the creation had to be locked away somewhere where even the most powerful of men were rebuffed. According to lore, the first and last beast that was constructed was eventually imprisoned underneath the most distant ocean. That's what the lore said, at least. Aeven knew how easy it was to change what was written within a book, though, so he took that story with a grain of salt.

Shaking his head, Aeven eventually threw his tattered cloak around his shoulders when the eyes of the stars started to blink at him from the sky. Vaulting off of the boulder, Aeven turned his back on the foggy ocean and made his way down the sandy shoreline towards Koronin before the sun completely set. Keyamir was not here and that meant that his plan needed to be reevaluated, as did his gossip that he'd gathered about the lone rogue. Either he'd been fed a lie, or Keyamir had found an escape route that Aeven wasn't privy to. It was nearly twilight when Aeven made his way through the front gates of the rustic town.

The few buildings that he could see were simple, small houses with curls of smoke snaking their way to heaven's doorsteps. The cobbled road that Aeven found himself on was more of a bereavement than anything and could be better labeled as a hole-ridden trail than an actual road. Aeven's fingers slowly found the collar of his dark, knee-length jacket and yanked it higher as he ascended uphill, his paranoia and anxiety screaming at him. Being a mercenary made you more enemies than friends. Aeven diplomatically nodded at a lone man that was smoking from a pipe, the stranger propped against a simple lamppost. The man turned away into the shadows. Koronin was not a very well guarded city, the town so isolated from the rest of the country that it oftentimes went forgotten when concerning the lords and ladies of the land. That's why it made it such a great destination point for thieves such as Keyamir. In lieu of that thought, Aeven couldn't help but loosen his bastard sword from its sheath. In Aeven's experience, you can never be too mindful in a forgotten city, even when you were just passing though it.

Skulking from shadow to shadow, it wasn't long before his eyes pinpointed an inn set discreetly back from the rest of town. He'd passed up this inn several times already, he was in too big of a hurry to investigate a shoddy inn. Now that he was sure that his information he'd gathered had been bad, he was in desperate need of a clue of where to go now. He also needed refreshed in the worst way, and the prospect of going for even a whole night without any type of food was not appealing in the least. Breathing deeply, Aeven pushed the thick oak door open silently, his eyes ravaging the room. It was empty of patrons. The smell of roast and potatoes caressed his senses. Finally deciding that there was no danger to be had, Aeven strode around the room carefully, a chuckle escaping his throat.

The furniture in here was gregarious and, for lack of a better word, obnoxious. Their were half a dozen cedar carved lounge chairs spaced sporadically around the lounge area, with dazzling orange and yellow striped pillows thrown atop them. Elegant, wooden barstools lined the bar haphazardly, and thick, oaken bookshelves rest against the walls that were bursting with books. Rugs and tapestry of all colors and sizes decorated the interior of the inn, some of the upholstery making

Aeven squint because of how bright they were. He seemed to be the only patron, which meant that hopefully he was free of danger for the time being. Aeven marched up to the well-used counter and hailed the owner, a tall, massive man with a wealth of scars and a thick beard that tumbled down his chest. The man's clothes were ragged pieces of cloth that have certainly seen better days, and the sword that hung at his side was speckled with spots of rust along its blade. His attention so focused on the spectacle of a man, it took Aeven a moment to notice that the grizzled warrior had company; a lady, very sleek and tall, and lack of a better word, she was simply majestic. Her clothes were immaculate, her dress a beautiful pale blue that could almost be described as transparent. Her face was serene, not a mar or scratch to be seen, and her eyes were the darkest of greens, akin to a forest right after a storm.

Nodding his head once towards her in a friendly fashion, Aeven pulled up one of the stools and made himself comfortable, his leather pack and hefty sword crashing to the floor beside him as he unburdened himself. Aeven had to admit that it took all of his guts not to get up and walk out that front door; this inn had a very disorienting vibe that he wasn't in the least bit comfortable with. He knew this town was small, but Aeven being the only patron here only singled him out for any that were looking for him specifically. Aeven could fight and defend himself, that was for sure; if several fighters tried to do him in at once, however, that would be a different story. Aeven had a sinking feeling that Keyamir didn't steal that artifact for himself, he was most likely just a middle-man for someone of higher power. If that person of higher power caught wind that Aeven was hot on Keyamir's trail, there would certainly be trouble. Aeven would just have to make his visit quick.

Two sets of eyes rested upon him; one set with curiosity, the other with knowledge, but both with a hint of wariness. Both waited for Aeven to speak. Fumbling for the right words, Aeven took a poke at an obvious statement, "Is that a pot roast I smell?" Beating the disgruntled man to the punch, the lady answered quite lightly, her radiant smile reminding Aeven of a caring mother.

"Why, yes, it is. Wait here, honey, and I'll be back with more food than you'll know what to do with." Murmuring softly, the elegant woman disappeared through a pair of double doors that led into the kitchen. Grunting, the man turned and headed up a flight of stairs that rested in the corner of the inn, his loud footsteps slowly fading as he reached the upper floor. Humming a familiar tune to fill the loud silence, Aeven wheeled around on his stool, taking another fleeting look around the room. A beautiful chandelier hung low from the ceiling, a semi-large piece of art comprised of polished antlers and runny candles. The candle's flames threw flickering shadows across the spacious den. Surprisingly, the one window that Aeven could find was placed above the crumbling redbrick fireplace. This small window was comprised of blue-tinted glass that depicted a mural of the sea.

Scattered around the room were paintings of various colors and sizes, though they all had one thing in common: dark undertones. Aeven's interest was piqued. Sliding off of his stool, Aeven found his boots guiding him to the closest canvas. It wasn't long before Aeven was making a small tour of the lounge, his background of attending countless noble festivities allowing him to gauge the artwork for what they really were; priceless and very rare as it turned out. It was once said that you could tell a person's motives, passions, and dreams by how heavily he paints. The darker the strokes and medium, the darker the personality of the painter. A thought that never seemed to have abandoned Aeven. Finishing his short-circuit of the room, it was the second to last painting that held Aeven in a trance of intrigue and question.

The painting was of a shadowed grove that possessed large, warped trees. In the center of the woods, and which seemed to be the focal point of the whole painting, was a large silver plinth with runes and engravings along the side of it. At the base of this majestic pedestal was a handful of blue roses, all thriving on the shadows and darkness that engulfed them. A faint, bluish light seemed to be emanating from the roses.

Sitting atop the dais was a large, leather-bound book. It was closed and no apparent writing could be seen to give this book any sort of name. It was a pretty thick tome and the leather looked fairly new, so Aeven assumed that it could possibly be just a blank book. With it being just a painting, however, it was just too hard to tell. Laying on the ground beside this plinth was what looked to be a small, blue harp, golden writing scripted at its base. Each string was depicted of a separate shade of blue; the smallest string being the lightest blue, and the largest being the darkest. Aeven could only imagine what thoughts were gripping the artist's mind as the falls from his brush strokes fell atop the canvas. Even though it was all Aeven could do to tear his eyes away from the painting, his thoughts never really stopped swirling the mysterious image through his head. A light pop from the fire brought Aeven back to the present, and with a small frown, he took refuge on one of the two large sofa chairs positioned around the fireplace.

Picking up on the quiet creaking of the kitchen's double doors, Aeven had just enough time to look up before the beautiful lady was upon him with the delicious smelling pot roast, she herself having acquired a plate of food. The powerful aroma was enticing, its fumes filling his head with thoughts of famish and starvation; he'd lived off of scraps for the past two days and he was ready for a full meal. Both parties made swift work of their food in silence, Aeven's eyes sporadically scanning the room as he waited for his stunning hostess to finish her meal. Naturally, his eyes inevitably came to rest on that mystifying painting. It pulled at him. Bringing his head back around, Aeven caught the lady studying him, watching him as a man might watch a horse he was about to procure. Her eyes were fierce, possessing both knowledge and desire with equal tenacity. Taking the initiative, Aeven haphazardly dropped his plate and utensils onto the warped floorboards beside him, words spilling out of his mouth with no forethought.

"I was wondering if you could tell me how that confounding painting came to be here in your quaint inn," he started, his thirst for knowledge getting the better of him. "The skill that went behind that artist's vision, his ardor and awareness for depth, it's nothing short of flawless. If I were to make an educated guess, I'd say that he had a legendary secret to share and lack of a better means to render his visualization. It almost seems as if the painting is a key, or, perhaps, a clue."

"No," she answered curtly. "I would describe the painting as a portrayal of a secret I wouldn't want to be known to all." She then chuckled lightly, her face becoming flushed. "What would you do if you had a secret to tell but had to make sure that it remained obscure? You can't just write it down for anyone to read. Sometimes you just have to get…*creative.*"

"I don't understand." Aeven scratched his head in bewilderment, his eyes scanning the painting once more. "It is just a painting, isn't it?"

"Well, it is in a way. As you can see, yes, it is just a painting. But with every picture, there are a thousand words to be told, as they say. So, you see that overly large book on the pedestal?"

"Yes, I noticed. To me, the painter depicted it to look as if the book could be empty of writing, or, in the very least, rarely used. You're telling me that their is a buried truth within this picture?"

"Well, the word "truth" can sometimes be subjective. But you are right. Now that book was painted to look as pristine as possible because why, do you think?" She then winked and nodded at Aeven, apparently wanting him to guess her answer.

"Because the tome's been hardly used!" Aeven proclaimed, standing up and getting a better look at the dark picture. Breadcrumbs tumbled off his shirt and onto the warped wooden floor. "Why would someone go to all of that trouble to hide a truth within a painting if the object of the painting is, for lack of a better word, an empty book?"

"Because to be able to tell a true telling of the story can be hard if the story itself wasn't jotted down correctly the first time. Especially if the artist knew both sides of the story. Who says that this is the only tome depicting a version of the hidden truth?"

"Great point." Aeven admitted. "Especially if the real "truth" isn't something that the majority would want known."

Leaning forward, the lady made sure to lock eyes with Aeven, her deep green eyes suddenly growing very intense and focused. "Not necessarily the majority, but more like the "powerful". I am speaking of the Eoghan Chronicles. Specifically the Saltheol Chronology."

"The story of the lost nation of Tai'drasial? If I remember right, the story was about how the realm of the aor'sii was brought down by a lone man with a very dark heart. Yeah, I've heard of it, nothing more than a myth, they say." Aeven leaned forward, meeting the lady's gaze, his attention fully grasped by this beautiful lady's implication of this myth being factual and not just some old wives' tale told to scare children into behaving. He felt guilty that he was giving into this lady's tale and not seeking out information about Keyamir and his whereabouts, however this knowledge *could* help him at a later date. Possibly.

"Correct. The Sanctuary of Peace, or more appropriately, Tai'drasial, was indeed a prosperous realm. Long before man was created, this world was inhabited by beautiful beings known as aor'sii. They looked like men but with slight differences. Where the average man was a bit stocky, an aor'sii was sleek and lanky, reaching about seven feet tall as an average height, for them. Generally, their skin had a golden glow about them, and their hair ranged anywhere from fiery red to deep-set black. These aor'sii were a very unique race. What set them apart the most from the race of man, however, were their grand wings. Usually the same color as their hair, these wings were sleek and gleaming, spanning anywhere from ten to twelve feet in length. Where an average bird feather is generally too light to give a description, an aor'sii feather makes bird feathers feel as heavy as boulders. Aor'sii truly did have the gift of the wind."

Shifting back in her seat, the lady continued with all the serenity of a queen. "Aor'sii also had a very deep intellectual capacity, making man look about as smart as a village idiot. These beings were no fools. Tai'drasial started out as a simple city but eventually grew into something much more, a phenomenon that words cannot even begin to describe. This one city stretched for leagues on end, shining walls and graceful towers marking the land with an overwhelming splendor. Every aor'sii helped in the construction of it as well. Aor'sii did not have any nobles or peasants, they did not have any defining rank into society. All were equal."

Shaking his head, Aeven settled back into his own chair, the crackling fire putting in its own input. "Yes, that is a grand tale, but some of it doesn't make sense. How is it possible that there weren't any ranks in their society? Didn't aor'sii have any feelings, such as thirst for more power? There had to be someone that was keeping the power-hungry in check. No being can be *completely* perfect. They had to have some type of flaw or else they'd still be here to this day."

"And they did. But you have to understand that this particular race of aor'sii had an overall sense of duty. Above all else, they knew that peace was the ultimate answer to a long life. They knew, like I'm sure that man does, that all war does is bring strife to the land and people. Every last aor'sii knew this. Working together, they created a vast, grand city that survives even today. But like I said, these were very intelligent creatures. They also knew that power does pull at a man's heart like the sun pulls at the moon; and the aor'sii were no exception to this. Their were few creatures more powerful than the aor'sii, and even less that wanted to confront them. And it was this theory that the aor'sii harnessed. With much apprehension, these brave aor'sii combed their own realm, along with surrounding lands for the surviving godlike creatures that held more power than they themselves did. They searched for creatures born of the planet that were on the cusp of extinction. For several decades they searched, scouring the deepest of canyons and the highest of mountains for any sign of life.

"Through vast forests they searched, rifling amongst trees as colossal as the titans of lore, and amidst the oceans they gleamed, flying through heavenly storms for the surviving beasts of old. And with much vigilance, they were victorious. They found dominant, territorial beasts that were more than capable of ravaging a city in one night. Beings so powerful that the very lands themselves quaked with fear. These mystical creatures were later designated as the chorr'galls. With each creature caught, the aor'sii created an immanent pact, a pact that served both races' benefit. Should any one aor'sii rise in power to try and dominate the rest, these newfound creatures would intervene and eliminate this power-hungry individual. Being as intelligent as the aor'sii were, they foresaw that this protection would only last for a short time seeing as how their own lifetime spanned well past that of any other living creature, including the lifespan of these new chorr'gall beasts.

"Hence the second half of this newfound pact. Like I had said, each creature that they had managed to find was on the brink of extinction, the rigors of age, and later, man, having gotten the best of each species.

And it was with this that the aor'sii used to bargain with. For having the aide against any rise in power, the aor'sii were willing to construct alters against the fabrics of time itself for each of these creatures to live in." Reaching for her ornately decorated cup, the lady took to studying Aeven over the rim of it as she took a long drink of her wine. Her attentive eyes held the crinkles of a hidden smile. She already seemed to know what he was going to ask.

"Against *time itself?* How is that even possible?" Aeven spat, his own simple cup plummeting to the floor. His own wine was long gone. Crossing his arms, Aeven tried to still his brash thoughts. With a slight glimmer in her eyes, the lady continued her tale.

"Well for all purposes, these aor'sii were very spiritual. Altering time was a small feat for them, considering that the god that they had revered with an undying passion was always at the center of their motives. Put simply, if Erenara didn't approve, then they didn't do it. To disrespect her was blasphemy to them. In a way, I guess that you can say that Erenara and the aor'sii had a pact themselves. The aor'sii gave their god holy and unyielding reverence, and in return, the aor'sii received slightly heightened powers and blessings that a typical creature is denied."

Aeven took to brooding this mysterious lady's story, all thoughts of Keyamir now gone for the night. For a time, all that could be heard was the slight patter of raindrops pelting the roof of the inn; that, and the soothing crackles of the dying fire. A few questions still bothered him though, and making sure he worded it right, Aeven finally spoke. "The race of the aor'sii seemed very powerful with their extraordinary city that spanned for leagues and their ability to even alter time itself with the blessing of Erenara. Who is this dark-hearted man that you'd mentioned before, the one that brought the aor'sii to their knees? Weren't the men of that age in support of the aor'sii? Not to mention these great creatures that were supposed to stop this rise in power, whatever happened to them, and why didn't they intervene? Wasn't that part of their pact?"

With a thoughtful look on her face, the lady gently set her cup on the floor, the sounds of the fire quieting down as if in anticipation of her answers. With an undertone of grief, she continued her sad tale.

"Towards the end of the aor'sii's existence, they had invited men to live amongst them in their grand city of Tai'drasial. They had an idea, a great idea in my opinion, that if aor'sii and man could live together in peace, the land would be just that much stronger. Hence, the Sanctuary of Peace. At first, the declaration that man was welcome in their land had no effect. The race of man was, at best, still fearful of the race of aor'sii. And who can blame them? The aor'sii were very intimidating. Of course the aor'sii knew this and so made an offer of peace towards the race of man. With almost little bargaining, the aor'sii convinced man to let them construct four cities exclusively for the race of man, no strings attached. And with each city, the aor'sii would teach them many trades, ranging from the ways of the artisans to the combat styles of the Drey'une Crusaders.

"With time, the race of man grew to trust the valiant aor'sii; the bond between the two races grew stronger with each passing year. It was a true miracle how these two races intertwined with each other, creating an exceptionally unique land full of ambition and knowledge."

"It must have been a dark day indeed when someone could bring an end to something so brilliant." Aeven interjected, shifting slightly in his chair. "So, how did it happen? The downfall of the aor'sii, I mean."

Taking a prolonged sip of her wine, the lady's eyes seemed to fill with an ocean's worth of tears, her voice tinged with more than just a little sadness. "When the aor'sii felt the need to keep their own civilization in check, they enlisted those colossal creatures that I told you about earlier to keep their power-hungry brothers at bay. But being as intelligent as they were, they failed to realize that the creatures had only sworn loyalty to the race of aor'sii. The pact said nothing about the race of men. The chorr'gall were still very much bitter at being imprisoned for eternity in temples that were hidden away in the most desolate of places. They were forced to hold up their end of the pact, but that didn't mean that they had to rise up any further than they had to. With the invitation of man into the aor'sii sacred lands, it gave just the opportunity that Kordethion Melelanis was looking for to bring the aor'sii to their demise."

"Kordethion," Aeven stated softly to himself, forgotten knowledge resurfacing. " If I remember right, Kordethion was a man that had surpassed all fellow scholars, reveling in what his writing had created for him. Fame. Grandeur. And if I remember right, he was also a sociopath; devoid of feelings, faith, or passion. To make his family name renowned, Kordethion had destroyed what so many tried desperately to create: unification between several realms. So he was responsible for the destruction of the aor'sii as well?!" Bowing his head in trepidation, Aeven waited a moment before speaking again. "This man was just flat-out bad news, it seems." Aeven worded his next question softly. "The chorr'galls were supposed to stop something like that though, right? I know that Kordethion was just a man, but still—"

"It was a technical loophole, but one that Kordethion saw almost immediately when he learned of this pact between the creatures and the aor'sii. You have to understand that Kordethion was indeed just a man, but a man with a vast amount of knowledge. And that's what gave him his edge. Like I stated earlier, the chorr'gall weren't exactly impressed with their side of the pact. Yes they got to live eternally, but what the aor'sii avoided to mention was that it would be from within a temple, a prison. The chorr'gall became *very* bitter, at that. In a way, you could say that the chorr'gall saw an opportunity for the aor'sii to fall, and as such didn't lift a finger to help them. In a way, the aor'sii set up their own demise.

"Testing his theory, Kordethion used every tool at his disposal to try and locate just one of these hidden temples. Obscure tomes. Family ties. Vast research. His hunt spanned the better part of two years, but alas, he succeeded. This temple was buried deep in the sands of Flayre'song; it was buried directly beneath the city itself. And, as I'm sure you've guessed by now, Flayre'song was one of the grand cities built for man by the aor'sii. The aor'sii thought that they were so intelligent, and they were. But like I had said, Kordethion was very brilliant, and dark-hearted at that. I suppose that he had no trouble at all with the rigors of scouring the sands for the lair of Eaerhon, the Great Beast of the Galaxy."

Finally standing herself, the beautiful lady started pacing back and forth in front of the dying embers of the fire, the patter of rain intensifying as if to urge her on. "His family, or what was left of it, had thought him dead when Kordethion entered the secluded temple for he didn't return to civilization until a fortnight later. And only his most trusted men knew what he was daring to attempt, his black ambitions already starting to plague the lands. Nobody quite understands or knows fully well how he did it, but Kordethion was able to make Eaerhon his own. Or so they say."

"What was Eaerhon like," Aeven spoke, a dark mood settling over the den akin to a blanket of smoke. "before Kordethion twisted its heart, I mean?"

"Eaerhon, like many of the other beasts, was the very last of its kind. The aor'sii found this poor creature on the brink of death, its potential grave no more than the skeleton of an abandoned barracks in the heart of the Flayre'song's wasteland. With many blessings, and who knows how many prayers to Erenara, Eaerhon was saved. With deep respect, Eaerhon gladly gave his service to the aor'sii. At least, in the beginning, it did. As for what this creature looks like, your guess is as good as mine. Although I do believe that I had read an excerpt once from a book that I had borrowed about Eaerhon resembling the form of a man but the heart of an inferno."

With a heavy sigh, the lady sat back down, her voice gently rising in anticipation. "But that is neither here nor now. Kordethion is now long dead, as are the aor'sii of old. However, I do have a question that I want to ask of you, and your answer can very well make quite a saga out of this age."

"A saga, eh? I like the sound of that." Rising out of his own chair, Aeven began pacing once again, his thirst for knowledge intensifying. "So, what's your question?"

"Only this. I have told you the tragic story of the aor'sii and the black-hearted soul of Kordethion. What I am proposing is a quest to the Sanctuary of Peace, to Tai'drasial itself. Some of those temples that I have told you about still stand, as do fragments of the lost civilization. You look like a mercenary, am I correct? Or, at least, a seasoned traveler."

"I am. A mercenary who is currently hunting for a bloody thief. After I find this man, I will be up for hire again, which then you can make your offer. Tell me though, this quest to Tai'drasial does sound grand, but what did that story have to do with the painting that I was asking about? What is the secret that that painting is supposed to hold?" With a speculative look, Aeven stopped pacing, one last question forming on his tongue. "And how come this inn's interior is so mismatched? It seems... well... almost as if it's an illusion."

"Why, I thought that would be pretty obvious. For both questions, I mean." Shaking her head, the lady stood up, hands on hips and a broad smile gracing her face. "As for your first question, through ardent research of my own, I have discovered the creator of that painting. While the secret of it is still very much hidden, I now have a destination for learning its hidden story. For obtaining the truth.

"I told you earlier that a story can be hard to tell if the story itself wasn't written down correctly, and this venture will shake the very foundations of that truth. I can tell you this. What would happen if a secret was discovered that the highest of lords wanted completely eradicated from history? A secret that would get your throat slit and your family assassinated if you but uttered it aloud? That is what this painting holds. Until you've finished with your current mission however, I cannot tell you anymore, and for that I'm sorry. If you want to learn more, you'll just have to come back when you're available for hire. But know this: this is not an adventure to be taken lightly, as I'm sure you've deduced. And as for the colors we picked for this inn, it's just to show that this inn is both of ours. We may be husband and wife but this inn is an investment. As strange as that sounds, it works."

Aeven whistled silently, his head shaking in denial. "Unveiling information that the nobles want to keep hidden? That *does* sound perilous. Gazing into the lady's green eyes, he thrust out his hand. "My name is Aeven Kvalheim."

The mirth disappeared from her face. "Alleta Blackiston, Knight of the Swan Wings. Retired knight, I should say. In any case, I am waiting until spring before I start this adventure of mine. Please consider my offer." With a nod of finality, Alleta's smile returned, sure that she had made her offer exceptionally clear. "The broom is in the closet right over there if you would like to go ahead and sweep up all those crumbs you dumped on my floor."

CHAPTER THREE

Sparks and Smoke

It was now well into night as Aeven stepped off of the slick steps of the Black Swallow inn and onto the meager, desolate road. The bleak sky was spattered with menacing black clouds, giant thunderheads streaking the skies as if to tear themselves through the land itself and down to the nine levels of sparodin. Heavy bolts of rain hailed down from the swirling sky, pelting nature below with a fierce tenacity. Gazing haphazardly through the onslaught of rain, Aeven could just make out the outlines of townsmen amongst the winding road, men and women that were desperate to finish their chores despite the impending tempest. With renewed exuberance at the thought of the adventure to come, Aeven stalked his way from building overhang to building overhang, the crashing of a thunderbolts making itself known to all within a leagues area.

A quick sweep of his eyes revealed a stout stone bridge close by, one that spanned over a roaring river that happened to run directly through the town square. It was late and he was tired, but Aeven had one last chore that he needed to complete before retiring for the night. Aeven reached the peak of the bridge and looked down into the town square. It was mostly empty. *I see him,* he thought carefully, *the man meandering there by the river.* Catching eyes with Aeven, the brightly clad merchant strode from the river's edge and to the base of a large weathered statue, the man's patched hat slightly catching in the wind. The statue was of a hooded woman embracing a jagged dagger clutched to her heart. The bright flashes of light from the storm made her seem almost godlike. Aeven tread across the slippery stone bridge with increased haste. It wasn't the statue that had Aeven's guard up, nor the presence of the mysterious merchant, but meeting a stranger in the middle of a brewing storm in a strange city was never a good idea in Aeven's book.

As he neared the colorful man, Aeven nodded toward a neglected looking pub on the corner of the muddy street and strode on by, the eyes of the statue digging a hole in the back of Aeven's head. The sound of silence caressed Aeven the moment he opened the heavy iron door to the Sea's Barrel, only a few glaring eyes roving around to see who had let the gale breach the entrance. Aeven could almost feel the heat of the fires escaping as he slipped inside. The room was dimly lit, and most of the patrons were either drinking their ales in peace or chatting around small rickety tables, whispering about current news or more foul matters. The look of the whole place was disconcerting; it reeked of dirty dealings and cheap ale. It was just Aeven's sort of pub.

Using more than a little caution, Aeven commandeered a filthy table of his own, dozens of speculative eyes hunting him across the dingy dark room. "I see that you've been doing well for yourself." A raspy voice choked out, immediately putting Aeven's hackles up. "I know that you don't remember me, but the man that hired you is a good pal of mine. I was there when you made your deal with baron Kaosa Brattian." Creeping into view, the merchant slid into a shaky chair adjacent to Aeven's, a strong stench of filth suddenly settling over their table like a blanket of smog.

"Well, at least we'll have our privacy now," Aeven muttered sourly, grimly watching as the occupants of the closest table make a swift escape after catching a whiff of the putrid man. It was all Aeven could do not to leave the table himself. Bracing himself, Aeven inquired carefully about the man's past. "You're a merchant, correct? If you were at baron Kaosa's manner when I met with him, then you must have been one of his guards. How are you a merchant, now?"

His eyes brightening, the harsh man leaned forward, clearly pleased at being asked a question about himself. "Why I definitely was, at that. I am a man of many trades. Golbart Camblin is my name. Like yourself, I was a mercenary in my younger days and quite feared, if I don't say so myself. For a number of years I was hired to protect the decks of ships when they set sail to foreign lands for trade and commerce. There's adventure to be had on the high seas and don't let anyone tell you otherwise. Why, some of the tempests that I had to navigate through would've left you spitless, boy.

After a time however, I wanted work where you weren't having the fear of drowning on your next quest. Of course, from my sailing career, I had acquired quite a repertoire of connections. Men that I had worked with, battled with, and ultimately grew friendships with had soon become my comrades.

"We had respectable battles we did, good memories and gallant bar fights. We soon built ourselves quite the notoriety, reputation of being able to get the job done. The Redtalon Mystics is what we called ourselves. But in answer to your question, yes I was a guard at lord Kaosa's manner. I'm sure that you realize how important this job is that he tasked you with, no? You think that he's just going to leave it in the hand's of one man? Like I said, I have more connections and friends than I know what to do with. Lord Kaosa knew how slippery Keyamir was, hence why he involved me on this quest. Looking like I am a merchant is more of a…*ploy*…than anything else. And it looks like it's a good thing that I *was* involved. Let me guess, you're having a hard time finding Keyamir? I *might* have some information for you. For a price." At that, Golbart shirked off his sopping cloak, his ashen skin and wiry, dark hair just as wet. Aeven couldn't help but stare at his forearms. They had several glowing glyphs that were tattooed up his arms and wrapped around his shoulders. Glyphs that glowed silver against his dark skin. His eyes growing distant, Golbart took to admiring the drab ceiling, obviously lost in reminiscences. Scooting back in his chair, Aeven left the man to his memoirs, wanting nothing more than to get away from the fetid stench. "Err... Golbart? I'm going to grab a couple of ales for us."

"I'll take dark ale," a familiar voice chimed in, her request just barely audible over the noise of the other regulars. "Actually, with the week that I've had, I'll take *two* ales. The darkest ones that they have." With a laugh that resembled chimes, the stranger took a seat in one of the vacant chairs, her feet immediately propping up on the top of the table. "What? Are you surprised to see me? I know that I'm late, but I've located Keyamir's whereabouts."

With a start, Golbart rocked back in his chair, his ears catching the tail end of the young lady's conversation. "Hey! That was my job! I was supposed to locate that dirty thief!" Shaking his head, the man stood up, a large frown slowly growing across his face. "I need a drink," Golbart spat, his large fists clenching in anger. The lithe man made his way to the ravaged bartender, his curses lost under the growing cacophony of the den. Turning his full attention to the new arrival, Aeven couldn't help but admire her impeccable timing, and for as long as they'd been traveling together, he wasn't in the least bit surprised. She seemed to make a habit of arriving just when she'd be the most needed. What did catch him off guard, however, was the new suit of armor that she'd managed to find in his absence. It looked like a work of art more than functional protection. Graceful, glimmering plates of metal enveloped her body, somehow perfectly accentuating her every curve. The metal itself was raven black, shined to reflect everything in its vicinity. Her leather boots, like her leather gauntlets, were dyed black as well, giving her overall image a somewhat morose and deadly look to her.

Thrush Balfourian's features however, were in stark contrast to her gloomy attire. Her light walnut colored hair was done up atop her head with two chopsticks, her nose and chin very dainty and elegant. To Aeven, her eyes were the most catching of all. Her left eye was a light hazelnut brown, the other the most brilliant of greens, and both held more than a little confidence. She only stood at about five feet four inches but her spirit well made up for her lack of height. Despite appreciating his friend's intervention, Aeven was still dumbfounded. What Golbart had said still rattled him. How many people had Lord

Kaosa hired to see Keyamir put in the ground? It made no sense. Their must be more to the story than he was being made aware of. Shaking his head, Aeven couldn't help but find the whole situation somewhat disconcerting. Whether this thief knew it or not, he was being hunted by what seemed like several groups of bounty hunters. Just as fast as Golbart could find another group to sell his information to, that is. With that last thought pervading his mind, Aeven reclaimed his rickety chair, leaning halfway across the table so as not to be overheard by any unwanted ears.

"I won't ask where he is hiding, not here at least. But in what direction are we to travel?"

Leaning slightly forward herself, Thrush pitched her voice very low, brushing a stray strand of hair back in the process, "We are to travel to the mountains that never forgive, where evil spawns new children every sunrise."

Aeven couldn't help it, he could feel his head grow lighter and a thin sheen of sweat coat his body. Leaning back in his chair, Aeven let this new revelation settle in his stomach; whatever appetite he might have had was suddenly lost in this new disclosure of where they were to journey; the Azaevia Mountains. Golbart might be able to sell this information to a group of bounty hunters that are new to the area and weren't privy to what the Azaevia Mountains can do to a man. But the chances of that were slim to none for almost everybody knew the lore of the mountains. Aeven didn't know the whole tale himself; he doubted that many who were alive did, but the few chilling fragments that he did know left a frosty ball of ice in the pit of his stomach. Shifting slightly in his seat, Aeven tried to suppress the rising images of the appalling beasts and gruesome clans infesting those tainted mountains, and what they did to the few who were brave enough to try and cross as a shortcut from Koronin to Ashenfelter. The remains of those poor souls were always devastatingly violent. If they were ever found at all.

His partner looked at Aeven with a bemused smirk. Leaning back in her own chair, a hearty laugh escaped her lips. "This excursion may be dangerous but it's nothing that we can't handle. Truthfully, we've been pitted against much worse. Not getting cold feet for this mission, are you?" As if to make her point, Thrush clutched the hilt of one of her swords and drew it from its sheathe, swinging the heavy weapon in the air as if the enemy was somehow floating above her. She rightfully earned several glares and bemused smirks from the surrounding patrons.

"It doesn't matter if we have to travel to sparodin itself to find this bloody pickpocket." Aeven smiled, his voice taking on stark contrast to his face. "We took this job and were going to see it through to the bitter end." With a sharp crash, Aeven slammed his hand palm down atop the thick table, his eyes glaring venom at all the regulars staring at Thrush and himself. "No matter what the cost." He finished solemnly. "What bothers me is the fact that I was hired onto this mission with being told only half the story, it seems."

"That's all well and good lad, but you're way out of your league here. Do you even have the slightest inkling on how to find the mountains that hide in the stars?" A raspy whisper arose, floating over Aeven's shoulder like a haunting tune. "And even if you did manage to find the mountains that ripple out of time, how are you going to be able to navigate the malicious trails? I know that I'm not as young as I used to be, but once upon a time, I created legends on the paths that I tread." With a sort of jaunt, Golbart twirled the spare chair around and sidled up next to Aeven, a conspiring glint gleaming from within his eyes. "Make me your navigator and I promise that you won't regret it."

"Legends are only as great as the man who tells the tale deigns them to be." Thrush muttered, more than a hint of regret painting her voice. "But he does have a valid point, Aeven. It sounds like we're going to have more luck finding this man some soap than we are of navigating the Azaevia Mountains. We need a guide, and he would do just as well as the next man."

The room itself seemed to fall silent as Aeven pondered this new conundrum, his mind working furiously at all the possibilities that could result from hiring this fellow mercenary. If what Golbart was implying was true, these mountains were going to prove very hard to navigate, much less trying to find a man that was hiding amidst them. It seemed inevitable, they need a guide. But for one to present itself at such a crucial time? It seemed perfect. Too perfect. Sometimes it takes some true skill to find the drawback of a "perfect situation" before it kills you and those closest to you. It was also very hard for Aeven to look past the fact that lord Kaosa had hired Golbart in conjunction with Aeven; and he was also sure that Golbart was being less than truthful with Aeven. What *was* the artifact that Keyamir had stolen? Hiring a man such as Golbart just reeked of desperation. Now he felt like a fool for not asking more questions.

With a final thought of regret, Aeven cleared his throat. "Naturally, it seems that we are left with little choice. Under the circumstances, we'll hire you as our guide. However—" locking eyes with the older man, Aeven made sure to imply in his face exactly what he was about to say. Aeven's face felt like stone. "If I catch even the slightest whiff that you're going to double-cross me in any shape or form, I will cut you down where you stand. Do we have an understanding?"

For a moment, Golbart's face contorted in rage, his eyes resembling the devastating thunderheads streaking the dusky sky outside. It was only for a moment, however, before that crooked, raspy smile reappeared on his dirty mug. "Despite what you may think of me, I do have some honor left in this old body. We have an understanding, and I'll even give you my word. I'll see to it that even if it takes me my last dying breath, you'll reach the dark heart of that mountain range alive. This I promise you. I just need one… favor. I *might have* gambled away my pay from lord Kaosa. And my armor." Golbart looked down at the floor in shame, his cheeks flushing. "It seemed like such an *easy* bet. An easy *win*. Well…it wasn't. I still have my sword, though. I still have that. I need to be outfitted with protection in case we run into trouble in the mountains. Which we most likely will."

Aeven, clearing his throat, rose up from his seat. He wasn't about to be outdone. "You promise quite a lot, Golbart, and I'll see to it that you keep your word. And now, I'll give you mine. So long as you travel under the wings of this group, no harm shall ever befall you. As long as the circumstances never waver, we'll protect you with sword and shield. That's my promise to you." Truthfully Aeven wasn't even surprised about his new comrade's revelation. With a nod of finality to his new companion, Aeven directed his voice over to Thrush, unconsciously readjusting his worn-out gauntlets. "It's going to be hell finding these cursed mountains, even more so without proper equipment. I know that we're without gold at the moment but, in any case, I want you and Golbart to find a suitable blacksmith and have him outfitted with functional attire. In the meantime, I'm going to find us some gold. Whatever that may entail."

With a wicked smile Thrush nodded in approval. "With functional attire, eh? This could prove interesting. Don't worry, I'll have this navigator of ours clad in something so magnificent that god's light will shine forth from this merchant's magnificence." Turning her full attention to Golbart, she leaned across the table so that their faces were only inches apart, her nose crinkling only somewhat from his stench. "The Redtalon Mystics, eh? Sounds pretty noble to me. Well, have no doubts that you're in safe hands."

"That's precisely what I'm afraid of." Golbart wheezed, his eyes darting from patron to patron. "I think the term safe with you two is about as safe as standing in the pit of an erupting volcano!" Sliding back from his chair, Golbart tumbled backward as a thunderous roar resounded from the other side of the table; Thrush's loud guffaws were drawing even more attention to the conspicuous table than was necessary.

"And what, may I ask, is so damn hilarious?" Golbart crowed, his old bearings getting the better of him. Watching Thrush himself, a bemused smile crept onto Aeven's face, a few flash memories flooding his mind.

There had been some close calls in his line of duty as a mercenary, quite a few instances where the kiss of death should have graced Aeven's soul. Chuckling, Aeven vividly recalled Thrush and himself scourging a monastery in the very pit of Flair Creek, which was coincidentally enough a volcano. To add a touch of irony to Golbart's statement, the volcano literally had started to erupt on them. It had been all right, however, they had found the loot.

Half-turning to Golbart, Aeven couldn't help but shake his head in amusement. "Don't ask."

CHAPTER FOUR

From Fist to Claw

An explosion of misshapen glass had shattered around Aeven in a rough, semicircular pattern of blood, debris, and ashes. The circular room was blurry, as if he hadn't used his eyes for days. He stumbled from his glass prison and fell to his knees, his wobbly arms shaking, trembling to just find the strength to hold him upright. To not let him fall face first into the shards of glass. His legs and feet wouldn't work correctly, as if they lacked the muscles to move the way that they were supposed to move. His shoulder blades ached something fierce. His memories faded in and out, as if they wanted a place within his mind but he didn't want them there and so denied them entrance. What he did recall was hazy. He remembered sand underneath his toes. He remembered the sound of the wind rushing by him, bringing with it the taste of salt on his tongue. He was little, the wind battered him something fierce but he laughed with it. He chimed in with the melody of the breeze. A man and woman approached him but he couldn't see them clearly. They were laughing too, though. All three of them were… happy. He couldn't hold himself up any longer. Laying his head down atop the back of his hands, he closed his eyes once more and embraced that fleeting memory of happiness. Laying halfway out of his shattered, glass prison, he embraced that one emotion that made him feel…human.

The night had been rough and restless; his reoccurring dream had haunted him to the point that he felt more drained after waking up than he did laying down. Sitting up halfway on his mangled bed, he leaned over and placed his head in his hands. For years he'd slept soundly without that dream, and now lately it was a weekly occurrence. A feminine hand came to rest on his back and slithered its way down his spine, her entire arm eventually falling around his neck and enveloping him in an embrace. Her lips fell on his cheek. "You were…extra restless last night." She whispered softly, her hand balling up and punching him on his arm. "You sure know how to keep a girl up extra late."

Aeven chuckled at that. They were both mostly naked and the morning sun was finally peeking through the small window. "Sorry," he murmured into his hands, "it's just something that I can't help."

"I know, this isn't the *first* time that I've slept next to you, you know. Far from it. You had that dream, didn't you? You always murmur the same things in your sleep when its that dream. Always. Lately its been more… consistent."

Aeven fell back against the bed and smiled as Thrush straddled him, her face now looming over his. He tried to stay serious. "Its like I want to remember more when I have that dream, but I somehow…reject it. Like internally I *don't* want to remember. But I know that I do. If they're memories at all. It could all just be one big hallucination made up in my mind, for all I know." His finger played with her bellybutton and then wandered up her stomach. She blushed at that, the sun catching her walnut colored hair as it cascaded down atop him. Eventually his hands made their way up her chest and to her face. "You're pretty perfect, you know that?" She really reddened at that.

They both jumped as a fist pounded at the door. "I'm not waiting all day for you two love birds to finish up! We need to be leaving soon and we still need my armor!" Golbart screeched from the other side of the entryway, "I'm not chasing Keyamir halfway across the continent! hurry up!" The sound of his heavy footfalls walking back down the hallway eventually disappeared.

"I'm going to *kill him!*" Thrush yelled into Aeven's chest, "I'm going to flay him alive and send the pieces back to lord Kaosa!" Her arms wrapped Aeven in an even tighter embrace, her hips easing closer to his.

"Well he's just going to have to wait on us, I think." Aeven whispered back, "because we're not done yet."

—⁕—

Not only had the storm subsided, but more townsmen were crammed in the ramshackle streets as Aeven finally made his way outside; he was already exhausted and it was only the early morning. It took Aeven a few moments to realize *why* exactly the streets were so crammed with people; it was the grand opening of an attraction that had been under construction for the better part of five years now. Aeven thought that it had been merely a rumor when he'd first heard of it, but it had actually been the truth, oddly enough. Why a resort would be built in a rundown city like Koronin was beyond Aeven. The attraction was so large that it seemed like an extension of the city itself, and it was constructed and hosted by the multinational merchant business known as the Goldenfist Corporation. Aeven was no stranger to the renowned merchant business; in fact, he had once been an employee of theirs before his life as a mercenary.

Aeven cringed at those thoughts, at some of the deeds that he had been forced to do. His life as their combatant was long since passed, and to be honest, he was not entirely proud of all that he had done in their service.

Aeven nimbly sidestepped a pair of hulking blond men who were marching in the other direction, one wearing pristine armor and the other elegant robes; both spit at his feet, one even taking the time to sneer at him. *Bloody city folk! Whatever happened to the respect you're supposed to show others?* Aeven fumed to himself, half reaching for the hilt of his sword before thinking better of it. *I've gotta keep my head today.* Aeven knew that it wasn't just the rude citizens of Koronin that had Aeven's insides all twisted up in a knot, it was the sea of flags that he was forced to walk under as well. A sea of golden flags bolted to the side of every other building and tower, flags that rippled amidst the strong breeze like an ocean of gold might ripple on a midsummer night. What really griped Aeven was that each of those flags had a golden fist embroidered across it to show the citizens who it was that had blessed them with their new attraction, the 'Silver Claw Theatre'.

Even with the plague of the golden flags, Aeven had to admit to himself that the money flowing in from the attraction, and the construction of, was helping in maintaining and upgrading parts of the rundown city. Parts of Koronin could now be considered majestic and full of life. These past few weeks had been so rushed for Aeven that he hadn't had the time to just *explore*. The new architecture was refreshing, and you truly had to take an afternoon to stroll the more obscure boulevards before you could say you have seen it all; all the more so when the rays of the sun reflected off of the wandering fog that always seemed to lazily glide down the grimy thoroughfares. Koronin was a sturdy realm full of tall towers, well constructed cottages, and stone bridges that gleamed as if built with thousands of dewdrops. What made the city even more grand in Aeven's opinion was the ancient, gnarled trees that were scattered sporadically throughout the city.

Towering hundreds of feet above the city walls, the one thing Aeven found the most mystifying were the large berries that these trees bore. Durable as clam shells and always changing colors, these glistening berries have been described by the townsfolk as edible prisms of hope, and the legend holds that if you're thinking positive thoughts and one of those berries drops on your head, you will be blessed for one year starting that day. Of course, Aeven didn't believe in that garbage; if a person wanted to have hope, he had to create it for himself. Aeven did retract his earlies sentiments about the city, however. It wasn't as run down as he'd first thought, and the city was certainly more expansive than he first believed.

Onwards Aeven pushed through the thickening crowd. A handful of travelers dressed in the fashion of Scarrow waltzed by, green feathered bowler's hats and short sturdy boots seeming all the rage from the warm realm in the deep east. Heading the other direction, past Aeven, strolled a handful of women from what looked to be the country of Dryden;

flowing red robes and golden ivy entangled amongst their hair. Each of them walked with a silver walking staff and dainty boots. Aeven pushed himself around the side of a particularly thick building and was rebounded by a crowd of several colossal men with flowing, braided red beards and women with thick, extended scarlet braids. Their clothes were drab and eyes red hot. They gave him one look and turned back around; they didn't budge. *Ashenfelters,* Aeven seethed, *the worst of the worst. Well, to sparodin to those that can't make room for strangers!*

A pedestal with a man standing before it was just up ahead. Elbowing his way forwards, Aeven stood at the forefront of the giant crowd as the announcer wrapped up his spiel. "It is with great pleasure that I can be the one to welcome you into the theater that the Goldenfist Corporation has created for your pleasure and entertainment; a three-mile race track for you to place bets with your favored kor'zhul. Visual games you can partake in, a delightful midnight theater presentation, and beautiful festivities for you to enjoy! Welcome to the Silver Claw, where the gold is always clasped in your fist!" Taking a swig from a shiny golden mug, the man stepped down to hundreds of hands clapping together. A giant pair of scissors were used to snip a beautiful colored ribbon that was strung across a tunnel entrance, and, as one, the entire crowd moved forward as if it was a single, living being. Aeven felt as if he was being washed out to sea by an ocean's worth of travelers.

Aeven lost himself in the giant silver-rimmed tunnel that supposedly led to this new theater, Aeven letting the bright, intense torches bracketed to the walls guide him to his destination. On either side of the tunnel was what looked to be a mural of swirling colors and intricate artwork, both sides overlapping at the top of the tunnel. Using the shaky torchlight, Aeven had to stop and admire what it was that he was sure so many would just pass by. Backtracking against the crowd as far as he could make it, Aeven inched forward until his nose was practically touching the tunnel wall. *This is a mural of how the aor'sii fell! And I have to say they really did their research. Aor'sii, Kordethion, and even the pact between the chorr'galls and the beautiful winged creatures. How amazing, and yet…coincidental.* Aeven thought to himself. *They even included the blue-lighted pedestal, with a small twist; instead of the dais being in a wooded area, it seems as if it's in a cave, or at least underground. This makes no sense, but perhaps a little more research on my part will reveal more.*

He finally reached the end of the tunnel. Stepping the rest of the way out of the darkness and into the wavering light of the entrance, the chamber was disorienting, even more so because of the array of brightly colored people waiting on the other side. Each attendant was standing so that they were the first thing that you saw when your eyes refocused, and while their smiles and eyes were as bright as a noonday sun, their clothes far outdid their perky facial features. Lively, lavender colored robes and fire red shoes were the attire that these personnel adorned. The flooring was rugged fool's gold all hammered into small tiles, not a smooth edge to be found, and reflected the light that the dozens of chandeliers emitted. Aeven squeezed past a rather large bearded man to come nose to nose to an attendant. "Welcome to the Silver Claw, good sir!" The red-haired lady quipped. "Which attraction are you interested in?" Spinning on her rosy heels, the lady's floozy lavender dress bounced up and down as she described what each attraction was.

"Across the room there on the right side is a red trapdoor that will drop you into the most amazing botanical garden that you could ever witness.

Exotic trees, man made rivers, and ancient artifacts are just the beginning of this adventure." Swiveling her dainty hand to the middle of the room, her finger pointed to a long blue flag that dangled majestically from the ceiling. She continued with her speech, "behind that flag is a rope ladder that will lead you to one of our most prized events, the kor'zhul racetrack. Kor'zhul are beasts that are about six feet in length and look like giant ferrets with claws and beaks like a chicken would have. Very intelligent creatures and very competitive in nature. If you want to be involved in the race, we have a kor'zhul that we trained ourselves. You would need to sign a disclaimer of course, and you would compete against other racers from around the world. Like I said, a very prized event!" Bobbing her head, the lady turned from the blue flag to the very leftmost part of the large room, glancing over two other sites that were obviously under construction still. "Our third and most exciting event is the infamous Gladiator's Halo; an arena of solid blocks of stone and nature that divides the warrior from all that he is familiar with. Who you battle is for the crowd to decide! Again, you will need to sign a disclaimer but the riches to be had are immeasurable. Tell me marauder, which attraction pleases you most?"

"Marauder? Can't say I've been called that one yet." Aeven mused. I'm supposed to earn money for our navigator's new armor; so, the question is which of these would be the most profitable? Or damned the most profitable, which would be the most fun?" It took him a few moments but he already knew what he was going to choose. "I think I've made my decision." Rubbing his hands together, Aeven couldn't help but smile.

Her insides roiled with anger and irritation. Stepping off of the doorstep of the quaint inn and joining the throng of townsman that were inevitably headed towards the big Goldenfist event, Thrush tried her hardest to ignore the lanky man that was following in her shadow. The hyena-like mercenary was the object of her hate, this morning. Thrush knew that Golbart would follow her because he was hard up for gold, like most of the realm was now. Ever since the country was plunged into chaos by those prestigious lords, the only work that was available was soldiering or merchanting; two careers that turned you from a caring person into a soul comprised of blades, blood, and money. She was sure that Golbart probably didn't care that he interrupted something special. Thrush hadn't seen Aeven for *weeks,* and this stranger had the *gall* to pound on their door and disturb their *one* night of solace because he was in a blazing *hurry*. Thrush wanted nothing so much than to turn around and punch him in the face, the need to do so was insurmountable. *To sparodin with this nasty scum of a human being; I told Aeven that I was going to do something, and I'm going to do it.* Thrush miserably thought, *I should just feel lucky that this* blasted *event is happening at all. What are the odds of us being here on it's grand opening? In a town like Koronin, no less? No matter, we certainly lucked out.*

Using her diminutive size to wriggle her way through the crowd, Thrush navigated her way through the river of people, merchants, fumes, and sounds until she arrived at a shiny tunnel that presumably led into the amusement park itself. The walls of the tunnel were dingy, cracked, and colored with so many paintings and murals that Thrush couldn't tell heads from tails out of it all. The torches were second rate, the light given off from them so sporadic that Thrush couldn't see more than five feet in front of her. *Knowing the Goldenfist Corporation as I do, they probably bought those bloody torches at a garage sale. Ha!* The end of the tunnel came fast, Thrush being swept up in a sea of people that wanted to get to the attraction just as much as she did. The entryway was overly bright and obnoxiously loud. *I hate being so short! All I can see are people's backsides.* Catching an attendant's attention, Thrush hustled across the rough golden floor with as much dignity as she could summon up. She'd seen posters scattered all across town of a huge event taking place here. Some kind of big new attraction. She knew exactly how she was going to earn money for this new armor that Golbart needed; it was also a great way to vent some frustration. Thrush asked the attendant if it was too late to sign up.

Thrush is an insufferable wench and that's all there is to it, Golbart thought to himself as he clawed his way past the last of the crowd and right up to her royal highness. *Aeven I am not sure about yet, he has too many questions and is too smart by about half. But this… this woman I could easily snap her neck in two and still get a good night's sleep.* Opening his mouth to rip Thrush a new one, the gaze she laid upon him made Golbart swallow his words just as fast as they were about to spill out of his mouth. *I don't know what this Scarrownian wench is planning but I do know that the Goldenfist Corp. always involves money; and where there's money, there is opportunity. I'll shut up and see what happens.* Quiet words were exchanged, and before he knew it, Golbart was following the two ladies through a large iron door in the leftmost part of the lobby and into a chamber that switched from tiled fool's gold to an inlaid silver bridge, complete with twin fountains on either side and raging waters below. Stopping short, the red-haired attendant spun on her glittering heels to instruct them on what to do next.

"Just across the bridge here is a large wooden door, as you can see. Wait just on this side with weapons ready until you are announced. Enter at your own peril and know that if you are in a life-threatening situation, our ratings will go up." Summing up, she finished with a curt "thank you and enjoy" before heading back through the entrance. Of course Golbart couldn't help but admire her strut as her skirt glittered by. She disappeared and he had a realization. Golbart had to admit that his nerves were shaken. Listening to the crowd jeer on the other side of that door and having his new partner weigh him with those cutting eyes brought his spirits to an all-time low. Trying to distract himself, he tried to start some semblance of a conversation. Golbart took to admiring the hilt of his sword as words tumbled out of his mouth.

"You and Aeven are both mercenaries, yet I notice that you guys seem to play by a set of rules that none of the other mercenaries play with. A set of rules dictated by honor. If I would have given that information that I had about Keyamir to any other mercenary in this area, I wouldn't have lived to see the next sunrise. I know that you already had the same information that I did, but still." Golbart didn't think that Thrush would answer; her grimace and constant glower was all he needed to see. She turned her back on him. Opening his mouth for a second time to really tell her what he thinks of her and her prince charming, Golbart was cut short as the large door burst open. Two burly men strode up to the pair of reluctant partners, one with a paper and pen in hand and the other with a nasty looking short sword and cudgel. Reaching his hand out for the pen, Golbart could only smile to himself. The arena was one place where he felt the most comfortable, and he would sign any agreement for that piece of mind. Even if it made his nerves scream.

—⚒—

The kor'zhul stalls that the Goldenfist Corporation had built alongside the racetrack were enormous and very flashy. Like the flooring in the previous rooms, it was constructed of tiles of fool's gold. Each stall looked to be assembled out of the finest of wood, very sturdy and polished to a shining gleam. Within each stall was an enormous illustration painted on the wall of various realms and cities; empires that each kor'zhul represented. Eight booths in all, Aeven strode up to the stall that had an enormous Goldenfist symbol daubed behind it; the beast that the Goldenfist claimed that they had trained for the public's use. Tipping his head over the railing, Aeven admired the beautiful animal with relish. His best friend, Curasi Enlan, had once told Aeven that kor'zhul had minds akin to great tacticians, they were always planning and always quick to adapt to a situation if need be. This specific kor'zhul was slumped out across the flooring of his stable, legs sprawled out behind him as if he was bathing in the noonday sun. Curasi had also told Aeven that no two kor'zhul were ever the same, and Aeven was starting to see why. This beast's short orange gleaming hair was immaculate. Much like a ferret's hair, it covered the length of its body and was very fine. Hundreds of bright yellow dots filled this animal's coat, much as if Aeven was staring up into the galaxy at the stars. This kor'zhul's large beak was akin to a falcon's beak, only was bright green like a lime, as was his claws.

"Beautiful, isn't he?" a voice piped up from across the room. "He has been the number one kor'zhul for the past three weeks; of course, since the Goldenfist Corporation own him, we are considered cheaters of one sort or another. But I know better. All the credit goes to this hardworking beast, Alken-thave." Sidling up next to Aeven, a rather tall brunette woman garbed in flashy, outdoor leathers leaned over the stall door and started to stroke the beast's beak. "Alken-thave has just finished a race and will be out for the rest of the day. I am sorry if you had your heart set on racing."

"It's of no consequence." Aeven mumbled, gloom setting in. This kor'zhul really was a beautiful creature. Glancing over at the young lady, Aeven noticed with disdain that her face had multiple welts and scars, some fresh and some looking years old. "I hope you don't mind me asking, but are the kor'zhul truly that rough when being handled?"

"My scars aren't the result of any kor'zhul, I'm afraid. I have three years until I am up for auction again, three years until I might be bought by a man that cares for his property. Until that time though, I serve the Goldenfist Corporation in its entirety, serving who I am ordered to serve; even if that means that the patron is abusive."

"That's horrible!" Aeven sputtered out. "I know that the Goldenfist is involved in some pretty shady stuff, but I never thought that they'd stoop so low as to get involved with slavery. Can't you escape?" Gathering his senses, Aeven rethought his words. "Forget I asked that, I know the Goldenfist Corp. well enough to know that cannot happen." Inadvertently, Aeven started to scrutinize that part of his mind that he swore he'd never touch for the rest of his life. *Yes, that energy is still there. And why wouldn't it be? The past is something that can't be so easily discarded.*

"These kor'zhul are the only friends that I have, unfortunately. Every morning I try to talk myself into stealing Alkin-thave here and bolting into the nearest woodlands. If I'm caught, however, they will chop off a limb of their choice, beat me into submission, and then lend me to the most horrific men imaginable for a month each. I have seen it happen two times now to other slaves. No, I have three years until I can be bought, three years. That is what drives me. It seems like such a long time away but I will persevere." Aeven couldn't think of a single comforting word to help the woman in her grief, so he went another route. "What is your name?"

Her brilliant green eyes were caught off-guard and she smiled. "Sylda Falconer." Grabbing Sylda's hand, Aeven clasped her fingers and gave her a smile, trying to give all the comfort that a mercenary could muster up. Aeven knew it probably didn't amount to much but when the world deemed you as a loner, any helping hand was greatly appreciated. He knew, he had been in her shoes not so long ago. When the Goldenfist Corporation had you in their claws, they didn't release you easily, if at all.

The gladiator pit was creeping with mist, smoke, and a haze of blood and ash. The ground was uneven terrain, rocky at best, with root snags and barbs that will catch a man's foot if he wasn't careful. Golbart knew that he was in trouble before he even stepped into the ring; he was wearing filthy brown robes for armor, had only a short sword for protection, and even worst was that he didn't know if having Thrush at his back was the wisest course of action that an old mercenary could take. Besides having constant worry for his life, Golbart couldn't help but admire the actual arena itself. Built on the very crags of Koronin, the coliseum turned out to be an intricate series of cliffs, crags, tunnels, and sandpits that was entwined with tree overgrowth and brilliant man-made traps. With the spectators seated on high benches around the rooftops of the Silver Claw, their roars and caws were barely audible amidst the clatter of swords and shields. It started to lightly sprinkle rain.

Golbart had already lost sight of Thrush; the battle had turned quickly when it went from scouting up on the crags to an all-out brawl on the whispering fields below. Golbart had to admit that the pair of them probably looked like the easiest pickings amidst the battlefield; an elderly man in tattered robes and a young woman that barely looked like she was a teenager. To be honest, if Golbart had seen the same opportunity, he would have taken it. *Gold is the lifeblood of Pry'ama, after all!* Golbart thought to himself. *I only need enough gold from this to purchase my own armor and decent weapons, so surviving is the key, here.* Stepping over the most recent corpse he'd created, Golbart felt the bright purple heather crunch under his boots as he scanned the fields for the next fool that needed slain. *Just because I wear dirty robes and carry a short sword, people think I do not know my way in combat. Such a foolish mistake! I'll take advantage of it.*

His boots were carrying him across the field before Golbart had a chance to think twice. His legs and body became more spry than even he had accounted for. Catching a shorter, fortress of a man as he was turning around from his own kill, his polished blue armor offered little defense as Golbart grabbed both of his shoulders and pitched him forwards and down the start of a giant knoll. Over and over the man tumbled, his horned helmet eventually falling off of his head as his body crunched through a throng of briars at the base of the hill. For good measure, Golbart watched as the man's body tore through the other side of the briars and down off of the edge of the cliff. *Say what you want about heavy armor, it might be fantastic against blades, but against gravity, it is no match.* Laughing, Golbart turned on his heels and braced himself as a second gladiator charged across the hill at him. A young gladiator with little to no armor, the man carried a short sword much like his own. Green cloak beating behind him, the bloke was on Golbart before he could position himself correctly; having no other options, Golbart sidestepped the man's downward sword swing and grabbed him at his elbow. Using his own momentum and that of the boy, Golbart pitched them both forwards down the very same hill that the first gladiator had tumbled down.

Doing his best to avoid the prominent crags sticking out from the side of the hill, Golbart ended up somersaulting to a roughly flat spot of the hill. Landing haphazardly on his feet, Golbart unsheathed his sword and spun around in a whirlwind of steel and robe, using his ungainly momentum in his favor. Like himself, the dark-haired young man had somersaulted to the same spot and had regained his footing in a crouching position. Golbart's bladed whirlwind caught the man in the shoulder as he was trying to stand up, forcing him forward and down the rest of the hill. The stadium resounded with a deafening *crack* as the young fighter's head hit the side of a boulder and colored it red. The man did not get up. The crowd jeered at that.

Tumbling down the hill had finally done his robes in. Sliding the tattered robe off of his body, he allowed them to fall to the ground in a pitiful pile as he crouched down, sword in hand. He knew that their were more fighters out there, even if he couldn't see them now. The ones that were left would be the most deadly. Golbart stood up and crested the hill, his eyes roving over the rest of the meadow with caution. Colorful was the only word Golbart could use to describe the grassland, colorful and vivid. Bright purple lavender waved amidst the sporadic wind, purple lavender and scarlet heather. Golden wheat shot up in droves, often as not spattered with blood as red as a setting sun. Hearing it before setting eyes upon it, Golbart tumbled behind a withering tree before a loud 'thunk' confirmed his suspicions. *Archers! Of all the dirty tricks of sending out on a big battlefield... I loathe archers! Blood on my toast!* Crouching on hands and knees, Golbart dove from his hiding place and into a large patch of wheat, hoping beyond hope that one of those dreaded arrows wouldn't find itself between his ribs.

Think Golbart, think! This wheat is going to be a poor shield when that fool figures out I'm no longer behind that cursed tree. I have no means of shooting anything back and if I try charging him, he'll riddle me with arrows. The rain will damper his skills, but only barely. Perhaps I can use that to my advantage. Golbart dropped to his belly and slithered forward as his ears caught the sound of air being punctured with another arrow, the twang of the string a sting to Golbart's nerves. *Why did I ever sign up for this?* Golbart thought bitterly. *I'm no spring chicken anymore!* Setting himself up on his haunches, Golbart raised his head just over a crop of bright blue plants, his eyes landing on a sight that somehow made his heart sink even deeper. *There are two archers! A robed man and a young woman in leather armor. This is just perfect. Where's my blasted partner? She's probably a corpse by now. That wench.*

Feeling the blood rush to his head, Golbart crouched back down and tried his hardest to think his way out of this one. He was at the brink of turning and running before a low rumbling sound caught his attention; chanting from the crowd all around him. Mistaking the repeated chant as cheers, Golbart had paid no mind to the spectators that were about to witness his untimely death. *Behind You!* The crowd chanted. Golbart's eyes widened and heels changed position as a sword crashed down where he had stood not three seconds before. *That same young man I sent cascading into the briars!* Golbart thought fast. The man's head was gouged where he had cracked it on some rocks, and he had what looked to be dozens of briar cuts across his face, but here he was, ready to slay Golbart with a renewed vigor. Having only one good arm now to fight with, the young boy smiled a crazy smile and gestured with his sword to Golbart, taunting him to make a move.

Feeling raindrops caress his bare chest, Golbart felt up to the challenge of putting this youth out of his misery. *A sword ready to puncher my heart and arrows that will surely embed themselves in my back. By luck has reached an all-time low!* Rushing forward, Golbart somersaulted underneath a set of twin arrows arcing through the air and underneath the boy's quick blade in a dance that only Golbart knew the steps too. Upwards Golbart's blade went, slicing the tendons of the boy's already useless arm. Ducking back in defense of the youth's reckless counterattack, Golbart hopped to the side and brought his sword up in time to avoid the detachment of his own head. Dropping down to a crouch, Golbart shot his sword out as a snake might strike its prey. Through the youth's stomach the sword went, piercing precious vitals and spilling the essence of what flowed through the boy's body. Dropping to the side, Golbart tumbled out of the way was two arrows punctured the boy's spilling guts. Spurting blood, the boy toppled forward in a heap, a soundless gasp escaping his lips. *That was the last of my energy,* Golbart thought dejectedly. *Thrush, the rest is up to you. I want my gold, so you had better come through! If you're still alive, that is. You'd better be.*

Thrush had only a moment to peek out of the wavering reeds and into the fray of what was left of the battle before one of the malicious archers turned around and scanned the area behind them; bad luck, that. They had eyes better than a hawk. A series of arrows shot through the tall grass and buried themselves at her feet. She screeched and backed up, trying her hardest to find some type of refuge or discarded shield. Almost feeling the tip of one of those nasty arrow heads slipping between her sweaty shoulder blades, Thrush bounded down the craggy slope of the scarlet hillside and towards the only thing that she knew would save her life at this point. It was the skeleton of a cottage that looked to have been incinerated during the battle. Lowering her shoulder slightly, Thrush let her new scaled armor take the brunt of the impact as her momentum carried her through the charred doorway and into the den that was spattered with blood and guts. Dozens of corpses were scattered around the blackened living room, some bodies freshly butchered and others looking as if they'd been charbroiled to a crispy finish.

Gagging, Thrush dashed through the red room and up a narrow stairwell. She crashed into a lean fellow who was hiding just beside the door frame. The floor groaned as both bodies toppled onto the same torched rug. Flailing her fists as fast as she could, Thrush felt repeated blows to the side of her chest as the man beneath her did the same as she. *Luckily, I have the power of steel to my advantage. Ha!* Thrush thought to herself, *this fool is wearing nothing but a jerkin. My blows will land hard. Now is a great time for my new weapon; I'll need some aid for defeating those archers. Praise the Drey'Une for their ingenuity!* Wrapping her arm around the warrior's hooded head, Thrush secured the man in place with her knee and then used her hand that was free to thrust down a switch that protruded slightly from the engravings carved on her armored leg. Mechanisms unraveled from the top of her right shoulder down to her steel boots as each piece of her armored puzzle was set free. A smile began to creep onto her face.

Thrush could feel two thin, spindly pieces of metal shift from their resting places on her shoulder blades to the top of her head, both pieces interlocking as a jaw might close, her eyes now protected with eye guards akin to an elk. Each pitch-black plate on her armor seemed to shift only slightly, emitting solid, golden wires, wires that snaked around her armored body, forming an exoskeleton as a second defense. Thrush watched in the reflection of a dusty window as her twin swords that she kept in sheathes strapped to her back attached themselves to her new exoskeleton, the hilts sliding into golden sockets, the blades protruding out and to the small of her back as if she had sprouted metallic wings. The man she was pinning down had eyes as wide as a frightened deer, his flailing arms now not trying to thump Thrush but instead trying to grasp anything to slide out and pull away from the beast that had appeared out of a simple armor.

Not wanting to kill the man, Thrush did the next best thing and bashed the top of his head with the new long, metallic cylinder that had appeared on the top of her armored forearm. The man lay as still as a sack of potatoes. Her head ringing from the rush of excitement,

Thrush had a hard time concentrating and eventually found herself dumbly gazing at herself in the grubby window. The man that had sold Thrush her newfound armor had told her exactly what would happen; her energy would be potent and powerful to begin with, she would feel like a god in human boots. That was the power of the keilance, the mystifying, green nugget that had attached itself to her right shoulder. The keilance is what powered her mystical armor. Without the aid of the artifact, her armor would useless. After only so much time though, she would become as frail as a child, her body unable to keep up the energy surge; even worse, if Thrush sustains any bodily damage within a month of using her new armor, her body will receive the damage with double the destruction. The merchant was very clear when explaining this to her.

Thrush did not fully know what the merchant meant when he had explained that the armor had some qualities that would reveal themselves over time, and the man also didn't know what the keilance was, he only repeated to Thrush what had been told to himself when he bought the armor; the man that had sold him that armor didn't even know. What Thrush did know however, was that she had a sleek, silver keg that had appeared on her back as well as fist-sized metallic orbs that spontaneously clinked down from a part of her chest that was exoskeleton, the orbs appearing from a golden spout at her side and falling into a deerskin pouch attached to her waist. She had always felt that her new armor was abnormally heavy, and now she knew why. Thrush did not know what she had gotten herself into with this contraption but the only direction to go was forward.

Thrush could see from the window that the light shower of rain was starting to evolve into yet another windstorm. *This seems to be the normal weather pattern for Koronin! It's either clear skies or monster storms. How lucky am I?* Thrush couldn't help but think, *those archers will be virtually useless in this weather.* Thrush bashed out the window she was standing in front of and poked her head out into the brewing storm. The shadows of the battlefield were still, save for the ravens circling overhead. Even the screams of the spectators had died down. *The calm before the storm. Wait, what was that there by the tree? Movement? No, it looks to be that archer wearing the robe. Someone slew him! Did we win?! No, wait, who's that?* Thrush was just able to discern the female archer before she assailed Thrush with a handful of arrows. *Fool! Can she not see? These winds have made her long bow virtually useless! She will be lucky if she can hit the side of this house from ten feet away let alone hit her mark from fifty! She'll have to hunt me in here if she wants me at all.* Thrush thought brazenly, *or, I can take the fight to her. Fight fire with fire, as it were.* Haphazardly remembering what the merchant had told Thrush of her new armor, Thrush tried to remember the sequence for operating her new toy.

The most basic of functions for her device was a compartment located underneath a trick latch on her breast; using her fingers, Thrush poked and prodded at the armor until a button gave way. Fishing her fingers in the new crevice of her right breast, Thrush found a small bag of rough, black powder. *Success!* Emptying the contents into the metallic cylinder attached to her arm, Thrush fuzzily recalled the next step of what the merchant had told her to do. Grasping a protruding latch from the end of the cylinder and pulling it slowly backward, it clicked into place. Another arrow whizzed through window, crashing into the door frame behind her. Thrush grasped one of the metal orbs from leather sachel and quickly popped it into the open end of the metallic cylinder that was attached to her forearm. *Almost done!* Thrush thought desperately. *I need to ram that bloody black metallic ball the rest of the way into the hole though!*

Water droplets crept down her neck and down to the small of her back as she scoured the dusty floor for some form of a ramrod; she had no success. *Rotten Drey'une! Of all the bloody pieces to leave out of such an intricate set of armor!* Crawling on all fours, Thrush soldiered to the far wall where the arrow had planted itself and yanked it free. Arrowhead pointing up, Thrush rammed the feathered shaft down into the metal barrel, effectively pushing the metal orb down to the bottom of the barrel and compacting the explosive concoction. Sidling up to the side of the window, Thrush hunkered down and took aim in the general vicinity that the archer was seen last. The storm was obscuring her vision, but Thrush was positive that the archer was still down there, waiting to just riddle her with arrows. *For as intelligent as the Drey'une were, this armor certainly needs some fine tuning. Overall though, I'm impressed! I can't wait to try and duel Aeven, he's going to get* roasted!

Thrush held her arm as steady as stone and carefully took aim of the obnoxious archer. One more arrow slung past Thrush's face. *So you* are *down there! Just a little to the left, though.* Using her free finger, Thrush pulled back a lever located at the bottom of the barrel and cried out in shock when her arm flew upward and then behind her. Thrush's ears were ringing something fierce and her eyes bleary from the clouds of smoke that emitted from the end of the metallic tube. Thrush couldn't move and so she just stood there and listened to the hundreds of cheering spectators; Thrush could only guess that she and Golbart had won the match. *I hope you're happy, Golbart, we've won your bloody armor that the Goldenfist Corporation was advertising.*

CHAPTER FIVE

Lurking Amidst the Snowdrift

It was cold. The weak cries of the baby slowly drifted across the snow-bidden plains, the soft wind caressing the resonance as if never having an intention of letting it go. Only slightly less audible, but just as constant, was the gentle crushing of snow under several pairs of boots. There wasn't a voice to be heard however, except for the intermittent grumbling and complaining of harsh weather and uneven terrain. No voices to be carried by the wind, no marching songs, nor jovial chuckles. Only the frail song of a small newborn. *There's something to be said for a warm fire amidst a snowstorm*, August Lor'odyn thought, his dark eyes sweeping the desolate horizon for an ounce of hope. Standing at six-feet tall and with blond hair and blue eyes, most women found August strikingly handsome in a cold, calculating way. August was a young man that preferred rigid law and order instead of vigilante justice, which was probably how he earned his current mission.

Keeping the only heir to the throne alive was more important that his own life, and August understood that. Even if the heir was only eight months old. August frowned slightly and shook his head as his eyes fell on his comrade's armor; frost was slowly taking its hold on the worn, stout metal. *Warm fire, indeed. It'll be half past noon before we all keel over from frostbite.* August raised his fist and halted the slow procession. Gazing down into the newborn's face, August sighed as the infant finally fell into a silent slumber, her slow rhythmic breathing disarming August. *How could anybody's anger hold out against something so precious?* But then again, it wouldn't be her specifically that anybody would direct an assassination against; it was what she stood for. She may be the rightful heir to the throne of Pry'ama, but for now she was an infant with a dozen political hands trying to pull her under and into sparodin. *It's funny how the smell of power makes swift work of the allegiance of the prosperous.* Closing his own eyes, August tried to hold back the deluge of memories that threatened to change him into a broken man, but they still came. They always did.

The smell of roses was strong in the air, August had noted, for this time of year. With a silent chuckle, he listened intently as his two fellow soldiers and siblings argued amongst themselves in the sunlit halls of one of the Chraonos garrisons, Namorhan Garrison. His older brother, Aeven, seemed to have a hold on the debate. As far back as he could remember, August had always been told that the creation of the noble class of drey'une had taken place the day of the downfall of the aor'sii; but then again had that been true, August supposed that the creation of them would have been a moot point. Almost nothing had survived that cursed day, least of all a small nomadic tribe of mediators determined on quelling the constant uprisings of political strife.

"The drey'une were created when the aor'sii met their demise just for the sole purpose of retaining important knowledge that the noble class tried their hardest to erase." Arma proclaimed, *"in the Saint Ivyn scriptures of Lu'guven, it specifically names the drey'une on three separate accounts, all of which pertain to them overseeing the land in times of great need. Aeven, they have the blessings of the aor'sii, no matter which view you decide to take."*

With an exasperated sigh, August studied his younger sister, her spirit for righteousness once again flaring up. Something that both her and Aeven had more than enough of. August preferred justice too, just more... discreetly. Just a head shorter than Aeven, Arma Kvalheim was never one to accept anything but the truth. In some ways, their father, Athrim, had been the strictest with Arma's training methods, instilling justice and valor in every bone of her body because he knew that her devoted focus for the truth would be what sees her to the end. She may have been the youngest of the three but in a lot of ways, she was the most dangerous, her cunning and precision on the battlefield naming her a deadly combatant. It had been eight months since her knighting ceremony and already her successful missions almost matched that of Aeven's and August's. She had been the talk of Chraonos for weeks, her accomplishments earning her a pair of golden-laced swords, the blades themselves resonating a thrill for violence, a thrill for passion, and a thrill for justice. A trait that their barer carried in spades.

Silently nodding his agreement with his sister's rebuttal, August fell behind the debating pair. Arma's fist slammed into her gloved palm, her voice becoming quite vehement to prove her point to its fullest. "With the reappearance of a drey'une in Pry'ama at so crucial of an hour just goes to prove my point. At Runa's blessing tonight, many think that the mystical knowledge of the drey'une will finally come forth. As I have debated with lord Baron Golgren quite often of late, the increasing number of renegade soldiers and refuges is alarming, to say the least. Both sides of the war are running out of supplies, soldiers are losing heart. Even the point of the war is losing its meaning. The winds of change are only bringing profit to the wealthy; the downtrodden are finding that what they're fighting for has lost all manner of reason and purpose. A good majority of our soldiers are turning to mercenary work, asking for money up front. The rest are leaving the country altogether and either disappearing into Tana'thial, Cour'seros, and even the Val'unei Isles.

"I've received reports that state even some of our Midnight Knights, mainly the Guilded Shields and the Solitude Soldiers, have abandoned the campaign as well. They say that the righteousness of the war has been tainted with corruption and deceit, something that they want no part of. If our land continues on this winding dark path of carnage and malcontent,

I fear that it won't be long before another country moves in on us." With a sad shake of her head, Arma slowed her purposeful stride. *"The seven lords of Cenaega, or as most of our infantry have taken to calling them, the Seven Devils, have laid waste to three of our nation's capitals within the last year. Fortunately for us, just recently one of our scouts had managed to evade the devils' forces just outside the fringes of Addel' Redara, his great stallion breeching our gates well after nightfall. Gosmodraii is on the brink of annihilation, all seven warlords moving in for the kill.*

As you well know, Gosmodraii is our nation's sole academy for training and educating young combatants; to lose a city such as Gosmodraii would leave a devastating scar on our country's morale. My point is that with Runa's ceremony at hand, we have an opportunity to raise our squad's spirit, an opportunity to show them that they are indeed fighting for something just. They're fighting for their future queen, Runa. They are fighting for their personal freedom. But most of all, they're fighting for their country. This drey'une will become the very blessing of this land and I'll see to it that it happens and that Runa stays safe." Coughing into her hand, Arma finished her speech with a hoarse throat. *"Even if that means fighting a devil of an enemy head on."*

August completely agreed. Despite the temporary allegiance with the countries of Cour'seros and Tana'thial, the seven devilish lords were banishing capitals to the abyss with little or no resistance. While their has been no allegiance struck yet with the Val'unei Isles, they have not aided the enemy either, so that was something. Reinforcements were scarce, to say the least, lords and barons from the great outlands were finding new reasons to pull their own troops back and reinforce their own borders; reasons that August could wholeheartedly agree with. He would have done the same. With Gosmodraii on the brink of crumbling, August imagined that each and every cadet of the school was fighting for their very existence. A fight that August wasn't so sure that they could win; this conflict had escalated to a war of surreal means. No more were the warlords fighting for any personal ideal or any personal purpose. It now seemed that the Seven Devils had a more sinister mastermind driving their motives. A force that had yet to reveal itself. What August did know was that the devious cause that drove the Seven Devils to wreak carnage was starting to seep into their own country; their was an ulterior motive happening that was twisting the war into something perilous. Some barons were seeing a chance at power that wasn't there before. Hence why the Midnight Knights withdrew. Pry'ama was rotting from within.

His ears catching Aeven's reprisal, August turned his head slightly to gaze upon his older brother. "I agree with you, but only on one point. I believe as well that this drey'une is here to bring our squadrons something, though I fear that what he brings isn't a blessing, but a warning. If you remember in the eighth passage of the diary of sir Luxesma, the diary that was recovered in Gorland Wall, Luxesma was one of the Squires of Dawn that was stationed in the Eighth Barrack, the barrack designated to the protection of Gorland's science facility. You know as well as I the writing in those passages. Inexcusable experiments completed by Chraonos' scientists, our ancestors.

"I will not utter those experiments here, not in these halls. But I am sure you are also well aware of how this war came to be? It came to be through the pure essence of truth. It is my understanding that this diary, as unfortunate as it may seem, was not recovered by a scholar of Chraonos, but of a scholar of Cenaega." Shaking his head, Aeven summed up, "Who could have known that a small diary would have such dire ramifications?"

Inhaling sharply, Arma's pace slowly came to a stop, her blonde braid catching the wind's breath. "I only assumed that the filth that had discovered this chronicle was a traitor to our cause. It never occurred to me that he was a traveler from another country. This puts the entire war in a whole new light. If he was a scholar from Cenaega, then that could only mean that he was—" Arma gazed upon both of her brothers, the gravity of the situation settling upon the three like an unwanted rotten blanket. Closing his eyes, Aeven exhaled deeply.

"Exactly. Being from the country of Cenaega, I imagine that the moment Boru Castellaw discovered sir Luxesma's diary, he found a means to a rise in power amongst his own people. Naturally, however, his actions spawned a beast with two heads, a beast that will prove hard to slay. Like I said, this war came to be through the truth. When Boru came across that diary, it was his sole obligation to deliver that treasure to his birth place Cenaega. And so it was that when the lords and ladies of Cenaega laid eyes upon this book, they not only gazed upon a long-lost treasure, but a subsequent way to finally bring their rival to their knees with the help of surrounding nations.

"The voyage back to our country must have been near ecstasy for Boru; he went from being a lowly scholar to a warlord virtually overnight. According to hearsay, when Boru embarked from his home to our country, he had with him an entire legion. The citadel of Scarrow never even saw them coming. After fortifying and making Scarrow their own landmark, Boru and his legion took to scouring our land. Searching for lords and barons that would listen to what this diary had to say. Through sheer force of will, or maybe it was just bad luck, Boru and his legion of soldiers was victorious, to an extent. When faced with being a turncoat or losing their life, you'd be surprised how quickly allegiances can change. Over the span of four months, Boru had managed to find seven warlords that would rid the land of its plague, of our ancestors. Through the truth of our past, we must now fight for the right to our future."

Reviewing Aeven's face, August took to contemplating his brother's words. Aeven was something of a philosopher; his ideals usually generated through the outlook of the greater good. Standing at about five-ten, his whole demeanor was that of confidence and righteousness. Aeven also had more vengeance and cunning in him than August was comfortable with, sometimes. A trait that August was still leery of, to this day. Aeven's body was muscular, if somewhat pudgy, with sandy, dirty dishwater colored hair that was tangled and wild. When their father Athrim had trained Aeven, most of his lessons had partaken in the use of knowledge and charisma. August had once heard that Aeven was described as "the knight that never had to raise a sword," and August wholeheartedly agreed. When he did have to raise a sword, it was certainly a sight to behold.

"The missing link here, in my eyes, is what was in that diary, exactly." Arma interjected, "You keep describing Luxesma's diary as a treasure of great importance. If this diary is as valuable as it sounds, the content of this book must hold some priceless information. It was not only able to sway a nation to attack us, but also turn some of our most precious troops against us as well. It is, after all, just a diary, isn't it?"

"It is. But you forget where Luxesma was stationed when he was writing this diary, and to what point and purpose he was posted there." Clasping his hands behind him, Aeven took a small step toward the hall's intricate balcony, his eyes studying the gentle sea below. "Like I mentioned earlier, Luxesma was stationed at the Eighth Barrack of Tai'drasial, one barrack of ten. According to the scriptures, many ages ago, the race of men was bestowed with a grand gift. A gift that would bring an end to the turmoil and distrust sowed between the race of aor'sii and the race of men, this gift being a city. I only know bits and fragments of this tale, but Tai'drasial was one of four capitals constructed by the race of aor'sii." Running his finger down the length of the balcony's barrier, Aeven's voice grew softer, barely audible over the crashing waves below. "It was to be that the race of men would inhabit this new citadel, a reigning influence over all other species and beasts of this land. But you know as well as I the hearts of men. Easily turned. Easily corrupted. Even with the race of men having dominion over the whole land, by and by, it still wasn't good enough for there was still one ancient race that held supremacy even over the most righteous of our kings. That was the race of the aor'sii. I wish that I could tell you how it happened, how the dawn of the new era transpired, but as far as I know, that information is lost to the compassion of time.

"From what little I do know, however, it was the murky events afterward that would shape history into what it is today. Through jaded words and underhanded endeavors, the ideals of men were finally brought to fruition. The wings of the majestic aor'sii were shattered—they fell." With his gloved hand reaching over the black balcony, Aeven's eyes followed a stray raindrop as it plummeted onto his gauntlet, his voice once again rising in volume. "It is said that some aor'sii became vigilantes, others took to hiding. The glory of the aor'sii was now just a fading chapter in the tome of history. Each aor'sii was now in a fight or flight response. The race of men knew this. And it was here that the most dismal of events would mold our atrocities. Tai'drasial was an empathetic gift to our race, one that we avoided to cherish in the least. A city created by a race we came to admire and loathe. Hence, we never came to fully inhabit this righteous citadel. On the contrary, we used it for the most part as a garrison, keeping only the barest number of soldiers stationed on the premises. We didn't want to utilize it, but, being the selfish species that we are, we didn't want anyone else to have it either.

"If you don't mind my cliché, it was a dark and stormy night when a certain event took place. It was a foot soldier who stumbled upon her first. Atop the tallest of towers, amidst the frostiest of clouds, a soldier by the name of Luxesma Coulter happened upon a beautiful tall maiden. A maiden with the finest of skin, with the most luxurious of hair, and with golden wings that would take even the most stalwart of men's breath away. Her name was Alathea Y'riia. I'll be the first to tell you that politics and virtue never meet eye to eye, and I imagine Luxesma faced the same conundrum. It was according to the king's own injunction that stated explicitly what was to become of any aor'sii discovered on the property of the royal's own. Death. Destruction. Yet in Luxesma's eyes, what he saw wasn't a deserter or a heretic. What he saw was an injured woman."

August watched as Arma coyly smiled, her words ringing clear and ironic. "An injured woman," she spat at her brother, her eyes smoldering something fierce. "Men were as predictable then as they are now. Let me guess, Luxesma went rushing to her aid? That wouldn't have been justice, that would have been foolhardy. There had to have been some point for a king to have issued a decree to a standard such as that. Like you said, you only know fragments of the story. The missing pieces could absolve the whole issue of whether Luxesma was in the right or not. You're a knight, what do you think about what he did? Emotion or law, which is more important? You can't have both."

"It doesn't matter what I think, this has already happened. It's done and he made his move. But, to answer your question, I probably would have done the exact same as he; can you really call yourself a knight if you go around killing people without a just cause?" Aeven retorted back, his own voice swathed in anger.

"A just cause?!" Arma chided, "the KING is the one that gave that decree! You can't get more just than that!"

"The king is only human! Can we just get back on point, here? Thank you. Luxesma did as his heart saw fit, and I don't fault him for that. Her wings torn to shreds and her leg crippled, Luxesma chose a side between justice and reason. He indeed rushed to Alathea's aid. I would expect no less from a knight to be." His face taking on a look of admiration and pride, Aeven watched the clouds slwoly roll in from the horizon, his voice never

wavering. "Through sheer force of will, Luxesma was able to carry Alathea down the spiraling tower to the only squad stationed in Tai'drasial at the time. He carried her to the only group of friends that he could trust. A group of soldiers stationed at Barrack Eight." Aeven gave Arma a sad smile, his eyes glowing with dread and remembrance. "I trust you remember what a squad comprised of back then? Back before the Third Chaining?"

Her eyes lighting up, Arma slowly relinquished this small piece of knowledge that most considered lost. She loved to read just as much as Aeven did."I do. Before the third king was hung from a chain for all to see for treason to his country, a squad generally comprised of six knights, four archers, and two medics. Not to mention a handful of squires. This entire squad served a single noble, and this noble would hire out his squad for a sum of money. But the most valuable member wasn't who you'd think it would be. It was my understanding that there was always a soldier that had infinitely vast connections and an arsenal of knowledge. A member of the party who made sure that the group did what they were supposed to do. He always lurked in the shadows, watching. Waiting. Who this soldier was, was ultimately decided by the Gale Magistrates, but it could have ranged anywhere from a knight to a squire. It just depended on the gravity of the mission. As it goes, this rogue would report back to the Gale Magistrates, and if the group had not fulfilled what they were supposed to do, or got sidetracked, then the noble in charge of the group paid a very hefty fine."

"Precisely. The overseer in Luxesma's squad was an especially ruthless man. With fast words and deep promises, Luxesma was able to convince his most valued friends in helping this aor'sii, Alathea. Tai'drasial was partitioned into ten separate sectors, and each division was bestowed with special academies and contemporary machinery that enhanced and helped govern the overall whole of the citadel. At the entry point of each sector was a colossal barrack, Luxesma being at Barrack Eight. I won't get into the specifics of each sector for that could take all night. For what it's worth, Barrack Eight was something of a phenomenon at what it was designed for, which was the progress of technology. It was just sheer luck that the tools needed for the medics to perform the various surgeries happened to be at the very sector that they were stationed at.

"The machinery bestowed upon this particular sector, along with the vast libraries and medical knowledge available to them, made Barrack Eight the pinnacle of society for those that resided in the grand metropolis. Which at this point, was virtually no one." Aeven's face grew darker, his voice now starting to taint with disgust. "Over the course of this event, Luxesma Coulter started recording a diary in which he kept on his person at all times. It was a chronicle. A chronicle of Alathea's surgeries, her rehabilitation methods, even the conversations they had. He recorded it all. You know as well as I what happens when you get to know another soul, when you share thoughts with them, share feelings. Over time, you begin to care about them." His pacing coming to a halt, Aeven closed his eyes and slowly knelt to the ground, his hand coming to rest upon that of a lone rose petal that had managed to drift all the way from the receiving hall. "They fell in love. It was an unclear feeling at first, one that I'm sure both of them denied. It was against what the king had decreed, against all laws, and it was unquestionably against all justification—it was heresy. You'd better believe that each and every cadet on that squad gave their all in trying to convince Luxesma otherwise, trying to make him see the error of his ways.

"Slowly he integrated her into his squad's everyday life. A dinner here, a walk there. Simple maneuvers, though, these maneuvers opened their hearts to new possibilities. Luxesma showing his team that Alathea was compassionate and life altering. Sharing thoughts and laughter with this beautiful aor'sii grated against the king's own injunctions; the very truth and laws in which each and every cadet of this squad personally swore an oath to uphold and protect turned out to be nothing more than black lies. They discovered first hand that the race of aor'sii weren't the malicious beings that they'd been told that they were. Their hearts weren't as black as winter's night, and they certainly didn't deserve to be hunted down like animals and slaughtered just because of the king's say-so. It was under this new revelation that each soldier's heart made a valiant change. With several pairs of eyes witnessing the couple, Luxesma Coulter and Alathea Y'riia were wed atop the very same tower that fate had first brought them together. Amidst the most formidable of tempests, wind and lightning as their choir, Luxesma and Alathea declared their vows to one another.

"*Each cadet renounced their loyalty to the king, forsaking their vows of protection to the crown. With rain at their backs, each soldier then declared a new oath, an oath sworn through blood, an oath of truth. No more were each of these soldiers going to adhere to false laws and injunctions created for self-profit. It was quite the opposite. It was here that each soldier swore a pledge to Alathea and to the aor'sii themselves that, through any and all means necessary, they were going to find and protect the last of her race, upholding the lands most valued and sacred law: truth. Sword in hand, Alathea blessed each soldier as he gave her their blood oath, bestowing them a new title.*

"*They were now known as the drey'une, or, in the language of aor'sii, shields of hope. What started out as an act of bravery, an act to uphold true justice, turned into a cause in which many soldiers responded to. With every soldier that rallied to their cause, their was a renouncement of vows. And with every renouncement of vow, with every drey'une that was sworn in to this new society, they came that much closer to their own downfall. For you see, like I mentioned earlier, the rogue of Barrack Eight's squad made his move at the pinnacle of these events. His ideals were not the same as those of his fellow squad members. What he saw was a citadel slowly growing in number of heretics and outlaws, outlaws sworn to the cause of overthrowing the throne.*" Slowly standing up, Aeven gazed into each of his sibling's eyes, the full meaning of his story implied on his face. "When Gawen made his move, I fear that it was checkmate for Luxesma and his cause.

"*Discreetly slipping out of Tai'drasial, Gawen used the political powers he was bestowed with in the neighboring citadel, coercing the town guard to carry a message to the capital metropolis of Scarrow. The message was simple, Gawen writing that a new coalition had formed and reinforcements was direly needed. The message was simple but the implication was vast.*

Slipping back into Tai'drasial, Gawen had one last objective to ascertain before he would be satisfied. Gawen found him in the Chamber of Prayer. Using his cleverness, Gawen shot Luxesma dozens of times in the back with bolts from a crossbow, each bolt representing every squad member Luxesma had turned from the crown. With a final spat on the corpse, Gawen slipped out the window and made his presence known to the progressing army.

"I wish that I could tell you that the drey'une stood fast with the impending onslaught. I wish that I could tell you that despite all odds, despite the betrayal of one of their own, Alathea and her followers defined what true justice truly was. I wish that I could tell you that, but then I'd be lying. Oh, they stood against the impending whirlwind of blood and blades, but against such vast might, the few just weren't enough. With the commander having Gawen at his side, whispering in his ear every flaw of Tai'drasial, it wasn't long before the night was painted red with blood. The retribution of the king was vicious. Alathea Y'riia had, once again, lost everything dear to her. Having to abandon her home, Alathea took to the skies with what fellow aor'sii comrades remained, the remaining drey'une defending their cause with blood. To this day, those last remaining aor'sii have yet to be found. And blessed be that a handful of drey'une were able to escape and spread the word of their cause to those that would listen to them."

Standing in stunned silence, August tried to gather his thoughts on this fragmented piece of history, Arma voicing her opinions first. "I realize that by our king's actions in the past, we must now mourn the loss of such a beautiful and nomadic race, but what does this have to do with our current affairs of warfare and political strife?"

"Only this. I told you that in the surgical and rehabilitation methods performed on Alathea, a diary was being recorded. A diary that not only recorded the outer physical structure of an aor'sii but internal as well. I also told you that every surgery performed on Alathea that day was everything short of a miracle. Technologies that we have not touched since."

The last pieces forming in her head, Arma crouched down on one knee, very faint words escaping her lips. "Oh lord, what have we done?"

""I'm sorry, I still don't understand. So the enemy has a diary with a picture of an aor'sii scribbled within it, so what?" August breathed, his sister's deep reaction catching him off guard. "This diary is obviously at the heart of the matter at hand, but why the importance of it?"

Spreading his hands, Aeven's face took on a look of deep sincerity, his voice full of harsh regret. "When I said that the scholar Boru had created a beast with two heads in his action of returning this diary to Cenaega, I fully meant what I said." Raising one finger, Aeven continued. "The first head of this beast is simply this. When I said that the ability to perform complicated surgeries such as healing aor'sii is something that we haven't tampered with since Luxesma breathed, I fully meant that. Boru is from the Citadel of Cenaega, a nation adjacent to Tai'drasial. Cenaega has been living beside a virtual goldmine with nary a clue, until now. With the resurgence of that diary, it's only a matter of time before the Terenris Project is fully revived again."

"If you don't mind," August interrupted quickly, "please explain what the Terenris Project is."

"The Terenris Project," Arma spoke quietly, "was an amnesty in and of itself. It had been the dawn of the next morning, the dawn after the disgusting slaughter of the drey'une, when they were discovered. six bodies. Or, more precisely, six aor'sii bodies spread throughout the citadel. Creatures that had been shot out of the sky when trying to escape. It was the commanders wish that they be burned or buried, however, it was Gawen's wishes that transpired. You see, he was the rogue member of Luxesma's waband, and being as such, was given temporary command even over his commander. He was a pawn of the Gale Magistrates, and they had other plans. The Magistrates were dark, cunning. Gawen had been there when Alathea had had her various surgeries, he knew what those machines could do. He knew what Barrack Eight comprised of.

"Gawen gathered every medic at his disposal and gave them only a single command: operate. It took raiding parties two months to recover that flaming diary that Luxesma had started, but it wasn't long before Gawen was adding his own debauched notes to that small book. Despite the commander's objections, Gawen soon took the whole matter into his own hands. Operations ensued. Using that bloody diary as a guide, five medics went to work on a single human volunteer. Using every tool at their disposal to give what man should not, no, cannot have. The gift of wings. They tried everything. If surgically removing the wings from an aor'sii cadaver didn't work, then, they tried the next option, and the next, until only one possible alternative was left. Selecting eleven female hosts, Sector Eight soon became a breeding ground for the next age of evolution. It was vile, wicked. With a murky hunger for power and supremacy, Gawen claimed that this new breed would be unto the land a gift of graceful soldiers that had the gift *of the sky, and the intentions of the king himself. An ideal that could have descended Pry'ama into a level of sparodin.*

Arma's voice picked up some strength. "It was the eighth month of the host's pregnancy that the rightful commander made his move. With the best of intentions and with the hardest of hearts, the commander did what he had to do in order to protect the sanctity of the realm; he rectified Gawen's mistake. Slashing down Gawen, this commander was able to assassinate two of the eleven women hosts before he escaped Tai'drasial with Sir Luxesma's diary, his actions halting the progress of these abominations. Not having ample information, and the king having been assassinated three months later by a rogue drey'une, the scientists of Tai'drasial proclaimed the endeavor a lost cause and left it at that. They only had so many aor'sii cadavers to work with and they did not want to waste them until the book could be recovered."

Slowly nodding his approval, Aeven picked up where Arma left off. "Precisely." *He raised his second finger,* "the second head of the beast, I fear, has already emerged. It was an ingenious tactic, I'll give them that, but by sending Boru back through our country with that bloody diary, he's plunged Pry'ama into a fit of chaos that is only rivaled by the amount of infighting that our own lords have started. Currents and rifts are running so deep through our various magistrates that I don't see how we're going to recover in time to defend ourselves. Both heads of these beasts are a powerful adversary. The question, which head is the more important to slay? Do we rally our forces and destroy Tai'drasial, and thus destroy the means of reviving the Terenris Project, or do we rally our forces and try and destroy the Seven Devils first, thus eliminating our opponent altogether? Our problem is that flaming diary; the longer that Boru has it in his possession, the more of our own forces he can turn against us."

"I just want to say this, and I am certainly not a sympathizer for our troops that are turncoats." *August spoke quietly,* "but if you learned that the entire reason for you fighting in the war wasn't for Princess Runa and her safekeeping, but instead was because of trying to defend a dirty secret that Pry'ama doesn't want known to the populace, wouldn't you be upset too? When put in that light, who are the real villains, here? Them or us? If you had to spill blood on account of the nobles, but was lied to on the reason, it just sheds a new light on why so many are defecting."

"Those are dangerous words, brother. I wouldn't speak them aloud again in these halls, if I were you. You never know who's listening. Don't forget that the hosts from the initial Terenris Project have supposedly been lost to the rigors of time. We all succumb to age at some point, I imagine." Arma spoke up, arms crossed and puzzlement marking her face. "All that is notated in our history books of the women carrying those aor'sii offspring is that they gave birth in the heart of some unknown fortress. There isn't a soul alive that knows which fortress it was, or what had ever happened to those babies. It is one of the greatest unsolved mysteries of this age." Arma quickly put in her last words. "I also think that there is a third head to that beast, Aeven, though it isn't one of Boru's making, but one that Chraonos had created. We need King Carrik VI to care enough to rally anyone at all. The task might just fall on the shoulders of what's left of the Midnight Knights, though they have pulled out of this war as well. Our country just seems to be losing heart."

A rough jab on his shoulder brought August out of his reveries; Runa Flockhart squirmed in his arms and then fell back asleep. *Our country has no heart.* Making sure all of his comrades were within talking range, August pitched his voice so it would carry above the howl of the wind. "Has there been any word on the progress of Sylaess Nicolson and what it is he's discovered?"

"Affirmative, sir," Keira McHaffie yelled, her arm shielding her face from the assault of the snow. "He's just returned, he's getting a bite to eat, now. By his reckoning, he estimates that we have less than a mile until we breach the outskirts of Aivunell." Promptly glancing at the horizon to get a better grasp on time, August began to issue orders to his squad. They needed to make haste and move on. His voice was lost to the wind, for the most part. It didn't take long to break camp, they were used to this pace by now. When the life of the princess was in your very arms, the last thing that you did was dawdle. Raising his gauntleted fist once again into the air, he signaled that they move onward, his mind slowly turning to brooding thoughts. They were dark contemplations, however, and only one thought continually resurfaced. *What happened to those lost babies and why did they never resurface into Pry'ama? Or did they?*

CHAPTER SIX

Blood of the Resolved

The rays of the shimmering sun glistened off of the wet sand, the waves from the low tide rumbling loudly in the background. The wind was cutting this morning, a coldness that cut through the clothes and chilled the very bones. Despite the chill and the wind, it didn't seem to deter the many townsmen that were busy working in the port of Koronin. In fact, unless Aeven completely missed his guess, the frigid air only bolstered them to hurry along and complete their tasks as quickly as possible. Thousands of glimmering eyes from the pink sky above looked down upon Aeven as his back rested against a battered crate in an abandoned alleyway. His breath materialized before his eyes as he sipped on his Koronin Salty Rush, the steam from the fresh drink making a small cloud above his head. Even with the constant murmuring and general clatter from the early morning bustle of the town, Aeven could still hear Golbart chomping on his deep-fried Coconut Zing, the smell of spicy fish permeating into the milling crowd before them.

Aeven could only shake his head; as much as he hated the smell of the food that Golbart was eating this early in the morning, they *were* in a port town. Aeven would be hard pressed to escape the smell of fish. As much as Aeven wanted to already be in the mountains tracking Keyamir, his small team was down for the count for now. Thrush and Golbart had battled in the Silverclaw Arena just two days ago, and as far as Aeven could tell, neither of them had sustained any form of injuries, and yet Thrush could hardly open her eyes the morning after the battle, let alone get up and equip herself. It worried Aeven something fierce and yet the local medic had said that she just needed to rest. Not being able to just up and leave his best friend, Aeven decided to make use of the unforeseen downtime and earn some extra gold for their expedition. It took a little digging, but eventually they were directed to a wiry young man that went by the name Polosim Bengtsson. He expressed his concerns about a local aristocrat and was curious if Aeven and Golbart were interested in investigating this minor noble. Aeven had quickly agreed. He'd failed at earning his own gold the other night, so this was a way to make up for that.

"How do we know that this man isn't just pulling our leg?" Golbart spat through a mouthful of fish, "what better prank to pull on a couple of travelers than having them get into trouble with a minor lord? I don't fancy sleeping behind bars tonight."

An exasperated sigh escaped Aeven's lips. "We already went over this. We're not technically doing anything *illegal*. Were just watching and then reporting our intel. It's an easy 300 gold pieces, and I can't say no to that. Who knows how far we're going to be tracking Keyamir."

"Well the longer we just sit here in Koronin, the angrier lord Kaosa is going to get. I don't fancy facing his wrath when he finds out that *you* lost the scent of Keyamir. We were both sent on this quest about a month ago now and I don't think that he'll wait forever for us. I know that you're close with your female friend, but perhaps we can hire us some muscle while she's indisposed? It wouldn't be a bad idea, even if you won't admit it."

The idea had crossed his mind, and Golbart was right, Aeven would never admit that. He just couldn't bring himself to just leave his friend, however, even if it did mean losing Keyamir, potentially for good. "Let's just concentrate on the mission at hand," Aeven spoke through gritted teeth. "We'll be well on our way into the mountains in just a few days. Let's just take this opportunity and earn some extra gold."

"You're the boss." Golbart stated sarcastically, tossing the remains of his fish on the shoddy cobblestone. Though Golbart had a thick cowl pulled up over his face, Aeven knew that he was snickering at him. The ashen skin man now wore his gleaming, golden armor with pride. With his earnings, he'd also purchased a mirror-like shield and a new sword. Aeven could admit to himself that the weapon was intriguing. It had a thin, curled cross-guard, just large enough for fingers to slip through. The cross-guard had a decorative orb on each side, and the blade itself looked scarlet red, like it was stained with blood. The man looked fearsome and could almost be believed when he bragged about himself and his mercenary days. Almost. Without another word to each other, both men strode out into the thick crowd as if they belonged there, cloaks sailing with the wind and heads down.

"Have you ever heard the tale of the Blood of the Resolved?" Golbart asked the back of Aeven's head. Aeven weaved and dodged around the townsmen of the milling crowd as he tried to listen to Golbart and his incessant rambling. The older man continued. "How the lords of the Eight Brethren stood atop a watchtower that overlooked Hexum Spine and could do nothing but stare down as their battalions were razed, pillaged, and beaten by the soldiers of Nyland's Isle?"

A memory stirred within Aeven, but it quickly vanished. The event sounded familiar though. "I vaguely remember," he stated briskly. "What of it?"

"This morning, and our task at hand, reminds me of the downfall of Olkwood. A city that rested at the base of Hexum Spine, a couple of wanderers were hired to keep tabs on a young man, a baron, who was making ties with Redwick Garrison. A citadel that was sworn enemies with the lords of Olkwood. These wanderers were hired because they wouldn't be recognized. These wanderers caught this young baron sleeping with a prestigious noblewoman of the enemy, and both were executed immediately. Well you can imagine how well that went over with Redwick Garrison; as you can see, Olkwood is no more. It was razed to the ground. Olkwood was razed, and several other lords that were in alliance with Olkwood joined in the fray shortly after. You may not have remembered the tale of the Blood of the Resolved, but surely you must remember the War Of Attrition? They are one and the same. Many lives were lost that year due to the subterfuge of two strangers just passing through town."

"You going soft on me?" Aeven piped up, his eyes scanning the handful of townsfolk for their quarry. They were on the boardwalk now, gulls screeching overhead and fog slipping around the fishermen like a second blanket. The wooden planks beneath their feet were wet, rotten, and even broken in some places, but that didn't deter the many fishermen and merchants from going about their daily business. The frigid water lapped beneath their feet at a steady pace. "I thought that you were supposed to be a hardened mercenary? This is just a simple task of spying, no more than that." Golbart huffed to himself at that, his muttering lost to the rumblings of the crowd of people. "And if you ask me," Aeven continued, "that young baron had it coming. You don't sell out those closest to you just so that you can save your own skin."

"And what about the entire town of Olkwood? Or the soldiers that died in the war after? Did *they have it coming* to?" Golbart spat, venom laced in his voice. Aeven didn't have a retort for that last comment, so he kept quiet, head tilted down and eyes ever searching. "All I'm saying is that sometimes, an innocuous deed can have a snowball effect that leaves many lives in the gutter, or worst. You just remember that."

Aeven whipped around, mouth open and eyes narrowed to mere slits. "That as may be, Golbart, but you're leaving out an important lesson of that story; accountability. If that baron had never started creating ties with Redwick Garrison, then *none* of those lives would have been lost. That man made a very bad choice, and it cost him..." Aeven's eyes finally spotted him standing several yards behind Golbart. An older man, lithe as a blade, face covered in a cowl and dark cloak draping down to the boardwalk. The man *was* conversing with someone, they looked very deep in conversation. Aeven just couldn't distinguish if the other man was of importance or not. He wore silver armor, also bore a cowl that shaded his head, and had an elegant blade draped at his side. The man certainly *looked* of importance. Aeven doubted that a sell sword would sport a sword that fancy. Almost as one, the pair of strangers started walking slowly towards the fringe of town, both heads down and conversing passionately. Aeven had no choice but to follow. He probably could have reported back to Polosim Bengtsson at this point, but Aeven wanted to know more. Something about the pair of these men intrigued Aeven something fierce.

Loose gravel crunched under Aeven's boots as he tried his best to be as quiet as he possibly could amidst a crowd of people without drawing too much attention to himself. He was sure that both himself and Golbart looked out of place, but that just couldn't be helped. The pair of strangers slowly wandered off of the boardwalk and into the old district of Koronin; cozy shops, quaint inns, and several merchants with their colorful wagons lined the streets to the brim. Golden flags waved amidst the cold wind, and the crowd of people only grew thicker and louder the further into town that they got. Aeven guessed that several travelers from the grand opening of the Silver Claw were still celebrating the festivities of the new attraction. The salty taste of the sea mingled with the sweaty stench of the growing crowd and the fragrant spices of the freshly baked food to create a miasma of fumes and tastes that Aeven was hard pressed to identify. Sweaty bodies pressed up against him from all sides, elbows jabbed him, and his thoughts were drowned out by the obnoxious rumbling of people talking, yelling, and roaring over the din of the other people. Though the milling crowd of people only grew thicker, Aeven was just able to keep tabs on his target.

They wandered through the streets for a good twenty minutes more, leaving the commercial part of town and entering a questionable and shady street that was mashed down to mere mud. Both men eventually stopped in front of a nondescript building that was caving in on itself. As both strangers stepped onto the rotten porch, the second man in the silver armor dropped his cowl as he entered the residence. Golbart, who had been following Aeven akin to a shadow, inhaled deeply, his spindly fingers coming to rest on his sword. The primary man, the lord that they'd been hired to track, quickly disappeared inside as well, slamming the cracked door behind them.

"Remember that story that I told you earlier, Aeven? The one where I stressed that the wanderers should have just left well enough alone and went about their own business? We need to just turn around. Now. Let's go get Thrush and just leave this place. I beg of you." Golbart muttered into Aeven's ear, sweat dripping down his face. "You do not want any part of this, I can promise you that."

Aeven inched away, his eyes narrowing. "What's going on here? You recognized that man, didn't you? Who is he?"

"You aren't going to like the answer. If *they* are involved then I want nothing to do with this. You can find some other navigator for your journey. I mean it."

"Come on, man, out with it." Aeven implored, hands splayed out before him. "Who is he?"

Golbart looked as if he wasn't going to answer, but eventually sighed deeply. "He is a war leader of the infamous band of renegade soldiers known as the Azure Skulls. I brought this upon myself for telling you that story, this is what I get, I suppose. My luck is worst than dog…"

Aeven cut him off short. "I don't understand."

"Remember how I told you about the War of Attrition? The Azure Skulls were a result of that. The war escalated into a far bigger one than even the lords could anticipate, and both sides needed soldiers. Badly. They made promises that they couldn't keep, promises of fame, of gold. Of glory. Of riches beyond belief. The war eventually ended, and the hired commoners that were pressed into war were left with naught to their name but blood and famine. Hundreds of them went back to their old life, but hundreds more wanted vengeance for being taken advantage of. Many thought that they had eventually died off, but as you can see, that isn't the case. That was only wishful thinking, on the noble's part. They have just been lurking in the shadows. Biding their time."

"So the two men that we've been spying on this morning were none other than…"

"Right." Golbart finished for Aeven, "members of the Azure Skulls. More specifically, the man that I recognized was Alexian Griffith. Hence why we need to just drop this now and leave. I met him, once.

Cold and calculating as the dead of winter. His story is sad, and I can understand his actions. Once a lord, he was stripped of his nobility and forced to live as a commoner when he followed the will of his commander and pillaged a town on the outskirts of Khraonos. The war crimes were placed on his shoulders, and his commander walked away with barely a slap on the wrist. Many thought that Alexian had taken his own life, but he emerged from the shadows just a few years ago. Well, *whispers of him* emerged from the shadows. Still, none could be dead certain that it was him. It seems that he's been more than busy. If he is making ties with leaders of a port town like Koronin, then he is well on his way of creating a revolution. A revolution that we just landed ourselves in the middle of, no less. You have a choice, Aeven. Report back to Polosim and fan this spark into a flame of war, or just leave this town now and forget that this ever happened."

"Don't these townfolk deserve the right to defend themselves? If we just ignore this then we are just as responsible for whatever happens afterward." Aeven's cold fingers clasped his time wedge that was nestled within his pocket, his adrenaline soaring high. Thinking of the deeds of the nobility always left a sour taste in his mouth, now more so than ever. Aeven himself was a noble, after all, even if he had a hard time admitting so to others. Perhaps that was the reason why he got so angry when thinking of the prestigious; he knew better than most what they were capable of. He was torn. Their were a handful of nobles that deserved worst than death, but did *all* of them truly deserve the wrath of the Azure Skulls? A piece of him wanted to say yes.

Shifting shadows. No sooner did the door slam behind the two renegades than a handful of young soldiers in pristine white cloaks emerge from the back end of the street, silver swords drawn and the look of vengeance glistening within their eyes. Aeven's eyes latched onto the golden clasp of the closest knight. The sigil of the house of Vanlanis, the house of the Eastern Marshes. Aeven's eyes raised to the rooftops of the simple houses; dozens of archers were creeping atop the terraces, arrows nocked and at the ready. The few townsmen that had been meandering through the street quickly scattered into the shadows like mice that had gotten a whiff of a predator.

Golbart quickly clasped Aeven's shoulder, terror stark on his face. "I know that look! Don't do anything stupid. We can still walk away from this unscathed! We have a mission to fulfill and this feud is none of our business!"

Aeven shrugged him off. "The Azure Skulls might be tactless, but no one deserves to be slaughtered in the streets like animals! Especially after how they shed their own blood in the noble's war. No, the least that they deserve is a fair trial." The memories of what the nobles were capable of, of what his own flesh and blood was capable of, started to drown him like an unwanted miasma of guilt and shame. Aeven wanted vengeance. Golbart yelped and dove behind an abandoned merchant wagon as Aeven slowly began to allow the energies from his time wedge to warp and twist around him. "I'm not going to hurt anyone," he whispered, "just deter both sides from shedding blood needlessly."

CHAPTER SEVEN

Heart of the Skull

One of Aeven's fondest memories of his father was of him defeating a band of renegade thieves singlehandedly while his guardsmen looked on in awe; his sword was akin to fire, his soul the embodiment of passion. It was part of this memory that Aeven tried to wedge into the present. Aeven wielding that sword and using his social status should be a surefire way of deterring bloodshed. Those knights wouldn't dare attack a noble of Chraonos, even one that is estranged. Lord Camdyn Vanlanis might be rash and young, but his fortress in the Eastern Marshes would surely fall swiftly if it invoked the ire of Chraonos. Aeven swiftly placated himself in the middle of the street, back to the ramshackle house and directly in opposition to the oncoming soldiers.

His internal energy was quickly depleting, but his memory was slowly materializing before his very eyes. Aeven focused on the crystalline blade that his father would wield with pride. The sword started out akin to a smoky mist, akin to a memory of a memory. It was hazy and uncertain. The more he concentrated, however, the more distinct and solid it became. The more that he focused on the minute details of the elegant weapon, the more certain that he became that the blade was in the here and now. Time warped and bent around him, crackling as Aeven's faint memory intruded upon the present. The blade itself was about four feet long, thick, and had tribal knots engraved into it. The hilt was just as stout, leather wrapped tightly around it, and golden, wire meshing to protect the hand. A few more seconds crept by and then the majestic blade came crashing to the ground. Aeven picked it up, a harsh smile creeping onto his face. His energy was still depleting, but now at a much slower pace now that the sword was here in the present.

Aeven could unsummon the blade, if need be.

No sooner did he heft the sword into his hands than a colossal crash boomed out in front of him; a giant, divine sword had materialized above the crowd of oncoming knights and struck down into an unsuspecting soldier, the sword dissipating into a holy thunderhead. The bolt pierced through the knight and lifted him up and off of the ground, the man flying several feet into the air before crashing down into the abandoned wagon. The soldier was charred to a crisp and lay lifeless. The door to the house cracked open and a petite woman in simple squire's armor rushed out, her own sword clasped in hand and raised high in the air. A second phantom sword appeared above the crowd of soldiers, two more knights being blasted off of their feet before an arrow plunged itself into the desperate woman. The fleeting confrontation escalated into a battle of madness and carnage at the drop of a hat.

Hardened veterans of the Azure Skulls spilled out of the alleyways and crevices of the street like thieves sneaking about the night. Lips pulled back in rictus snarls, their blades glinted in the sunlight as the hunters quickly became the quarry. These noble knights might be from prestigious academies where only the finest of scholars taught, but they were no match to the renegade soldiers that had lived and breathed battle for years on end. Violent screams erupted all around Aeven, blood and bodies alike spattering across the ground in droves. Aeven backed up against an abandoned shop. He couldn't decide which side he should be fighting for, or if he should be fighting at all. He only had a moment to ponder before the decision was made for him. Two young knights lunged for him at once, one sword coming high, the other low, but both came as swiftly as the wind. Aeven was faster. Rolling to the side, Aeven brought Cinderforge around in a wide arc, effectively blocking both incoming blades. His sword clashed and clanged against his opponent's blades, and every time it did so, Aeven could feel his own energy depleting internally. He couldn't keep this up for long. Possessing his father's sword had done nothing to deter the oncoming knights, it was time to try a different tactic. Deflecting a few more thrusts, Aeven brought his sword up and around in a shower of blood and guts, both knights falling to their knees in unison. Their armor and swords might have been the best that gold could buy, but their skills had been weak and fruitless. Pain panged at Aeven's heart, but it wasn't something that could have been helped. Hanging his head, Aeven allowed the sword to dissipate in a shower of smoke and time.

"You've done it now!" Golbart hissed at him, the heavily clad man grabbing his elbow. "What's gotten into you?! Killing two of lord Vanlanis' men? Are you trying to start a war? If just one of those knights recognize you, word will get back to the Eastern Marshes that a Kvalheim is helping the Azure Skulls! Helping with a revolution! The entire country could be plunged into war for this. We need to leave. Now!"

"It's not like I had much of a choice, did I?" Aeven spat back, "should I have allowed a blade to pierce me just so that I don't upset the nobles? Don't try and turn this around on me. I didn't send those knights to slaughter these people, I was just at the wrong place at the wrong time."

"You weren't here by accident, and that's a fact." Golbart stated solemnly, "and now is not the time to debate this. We need an out, but it seems that both ends of the street are clustered with bodies and blood." Golbart was right. The local guards had joined the fray now, as did reserves of the Azure Skulls, and the entire street reeked of butchery. Shields and blades crashed against each other in a din that pierced the ears, and bodies pushed up against each other so closely that spittle and curses were shared just as passionately as swords and daggers. The salty mud was now a thick river of blood. "Wait, I see an out for us. With any luck, no one will notice. Follow me!" Golbart dashed and dodged through the onslaught of soldiers towards an alleyway that was adjacent to the house that the original Azure Skull leaders had disappeared into. Like a rat in the night, Golbart scurried through the alleyway and to an obscure trapdoor that looked the worst for wear. Rust had worn down one of the two small doors, while the other one lay broken into several pieces. Having no other choice, Aeven followed his stealthy comrade as he kicked open the entrance and hopped down into the unknown.

A squad of knights *had* noticed, and before Aeven could escape all of the way through the trapdoor, thick fingers snagged the hem of his cloak and yanked him back out into the darkened alleyway. "You think that you can escape your fate so easily?" The rough faced man spat, a solid fist belting Aeven in the stomach. Their were two more knights behind him, both snickering, eyes alight with a passion for destruction. Aeven doubled over, bile rising into his throat. These knights were dressed just as pristinely as the others. Armor immaculate, weapons unscathed. Aeven wouldn't have been surprised if this was their true first battle. He would use that to his advantage. "You and your kind are filth. No, worst than filth. Woe to the realm when your pig of a mother sired you! You commoners are all alike." The stout boot of the knight came up and connected with Aeven's chest, sending him sprawling backwards and into the mud. "You cause havoc and mayhem, and then complain when the nobles aren't doing enough for you. Pitiful!"

Good, Aeven thought desperately, *so they don't recognize who I am. Or, at least, this man doesn't.* The knight grabbed another handful of Aeven's cloak, and that's when he made his move. Snagging the knife from behind his belt, Aeven plunged it deep into the man's chest, a look of pain and surprise sprouting on his face. His body fell to the side, life quickly draining from his eyes. Springing to his feet, Aeven drew his sword and spun around in a flurry of mud, prepared to fend himself from the other two soldiers that were directly behind him. They both had snarls on their faces, eyes narrowed to mere slits. One woman and one man, swords drawn. *I don't have much choice here. A mob of blades and blood behind me, and these two cadets in front. We're supposed to be on the same side! Do I really want to cast my lot with them, however?*

The woman's sword lowered just a hair, recognition blossoming in her emerald eyes. "I knew that I recognized you! I trained at your castle, years ago. Back when I was first enlisted. You're a Kvalheim!" Her comrade glanced over at her, speculation and surprise marring his face. "Do you know what Vanlanis could do with that information? That a Kvalheim is fighting for the Azure Skulls? Multiple factions of knights would come together and slay your wicked family, and that's a fact. I just hope that I'm there when a noose is draped around your neck. You and your kind deserve it. As soon as I find liege lord Polosim, your *hide* is mine!"

Aeven felt as if he had been belted in the stomach once again. He felt lightheaded and that he'd been played for a fool. Which he had. *Polosim was in on this?! He knew who I was and intentionally played me for the fool. He might have just started a revolution by involving me in this! I bet my entire stash of gold that he has a messenger on his way to the Eastern Marshes saying that they "saw" me helping the Azure Skulls. No. No, I don't know that for certain. But I have a hunch.*

The young blond knight lifted two fingers to her lips and gave three sharp whistles. The din of the fighting was just too loud for her comrades to hear. None behind Aeven acknowledged that she needed help. She attempted to give a fourth whistle when her face blossomed into a look of anguish. She looked down at her stomach as a blade appeared from the middle of it. She crumpled into an unmoving heap on the ground.

Aeven rushed forward and took a savage swing at the last remaining cadet. His sword came up just a hair too late. Bashing his blade aside, Aeven swung the dagger around that was still clasped in his other hand and connected it into the side of the man's head. He crumpled into the mud like a sack of potatoes. "Great timing, Golbart. Not a moment too late. I'm impressed."

"You should count your blessings. I came this close to saving my own skin and leaving you to your own fate. The lord knows that you certainly deserve it." Golbart bent down and wiped his sword on the deceased cadet's cloak, his eyes coming up to meet Aeven's with a dull fury. "We need to leave before another knight recognizes you. Come on."

The passageway down into the storm cellar was dark, damp, and musty. The steps were slick with grime, and the smell that clung to the air reminded Aeven of a rotting animal. Their footfalls reverberated against the crumbling walls as they made their way down into the dark abyss. The descent down didn't take long, and the narrow stairwell eventually led into what appeared to be a small lounge type area. Three small bookshelves lined the walls, and a ratty chair rested in the far corner of the room. Blissfully there was a door against the far wall, opened part way and busted to pieces, but a door nonetheless. So this cellar did have another exit. A means to escape the massacre above. *The damage might have been done already before I even started this "mission". What choice do I have now, though? None. Polosim recognized me and played me like a drum. I need to find Thrush and disappear from this cursed city! I have my own mission that I need to focus on. I'll just write a letter to my brother in Chraonos and explain what happened. I'll explain that he needs to be prepared and I'll check in as soon as I can.*

Aeven was so focused on this predicament that he didn't realize that Golbart had stopped at the entryway, his eyes fixated on something just above the door frame. "Well I'll be," He murmured to himself. "Someone must've been in a bleeding hurry to do such a shoddy job of hiding their treasures. Well, you know what they say, a thief can't outsmart a thief. As my personal motto goes, 'if it ain't glued down, it's now mine to own!'"

"Do we really have time for this?!" Aeven hissed, his attention drawn to the door that was just behind them. "All it'll take is one person noticing that were down here before that brutal fight descends upon us! We need to be gone. Now!"

"Now just hold up here. This'll take all but a few minutes and, believe me, this treasure is more than worth it. Besides, *you* drew *me* into this fiasco, remember? Don't blame me if I don't want to walk away empty handed. You just watch that door and be sure to defend us, if need be." Golbart unceremoniously drug over the chair to the doorway and stood upon it, hand ripping away a false board that had been loosely nailed above the door frame. After a few moments he was hooting and hollering, his thick hands dropping a small, silver inlaid chest at Aeven's feet. "Here, you can have whatever is inside of *that*. I'm feeling mighty generous. But all of this gold, and these gems here, they are *mine*!"

"You're only giving this to me because you can't possibly carry all of this back to our room without raising suspicion. How under the stars are you going to even carry all of that treasure, anyways? I'm not going to carry it for you, that's for bloody sure."

"You know what you're exceptionally good at?" Golbart barked down at Aeven, hands plunging fistfuls of gold and gems into his pockets. "You're great at *complaining*. Just take the bloody treasure box and be grateful. Again, whatever is in there is yours. I have enough here as it is."

Eyeballing him sideways, Aeven let out a frustrated sigh and opened the small treasure box so that they could move on from this musty, stinking room. Resting within the red padded box were three thick anklet cuffs that looked to be made of a silver type alloy. Simple runes were etched into the treasures. "I don't believe it!" Golbart snapped, jumping down from the chair and snatching up one of the artifacts with a surprising deftness. "These here are worth a hundredfold more than the gold I'm stuffing in my own pockets. No, a thousandfold! My luck just gets better and better. Or worst and worst, depending on how you look at it."

Aeven was at a loss for words. "Well? What are they?"

"It amazes me sometimes how little you know, especially knowing that you are a noble. How can you now know what a Hex Adaptability Lunar Operant is? HALO for short. The company "Lunar" is in direct opposition of the Goldenfist, and these are ways for a warrior to imbue themselves with a skill set from only the best of the best. I'll be the first to tell you that these are very versatile, and *extremely* coveted. When you equip this to your ankle or wrist, you are, in essence, putting a hex on yourself that will imbue you with the fighting style that these runes are derived from. These artifacts are specially crafted and use a concentrated amount of lyvah and nyvah to achieve the desired effects for exploits, adventures, and deeds from past warriors that have worn these anklets before you. There are only a small smattering of these across the realms, and only one can be worn at a time. But the value of them? Priceless. How these got to be here, in this dump of a city, in this dump of a cellar, is beyond me. But, here we are. A HALO Prism is a tool, just like a time fragment, that will aid you when you need it most. You don't need *three* of these, right? You don't mind if I just take this off of your hands, right? And look here. There are even three Chraonos Slots in this here anklet where you can insert the time fragments that I just mentioned. Again, like I said, these are truly versatile artifacts. It's just a shame that Lunar is no longer a functioning company. Well, as far as I know they aren't functioning. But who's really to say? This is a vast realm, they could be anywhere."

Aeven picked up one of the anklets and stared at it, completely at a loss for words. It was pleasingly aesthetic. The metal was sleek, thick, and a cool, crystalline blue, whereas the one that Golbart had was dark and smoky. The one in the box still was scarlet red and had sparkling black gems inlaid into it. The runes on all three of them were smoldering orange, as if alight with the passion of just needing to be used. His eyes strayed to the bottom of the anklet. It was small, but there was an inscription beneath the runes themselves. "This says "Azure Trapsmith", Aeven muttered, his interest piqued. "It certainly can't hurt to have more tools at my disposal, I suppose." Against his better judgment, he snapped the tool to his ankle. It was snug.

"A trapsmith, eh?" Golbart chuckled, his fingers deftly snapping his own anklet to his body. "Well I can certainly see where that one fits you like a glove. You are sly as a fox and too smart by about half. As for me, mine says 'Corsair Starshard'." I'm excited to see what knowledge is passed down to me through this! I'm itching to battle. I would bet my right arm that there is one more of these up above where the battle is raging, but I'm smart enough to just be happy with what I've found."

It took a moment for Aeven to catch on to what Golbart was harping on about. "That girl that was summoning those swords out of thy sky! I've never seen anything of the like before. No matter. Let's just go! I'll nab this last one here for Thrush. She should be excited about this, she's all about the artifacts and new equipment." Aeven glanced over at Golbart, but he wasn't listening. He had a handful of his time fragments in the palm of his hand and was staring at them intently, presumably thinking about which ones to put in his anklet.

"Do you realize how important of a decision it is on which of these to put in the anklets?" Golbart whispered, hand scratching his head. "The combinations and possibilities are endless!"

"That's a conversation for later!" Aeven snapped, "Lets just go. When we get back to the room we can toy with these HALO Prisms. But not now. This day I'm sick of the bloodshed."

CHAPTER EIGHT

Spider Eye Canyon

Mist. Mayhem. The imagery of violent waves, distant thunder, and screaming that pierced the heart wouldn't leave Kordin St. Khaun's mind, even after several hours had passed. The violent screams of the soldiers that he tore asunder still reverberated inside of his head. He always sat in silence after a brutal slaughtering, reminiscing and praying to his god that what he had done was indeed the righteous path. The garrison's balcony was cold. Blazing fires could be seen far below, the fires of dozens of soldiers and members of the New Sect coming together as one, finally. The frigid stars gazed down at him, judging him. Each fire spouted at least five feet high, some even higher, but none of the heat had found its way upwards to Kordin and his twin sister that sat beside him, cross-legged and just as silent as he. She too was praying to their god, praying that demons such as they could one day find peace. Both he and his sister Rhea were twins, born to a high lady of Golub sixteen years ago. Both had completed the knighting academy in lockstep, and soon after that they had both attained the rank of h'arai not three years past. Gifted was the term most had used when describing the young, dark pair of siblings, though the soldiers down below called the pair of them demons, and for good reasons. The battlefield never goes as planned for the enemy when the St. Khaun twins fight, and that was a fact that none could dispute.

Breathing deeply, Kordin allowed his eyes to close and his memory to sweep him yet again through the slaughtering of this morning past. The legion of the Seven Devils was exotic. Exotic and elusive. Rumor had it that most of the original legion that had sailed to Chraonos from Cenaega were raised in rank after they had pillaged and plundered some of Pry'ama's most iconic cities. And they didn't just plunder gold and resources; they had no problem taking hostages and soldiers as well. The Seven Devils could be very devastating, when they want to be. There was resistance at first from the Pry'ama natives, but the Seven had made such an example out of the first stronghold that the other notable cities gave in after a heartfelt fight.

It wasn't long after that the Seven Devils were marching around the Azaevia Mountains, searching for a way to lay siege to Kordin's home without actually passing through the Azaevia Mountains. Those mountains slew even the bravest of soldiers. Amdaer'lael was very unique in a handful of ways, the first being that most of the realm resided underneath the very grounds that the foreign legion was trying to lay siege to. They just did not realize it. The only structures that were topical were a multitude of stone garrisons and a handful of prisons. Amdaer'lael was *compassionate.* If a man was convicted, he was given a robe, scripture of the New Order to read upon, and a special drink. The drink was made of a concoction comprised of caordin'torr, or liquid energy that elevates mental and physical power to an extreme degree. It elevates the bearer to a degree of hysteria. These drinks deteriorated the mind but were excellent for battle. Left in contemplation, those very convicted felons were the first to be called upon when a dangerous mission came available. If they survived and obeyed their commander, then *one* year was taken off of their sentence. This process could be repeated multiple times until the sentence was finally paid in full. Amdaer'lael was on the fringes of the Spiral Rift, a great, broken plain that spanned for hundreds of miles. Thieves and rogues loved Amdaer'lael because it was easy to disappear if the law came looking for them. How they handled prisoners was supposed to be a strong deterrent for thieves such as them, but some just never learned. Those ones made the best soldiers.

Memories from the past day haunted him like an unwanted smog of darkness. Kordin remembered the sand beneath his feet, the feeling of sharp seashells pressing against the softest tendons of his toes. He and his sister had opted to spend three consecutive nights on the roughest crags of Amdaer'lael's rim. Waiting, anticipating, and watching. The commanders of Amdaer'lael had not ordered the two of them to do this, nor had the council, or even the local baron; they did this because they wanted a test of their strength. They needed to *know* what exactly they were up against.

Being a mindful tactician wasn't all about sheer strength. It was about being smart. It was as simple as that.

The mist of the sea was dissipating as the sunlight from high above pierced it's heart. Kordin and his sister watched in awe and horror as a legion with armor like fire birthed the entryway of the dual canyons known as Spider Eye Canyon. The first to crest the canyon walls were giant, elegant birds with piercing, long, spiral type horns that protruded from the animal's narrow head. Riders, wearing armor as scarlet as the beast they rode, were hunched low on each of their beasts, barbed spears each slanted at exactly the same angle. Marching almost directly underneath these flying creatures was a type of soldier that Kordin had only heard whispers about.

Known as the psych'une'torr, or as most people have started labeling them the 'lamplighters'. Red-skinned barbarians, these men and women were more akin to human juggernauts than mere soldiers. Garbed to the teeth in silver rimmed plate mail, each hooded psych'une'torr carried various battle axes and long, thin throwing knives that draped from their thick belts. If Kordin was prone to be frightened, which in fact he was not, he would say that the most feared attribute that the psych'une'torr possessed was the piece of equipment that resembled a lamp, an item that swung over the tops of each of their heads. Never seen in action, Kordin had heard only whispers of what was possible with those light sucking machines. This was the power of the Seven

Devils; this is what called him and his sister from the depths of the city known as the Bone Realm to stand before a tide of scarlet and doom.

Rhea and himself had gained the attainment of the rank of knight from that fool academy in Chraonos, they had also unlocked a barrier in their own mind to achieve the status of h'arai with the Goldenfist Corp., and yet the definition of fulfillment went unfulfilled in their lives. Serving a glutton of a pig who wears a crown was not the path that they wanted to tread, nor was the path of fighting everyone else's battles for a thankless people. No, Kordin and his sister had found a new 'family' now and all that entailed was the sacrifice of their very souls; not a hefty price at all. Lanky soldiers in red-shelled armor climbed the cliffs just as a swarm of ants might invade new territory. Leathered scouts paraded the trails behind Kordin, hefty legionnaires bulwarking below. When one of those ghastly birds rose high in the air to meet him eye for eye, Kordin knew that now was the time to demonstrate what it meant to be considered one of the kul'sadar. It felt as if time stood still, for just a breadth of a second. Kordin gently pulled his Mask of Sorr'raa down over his face, anger touching his eyes. In one fluid motion, Kordin tossed his most precious time spiral in the air and let the confounded soldiers watch as all eyes followed the trajectory of his royal blue item of power.

The soldier atop the winged beast whistled once and the bird's talon slashed out at Kordin, the razor sharp claw barely missing Kordin's face. Allowing his sister to assume control over his time spiral, he could feel Rhea's energy in her own Sorr'raa build up as he unleashed his own mask's secret. It's funny what the mind creates from such a surreal experience, Kordin realized. Time slowed down, he remembered as his sister's energy went rampant, but what happened after that burst of power seemed hazy and distant. Kordin's thoughts shimmered and then were gone, replaced by either a peace that his God had given him, or a peace his own body supplied Kordin knew not. What he did know however, was that his sister snapped back to reality the same moment that he himself did, and like himself, she had taken to studying the masses of servants and soldiers that rested far below. Kordin was sure that she was thinking the exact same thing as he, for some twins worked in that frightening way, having the same thoughts at the same time. Tonight was a victory of celebration. They had struck the first blow, that was all that mattered.

The intention had been to initiate the voyage within the month, when they had enough people recruited. Now their attention was focused on the beast that was clawing at their doorstep. Only a select few of those people down by those fires knew what was in store with the voyage to come, the voyage to the new realm. The *voyage*. Even that simple statement left a bitter taste in his mouth. The *voyage* had been lord Leothelias' idea. An attack on Pry'ama from the realm created from the pit of the sea. Rhea and himself might be adopted and used for the benefit of lord Leothelias when and where he saw fit, but their endgame was going to be something that *none of them* will see coming. The rest of those men and women, though they might be pawns now, will be Kordin's weapons of shadow and deceit. They were much like him and his sister, duped into joining a trek to a promising new realm and then, upon arrival, forcibly converted over to be weapons of war by that awful well of dark energy. Kordin visibly shuddered. The voyage. The deception. It all reeked of political rot. So many lords and barons were vying for the seat of power, and they were *all* willing to use anyone that they could to attain it. Even a pair of distraught siblings that just wanted to be left alone. Hearing the gong that commenced the meeting of the kul'sadar, Kordin and his sister Rhea basked in the cold wind one last time, anticipation of the night's events drowning them in excitement. Tonight would be a night like none other. This was going to be the night that the Seven Devils lost an entire legion of precious soldiers.

Aeven's nose crinkled. Forced to tread the only path wide enough for an unbalanced merchant's wagon to traverse, the small team was submissive when Golbart dictated from the front of the group which trails they would ride. The Azaevia Mountains was an ungodly sight full of deserted shacks, desolate crags, and chilling winds that cut to the very heart; when Golbart started to choose the paths that led down and out of the heart of the Azaevia Mountains, there wasn't a murmur of complaint from either of the other two companions. Veering his wagon downward to a burst of warm wind, the smell that greeted the team after rounding a particularly long bend was sweet. The trail had finally descended to the mouth of a great plain, and yet the valley that they looked down upon told a very interesting story. For miles on end, Aeven could see steel wrought buildings that looked the worst for wear. Some of them had fallen over completely to be consumed by the planet, while others were still erect but punctured with holes of rust. Heaps and mounts of discarded junk lay scattered within, the land itself tainted black. Thick vines and gnarled trees grew over the top of most of the debris. He could only shake his head at what the purpose had been of a place such as this. It stunk of the Goldenfist somehow, but Aeven couldn't quite place his finger on it. His eyes scanned the rest of the valley; thousands of small, red berries floating in vast lakes overtook the rest of the gully. Farmers could be seen as well, though not nearly as numerous as the bogs. Each small stead had a rustic cottage with various cattle spread out around them, the mere sight of the setting stirring something deep within Aeven. Just the simple act of watching these farmers do their day to day work as they walked by gave Aeven such a sense of contentment that he briefly contemplated sheathing the life of the mercenary for good. Oh, how sweet that would be.

"I see that look in your eyes, boy. At one point in time, I felt the same way." Golbart rumbled from the seat of his wagon. "This small village is just one of many that creates what is known as the External Rim. When that longing look shakes itself out of your head, take a closer look at those unfortunate souls."

"Honestly they just look like simple farmers with a great deal of more sense than I possess. I can admit that they're smart to live on this side of the valley, able to hide from the woes of the rest of this realm." Aeven answered. "And frankly, it wouldn't take a lot of convincing for me to sell this scarred sword of mine and buy myself a clean shovel."

"While escapism is a beautiful art, I think that you mistake them, Aeven. Look at those 'rustic cottages' hiding beside the face of the mountain; the windows are just large enough for an archer to shoot through, and the outer layer of that house looks to be made of granite, mortar, and even a few barbed spears! I would bet my life that those "cottages" have access to underground tunnels that are beneath those bogs."

"These poor souls live in the depths of the Azaevia Mountains! Of course they need fortification! You senile old bat, these farmers are poor, not stupid!" Aeven shot back. "This valley is the very centerpiece for the entire realm of Pry'ama, who knows what vile miscreants plague their doorstep? I would bear arms too if it meant being able to lead a relatively safe life."

"Well, blood on my eggs, why do I even bother? I know all of that kid. However, why do you think that they even call this the 'External Rim' if it is the centerpiece of Pry'ama? It isn't because of its beautiful view, that's for damn sure. Here, I'll do you a favor and point out a landmark for you. Do you see that overhang there? The one looming over those dozen 'cottages'?" Aeven did indeed see what the old coon was rambling on about and from the looks of the layout of the square building, it was an old prison; from what Aeven could tell there were at least three guards posted around the side of the solid building, as well as a lone legionnaire standing stoically above the large gate. Behind the building itself, off in the distance, was a pair of ridges that made Aeven squirm. He recognized that landmark. Spider Eye Canyon. He would cut off his own arm before walking between those peaks.

"I see a crumbling building if that's what you mean," Aeven answered dully, "though its so far up the mountain there that I can hardly make anything out on it."

"It's a sturdy prison, but not one to keep in your average felon. You wouldn't believe it, but inside that landmark is a very unfortunate legend."

Holding his head high, Golbart waited for Aeven to take the bait.

"The anticipation is killing me here, man. What's the legend?" Aeven knew the old crow was glaring at him. But to be frank, Aeven didn't really care at this point. He knew that Golbart was working up to something.

"Inside of that tower holds what's known as the Well of Screams. When I was just a youngin', news spread like the wind of an extraordinary team of fighters that had to rectify a mistake that our researchers of Chraonos had made concerning a small handful of h'arai that deviated from the Goldenfist Corp. For years these young fighters eluded the king's military, and as time progressed, these h'arai's actions became wilder, more demanding, and more chaotic. Their young minds just couldn't handle the temptation of the ever-present energy source known as lyvah, an energy source that is drawn from the cosmos itself. You see, when a h'arai is trained, he is trained to use nyvah, the energy source of the planet. Nyvah is relatively safe and does not try and pull you under into its succulent enticement like lyvah does. In any case, most of the countryside was razed and pillaged before these soldiers were reigned in. And it wasn't just *them* that the capitol had to wage war against. People from all nationalities flocked to these rebels like flies to… well, you get the idea. They called themselves the Crimson Swarm.

"The Goldenfist Corp. tries to train only the best suited to become h'arai, but sometimes the lust for power is just to great. In any case, these young h'arai weren't just "accidents". Rumor has it that the king wanted living, breathing weapons to have at his disposal. You see, these soldier's weren't just enticed by the thought of more power; they were pushed over the edge. They were each taken to the Well of Screams and 'blessed' with some of the darkest energy known to man. Eventually those h'arai were captured and contained, indefinitely frozen in time by means of the very well that they'd been corrupted with. Scattered across Pry'ama are prisons such as these, containing the corrupt soldiers that were later deemed as the "kul'sadar". Until the energy of that pit is released, we are relatively safe; only a very knowledgeable disciple of Nemeth would even know a hint of how to unlock that prison. And even then, its not that simple. Some say that the ideals of the kul'sadar live on in those that have been taken advantage of. But believe you me, do you think that the Goldenfist Corporation learned from their mistake? Of course not. Keep your eyes peeled, you may see some atrocities that will leave you in fear around these parts. These mountains didn't get infested with abominable creatures by mere accident."

Leaving that last statement floating in the air, Golbart clucked at his horses and his wagon picked up its speed, his parting words being "I believe I need a drink."

Aeven couldn't bring himself to tear his eyes away from the monstrous building perched high atop the cliffs. Aeven knew better than most what it was to be a h'arai, for a handful of years he himself had been one. Aeven had trained with the Goldenfist's best to become a soldier that was capable of the worst of destruction. And Golbart had been absolutely right, nyvah was the safest energy to use. Lyvah had been outlawed for precisely the reasons that Golbart had mentioned. Shaking his head to bring himself out of his revelries, Aeven barely noticed as the team cleared a large stone entryway into a central square containing hundreds of meandering townsfolk, all intermixing and bartering with visitors from outside the city walls. Aeven watched in humor as Golbart's wagon found a spot to park beside a red roofed tavern, half a dozen young men coming over to give the elder man a helping hand. A dingy sign beside the stone entryway read that this section of town was named Outter Daile.

"Fumes in my mouth but I've been looking forward to a dark ale for some time now!" Thrush finally spoke up, her eyes lighting up with enthusiasm. "I imagine that we're going to rest up for tonight and resume our search at dawn. There aren't a lot of choices of where Keyamir could have disappeared to from here. He'd be a fool to stay within the confines of these walls, and anything south of here would just lead to small farming villages. No, I bet that he's headed to Spider Eye Canyon, the valley that leads to Amdaer'lael. I'd bet my left eye that he's making his way to the Spiral Rift; once he's out in those sands, the law will never be able to reach him. Nor would they want to." Thrush clapped Aeven on the shoulder once and then disappeared into the Floating Cranberry. Aeven was left with naught but his thoughts.

The sun was starting to disappear behind the mountaintops and there was a chilled bite that hung in the air. Most of the residents seemed to favor various garbs of deep green and black hoods, each of them carrying large scythes strapped to their backs. *Those scythes look more for self defense than harvesting food.* The population of people was surprisingly large for such a small town, and that made Aeven anxious. He just did not want company right now, especially a crowd of boisterous strangers bustling around him. *This could be the last time that I get to have a drink with Thrush, however. And I don't want to hurt her feelings.* Hanging his head, Aeven took a deep breath and pushed open the splintering door to the tavern. Maybe a drink didn't sound too bad after all.

CHAPTER NINE

Kul'sadar

Rhea St. Khaun was one of this age's kul'sadar. A living ideal of how life could be without a reigning dictatorship. A living weapon that people were terrified of. People whispered about monsters such as her, and for good reason. Herself and her brother were so adept at using lyvah and nyvah that they could perform almost any feat, within reason. Having powers of this magnitude left her feeling isolated most of the time, which she was more than okay with. Friends just got in the way. Thick mist clung to her armor like a second skin as she sat on the slick rocks of Skulter Cove, watching the small rivulets of caordin'torr filter down with the rainwater from high above the ridge and down into the gully below. Chaotic, mystical light from the energy splashed against the wall of boulders, highlighting the natural nuances that made this cove so special to her. This fjord was her place to meditate on life when she was feeling out of sorts.

She should be scared; the legion of the Seven Devils was swarming across the mountains like an anthill that's been ruthlessly kicked. The soldiers of red could just as easily attack her here, in the dead of night, as they could amidst the battlefield. But she wasn't scared. She's almost forgotten what that feeling even feels like. She was one of the kul'sadar.

She might not be invincible, or even come close in power to one of the original kul'sadar that were indefinitely imprisoned, but in this age? When there are none to contest her? She was a magnificent weapon that all lived in fear of. She shifted her back against the rough wall, her dark skin shrouding her amidst the cold darkness of the looming night. Although she was here for meditation, that didn't mean that she had to be unprepared. She was fully adorned for battle. Her barbed spear lay close by, propped up against a nearby boulder, and her steel ring-mail armor gleamed against the stars as she shifted into the light of the moon. Her black cloak lay draped around her as she absentmindedly flung her thick braid around her shoulders, her eyes scanning the ridge line for any sign of movement. None caught her eye.

"We may be kul'sadar, but it still isn't healthy for you to isolate yourself like you do." A deep voice claimed, Kordin striding out of the shadows from a cleft in the wall of boulders. The same towering height as her, Kordin was stark muscle where she was lean mass. In the shimmering ocean light, he did look impressive. His full plate armor was silver with splashes of red on it. He had long hair with streaks of silver, and a great sword that hung across his back. Kordin was intimidating at the best of times, and terrifying when he meant harm. He was very charismatic, and where Rhea liked to keep to herself, he liked to surround himself with people of status. In most ways they were identical, but in other ways they couldn't be more different. Despite their contrasts, they still held the same ideals. Torn from their mother in Golub, they now served a ruthless man that was vying for supremacy over Pry'ama. And he was intending to use herself and Kordin to achieve his goals. That was what drove the pair of them to fight. To rebel against those that would use them. That was why she chose isolation, she could trust *no one* except for the man standing before her. Her brother.

"What is it about this place that draws the energy so?" Kordin mused, "why does the caordin'torr flow so freely here? Those lights are just dazzling."

"I've thought long about that very question. The answer might even be the very reason why the Seven Devils are poised to strike." Rhea replied solemnly, "if you walk down this beach just a little more, you'll find a shallow cove that holds something rather curious."

"It is rather curious why the Seven Devils would choose us at all as a city to try and sack," Kordin responded thoughtfully, hand coming up to his chin in contemplation. "That is an area of contention between myself and my advisors. Why *did* they choose us? Well, your answer is just as good as theirs. What do you think?"

"There is a pedestal, of sorts, resting within that cove. I've walked to it many times; the cove looks as if it could have been part of a temple, once upon a time. The pedestal survived, somehow, but not much else did." Her brother looked askance at her, eyebrow raised. She hurried on with her explanation. "Its an artifact from Tai'drasial! Several temples holding these pedestals were built within Pry'ama by the aor'sii. There is a link between those pedestals, the aor'sii, and the caordin'torr. It could be that the Seven Devils knows something more about the matter that we don't. In any case, I can see them seeking out those artifacts more than them trying to commandeer our farmland."

"The Seven Devils have a very large army to feed; don't underestimate their need for food! And this pedestal has been resting on our shore for all of this time?! Why was I never made aware of this?" Kordin sputtered, "what do we even know about it?"

"It hasn't been mentioned because their isn't much to know! I've told you as much as any scholar can tell you. It doesn't even look like much. Part of it is shattered, and their is sea lichen growing on the rest of it. But it is unmistakably one of the sacred pedestals. They were an integral piece to Pry'ama's past, but other than that, not much is known. No one even knows what they were originally intended for. I know that they helped seal away the ones that were forsaken to us, but not much more."

"Is it something that nyvah or lyvah can help us with? In uncovering what it is that they do, I mean."

"Well, yes and no. I tried using a trickle of nyvah, just to see, and the pedestal did react. It glowed, for the merest of moments. That's what made me certain of my theory. But I dared not try more than that for fear of what would happen. Can you imagine if we broke the seals on the prisons that are holding the original kul'sadar? We'd be unleashing a devastation upon the realm that none have ever known. They weren't just powerful. They were *feral*. It's true that we hold the same ideals as they did, the difference is that we are more *controlled*. We have a *purpose*. They did not. They just wanted to destroy and slay in the name of Todraganian, the Forgotten One . If these pedestals are being used as a means to keep the original kul'sadar imprisoned, then we may just want to let the artifact be and just forget about it."

Kordin stared at Rhea in silent contemplation, and then finally asked "so what *are* the names of these archaic pedestals, exactly? Someone has got to know. They cannot be *that* obscure."

"They're called the Pillars of Eraa'saara. The name had escaped me until now. And the only reason that I know that is because of Lindy." Lindy was the closest thing that the pair of them had to a true parent, and she was actually a traveling scholar for lord Derrond. He would send her on obscure quests to investigate ruins that most have forgotten about.

A Grey Garbling cawed from the ridge above, the small, vulture-like bird's cry akin to a weeping baby. Kordin and Rhea looked at each other knowingly, neither having to voice what the other was thinking. "Did you bring any of your guards this night?" Rhea finally asked, "or any of your diplomats, for that matter?"

He shook his head no. "None know that I came to visit you down here in this cove. And the thought of having guards is laughable. *Me?* Guards? Ha! I'd just end up guarding *them*."

"You just be careful. An arrow can just as easily pierce your heart as it can anyone else's. We aren't *invincible*. Just powerful." Rhea sputtered in indignation, "and if you didn't bring your guards then that means that we have company." The bird cried out again, and then several others slowly took up its disconcerting scream. Rhea might have been down here alone this night, but she had several beady eyes keeping watch over her. This cove was a giant Grey Garbling nest, though almost none knew that. "They have us surrounded," she whispered, eyes roving the canyon walls.

Rhea jumped in place as a sharp clicking sound reverberated off of the boulder beside her, an arrow spinning off into the frothy waves.

"Arrow indeed," Kordin chuckled, "I think that they must have heard you. I fear that we are in for a very long night. The first of many skirmishes begins, it seems." He gathered himself and stated more solemnly, "I may have left my personal guards at camp, but I am no fool." With those last words hanging in the air, Kordin brought two fingers up to his mouth and gave three sharp whistles, the high pitched sound drowning out even the cawing of the birds. A few seconds crept by, and then arrows fell from the darkness high above like bats swooping down for the kill. Sharp screams of pain trickled down from the ridges just as sporadically as the arrows, Kordin's soldier's as deft and silent as the wind.

"How could they have known that we were down here in the first place?" Rhea whispered, "Was it just happenstance, or did they have some intel?"

"A speculation for another night!" Kordin spat, sidestepping an arrow that narrowly missed his chest. "It could be that you're correct in thinking that they're here after the Pillar of Eraa'saara, or perhaps we have a turncoat within our camp. In either case, right now we just need to *fight*! Did you remember to bring your mask with you?"

"No, I came down here for some peace, not to display my prowess!" Rhea shot back, "its up at the garrison!"

"Then we do this the old fashioned way." Kordin chuckled, hands clasping the hilt of his sword and eyes focusing on the bodies creeping towards them amongst the mist. "Well, as old fashioned as you and I can get, I suppose! Which isn't saying much. In any case, we aren't alone! As soon as my soldiers are done with the archers up on the cliff, they'll help us down here."

Rhea wasn't even listening to her brother; she was concentrating on the steady lap of the waves and the cool, refreshing mist kissing her skin. Where her brother focused on tactics and guile amidst a battle, she sought out *blood*. She needed to be *calm* and have a lucid mind in order to direct her mounting rage. She counted no less than eight red armored soldiers creeping about the sand and boulders, their bodies no more than shadows amongst the ocean spray. Her mind became clearer as her inner spark ignited. She needed a clear mind so that she could focus on her *anger*, her *frustration*. Her *malice*. She needed all of her *spite* clearly directed to those that would deprive her of even trying to live a meager existence. "*Yes*," her brother whispered within her mind, "*harness that anger.*" One soldier by the outcrop of boulders, three creeping towards them on the strip of sand, and four slithering through the fringes of the water. All with weapons bare and lips pulled back in a rictus snarl.

Rhea couldn't control herself. The canyon reverberating with her violent scream, a scream that even dwarfed the cawing of the birds, she rushed forward in a blaze of sand and blood. Rhea's rage consumed her, her clarity of mind lost to adrenaline and blood lust. The soldier that hid amidst the shadow of the boulder barely had time to pull up his curved scimitar before Rhea's great ax was cleaving down upon him. Though his sword was durable, the man's eyes widened in fright as the head of her ax broke the weapon in two. With a sickening thud, her ax lodged itself in the legionnaire's head, effectively spraying her in a shower of blood and brain.

Rhea no more than yanked her ax out of the man's head when a resounding explosion erupted beside her, the force from the impact throwing her off of her feet and into the sand several yards away. Coming to a rolling stop, she barely had time to cover her head before a shower of shrapnel and seashell rained down upon her, violent flames licking at her skin. "So they can use nyvah as well, eh? This should prove *exciting*. All that they've managed to do is feed my *rage*." Her fingers tightening on the long handle of her ax, she rolled back onto her feet and dashed towards her next victim, a young woman with scarlet hair and magenta armor. The legionnaire's scimitar out and round shield at the ready, she taunted Rhea with a smirk and swing of her weapon. Taking a running jump, Rhea swung her weapon around in the air and brought the weapon upwards and under the woman's guard, knocking both her shield and sword away to the side. "That fireball was *your* doing, wasn't it?" Rhea whispered in her ear, grabbing a handful of the woman's beautiful braid. "I didn't like that." Dropping her ax into the sand, Rhea punched the woman in the throat three times and then threw her into the churning waves. The woman did not get back up.

Spittle flew from her mouth as a gloved fist belted Rhea in her stomach. Salt water cascaded into her ears, mouth, and eyes as the savage soldier kicked the back of her legs out from under her and dunked her down into the churning water, the handle of her ax well outside of her reach now. Her hands grasped for anything and everything to try and help her pull herself up and out of the water. The man's ankle was solid as a tree trunk as her fingers weakly wrapped themselves around his iron boots, however his other foot came crashing down atop her head to ensure that she remain where he wanted her; drowning to death in her most favored grotto. Blood floated before her stinging eyes as the side of her face was smashed against sharp lichen and seashell that was trapped within the sand. Her arms flailed around in wild motions, her legs as restless as an enraged ridgecat. *This is it,* Rhea thought direly, a sense of loss and peace settling into the depths of her mind as she realized what was about to happen. *This is when I meet my maker. This is when I finally get to meet Todraganian, the Buried One.*

Wait, what am I doing? I am such a fool! Is this how I prove myself to our great master? By laying here and dying like a starving hound? NO! I AM worthy of his FAVOR! I cannot let him down! Like the evening tide, Rhea allowed the influx of the caordin'torr that was spilling down from the rocks not fifty yards away to flow freely within her, the energy waning and waxing just as the waves were doing. Internally she knew that what she was about to do was more than a little dangerous. If most of the caordin'torr here was comprised of lyvah, instead of nyvah, then she could give herself a permanent ailment of the mind that she'd have to live with for the rest of her days. A permanent bout of psychosis. Is that something that she could live with? *Yes.* It was better than dying. Trying to use an energy source that was derived from the cosmos itself was never safe, which was why most tended to use lyvah, the energy of the planet. But with her head being slowly crushed underwater, she had little to no choice.

She could...*feel*...the energy that was trickling down from the ridge high above rush towards her in a shower of prisms and light. Darkness was starting to consume her. Water inched its way down her throat as she tried her best to stave off the need for oxygen, her arms and legs growing so heavy and tired. And then she felt a welcoming warmth embrace her. Her body felt rejuvenated, her mind as sharp as a knife as the familiar feel of nyvah energized her body to the point of euphoria. The stinging sensation went away, the man standing before her crystalline clear. He pressed down harder on her head, his heavy boot crushing her jaw to the point where it felt like it was about to snap into a mangled mess. Her eyes followed the prism of light that gracefully rose up from the ridge-line and down in a refined arc. The stout, armored man no more than looked over his shoulder before the intermixed prism of energy showered *through* his body and down into the water where Rhea was drowning. The man's eyes widened in horror as his armor was torn asunder, blood spilling out in waves. He crumpled in place.

The energy that rushed into her didn't just reinvigorate her, it jilted her mind. Made her sick to her stomach. Her entire body felt nauseated, her muscles cramping and spasming. A hand grasped her own and yanked her up and out of the water. She stumbled forwards a few steps and then fell to her knees in the wet sand, her fingers clasping the seashore as her mind tried to keep its grasp on reality. "What did you do?" Her brother whispered in both awe and fear, his large hand coming to rest on her shoulder. "Even the warlords that possessed the Twelve Orbs of Laedrea never dared touch lyvah to the extent that you did this night."

His voice wavered in and out. Paranoia stabbed her heart. "I...I didn't have a choice! I didn't know how much of that energy was nyvah and how much was lyvah. That man was crushing my head underwater, I...I had to do *something*!" Rhea sputtered, "And where in oblivion's light were you!?

Where was my brother when I needed him? Were you just *waiting* for me to *die*?!"

"Did you forget that we were in the midst of battle? Or did you suffer more damage to your mind than I originally thought?" Kordin uttered darkly, "Take a look around you."

Rhea obliged and was surprised to not just see a dozen more armored bodies strewn across the strip of beach, but also soldiers stalking in the shadows along the ridge-line. Men that wore leathered garbs and possessed wicked looking long swords that were more than capable of skewering between the Seven Devil's stout armor. "How long was I under water? It couldn't have been more than a few minutes."

"And it wasn't. A lot can happen in just a few minutes, especially amidst a battlefield. If you'd have just waited a few seconds more then you wouldn't have had to take such a foolish risk." Kordin spoke plainly, "Its of no matter now. What's done is done. Come, let us check out this Pillar of Eraa'saara. It needs investigating."

CHAPTER TEN

Crystalline Sun

To call the tavern dismal would have been a compliment; moonlight pierced the deluge of dust in the air like an arrow puncturing a heart, and the amount of sand and dirt that caked the floor would have made even the laziest of house-mistresses blush in embarrassment. The wind was blowing westward this night, down across the rolling sand hills, and bringing with it a cool bite to the air that made the fire even more comforting. Men and women both were stooped over their tables with heads nearly touching, whispers and murmuring coalescing around the lounge like rancid smoke. Bowls of stew and mugs of ale sat forgotten as rumors and secrets were exchanged like the finest of gold.

Though some of the lounge was filled with regulars, there were just as many disheveled patrons that looked to have traveled from the furthest reaches of Pry'ama. Most wore heavy, green cloaks and navy-blue garments, but she couldn't quite place where they had traveled from. The women wore their hair up in thick braids, while the men had wild beards and even wilder hair. Most of them looked beaten, sad. Defeated. Like they'd lost something precious to them that could never be reclaimed. Thrush felt cold, inside and out. She understood their anguish, even if she didn't understand their situation. These were hard times, even for the nobles.

Thrush wished that the cloak that she wore was heavier this night, or that she had worn extra undergarments, but no doubt that she would warm up soon. Truth be told, for it being a storm month, it was relatively warm compared to previous years. Asvuldure was never a pleasant time of year for someone that grew up in a capitol that was renowned for its heat. Not a day crept by that she didn't think of Amoriah and its onslaught of intrigue and political strife. The weather their was as stuffy as the pride and political rifts. Thrush shook her head in annoyance. That was neither here nor now. Readjusting the bow in her hair for the dozenth time, she smiled. It was a godsend that she could finally take off her heavy plate mail, even if it meant leaving it in her questionable room. She loved that armor, it was something that kept her alive in the deadliest of times, but it was as cumbersome as carrying around a mountain. Her body ached something fierce and her skin was chaffed in places that she wouldn't mention. She still didn't feel quite right after that last battle in the arena. She felt drained, like her stamina just wouldn't replenish.

She stood in the entryway and watched as Aeven made his way through the crowd of people like a boulder that would not relent in the stream. Aeven was something of a peculiarity, a young man with sun-scorched cheeks and weathered armor that most would chuckle at. While others laughed at his unkempt appearance, Thrush found him endearing and one-of-a-kind. The son of a noble lord who defied the traditional lifestyle of luxury for one of battle and blood. That was a lot of the reason why she related to him so much; she, too, was the daughter of a prestigious lord, and like Aeven, she wanted nothing but the dirt under her feet and the wind in her hair. She absolutely hated the noble life, detested it with her whole being.

House Balfourian, her family, was renowned for intrigue and politics; more than a family should be. When both of her brothers started to dabble in the affairs of other lords, she took to her horse and never looked back. If she was to die by a blade, it'd be on her terms and in her fight, not because of a short length of steel plunged into her back.

Her family was respectable, but they also played their part in the War of Attrition, and she wanted no part of *that*. It was still too soon after the war to advertise that her family had made cut throat decisions that had cost many soldiers their entire livelihoods. A slender woman whisked by her, bringing her back to the present. Snagging a maple cake off the smudged platter, Thrush tried unsuccessfully to push her way through the thick crowd of people.

Though she tried her hardest to follow Aeven, she eventually wound up in front of a broken, ramshackle stage that a young, lone woman was performing upon. Thrush bit back a laugh and watched her, her mood successfully rising and her thoughts receding from the darkness. This young woman was dressed very peculiar. Her pants were simple, nothing more than peasant trousers, and her shirt was cut low and showed more than her fair share of cleavage. What caught Thrush's eye though was her simple black mask and colorful, diamond shaped patches that decorated her outfit. Her fingers deftly tossed five colored balls in the air before the crowd of onlookers, the balls somehow maintaining a perfect oval shape. Her spirited laughter dwarfed the cheers of the crowd.

Thrush ate her snack with a foolish grin on her face. The young woman was supple and robust, with blonde hair that was pinned up atop her head with a couple of carved sticks and a smile that spread from ear to ear; she was very charismatic, and it showed. Her laughter was like chimes, and she belted back insults just as quickly as they were delivered from the small sea of people. Thrush hooted and hollered along with the rest of the patrons, and when the performer's act concluded, she was surprisingly disappointed. The young lady was showered with coins as she gave a small twirl and then a curtsy.

Though the tavern was horrendously dirty, Thrush suddenly felt as if she could have chosen her own outfit more thoughtfully. Her attire was comfy, a pair of loose trousers and a simple shirt, but it was far short of flattering.

Wait, why do I care all of a sudden what I look like? Thrush thought furiously, *I'm just wanting to talk to her, after all.* Wiping away the loose crumbs from the maple cake, Thrush climbed her way up to the stage and helped the young woman out. "You really don't have to do that," the performer stammered, "this is what I do for a living. I'm an artist. I sing, I dance, you know. Tell stories of heroic deeds, recite poetry. I work for the Crystalline Sun."

Thrush was amazed. "You work for the Crystalline Sun?" She asked in amazement, "what are you doing in a dump like this? Aren't you normally contracted out to the High Courts of Chraonos?"

The young woman's face became flushed. "Yes, I work for them. Why wouldn't I perform here? Even the lowly places like this need some entertainment, yes? And I had other business here, as well. Why not make a few extra coins?"

"I didn't mean to offend, you just caught me by surprise. If I remember right, the Crystalline Sun has many guilds associated with it, doesn't it? Different places that you can train at? Which did you attend?"

"Roothold. I've lived there for most of my life. I'm sorry, what was your name again?"

"Thrush Balfourian," she stated as she handed the performer the last of her equipment, "and yours?"

"Fre'ja Nyland," she stammered, her cheeks flushing once again. "Come, let us take this outside. It's hard to hear you with all of these people yammering, and there's another band that is getting ready to set up on this stage here."

Thrush wasn't in the mood to argue, Aeven could take care of himself. What they all just needed was an evening to relax and recuperate. Freja was like an eel in the water; she slithered and swam through the throng of people like a shadow, never bumping a single patron even though she was lugging around a leather pack full of performer's equipment. Thrush, on the other hand, felt like an ox in a crowd of cows. No matter which direction she moved, she was bumped, jostled, and pushed around like an animal waiting its turn for the grain bucket. She received more than her fair share of dirty looks and elbows in the ribcage. Eventually they found themselves outside the tavern but inside the ruinous stable, the smell of rancid smoke replaced with the stink of horse dung. Thrush leaned up against the shoddy wooden railing and fiddled with the artifact that Aeven had given her a few weeks back, the HALO Prism. Standing in the impending twilight, the wristlet glowed a brilliant scarlet, the runes on it alight with an orange passion. The runes upon this artifact read 'Sun Singer'. That resonated something fierce with her. Fre'ja's voice washed over her.

"I'll be honest with you; you asked me earlier why I am not singing and dancing amongst the High Courts, and its not just because I had other business. In truth, I don't agree with the ideals of the nobles, as of late. In fact, they make me sick. Especially after the stunts that they pulled after the war." Fre'ja's voice now contained more venom than a Chittering Mine snake, her fingers shaking as she gripped the railing of the stall. "How can the noble's deceive the commoners so easily?! They fought hard in the war too. No, they fought *harder*. They didn't have the luxury of standing in the back and shouting commands. The commoners…they were slaughtered. And the ones that made it back from the war? Thrown out on the streets like sick dogs. No, I won't sing and dance for them. Never again."

Thrush didn't know what to say. If Fre'ja knew that she herself was a noble, she probably wouldn't be so open and friendly. And if Fre'ja found out that she was of house Balfourian? She would expect a knife in the gut, no questions asked. Thrush herself was bitter about how the War of Attrition ended as well. The nobles should never have made promises that they couldn't keep, even if they sorely needed soldiers for the war. Now Pry'ama had an uprising of destitute soldiers and thieves that were just as bad as the Seven Devils. "Why are you telling me this? I could be a knight of the Ruinous Shield, for all you know."

"Yes, you could be. But you're not." Fre'ja spat, "you think I can't tell the difference between the law and a ruffian? You do look like someone from the higher class, but whether your disenfranchised or just a runaway I can't tell, nor do I care. I'm telling you this because their will be a revolution soon. One that you may want to be a part of. My business here was to meet with fellow commoners, ones that were taken advantage of. You think that the Seven Devils are a pest? You just wait. The king and all of his henchmen are going to be taken down."

"You're part of the Azure Skulls." Thrush breathed, excitement tinging her voice.

"Yes, and proud of it."

"Fre'ja whispered, "no more are we going to be slaves of the nobles. They don't understand that while their actions may have just caused an echo at first of what's to come, in a few months it will be an avalanche that will sweep the nation. Whether you want to be involved or not... hey, look out!"

The ground outside of the stable exploded upwards in a shower of dirt, rubble, and manure as a nameless creature burst forth from the ground akin to a badger that's just had its peace disturbed. Thrush stepped back in horror as the moonlight illuminated this darkly divine beast, the creature something that looks to have been created out of the darkest of nightmares. It looked to be a woman, but with pulsating wings of energy and armor born of the roughest of stone. Her eyes... they were fiercer than fire and wrought of anger. Strapped to one arm was a shield that protected the whole of her body, lichen and moss growing atop the front, and in the other hand she grasped a curved sword that glittered in the moonlight. More holes exploded around the streets of the town, rubble and flagstone flying upwards into the air as stout creatures half as big as the winged beast crawled out of the pits akin to bears coming out of hibernation. These fiends looked like stout, bald men with tendons of muscle that were taut in the moonlight and silver beards that spilled down their taut stomachs. They, too, had wings, though they weren't wrought of energy, but of sinew and bone. Hanging around their necks were thick chains of gems and stone, and their clawed hands held crude weapons of varying origin. Thrush's hand bolted for her sword and then realized with dread that she left all of her gear in her room. She could feel the blood leaving her head as the winged woman elegantly dropped down to the ground and took one step toward her, her stone shield leaving a gouge in the dirt.

CHAPTER ELEVEN

Scars and Embers

Tobacco smoke, the sweet aroma of food, and the stink of so many bodies pressed up against one another intermixed in the boisterous den of the Floating Cranberry. The lounge was spacious, and yet every seat and table was occupied with both locals and travelers that were just looking to have a festive night. Aeven's ears rang from the dull buzz of people exchanging stories, from the raucous laughter, and from the horrendous noise that some deemed as 'music' that was coming from a couple that looked as if they had a hard time trying to figure out how to even hold their instruments properly. Bars of moonlight cast through rotten rents in the wall that highlighted motes of dirt, dust, and filth that was smeared across the floor of the establishment. After a second glance around, Aeven noticed that most of the soldiers sitting around the den were adorned with the same suit of worn, silver armor; they sported crests that Aeven had never seen the likes of before. These soldiers bore thick, green mantles, each mantle sporting an embroidered soaring hawk with a glove in its grasp. The hoods of these majestic, thick mantles resembled the head of a bear, and these men wore gauntlets that looked like beast's claws. Their demeanor and appearance was just as feral, the men and women looking the worst for wear. Their clothes were mere rags of what they used to be, and their armor held only a glimmer of the splendor that they once did.

"Any guess on who these soldiers are?" Aeven had to practically yell into Golbart's ear. "I've never seen that sigil before that they wear, and when I was a squire serving my father, I was made to learn every country, where they reside, and what their emblem is. I've never seen the likes of them before."

"I would keep my voice down if I were you, these are no ordinary soldiers. I poked around and sparked conversations, but my family be slashed if they revealed any more than the most basic information about themselves to one such as I. I was a pathfinder for my band of warriors, for blast's sake! I pride myself in gathering intel, was renowned for it, and that upstart of a girl that you travel with pries where these soldiers are from faster than a Scarrow wench flips up her dress! Just unbelievable. In any case, these soldiers are all disenfranchised from the nation of Calder; the work of the Seven Devils. These fighters and an encampment of townsmen that are on the fringes of town are most of what's left of the Calder kingdom. These fighters followed the vile devils across the mountains to try and waylay them and do our country a favor. Unfortunately, by the time these soldiers had caught up to that specific regiment of the Seven Devils, the Devils had already been annihilated by an unknown force. All they found was blood and ruin.

"Some villager's rumor that the surrounding barracks of various realms all came together and overcame the Seven Devils, while others say that a legion of knights from Chraonos itself came from behind the unsuspecting force and slaughtered them. I don't need to tell you what they say about listening to rumors though. I personally don't think that king Vanlien cares enough about a small town such as Calder to send a legion of knights to reap justice. Nor do I think that the surrounding cities are mature enough to collaborate together to pull off a unified assault. Putting the Seven Devils conundrum aside however, I did learn something that was all my doing; these soldiers are now headed to Amoriah. Without a kingdom, these men and women want to lead their people to a new realm, to a realm where the baron will cherish them. And who can blame them? I wouldn't want to reestablish a kingdom atop the graves of all of my family, friends, and acquaintances either. The dirt of Calder is too tainted now with blood. Politics is no place for us mercenaries so I didn't dabble in their affairs, but they are dead set in helping the distraught students of Nemeth reestablish their new home as well in Amoriah. The academy of Nemeth might be no more than a ruin now, just as Calder is, but Amoriah will shine in all of its glory and provide a new home for so many. Even a rugged mercenary such as I can appreciate that."

"The Seven Devils sure have laid waste to our home," Aeven muttered darkly, his mouth twisting in distaste. His eyes laid upon the soldiers in a new light. "And I loathe what our king has become. No, I loathe what our *nobility* has become."

Golbart nodded forebodingly. "I was able to convince them to let us tag along with them until we catch wind of Keyamir again. With the arid sand surrounding us, Keyamir's tracks will have been blown away long since.

We need a new lead, and so far these soldier are our best bet. What are your thoughts. *Lord* of *Chraonos*?" Golbart spat that last part out with more than a little sarcasm, his eyes alight with fire and mirth.

Aeven followed Golbart over to his table in dark silence, studiously ignoring the snub. Though Aeven had deviated away from the life of servitude as a knight, it was always bitter medicine when other comrades of his kind were not able to defend the people that they swore to protect. It was true that he longer served Chraonos as he once had, but the predicament still irked him something fierce. Not to mention the secondary problem that they faced concerning their current quest. The lord knew that the longer that they searched for Keyamir, the harder he'd be to find. Their stash of food and gold was starting to look a might measly, and this expedition was far more hectic than even Aeven could have anticipated. Nodding his head once in acquiesce to the old man's request, Aeven slowly grasped the mug of frothy ale that was set down before him and watched in silence as the old man disappeared into the throng of destitute soldiers to confirm their negotiation. Their eyes held so much conviction and loss. Aeven had lived that life once before, and by no means wanted to dawn those shoes ever again. Amoriah would be a welcoming home for both the wandering students of Nemeth as well as the destitute survivors of Calder. Perhaps the two nations could form a new, unified alliance. One that will help slay the Seven Devils.

Aeven took no more than five breaths before the empty chairs at his table became filled with strangers that were looking to just enjoy the music and festivities, much to his dismay. The first man that sat down looked as if he had been a nomad for the better part of his life. Tall, elderly, and scarred with more wounds than even Aeven had, this man was garbed in deep blue traveling clothes and held his dark hair back with a muddied green bandanna. Interestingly enough, the man had what looked like three metallic fish entwined in his braid, each fish colored as if they had just jumped out of a rainbow. His skin was as dark as ash, and his eyes as bright as the radiant sun. This man was highly intellectual. Perching his tall walking staff beside the table, the man nodded to Aeven and hailed down a distressed waitress. Before he could voice his order, he was talked over by the other man that had sat down."I want in on that," the man stated to the frail server. "I will take an Ashenfelter Bomb with a shot of Nalangan Hail. I do not want to wait long, you hear?" the man barked, "It took me long enough to just find a place to sit. I do not have all night!"

This man was hard, Aeven surmised, and held an air about him that made you second guess yourself. He held just as many scars as they did, if not more so. This man wore a long, leather jacket with a collar that rose almost to the man's earlobes. Ranging on the thinner side, this young man's eyes burned with a fervor that you weren't soon to forget, his gaze alone dissuading Aeven from even commenting on the man's ill manners. His hair was very dark, long in the back and formed into a sharp peak on the top. He wore red warpaint underneath his left eye, the design creating a symbol that Aeven was somewhat familiar with. Two jagged stripes and a strong, thick line down the center. He lugged a heavy pack with him, and carried a sword that looked born of ice. No, his eyers weren't filled with fervor, but filled with a heat akin to that which burns the heart. The man's eyes taunted Aeven to comment on what he had just said, to bring justice and save that woman's pride. "You come from the Gates of Keiadanis, don't you?" Aeven whispered, awe touching his voice. "What brings you all the way here, I wonder?" The man only gave him a sidelong glare and sat back in his seat, studiously arranging his gear.

The waitress quietly brought them their drinks, along with some much needed food. She left just as quickly. "The blessings of the chorr'gall are all around us, if you take the time to look. I could ask you the same question," the stranger stated studiously as he dribbled some sweet Sydina oil over his peppered turnips. "Why are you so far away from your castle walls?" He looked up and stared Aeven down, a cold silence settling over the table like a sheet of ice. It took Aeven a few minutes to collect himself.

"I was once told that a man's scars were memories made impression on the skin." Aeven spoke, purposefully avoiding the heated man's stare. "And from the looks of us, we have had some breathtaking experiences. How about we exchange stories while playing the game of Triple Slots? I'll pay for drinks, and I deal." Sliding his own deck of cards out from the many pockets that comprised his jacket, Aeven noted that each man looked more than a little reluctant to participate; the elderly because he was tired, and the younger man because he was just plain spiteful. Nevertheless, Aeven dealt the cards and started off with his own encounter of years past. "My own story starts when my father, lord Athrim Kvalheim, was reigning baron for the realm of Chraonos. I had just achieved my standard sword and shield for completing the knighting academy and was west bound through the wilderness of Flayre'song on a steam wagon that held other warriors such as I, soldiers that had never seen true combat had never had the displeasure of watching their friends stabbed to death or beheaded. Each of us was garbed in pristine Chraonos uniforms however, heads held high and ideals that none would waver from. We were plainly fresh out of the academy and could conquer the realm." He snickered at his own joke and then fell silent when he saw that none of the others at the table even cracked a smile. He cleared his throat.

"The rough road that our steam wagon was traveling on was lit up by the stars overhead, our driver having to keep a slow pace on the off chance that what we had been sent to hunt attacked us first. Honestly, I couldn't have been more excited. I had all new time spikes and a sword that had never been bloodied."

"Hold up." The younger man spoke. "You carry time spikes?" It was not a question but a statement. Aeven wasn't sure whether to be glad that he was finally talking to him or perturbed that the man had interrupted his story. In either case, Aeven just nodded. "How about a wager then? I tire of betting mere gold." The young man claimed. "I carry a time wedge. How about we bet your time fragment against mine, and this here bloke can throw in the towel unless he has something of equal value."

The aged man had not murmured a peep the whole time Aeven had been talking to him, but as soon as that wager was made he dove his hand into his leather skin pack and came out with a spiral shaped crystal, green in hue, gently propping it up on the table. His voice was course and gravelly, but very audible. "I'll take you up on that wager," he claimed. "Here is a time helix." Thrush had always thought Aeven a fool for carrying a time spike on his person but Aeven always rebuked her on that point. She claimed that they were obtrusive to the mind, had powers that man had not even scratched the surface of, and left the holder of the crystal overly exhausted and to the point of collapse if overused in one sitting. All of her points were valid, Aeven could admit that. But a time fragment could change a failing battle into a victory and that was a price that any soldier was more than ready to pay.

It was widely known that caordin'torr was the energy force responsible for creating these exotic crystals known as the time helix, time spike, and time wedge, otherwise known as time fragments. Time fragments are developed in various pools of caordin'torr, whether it be rivers, lakes, or even caverns that are ripe with the raw energy, and none that are produced are ever the same as another. Some borrow energy from nyvah, others from lyvah, but most hold an inkling of both. These time fragments are scattered all over the realm, and as such a person never knew when he would come across one of these rare items. Aeven also knew that if the aor'sii had never created those mystical temples of time for the chorr'gall to live forever in, then the energy pools known as the caordin'torr and these very shards of time would not even exist.

Aeven thought it was ironic how such an innocuous event had such an impact on Chraonos. Well, as innocuous as it is to build a temple where time did not effect it. One event just led to another.

Dealing out the rest of the cards, Aeven picked up on the story that left him scarred not only on his body, but his soul and mental stability. "My best friend was with me that day, Curasi Enlan. He and I had always competed with each other on who could win the most duals, stealth missions, you name it. That night however, when that creature crashed into the side of our steam wagon, both of our faces looked identical; full of fear and exhilaration. There we were, just two knights in our basic military attire ready to conquer the world. I remember our steam wagon taking a hit on the right side, the cheaply constructed contraption crinkling and smashing like a poorly made Lilien'thel mug. The back door of the wagon was ripped open by this beast's talons in one fell swipe, and before I knew it, my whole team is sprawled out on the murky ground. Only one man in that whole crew was able to stabilize himself in an orderly, swift fashion. His name was Grestalt Danner, a man I idolized greatly and one of the last four Loreguards willing to fight for our king. He was best friends with my father. Raising my head, I watched as Curasi found his feet and took a stand next to Grestalt, last to find his feet was I.

"The beast that waylaid us was known as a Great South Cloudstrider, one of many predators that had found their way into the midst of a project that the Goldenfist Corp had undergone. Experimenting with these very stones that we gamble with tonight, the Goldenfist Corp wanted to create an energy source that superseded even the great caordin'torr rivers. Unfortunately, this beast had swallowed a time helix, and small comets and cosmos debris crashed around us as we tried to slay this disoriented animal. This fight was over before it even began; Curasi was the first to take a hit, crumpling under the weight of the beast's great paw. Targeting me next, it got no more than a step away from my best friend when it was struck down by a bolt of fire from above, Grestalt having used his own time spike. The beast laid dead, and as I rushed over to check on Curasi, a fist-sized comet crashed down into the side of my body, effectively giving me the best scar in all of creation." Wanting to prove his point, Aeven stood up in his chair and lifted his tunic up, revealing his scarred, smashed up left side. Aeven's audience was mildly impressed. *Well, I thought it was a great story,* Aeven thought miserably. Sitting back down, Aeven peeked at the three cards that he had dealt himself and chose the one that was the most promising, a Golub Spiral Nine. Sliding it to the middle of the table face up, Aeven waited expectantly for the next traveler to reveal his tale.

The elderly man spoke next, his mouth just barely visible over the great, green woven scarf he had wrapped around his neck. "Great story lad but I think I can do one better. My accident took place before I became the proctor for the academy of Nemeth; I was young and dumb to put it lightly. I remember that it was winter time and the ice was especially fierce that year. The fishermen village I was living in at the time had become a ghost town over the course of just a few weeks. Rumor had it that the leader of a renowned group of warriors known as the Genoba'sii had defeated a chorr'gall, one of the rare creatures that the aor'sii had brought back from the brink of extinction. This chorr'gall, in defeat, had divulged some scars of the tribesman's past that none had known about, causing each clan to fan out from the citadel of Opel'sung, down the goat trails of the Azaevia Mountains, and into Pry'ama itself. They were searching for someone, a lord that would complete their clan. This knowledge involved the completion of a divination, but none can truly be sure.

"Villagers from all surrounding regions abandoned their farms, taking only necessities that would get them to the closest stronghold. I was a wanderer, a writer that traveled from nation to nation in search of what life truly meant and in search of inspiration for my next book. Though I had naught but my leather skin pack and my ancient pike, I was empathetic for these farmers who had no royalty to defend them. Or even any local guardsmen, for that matter. In all honesty, I think that most of these farms were forgotten due to them being so isolated from any sort of city. Jai'bens Meadow. That's what the town was named. I gathered my own belongings and joined the chaotic crowd of people rushing towards the nearest hold, fighting and protecting where I could. I suppose that's just the sort of man I am.

"The wind was whistling and whaling something fierce of course, what else can you expect from the coastal weather of Jai'bens Meadow? I know in my heart that a staff cannot protect against much, but mind you, it can protect against something. Its all I had, really." Pausing to take a prolonged drink of his ale, the elderly man continued. "Three days we marched, and when night fell, we set up camp as a military band would. We rationed what remained of our food and remained vigilant. I was looked on as their leader by most of the party, and as such I led as best as I could; it still did not prevent an ambush on the fourth day however. Ironically, the Genoba'sii had never found us, though I really doubt that they would have harmed us anyways. What would prophecy want with a couple farmers? No, we had the misfortune of getting in the midst of a brawl between the prized Goldenfist scientists and a band of contraband mechanics. They had been thieving, and the Goldenfist wanted their artifacts back. Dozens of the Goldenfist specialists lined the muddy road, ready to impale any that tried to push through to the next city. Behind us, rumbling just to the southeast of where we had marched from, was a large shuttle that was bigger than any wagon you could imagine. Only that it was sleek, and had deep, dark smoke emanating from where the metals connected together. Can you imagine that? I thought that I was dreaming!

"Painted on the side of this exotic vehicle was elegant writing that I had never seen before, as was a picture of a purple dragonfly. That was the name I later deemed it. The specialists charged forward with pikes out as if we weren't there at all! Women and children scattered in every which direction, some retreating into the nearby woods, and others towards the shuttle that was sitting idle. Myself, I did what any sane man would do in that type of situation: I ran like hell! Their were just too many villagers scattering in too many directions for one man to try and help. I yelled at them, but they paid no mind to the likes of me. I bolted for the shuttle and tried to find passage onto it, just as others were doing. I would not be here to tell this tale if the pilot of that vehicle had not had a heart. I was the last one to whip through the wind and jump onto the ascending ramp, three arrows impaling my poor leg in the process. I cannot complain, I lived and every one of those folks that ran with me lived as well. Barely." The elder man stood up and propped his leg across the table, the appendage horribly misshapen and scarred. Aeven's thoughts reeled. *How simple would life be if we had one of those 'dragonflies' that he just mentioned?* Opening his mouth to ask just that, another sound emanated throughout the room, and it wasn't Aeven's begging. The sounds of steel clanging against steel out in the street, bloody screams quickly following. Every patron came to a standstill as their ears picked up on the distinct yells of the guards outside. "We're under attack! To arms my brethren, we are under attack! Unnamed beasts wander the streets!"

CHAPTER TWELVE

Ca'or

The tavern door blew open in a shower of splinters and iron, the patrons that had been lounging before now scattering like smoke on the wind. Aeven barely had time enough to pick himself up off of the floor before a ghastly monstrosity with wings like a depraved bat sauntered in, its crooked, gem-like claws grasping a crude weapon fashioned out of bone, leather, and steel. Its face was a smoldering furnace of hate and malice. Aeven couldn't tear his eyes away from this beast that seemingly appeared out of legend. The creature took no more than three steps into the establishment before a sword found its way through its throat, one of the local guards dashing forth and ending the miserable beast's life. "The ca'or…they're…real?" Aeven whispered, murmurs of the same sort arising from all around the tavern. The gnarled beast no more than fell to the ground before two more were there to replace it, both the same as the first, crooked, leathery wings and beards that flowed down their muscled bodies. They had distinctions from one another, eerily human distinction, but you could tell that they were from the same breed of beasts. Leaping over their comrade with vicious snarls, the two creatures started swinging their weapons in a fury of malice and blood. Taking a quick look around,

Aeven saw that the two men that he'd been dicing with were both gone. He spit on the ground and stood up, drawing his sword in the process.

Very few patrons rushed forward to meet these nightmares in combat, most darted behind tables and jumped through windows to escape the wrath of the ca'or. From the blood curdling screams coming from outside, however, Aeven guessed that their were more of these creatures in the midst of town, slicing and chopping their way through what humans they could reach with their crude weapons. Their wasn't room for Aeven to rush forward and attack, to many soldiers were clustered around the ca'or as it was. Fire started to erupt from the walls, waves of smoke billowing into the lounge and smothering those that remained. *I need to finish this. Fast.* Aeven searched the recesses of his mind for the vibrant energies that were ever present within himself. He still couldn't get used to the feeling of the energies from his various time fragments resting in the back of his mind. They were akin to… *souls*…almost. Living entities that he could draw power from. And those powers grew and evolved the more he interacted with them, and not just in battles. He could be sitting around the campfire and bonding with them, discovering what makes each of those fragments unique.

His mind scrounged for an energy source that had the personality of a wild bull; unruly and temperamental. It was his time helix, a scarlet colored one that he'd found years ago for sale in the slums of Chraonos. Time helixes were unique in the respect that they combined experiences with the past and present, and intertwined them to create something surreal. Most people steered clear of them because of how erratic they were, and the one that Aeven found was in its own league of wild and impetuous. That was probably why he found it for sale for so cheap. But Aeven loved it. It fit his own personality perfectly. With the fingers of his mind he grasped the pulsating energy source and felt the vitality of his time fragment seep into him akin to dipping into a hot bath. He didn't just feel rejuvenated, he felt chock full of piss and vinegar. And anger. So much wrath and anger that he couldn't see nothing besides the beasts in front of him. He *hated* them, hated what they stood for. Aeven couldn't think straight, he just knew that those nightmares needed destroyed. Now.

His memory from the past that he fixated on was from not that very long ago, from his battle with the Azure Skulls. He remembered that female warrior summoning giant, divine swords that had materialized above a crowd of oncoming knights striking down and obliterating them. Aeven fixated on that thought and poured all of his newfound energy into summoning swords very much like those that he had seen. The few soldiers that had rushed forward to strike down the ca'or were on their last legs; only one more soldier remained, and he was now trying to protect his brethren from sure death. Aeven had to hurry. He could feel the energy pouring out of him and into the surrounding room. It left him drained to the point where he had to fall to one knee. His sword clattered to the ground but his eyes looked onwards towards the beasts. Both still remained, if a little bloody. And then he saw them. The swords weren't divine, they were smoky and held more than a little sinister energy. They crackled bright red. The five swords created a circle above the ca'or and started to spin around slowly at first, and then faster. The swords were now moving at a rapid pace, and as they did so, vibrant lighting crashed down from each smoky blade and pierced through the nightmare creatures and down through the floorboards of the tavern. Both ca'or looked up for only the briefest of moments before the firebolts incinerated them on the spot. The last of the soldiers cried out in dismay as he fell backwards, his friends now no more.

Aeven gagged at the smell and vomited to the side. "What did you do?!" The soldier stammered, his eyes glued to the swords that slowly dissipated into the rampant smoke. "How can you live with yourself?" Aeven couldn't speak, his mind fuzzy and his body sapped of strength. A woman screamed from just outside. It was a scream that he was very familiar with. *Thrush!*

Using his sword as a means to get back onto his feet, he jabbed it into the ground and pulled himself upwards. *I'm coming, friend!* Dashing forwards, he leapt over the remains of the bodies and rushed towards his best friend.

"Warriors of the planet?!" The man had exclaimed in incredulity. "That's probably the most ridiculous statement that I've heard this night. And I've heard some that'll make you spit out your ale in laughter. It had been a conversation that Johauna had heard earlier that night. Before the attack. The first man had been talking about how the planet was starting to create creatures that could defend the planet from the plague of man, and a resistance group of soldiers was starting to form. A group that would defend humans from the wrath of the planet. The man got laughed at. None had believed him. If only they saw what Johauna was looking at now, they might not be so quick to jest. Johauna Beybridge whipped his gnarled staff around his head and plunged it down into the planet with as much might as he could muster for being sixty-eight years old. He was within spitting distance of his shuttle's rusty ramp and was now surrounded by vibrant cactus, thirsty sand, and creatures that looked to have been wrought from the pages of legend. His scarf rustled with the constant wind, and like the wind, each warrior's stance was restless and ever moving. Unlike the barbarians you read about in those fictitious children's stories, these men and women he was combating were as refined as the best of books, both knowledge and wisdom holding their place in each of their eyes. That was why Johauna had to keep them guessing; if they knew he was playing for time, sure as spit they would have run him through already. *How can it be that both of those men I was carding with were holding time fragments? The fates hold an ironic sense of humor. Most residents of Pry'ama want nothing to do with those cursed stones.*

Fading in one direction and then the other, Johauna tried to work out how he was going to make it the last five yards without getting impaled by a sword. *If there is one thing that age has taught me, it's that the Great Mighty One makes things happen for a reason; and the reason for this battle? I have yet to see.* The first brute stepped forward and brought his sword crashing down in front of Johauna, the crude blade nearly missing the soft part of his neck. A second creature, a stouter one with a glowing stomach, rushed around and brought his scythe soaring towards the heavens in a bursting uppercut, Johauna just barely hopping back in time. There was a third warrior as well, a lanky woman-like creature with not near-enough clothes on for this type of wind, held her ground to assess what Johauna would do. Her thick shield and stout sword making Johauna's escape impossible.

You leave me little choice, here. Harnessing his energy from within, Johauna directed his mind to the power of nyvah. *Oh, such sweet energy of the elements! I embrace you. Now, for my last trick!* Directing his inner mind to his own time fragment that he carried in his pouch, Johauna brought forth the soul that he had melded with years ago. Johauna initiated his mind-link. "Dao'Sirakas! Aid me! Come hither friend and help me change the tide of battle!" Johauna yelled into the wind, his staff whirling above his head. The tingling from within was the same, and he winced at what was to come. He felt euphoria, and then just as suddenly he felt like the very fabric of his skin was being shredded piece by piece. He felt on fire, and then just as suddenly, as if he'd been dunked in glacial water. The three creatures took a step back as they watched Johauna cower before them, his body emanating a whirlwind of energy, wind, and water. Johauna heard the faintest of laughs in the back of his head, in the deepest recesses of his mind. The lush ground didn't just erupt from where Johauna and his staff were perched; it imploded downward in a sonata of rocks, wisps of light, and shrapnel.

Downwards Johauna tumbled, the chasm growing deeper and darker. He could feel the change from within, like teeth sinking into his throbbing mind. Lyvah came first, the dark, corrupt energy from the astral planes plaguing his very sould. Johauna's fingers dug within his pouch and clasped the golden time spike that rested within. Depression and anxiety threatened to engulf Johauna just as it always did. *If man had not gone and corrupted the delights of the land and life, I bet lyvah would be the sweetest sensation instead of a nauseating and dreadful experience. Lyvah, it is just so... succulent.* Johauna concentrated on the second source of energy that swirled about him, the safer one. Nyvah. Through the air Johauna fell, the darkness snapping at him like a stray hound hunkering in the shadows. Johauna had lost track of the barbaric creatures, whether they be floating above him or below, he knew not. Staving off the impending psychosis, Johauna welcomed the next current of energy that consumed him, which was the energy from the time fragment itself, or more appropriately from the chorr'gall in which Johauna was linked to, Dao'Sirakas.

We must've fallen into an underground lair; that's why this chasm seems so big! It was only supposed to be a deterrent for this beasts to leave me alone! If Johauna could describe the sensation of drawing energy from the chorr'gall, it would be described as cold, frothy water flowing from the pores of his skin outward, only instead of water it was energy. The sensation was the strongest in the shoulder blades of his back, where the chorr'gall's mind and Johauna's body combined to give him wings of spiritual energy. Johauna knew that their were different ways that a person could access a time fragment, and as far as he knew, man has not even begun to tap or understand what a time fragment could truly do. In fact, it was not absolute fact that the energy that came from the fragments of time was from the beasts of old at all; it was just the most likely scenario that man knew of. Producing celestial wings that the chorr'gall offered was just a learned skill that one could acquire if they worked with their time fragment long enough. *Time fragments…they are living things. Sentient. Most do not realize that, they treat them like tools to be used and little else.* His descent finally slowed. Johauna smiled at his own success until he felt elongated fingers and forearms wrap around his shoulders and neck.

Cascading back down into the valley of darkness, Johauna began his mid flight fight with the mistress beast.

The smoke was daunting, the sheer amount of it causing the battlefield to be swathed in shadows and darkness. His eyes watered, his throat felt like sand paper. The yelling and screaming of the carnage and mayhem in the small town was even more unnerving, and whether it be the local farmers with their scythes, or the disenfranchised soldiers from up north, each warrior stood shoulder to shoulder as the onslaught of vile creatures crept their way deeper into the smoldering village. Bodies were scattered amidst the streets like litter, and some of the buildings, the ones not on fire, were starting to take a new shape. They glowed a dull luminescent color now, and a thin layer now covered the surface of them like a second, gray skin. A skin that pulsated and moved on its own like a heartbeat. Looking at them made Aeven's skin crawl, the taste of vomit souring his stomach. *It doesn't matter what the Seven Devils do,* Aeven thought direly, *if this new plague of creatures aren't contained then we will be no more than fodder for them. We all face this problem as one, or we die as one. There is no middle ground here.*

The ragged line that the soldiers and townsmen formed was starting to break into small groups, each regiment drawn into their own fight as more men fell to the might of these ruthless beasts. *The timing of it makes no sense! Why attack this town now? Why reveal themselves like this?* Aeven hated to admit it but his internal struggle of whether to leave the battlefield was almost as strong as his urge to try and save everyone that was still alive fighting. He wanted to stand shoulder to shoulder with the guard, but he also knew that the High Courts needed to know about this new plague. These beasts could sweep the realm and catch most lords off guard. Aeven wanted to do what was smart, but his heart was telling him otherwise.

Thrush was the only fighter still left in Aeven's immediate vicinity and her vigor had long since gone this night; in fact, if Aeven didn't know any better, it looked as if she was about ready to pass out from exhaustion.

Thrush was one of the best fighters that Aeven knew, she could easily stand alone in the heat of battle and come out on top. But this night she looked like her energy and stamina was nearing its end. Especially after that last battle where Aeven had to save her from that winged wench. That had been too close of a call. As for Aeven, it was all he could do to stand up and swing his own sword; that brawl at the tavern had depleted him something fierce, and him and his own were going on two days now without rest. Smoke snaked around his ankles as his eyes tried to pinpoint the airship that the stranger had been talking about. That was Aeven's beacon of hope. While an invitation was never extended to Aeven to actually be a passenger on the airship, it was the only way to make it out of this carnage. Make it to that airship so that they could spread the word to the rest of the nation. An infestation was coming.

CHAPTER THIRTEEN

Prowess

Aeven was deaf from the screams, his eyes bleary from the smoke. His boots were caked with blood and mud, and his armor was shredded and torn. But they still clung to the hope that the airship was still available. Golbart had somehow managed to find Thrush and himself, and even more amazingly, with his merchant's wagon still intact. Aeven was disgusted at first that Golbart would put the priority of his merchandise over the wellbeing of the helpless, but in the end it turned out to be a godsend. A handful of strangers were now riding in the back of his rustic carriage, which happened to include a small family, a stoic bearded man with a thin sword and a sour look in his eyes that had taken a knife to the knee, and a young woman that Thrush apparently knew from the tavern. There were others yet still that fought alongside Aeven, including a tall woman of the culinary arts; Lucia Serafin was her name. Just through idle talk Aeven had learned that the busty, raven-haired woman had graduated from one of Pry'ama's greatest culinary academies, and even owned her own restaurant here in the External Rim. Well, she *did* own one. Who was to say what became of it now? She never did reveal if her restaurant had been torched to the ground or not, like so many others had been, though the look on her face was enough of an answer.

Though she was just a chef that was armed with a short bow, having one more fighter this night could mean the difference between life and death, and that was no joke in Aeven's book. The more that they traversed the broken, cobbled streets, the luckier they became when another able bodied soldier joined their ragtag crew. *But when does our luck run out? That is the real question. These might be all of the soldiers that we get. Everyone else is either laying dead in the streets or well on their way to the next town.* The rushed feeling that the whole group had been swept up with was now starting to fade as the dead of night was turning into the birth of dawn. Most of the ca'or that had assailed the town lay dead in the streets alongside the townsmen, however a handful of buildings still had that outer skin attached to them, like they were mutating into a living organism. *This feels like just the beginning of this nightmare. But why now? What's changed?*

Aeven didn't think that they could survive another fight. Most of them that trekked along the silent streets barely had the energy or willpower to put one foot in front of the other, let alone swing a weapon. Each warrior was haggard and looked as if they had wrestled with death and came out on the losing side. Blissfully they were approaching some foothills, which meant that they were approaching the fringe of the city. The trail down from the ravaged town and into a deep ravine was treacherous, and Golbart had to get more than a little creative to maneuver his wagon down the sloping hills. The base of the gully was heavily shaded and well protected with rocks and boulders; it did not take long for a very small fire to spring into existence nor for an assortment of jerky, bread, and cheese to be passed around for all to enjoy. Aeven would have loved for them to hike a few miles more, but none of them had it in them. Despite how tired the group was, each was in high spirits as they finally settled into the dirt; smiles and laughter floated into the sky alongside the faint smoke of the fire. Many tears were also shed at what was lost. A steep price was paid this night for an attack that none saw coming. The External Rim was nothing more than a graveyard, now.

Thrush looked like she was ready to pass out and yet she still volunteered to take the first watch, which Aeven knew she would do; Thrush was not a very sociable person when it came to complete strangers, a flaw that Aeven had always assumed came from an incident in her past. He never pressed the matter, instead watching as the performer that she met at the tavern, Fre'ja, and herself climbed a ledge and perched together, watching and waiting for any signs of the ca'or. They both sat shoulder to shoulder, heads together and talking about something that only the sky could hear. Morning was just starting to break. *Did we really fight through the whole night? I feel like someone took a wooden staff to my whole body.*

Aeven finally crouched down beside the smoldering fire once everyone else was settled. Truthfully the fire pit wasn't big enough for all of the stragglers that had managed to join their group, but most just wanted to curl up in the dirt and sleep. Aeven had managed to sit between Lidarian and Keegan, sister and brother that were also knights in service of Synlox, a city far, *far* from where they sat now. A city that was leagues away. "What brings you to the External Rim?" Aeven inquired, "knights all across the realm are disenfranchised because of those bleeding Seven Devils. I'm surprised that you strayed so far from your own kingdom. Especially when our king seems to support treachery more than justice anymore." That last bit Aeven barely whispered into the fire, his thoughts swirling as bad as the smoke. "The king keeps himself holed up within his own kingdom when the rest of the realm burns to the ground." The young knight started talking, but Aeven was now lost in his own thoughts.

The table was rough, charred, and had more than its fair share of scars on it. The ashen table was about eight feet long and was completely bare except for one wooden bowl full of fruit and a candle that was flickering shadows across the small chamber's brick wall. After the door was closed, Aeven had to stand up and start pacing around. This room was suffocating, and the dancing shadows only made it worst.

Aeven was alone in the room, and his thoughts started to drown him. It was no secret that he'd left the order of knights, nor that he was a mercenary for hire now. How did they know that I was here though? The location for this meeting was unique, a catacomb at the base of a mountain that had hundreds of yellow roses growing around it. The Edging Gaps is just a mysterious place.

It had been a week gone since a mysterious rider requested that Aeven meet with the Baron of Seven Souls, finding him travelling alone towards an unknown destination on a road that had no name. The winded horse had come barreling up from behind him, slight man hunched over the mane of the animal, mud raining down on Aeven akin to an Opel'sung storm. and now here he was alone in this chamber with nothing but his dark thoughts; if Thrush knew he was here she would beat him into a pulp.

Thrush always warned him about taking a job that values gold over integrity. She says that it never turns out how you think it should because you never know how many fingers are in the pile of gold that was promised to you. That was all well and good when you had constant work, but in Aeven's book, watching your father get a public hanging and being cut off from knighthood all in the same week was enough to make you take actions that you would normally deem 'crazy'; two months ago his father had been wrongfully executed, and ever since then, Aeven felt that he has been a whirlwind of questionable deeds.

Becoming an advocate himself for the Seven Devils and doing their grunt work is by far his most onerous deed as of yet in Aeven's own eyes, and to be completely honest he did not feel guilty in the least bit. Being told to his face by a fellow knight that Aeven himself would no longer serve the king through knighthood was an experience that had scarred Aeven through and through. Aeven knew that his sister Arma and his brother August had been treated with equal cruelty, though where their own paths were leading them was beyond Aeven.

The journey to this lonely underground chamber was treacherous enough, if a man didn't know the foothills of the Edging Gaps like the back of his hand, then finding this spot could have taken a lifetime; the only visible indicator that the messenger had relayed to Aeven when giving directions were the yellow roses growing on top of the trap door that lead to this catacomb. Yellow roses did not grow anywhere else on the whole continent of Pry'ama.

"I see you have made yourself comfortable." A man in a thick fur coat spoke, his entrance through the large wooden door anything but anticipated. The man was in his later years and very lanky. If Aeven had to guess, the man was almost seven feet tall and then some. The man's face was rough, like it had been hacked and carved with a wood knife, and his eyes were so dark of a green that they appeared to be black at first glance. The most notable feature of the man in Aeven's eyes was a golden circlet that sat on top of his shaved, stubbly head; the circlet held an engraving of what looked like a feral cougar pouncing on a flock of birds.

I know I have seen a circlet almost identical to that one before! Aeven couldn't help but think to himself. *I can't say where though to save my life. Something I will just note to myself for now.* "Since you aren't using your chair, I'm going to. These knees aren't what they used to be." Pulling a chair back from the other side of the table, the man sat down and coughed into his hand, his whole chest heaving and jerking. "I want to get right down to business, Aeven, for both of our sakes. Not just because I don't have a lot of time left here on Pry'ama, but because these chairs are so damn uncomfortable! And yet I am too cheap to replace them.

"I know that you have heard of me; my name rides on the wind faster than a forest fire. I am Kaosa Faydenfell, the general of the Seven Devils, or as most know me, I am the Baron of Seven Souls". Kaosa excused himself as he started another fit of coughing, blood and spit splattering the floor and table. "I am not well. I can barely walk from one room to another, and eating has become more of a chore than a treat anymore; I am dying, this body rejecting the implant that the Goldenfist Corp had injected into me.

"This implant was supposed to make me more agile, intelligent, and powerful. The imbedded vial was supposed to release shots of energy into my body, a solution from an energy source that you know quite well. Can you guess it?"

"Caordin'torr" Aeven whispered, "why would the Goldenfist try to harness such a wild and dark energy?!"

"Yes, the Caordin'torr. It was an experiment. I wanted to be more than what this body of mine had to offer. As of now, I feel that I have been poisoned by a turncoat. I am telling you this because I want you to grasp how important this is for both of us. I represent a band of soldiers that have evolved into a legion that want to right what was wronged concerning the Goldenfist Corp experimentations. You must know what I am talking about. Luxesma, that diary.

"Those poor women that your nation refers to as the 'Hosts' need to finally by avenged. Pry'ama has a rot, a sickness. You must see that! Of course most of your realm refer to us as the 'Seven Devils', and why shouldn't they? We have pillaged and plundered a handful of your nations in order to prove a point; to create a healthy country again, the rot is going to need to be cut out of it completely.

Templars should be able to walk from nation to nation and protect those that need protecting. Knights should be at the forefront of our armies directing and commanding; even drey'une should be at the center of our political régime, developing theories and solutions for problems with mediation. Instead, each of those factions have been run into the ground and annihilated by your king because in his mind they could have become a potential 'threat' to his position.

"I called for you personally because you are a man that has been trained in honor and respect, with values that are virtually lost in the rest of Pry'ama. You have more ties and connections via your family name than any other man I could have called upon. You also have been trained as a h'arai through the Goldenfist Corp, which gives you yet more connections as well as insight into how they operate and what their motives may be. Rumor has it that you are now disenfranchised, just a man on the wind. A man that can be hired.

"Now, I will give you a secret of mine that I was prepared to take to my grave. That journal that Boru is preaching about, the journal that is driving our whole army to seek justice, is the very tool that we are using to beckon back those last few aor'sii that had departed across Pry'ama's ocean decades ago. In it contains directions on how to operate a handful of the Goldenfist machinery that was left in Section Eight of Tai'drasial. Machinery that had been used for the Lost Project."

Wanting to add emphasis to what he was saying, the man's hand lifted from his weathered coat pocket and placed a small diary on the table in front of him. The book was slight but the whole room seemed to reverberate with the 'thud' of it landing on the table. Luxesma's diary, Aeven would *have bet his life on it. In Aeven's mind, all of Kaosa's words rang true and it set forth a projection of thoughts that startled Aeven to his core. Here was a warlord, the leader of the warlords to be more precise, that was sitting alone with Aeven in this small, dingy chamber and was apparently more ill than a dying dog. Aeven knew full well that all he had to do to rid Pry'ama of its plague of the Seven Devils was to slay this man where he sat; in doing so, Aeven would then possess the diary that had started this whole war to begin with.*

What would be the point to that end though? What Kaosa had said was true, the king was greedy and insolent, and if Aeven killed off Kaosa, then all it would be is a favor for the king. The very same king that had his father hung and his family ousted from nobility. Aeven would rather cut off his own hand than help the king. Perhaps Kaosa had a point, sometimes you just had to cut the rot and repair the damages afterwards.

"Why am I here," Aeven asked in a rush, "why should I help a crime lord achieve his goals?"

"A crime lord?" Kaosa chuckled at that, his body heaving. "Simply put, I need you to recover a priceless artifact that was stolen from me; an artifact that is needed in operating those machines in Section Eight of Tai'drasial. Think of the artifact as a key. The machines are locked without that key. Without this artifact, those machines do not have any energy to operate and that puts a halt on our entire tactic of resurrecting a glorious race.

"The man your after is a rogue, a thief. He appears and disappears as easily as the wind. His name as I know him is Aneiyrin and he was working as one of my lead scientists in Section Six for weeks before the discovery of an access way was discovered to enter Section Eight; after that, the man disappeared and so did my Sky'un'grael. This one single artifact can operate an entire Section, and if we could get the whole nation of Tai'drasial operational then my army will finally have a home, as will all of Pry'ama's disenfranchised citizens who are tired of the king's antics.

"Here, however, is the catch. Like anyone who uses a Sky'un'grael, once you attach yourself to the soul within, there is no going back; you have to keep the artifact on your person at all times due to part of your own soul being given to the Sky'un'grael to keep it powered and ready for use. I have uncovered the mystery of what happens when a Sky'un'grael is stolen from

you after having used it—a small piece of your soul disappears each day and is replaced by a small piece of the soul that inhabits the artifact. A soul exchange, if you will.

"I can see the question on your lips. How do I know this? Because I've been getting sicker each day that Aneiyrin has been gone, and I now hear a voice. It was subtle at first, but each day it grows stronger. And my soul feels…tainted. Scorched. I do not know what will happen fully when our souls are exchanged but I can tell you this; I feel more feral and vicious each morning I wake up." His other hand came up from his pocket and dropped a leather pouch of coins on the table, one of them spilling out. A golden Chraonos coin. "This here is just the trust money. There is a lot more for you once you deliver my artifact, and a rogue's head, to me. Soon."

Aeven had so many questions. They were planning on resuming the Lost Project? And Tai'drasiel could only be powered by the Sky'un'grael? Aeven was ready to call Kaosa out on being a hypocrite for wanting the Goldenfist Corp. infiltrated if he wasn't going to act any better, and then he thought better of it. That gold looked just too good. Swiping the pouch from the table, Aeven made his decision.

CHAPTER FOURTEEN

Upheaval

Sunlight beat down on Golbart's back as he navigated his old merchant's wagon down an obscure road and out of sight, rounding a gnarled bend in the road that supposedly led to the base of the Azaevia Mountains. Golbart swore that he knew where he was going and that for better chances to catch the rogue, they would need to split up this time. They would need to catch him off guard. Aeven could admit that it made sense. Thus far they've had no luck in tracking Aneiyrin, though they all had a pretty good idea of where he was going. They just needed a different tactic.

Aeven watched as his comrades slowly started to pack up their camp, if you could even call it that. Each of them had only escaped with the barest of necessities, and it showed. He did feel as if he owed them an explanation though. "If you want to depart ways with me now and travel your own path, I completely understand." All eyes turned towards him as if frozen, their weary eyes measuring him. Aeven cleared his throat and tried again.

"This might come as a surprise, but I am on a mission for the general Kaosa of the Seven Devils. I want to be clear that I do not work *for* him, but with him. For now. I actually agree with what they are trying to accomplish."

Both of the Barr siblings laid hands on the hilts of their swords, outbursts from both. Aeven held up his hand. "I *do not* agree with the destruction of Pry'ama. I do agree that we have become corrupt from within. Think about it. When the Seven Devils' ships landed on our coasts, they were but a few. Just a vanguard. Easily manageable. And what did the king do? He called forth three of our finest cities cavalry to protect *his* castle. He *allowed* them to pillage our fine country with naught a worry except for his own skin.

"He left several small cities and towns to fend for themselves! It's insanity. I won't even mention the destruction and decay that has infected our knights and legions." Both of the Barr siblings slowly sat down after that statement. "That is why I am helping the general Kaosa for now. We are rotten, through and through. So, follow me if you want to help in trying to purge our country of filth, or you can be on your way. I am going to stay here one more night though to give Golbart a head start."

His comrades resumed their packing, but now it was hesitant. Wanting anything to distract him from his perilous mood, Aeven resorted to nabbing the hardbound book he had found months ago that was now buried in his pack, his mind niggled him to read a passage that Aelora Aegus had written on her own journey so long ago. Using the struggling firelight that had sprung up in the fire pit like roving fingers drowning in ashes, Aeven hopped down to the base of the boulder he had been camped atop on and propped his back up against the solid stone.

The words from the journal jumped out at him and pulled him in as if he had fallen from a tedious ledge and was plunged into a sea of emotions. *Elinel, year 1331. My journey feels as if I am bound on a ledge with no easy trail down to the bottom; each of my comrades that I have grown accustomed to traveling with and fighting beside has their own set of problems and goals that are almost too hard for them to overcome. We are poised against such a monstrous and malevolent nemesis that any hesitance that anyone of us shows is surely the ruin of the whole team. Each soldier is pushing and pulling for self-fulfillment instead of unity for the greater good of all. My breath stays caught in my throat as I wait for the plunge downward from this desolate cliff of despair that is surely going to be the death of us all. I wait and I listen for the man known as Kordethion, surely he is strong enough to change this tide of depression. With much faith and misery, Yours truly, Aelora Aegus.*

The passages' words hit Aeven like a coastal wave, leaving him frigid and shivering from his spine down. Aeven knew it was just coincidence, but Aelora's words seemed to grasp Aeven's worst fear about forming a coalition and spelled it out for him on the old, musty page. Aeven couldn't say if hours had passed by or only mere minutes, but when next he looked up his eyes saw his whole crew lined up before him, all activities and preparations for camp stowed back away like they had never been this night. All that remained was the flickering fire licking at the clear night sky.

Thrush stepped forwards. "That must have been one bloody fine speech you gave, boss; they have all been scathed by the current political system in one form or another, and they are ready for change. Change that they want to be a part of." Thrush was all smiles. She was ready for different company to travel with besides the sleezy mercenary.

Aeven hung his head down, relief washing over him. They were now on a course of purging Pry'ama of its 'rot', and there was no turning back. "If you guys are remaining here, shouldn't you leave your camps in tact?"

"I apologize, that is my fault." Lucia spoke up. "I am sorry that I didn't think of it before, but we were in such a rush that I got disoriented. I know of an underground tunnel not half a mile from where we stand; I know because I used it to travel from my own homeland to the External Rim so that I could bypass all of the renegade soldiers lingering around this mountainside! The Azure Skulls have become infamous around these parts."

The woman's full lips pursed, and her eyes slanted down as her anger at herself started to show. "It would mean abandoning that mercenary that we were supposed to meet across the mountainside, but to be honest I think we are better off that way. He makes my skin crawl."

"This is brilliant!" Aeven declared as he regained his feet. "How far is this tunnel supposed to stretch? Can we reach the Azaevia Mountains this way?"

"Now this is only speculation, but these tunnels look as if they could snake around almost the whole realm of Pry'ama; I needed a map to navigate the passageways. To say that they are vast would be an understatement, I'm afraid! There are several waypoints that are good indicators of where you are, if you can find them. Each waypoint is overgrown with patches of blue roses. And where there aren't blue flowers, there are yellow ones. Curious, no? In any case, if we camp in the tunnels for the night it would be much safer than here."

"That is interesting." Aeven mumbled to himself, not sure what to do with that information. Louder, he said, "This underground tunnel system sounds perfect. We just need to find our way to the heart of the Azaevia Mountains. There are only so many routes that lead to the Spiral Rift, and Aneiyrin is sure to travel the most obscure one. Shaking each warrior's hand and thanking them personally for joining him on his quest, Aeven finally beckoned Lucia to lead the way to what was surely going to be the band's deliverance into completion of this mission.

The evening was still young as the haggard group surpassed the withering barrier of foliage that had hidden them for camp and started their trek up a nameless dusty hill with only the glowing eye of the full moon for company. *Lucia told us that this passageway was less than half a mile from where we were standing, and if we are traveling back uphill then the access way is probably at the crest of this hill. Possibly.*

Only a handful of minutes passed underneath the blanket of darkness before Aeven's worst fear for this night sprung to life. The hill was crawling with the shadows of men as soldiers in golden cloaks and white attire appeared like ghosts. There were dozens of them.

Raising his hand just high enough for his band to stop in their tracks, Aeven pointed out the closest one without saying a word. *How could they have known that we were here, of all places?! The Goldenfist Corp wasn't even involved in the attack of the External Rim! Someone pointed them in our direction, and I would bet the clothes on my back of who that person is. Some people just love gold more than life itself. But am I any different here?* Lucia, who was standing shoulder to shoulder with Aeven, grabbed his forearm in midair and then pointed almost directly to their feet. *Blood on my eggs, I almost stepped on that one!* Of course, the man hidden on his belly like the snake that he was, slithered to his feet the moment he saw that he had been spotted, and just as quickly Aeven grabbed the man's collar and jerked him forwards, ramming him through with the knee blade that was concealed in his armor.

Taking note of the golden emblazoned fist embroidered on the shoulder of the man's mantle, Aeven quickly threw the lifeless body back to the dirt as several more Goldenfist specialists emerged all around the surprised group; there had to be over four dozen of them. Specialists intent on finally slaying Aeven and those that traveled with him. Aeven wondered how high the price was on his head.

Approximately fifty soldiers against Aeven's fatigued six? That was not a gamble Aeven was overly keen on. *I would have to be really drunk to bet on those odds. Betting against men of this capacity? That would just be plain foolish. These soldiers are wearing silver cloaks, elegant ebony armor, and matching winged helmets; if I am guessing correctly here, then these men are Specialists from the main Goldenfist headquarters itself. These men mean business, I'm afraid. They're only given the bests of equipment, the best time shards.*

A long, deep sound caught all ears. It was a long winded sound, and deep. *That's the wail of a battle horn!* Again it roared, blaring from the very destination that Aeven and his team were so intent on getting to. All eyes drifted to the crest of the hill, the moon's light revealing tall, elegant bodies with wicked swords. A second horn chimed in, this one wailing from far to the west. *So, the barbarians have finally caught up with us, and if those bleeding Mind Magistrates are with them then this battle will be a very short one. The specialists are a force of their own, but how does one combat lyvah and nyvah with naught but a sword? I am sure that these Goldenfist cronies realize this as well.*

Indeed, as the specialists realized who it was that started rushing down the rolling hill like wolves loping towards a kill, more than half of them turned their backs on Aeven and his team as they dug themselves in for what was sure to be a bloody and costly battle. Screaming, spittle, and blood erupted all around them as men collided into men and swords tore into flesh. Aeven and his team were swiftly forgotten as the fight for life descended upon the prestigious soldiers.

Aeven was whipped around as someone grabbed his shoulder and steered him to the west. It was Thrush, and she was pointing to yet another battalion that was sneaking up the rolling hills behind them. They only had about a mile left until they joined the fray.

"I want to get to that tunnel just as much as you do, but this is reckless and foolhardy! We can't fight our way through this," Thrush squeaked, "we need to disappear. And fast!"

"I can think of only one solution to help us here, but you aren't going to like it. The cover of darkness and confusion is only going to protect us for so long!" Aeven responded, and without even looking at Thrush he knew she was staring daggers at him. She knew what he was thinking. It didn't matter how she felt about his time fragments, they were few against many and they had little to no choice. They needed help and it was not forthcoming from anywhere else.

Lucia was the only person in the group who wasn't a fighter, and as such Aeven pulled her into the center of the group as the rest of the warriors circled around her facing outwards, weapons out and ready for the onslaught of warring soldiers. Delving his hand into his cloak's pocket, he grasped the blue glass shard and concentrated on the energy pulsating in the back of his mind. *I need a mindlink here! Don't fail me now.* Trying to grasp the elusive spirit of energy was like trying to catch a fish with his bare hands.

The clanging of steel against steel, of screeching and bantering sure wasn't helping. Bodies pushed in all around him as his friends tried to stave off the symphony of screaming soldiers. His father's words suddenly burst into his head, Athrim's warning of what a time spike could do, if used in haste. *Remember son, a time spike is special, it is different than any other tool! A time spike makes use of the environment that you are already in, not from a memory or event you remember from the past.*

A time spike is unique in the respect that it takes a sliver of the past in where you are standing, though forgotten by this age, and brings it back to the present. It could be anything! Remember this. You cannot choose what piece of time for it defeats the whole purpose of the mystique. the chorr'gall that you draw your energy from chooses the segment of time in which it draws from. They choose for they have been alive for countless ages and know all there is to know about man. Remember this.

Soldiers were closing in, silver cloaked specialists in front of Aeven, and rabid, barbaric soldiers from behind. His team was in between a rock and a hard place and that was a bloody fact. The diminutive scout from Sa'thagrias, Scaldala el'Connor, was on one side of Aeven, javelin out and ready, and Lidarian Barr, the ranger that hailed from Reinhart Shrine, was on his other side, both glancing at him in wonder of what it was he was planning to do. *If these men and women are going to die defending this hill, I am going to remember who they are, and where they lived. They deserve at least that much.*

Darkness clouded their vision, and tendrils of fog wrapped around their legs like thick fingers looking for the unwary to ensnare. *I've got to focus! I only have a few precious minutes before the chaos descends upon us. Ha! Finally.* His mind finally grasping the elusive energy, his mind and body exploded with violent, vermilion light that he knew all could see for miles around. He knew that there was no more hiding amidst the shadows of night as the hill lit up like the grandest of firework displays. All hands tried to shield their eyes as all were temporarily blinded by the vibrant burst of light.

His very bones felt as if they were expanding and contracting of their own accord, to a tune that he didn't know or recognize. Aeven dropped to his knees, eyes swimming and muscles aching. That was the work of the ancient creatures known as chorr'gall. For a time spike to work properly, it had to draw its energy from both the chorr'gall as well as from the energy that Aeven had within him, which right now wasn't much. He had known the ramifications for trying to perform such a miraculous feat.

Aeven's body was the catalyst, and as many times as he had tried to use this particular time spike, he had never had much success with it. Oh, he had tried plenty of times, more so out of curiosity than anything. Why would there be a time fragment that had no purpose?

His inquisitive mind wouldn't allow him to quit. Eventually he just kept the curious fragment in his pocket more so out of habit than anything. This night, something drove him to use it. Beckoned him, enticed him.

Cringing, Aeven prepared himself for the voice that he knew would surge into his head from the chorr'gall that was linked to this fragment. It spoke, its words pounding Aeven's concentration into submission. *Aeven Lionrose. It feels like just yesterday that your great grandfather was begging at my feet, crying for my support against those that shackled me to this infernal temple.*

I loathe those aor'sii! I loathe them to my very core! I was once so happy and at peace bathing in the depths of the raging seas, and now I am nothing but anguish and sorrow. I denied your great grandfather support because he was arrogant and a rutting fool; you though, you are a man cut from a different cloth. Perhaps a man that can change life as we know it. I am going to help you, Aeven, but not for the reasons that you believe. My name is Kael'thalian, remember me.

His head reverberated with the creature's voice, what was left of his internal strength being used to stave off the deluge of darkness that was threatening to drown him. Aeven distantly felt the shard gripped in his hand turn searing hot, hot enough for his palm to start blistering and bleeding. He screamed and writhed on the ground, and yet Aeven could not drop the fragment. To do so would mean that all of the rampant energy would backlash into him, and that would mean utter destruction for his body and those standing closest to him.

Aeven was close to succumbing to the darkness, he could feel it in his bones. He was on the doorstep to true insanity. Again, his father's voice protruded his thoughts, beckoned him to fight on. *Aeven, I am giving you this shard because it is a family heirloom; an heirloom that is precious. When we found you, you were not but a few years old. Naked save for this time fragment dangling from a cord around your neck. We found you near the Gates of Keiadanis, alone and shivering, huddled beneath an alcove of boulders. I thought for sure that we'd find the rest of your family somewhere. We never did. You couldn't talk, could hardly walk. I was amazed that you were alive at all. So, you became a Kvalheim that day. I kept that time fragment until I thought that you were ready for it, and I had our family crest engraved in it.*

The ground started to upheave. Chunks of dirt, shards of stone, and half-rotten logs tumbled across the ground as something underfoot started to rumble and quake. Screams and taunts from fighting soon changed into cries of anguish and fright as soldiers from both sides were ruthlessly impaled by shards of stone and splinters of trees. The bodies of the deceased tumbled haphazardly down into new ravines as the terrain gave way to rents in its crust. The planet itself seemed to groan in anguish.

Aeven's fingers grasped at the ground as he himself fought against falling into one of the newly made chasms. All fighting came to a standstill as landslides of boulders and dirt cascaded down from high above, each warrior now fending for himself. Lifting his head, Aeven could see that the devastation wasn't just in the immediate area; the planet for miles around was roiling like boiled water. *What have I done?!*

Aeven's team crouched down next to him in a crooked line as the devastation took place, the impenetrable line of soldiers now dissipating like smoke on the wind. Those that tried to escape uphill were met with boulders, shrapnel, and mud, and those that tried to sprint downhill had to navigate the new chasms that were forming. Aeven's ears were screaming from the thunderous rumbling of the planet.

Then the reasoning behind the tremors was apparent, and for once, Aeven was at a loss for words. Emerging from the soil like a whale peering from the surface of the rolling ocean was a colossal fortress. The emergence was slow; as slow as fog rolling over a forgotten plain, but emerge it did. A thought struck Aeven as his jaw dropped at the sight before him. *Those tunnels that Lucia was so keen about! They were the... tunnels of a castle!* The keep was colossal, lichen growing abundantly across the dark, rough stones. The curtain wall was in shambles, and the courtyard itself was overgrown with vines and briars. But overall, Aeven had never seen such a majestic castle. It had a dark beauty about it.

Aeven's eyes latched onto one of the battlements appearing out of the many chasms; there was a red, vibrant script painted across its stonework. The language was foreign to him, it kind of resembled the language of the aor'sii but only in the loosest of sense. The ground vibrated again, more chaotically. Like the planet was heaving.

His whole team was now lying flat on their stomachs now as the ground lurched beneath them and the castle emerged far below. Scaldala whispered out loud into the fresh ground turf, "can that race really be destined to come back into Pry'ama? Let us pray *not*!" Despite himself, Aeven jerked around and stared at the small, stout man. *He knows something about this!* Aeven thought bitterly.

At each corner of the castle were peculiar statues of monstrously sized golems, their heads tilted to the sky in ruination and their mouths gaping open in obvious pain. Upon closer inspection Aeven saw that the mouths were actually windows into the castle. He did a double take. A person's head was poking out of one of the gaping mouths, the figure staring down at the ruptured hills as if he couldn't believe what he was seeing. Dawn was just starting to break and Aeven could barely see the outline of the man, but he had a strong suspicion of who it was. It was just too much of a coincidence to think otherwise.

Aeven watched the man's head swivel from one side of the hills to the other as he slowly rose into the air with the rest of the fortress. The man pulled a green hood up over his head as his eyes latched onto the hillside that Aeven was resting on. He couldn't tell whether the man was able to see him or not in the birthing light.

He must've seen him. The stranger's arm waved out of the golem's mouth; a bright orange orb clutched in the man's hand. He was taunting Aeven, and he took the bait. His newfound anger was stemmed entirely from anger. Springing to his feet, Aeven dashed towards the rough outer wall of the castle. Towards the gate that was wide open. *That man I saw knew me, and I bet if I saw his face, I would know him too.* Aeven now knew how Aneiyrin had been so elusive. *I was one of the best scouts when I was a knight, and yet this man has been as obscure as a raindrop riding the saddle of the wind!* It all makes sense now.

CHAPTER FIFTEEN

Puzzles

Aeven dashed through one of the castle windows as it slowly rose into the dawning sky, glass shards exploding inwards as his boots connected with the rough floor. The inside of the room was overgrown with vines and roots, the air thick with dust and darkness. The stone flooring that Aeven tumbled onto was as cold and dark as the fineries and tapestries that decorated the long room. Long, elegant scarlet rugs lined the shadowed halls, and faded portraits hanging skewed on the walls disappeared into the darkness in several different directions.

Aeven couldn't tear his eyes away from the ceiling. Grim, barbaric statues could be seen hanging from iron crossbars embedded in the ceiling high above, the rusted metal supporting grotesque terracotta bodies that were positioned so that they looked like their sinewy bodies had been mutilated in the most disgusting of ways. Each statue was different; some were young men, others woman, but all were unique, and each was made as if their eyes sought out any strangers that trespassed through their dank hallways. Aeven's feet were rooted to the ground, his skin starting to sweat. The statues felt as if they were sapping his remaining strength. *Just…why? No, must not linger. Must persevere. I hope to never meet the man that created something so hellish as this.*

Aeven was bathed in fading, luminescent light that spawned from the statues themselves. There didn't seem to be any chandelier, torches, or even flames, and yet they somehow produced a dark light. *I can't even begin to fathom how this room works. My friends need to hurry, I am losing energy. Fast.* It wasn't long before each member of his squad came tumbling through the very window that he himself had; all except for Scaldala. Lucia voiced his unasked question. "Scaldala was too short to jump through this window. Salt in my milk, I was almost too short to tumble through this window! He was a good distance behind me when I bolted through, whose to say which floor he wound up on."

Aeven was livid with himself. He always did stuff like this, rushing into trouble without taking the time to stop and think of others and what they might need. *Blood and sugar!* "We need to find Scaldala first, now, instead of chasing after Aneiyrin. It's not his fault, nor is it ours, but he is part of our group and who knows what surprises are lurking in this nightmare. Let's find a staircase to a lower level and then we will just have to backtrack when we find him. Aneiyrin will invariably be on a higher level. I'm positive of that."

"No need for that," Thrush said. "Aeven, you need to chase after Aneiyrin; we've been on this hunt for weeks now, and if you lose this chance then there might not be another. You know that I am right. Scaldala knew what he was signing up for when he joined our quest. Well, maybe not *this*, but you catch my drift. And you need to give him credit where credit is due. I saw him on the battlefield, he is a lot more capable than you recognize."

Aeven opened his mouth for his rebuttal and Thrush cut him off again. "I see no reason why Keegan and I can't break off from our group and find Scaldala ourselves. You do what you need to do and we will do the same. This castle is huge, but we will be able to find you. Eventually." Aeven nodded at her in agreement and watched as the duo disappeared down one of the many hallways, both having swords at the ready.

Aeven looked around and spotted an elegant chair that was resting beside a redbrick fireplace. He really needed to sit down, he felt like he was about to collapse. He found his seat and watched in mild interest as an explosion of dust ensued. Whichever direction they were going to travel in this monstrous castle, it had to be quick and thoughtful. He didn't have enough energy to just go blundering into problems like he was famous for.

His newly formed team was now scattered like dandelion seeds in a river, each floating in their own current and yet still all headed in the same direction. If Aeven was to unite them once more then he was going to have to make a smart move. Somehow. Sitting on his chair, Aeven couldn't help but look out the window that was directly in front of him. This fortress seemed as if it had finally ascended completely from the ground; at least, the rumbling and tremors had come to a standstill. The weathered chef and the isolated knight both stood within the room, lost in their own thoughts as they too gazed out the window.

It was time for a smart move and Aeven believed that Lucia had the answer whether she knew it or not. "Lucia, can you describe to me where those blue roses were growing when you traveled this fortress when it was underground? I know this is all disorienting but please try and remember. It could save our time and our lives." Aeven asked.

"That is a mighty fine question," Lucia mused out loud. "It's hard to explain but it looked as if the patch of blue roses was growing behind a row of long, thin jagged rocks that didn't quite reach the ceiling. The room that the roses were growing in was dark and dank, and truth be told, it looked more like a cavern than a room."

Aeven walked to the window and stuck his head into the crisp air, looking upwards at the great stone golem's head. He beckoned the others to look with him. "I saw that man in the window right above that golem's head. Lucia, I think those jagged rocks you saw the roses growing behind were the golem's stone teeth."

"Aeven, you're a genius!" Lidarian quipped, "It's as good of an idea as any I've heard yet this morning. To the golem's mouth we head then."

The air tasted moldy, stagnant, and the darkness of the hallway smothered her like a pillow to her face. They had been walking for no more than a handful of minutes before she had to stop and lean against the wall. It was humid, she was sweaty, and her body felt as if it was covered in spores and dust. She itched, bad, and the sweat rolling down her scalp, breasts, and body was driving her mad. Keegan Barr, the young, gentle knight that he was, turned his head away as she tried to itch in places that wasn't very ladylike. "I need some air. I'm sorry, I know that were on a mission to find Scaldala, but I need to bathe in the morning wind. These pungent hallways are *killing me!*"

"No, no I understand. I, too, am itchy." Thrush gazed at him sideways but didn't say anything. He looked perfectly fine. He certainly *wasn't* sweaty and itchy. He looked like he was just out for a morning stroll. "In fact, I see a window from where I am standing. A tall, oval one, in fact! It's a godsend, no doubt. Look, it's not even ten yards from where I stand."

Thrush bolted past him and jumped onto the window's ledge, the cool wind washing over her like a perfumed bath. He sauntered over and joined her, both hanging out of the window like clothes hung to dry.

"Having fun?" A voice whispered into her ear. Thrush no more than whipped her head around before a hand shoved her out of the window, Keegan not far behind her. The ground came fast and hard.

Thrush lay sprawled under the morning lowlight, and let her head come to rest against the dewy grass, Keegan coming to a rolling stop beside her. The land had stopped rumbling, which meant that the window that they had initially been aiming for was leagues above where they now lay. *Well, perhaps not leagues, but it sure felt like it.* If Thrush had the energy to stand up, she probably would have puked at the gravity of their predicament. Fortunately, she did not have the energy.

Keegan was the first to his feet, the stoic young knight favoring one leg over the other. *By my mother's blood, that young man has an immense amount of fortitude! He's not too bad to look at either with that chiseled chin and strawberry blonde hair.* Thrush thought to herself as her new partner started talking quietly. She sure liked his husky voice too.

"We must have the Elder's own luck to have survived that fall! And now, here we are outside of fortress walls with who knows how many enemies roaming these fields in search of Aeven, and invariably, us. And worst of all, my sister is up in the clouds fighting alongside Aeven while my bruised behind is down here with you!"

"Pipe down and help me up," Thrush hissed. "Aeven is the best fighter I know of and has more skill than any five warriors you can find. It isn't him or your sister you should worry about, I can guarantee that."

Keegan shut his mouth and stuck out his hand, his eyes opening wide and his mouth dropping slightly. "Thrush!" the man grunted, "your armor, it's... it's glowing!" Thrush had been so caught up in admiring her partner that the vibrant pink aura that had sprung up around her had been only a quick second thought until now. Bringing her gauntleted hand up to her face, Thrush watched as the bright pink light emanated from a point beneath her armor's plates.

Is this light coming from my armor or from me? Thrush couldn't help but think to herself in desperation. *My face doesn't seem to be glowing so it must be emanating from somewhere in this plate mail!* Thrush looked down at the rest of her body and noted that the light was the strongest at the center of her chest; it was beating, like a heart.

Keegan was curious. Kneeling down in front of her, he proceeded to try and figure out how the metallic plate shifted to reveal the source of the light. Thrush's own fingers were covered in thick leather hide from her gauntlets and felt clumsy at best, so she let the young man try and find the light that hid just above her heart. The man was quick; in the space of fifty-two breaths, Keegan had found a small lever hiding amidst the overlapping plates on her chest.

Keegan clicked the lever down and the plate at the center of her chest swung upwards and outwards, bathing him in all of its brilliant light. "I can't see what it is!" Thrush yelped, "I can't get my head down that far. What is it? Can you describe it to me?"

"Well, underneath this plate that swings outwards is a crevice about as deep and long as the palm of my hand." The young man stated bluntly. "And I don't know how else to describe this so I will just say it and hope you believe me, but inside of this crevice is a black orb that is floating of its own accord. The orb looks as big as a person's eyeball and is as black as the darkest of nights; oh, and it looks like some of your blood is dripping onto the top of it. You probably busted up one of your arms with that fall and it looks like your blood touching that orb has set off some kind of chain reaction. Besides that light radiating from you, do you feel any different?"

Thrush had to sit there and think about that question for a second. Trying to isolate which pieces of her body hurt from the fall and which ones felt different from this new revelation of her armor was quite the task, but after ten minutes she finally had to shake her head no. No, she did not feel any different, she only felt tired and confused and frustrated. But then, how was that different from any other day of the week? Letting her head fall back into the grass, she stared up at the morning sky. They needed to come up with a new plan, and fast.

Scaldala el'Connor has always considered himself renowned for getting himself out of sticky situations, and it always surprised other people because of how short he is. People just assume that because he was short on stature, he was just as short on wits; a misconception Scaldala was always keen on correcting. Oh, how wrong they were. Scaldala might be short on height, but he'd be damned if he was any less capable than the next man.

Scaldala knew that pulling himself into a different part of the castle was a very risky bet, but first and foremost, Scaldala was a scholar, a genius some called him. When this fortress burst out of the ground like smoke springing free from a fire, Scaldala knew in his heart that he had to scope it out and gather as much information as he possibly could. He needed to scout this new landmark for himself so that he could better prepare his lord of what's to come. Battle, surely. The room that he had crawled into was frigid cold and smelled as damp as a wet blanket. The stone room was also as bright as the noonday sun, even though it was barely morning outside.

Bright energy seemed to be emanating somehow from within the very foundation of this room, casting the elegant, dark-wooded furniture in a ginger glow. The mysterious light seemed to seep through the cracks of the intricate stone walls and flooring, bathing all within the room in spackled rays of orange and magenta. Squinting, Scaldala tugged his heavy mantle closer to his body and carefully crept his way to the large fireplace that rested against the far side of the room.

A towering bookcase was perched against the mossy wall, and Scaldala was drawn to it like a bee to nectar. Using his javelin as a walking staff, the stout man began perusing the dusty tomes. Thousands of books comprised of various colors and sizes towered over the Scaldala, and despite how bleak the situation was, Scaldala was immensely proud of himself for having chosen this chamber out of the many that he could have wound up in. He admitted to himself that their might have been *some* luck involved. Nevertheless, his eyes roved the shelves and he eventually settled on three tomes to take with him. His knapsack would hold no more than that, and he needed his hands free in case he needed to defend himself.

Scaldala chose the nearest doorway to exit the chamber and disappeared from the glowing coral room and into a hallway of luxury and death. Elegant, black drapery decorated the walls, and long benches with scarlet cushions rested beneath the tapestry. Metal wrought sconces that were made to look like roses also lined the walls, the torches resting within them freshly lit. Scaldala had been a captain for Sa'thagrias for many years, he has seen his fair share of blood, guts, and political strife. Nothing compared to this though. It took all that it had within him to put one foot in front of the other.

Aeven watched Fre'ja Nyland sway ahead of him, one foot elegantly in front of the other. Aeven could see why Thrush liked her; both were free spirits, travelers. They were filled with wanderlust and allowed their hearts to lead them. Aeven felt a stab of jealousy and then quickly beat it down. *It's not the time or the place for that! I'm sure that Thrush is safe.*

I love her as a friend. Don't I? Fre'ja reminded Aeven of a painting. Her clothes were so bright that they made Aeven's eyes hurt, and she had a way about her that was just creative. Slung across her back was a harp, and at her side a rapier.

Each was lost in their own thoughts, moments fading into minutes as the hallway that they'd initially chosen dwindled from being grotesque into a plain passage that was unremarkable. A few more minutes crept by and then the group came to a grudging halt. "Is that a…trapdoor?" Fre'ja whispered, looking up at the ceiling.

"Wait, there's another one!" Lidarian blurted out, pointing to a section of wall about five yards away. The grotesque statues might have been gone but that didn't stop Aeven's hackles from standing on end. There were dozens of them, and each trapdoor was slightly different, some made of steel, some were built of thick wood, and yet others comprised of slick stone. From what Aeven could tell, it was virtually impossible to proceed any further without going through one of those trapdoors for the hallway was a dead end about thirty feet from where him and his team were standing.

"This is ludicrous, we need to find stairs that take us up to the next level! Each of these trapdoors leads to the levels beneath us, and none of us are tall enough to reach those trapdoors on the ceiling." Lucia spat from behind Aeven, "At the rate, we are going to lose Aneiyrin before we even have a chance to catch him!"

Aeven could feel the chef's temper building up to a fiery tempest so he quickly interjected with his reasoning. "Let's not be so hasty now. Look at the walls of this hallway closely. I think it holds the key to choosing our way from this point forwards; those trapdoors are there just to distract us."

"I don't know what's gotten in your head, Aeven, but I do not see what you see," Lucia smoldered. "It looks like a wall made up of rough stone blocks and crappy, cheap mortar. There aren't even any windows to tell which end of the fortress we are at, for all we know we could be at the bottommost level, and we wouldn't even know it!"

Aeven could have sworn that Lucia was joking but from the long frown on her round face and the tone of her voice said otherwise. "How can you not see it?!"

If Lucia's face was red before, it was scarlet now, her eyes mere slits. *Okay, okay. So she is either a superb actress, or something here is amiss.* "You really do not see that blue and green mural surrounding us right now?"

The look she bathed him in said that no, she did not. Was he starting to lose his mind? Or was there more to this than met the average person's eyes? Looking over at Lidarian told Aeven that it had to be just him that could see the colorful mural for her stare was just as blank as Lucia's. Fre'ja looked just as perplexed. "If neither of you can see what I see, then this means that this test is meant for me."

Aeven's reasoning seemed so simple to him, even if the women gave him withering gazes. Perhaps they thought that he had finally lost his mind, which was completely understandable. Maybe he thought the same thing of himself. Stepping up just short of the first trapdoor, Aeven turned to inspect the first piece of the mural. The mural, if you could call it that, seemed to be a painting depicting what Pry'ama looked like in times past; A Pry'ama with several cities and realms that Aeven had never even heard whispers of.

The map was gigantic, taking up at least ten feet worth of stone wall, and the detail was so amazing that Aeven lost himself in it for a time, imagining himself walking a land that was cherished and taken care of instead of one that was abused and mistreated. It was a paradise. *What a treat that must have been*, Aeven thought sourly. Looking down the length of the wall, Aeven was able to distinguish more murals, a panorama that depicted events that had taken place in times past.

To Aeven's eyes, the color of the mural kept bouncing back and forth between deep blue and vivacious green, the more he concentrated on one color the less the other one seemed to appear. What really made Aeven's breath catch was that the more that one of the two colors showed, the more that the events depicted seemed to shift as well. The first mural of history showed what looked like the aor'sii constructing colossal humanoid figures together. *Golems that look very much like the ones here 'guarding' the castle.*

Aeven's thoughts wandered. *Why would the aor'sii go to such great lengths to create something as powerful as that golem? Or perhaps there's more than one golem? From the looks of this mural, it looks like there is more than just the one golem that was created. This begs the question however, for hundreds of years no one has seen the likes of these golems. Which means that they are either fictitious, or very well hidden.*

When Aeven focused on this painting with the mindset of seeing the blue pattern, the aor'sii seemed content and happy, and the golem itself looked lifeless; focusing on the green pattern however showed imminent discontentment amongst the aor'sii, each of their faces held a rictus sneer and shadows pervaded their eyes. The golem was illustrated as raging across the cities of Pry'ama, tearing citadels asunder. *Such a sharp contrast! But what does it mean? Two different perspectives perhaps?*

Aeven continued to the next panorama. It was a simple mural but spoke volumes of where the rest of the paintings were headed. This piece of the puzzle was of an aor'sii again, only he was standing upright and was holding two objects; the first was irrefutably a sky'un'grael. It was a vibrant blue, and smoky mist spilled out of it in waves. Nestled within the arms of this aor'sii was a small baby, a human baby, unless Aeven was mistaken. This baby was being held at the aor'sii's chest and seemed content. It looked up at the aor'sii lovingly. Both the aor'sii and the baby were bathing in the mist of the orb.

Again, Aeven shifted his perspectives, the blue versioned mural depicting peace and tranquility between baby and aor'sii. When Aeven shifted to the green version however it made him frown. The aor'sii was hunched over the baby as if he wouldn't let it go, and there was now a woman on hands and knees looking like she was begging the aor'sii for what Aeven assumed was the baby. Aeven couldn't help it, he shivered and was filled with anger. Both versions still contained the sky'un'grael.

The more I hear and read about the aor'sii, the worst off they appear. How majestic were they really? The final mural was the most powerful of all. In the center of the last mural was the same lifeless golem, only clasped in both of his hands was the smoky orb, the orb appearing so small in comparison to the golem that it was almost too hard to distinguish. On one side of the golem was the same baby that was in the previous mural, or a baby that looked like him at least, and this infant was sprawled out on a stone table.

On the other side of the golem was a creature that was as large as the golem itself, this creature looking as if it was shackled to a stone temple.

The creature looked livid. *I would bet my tanned hide that this creature is a chorr'gall!* Aeven thought excitedly. When Aeven tried to focus on the two separate colors of the mural, the illustrations stayed exactly the same. *At least on this point, the two perspectives could agree. What could these golems, the chorr'gall, and us humans all have in common with each other? And these orbs, the sky'un'grael, seem to play a key role as well, though the artist here isn't revealing of what.*

Aeven's fingers absentmindedly strayed down to the orbs strapped to his belt, orbs that looked very much like sky'un'grael. The very orbs that he'd found on that beach weeks ago. *There's absolutely no way that I have two sky'un'grael. Impossible. Who would leave something so precious laying around on a forgotten beach? I'm sure mine are nothing more than decorations.* Much to their credit, all three women stood vigilant as Aeven continued to assess the mural; and as much as Aeven's heart and mind wanted to stay and admire this revealing piece of history, he knew that they just did not have the time for such luxuries. Aneiyrin was here in this fortress and Aeven knew that he somehow had the answers to Aeven's questions; Aeven just had to catch him.

Aeven knew that the key lay in one of these paintings. Searching the paintings felt like it took centuries, and not just because of the time-crunch. Whoever had created this fine artwork had put so much time into it that they could have hidden a cosmos worth of information without the viewer being any the wiser. *I have the original mural, the blue mural, and the green mural to scrutinize, each with their own plethora of details! This could take years!*

Finally taking a gamble, Aeven's eyes settled on the second mural and concentrated. This painting seemed the most important. *The original mural is confusing enough to look at! What if they hid the key in the blue version, or the green? This could take centuries to depict! Literally!* And then he saw it; it was very distinct and miniscule, but there it was right underneath his nose. The baby that the aor'sii was clutching was pointing eastwards, directly at one of the trapdoors that was but a few feet away.

Aeven didn't have any choice but to follow his gut instinct on this one. It could have been a fluke of the artist, but it was all Aeven had to go off of. He would just have to bet his fine azure luck on this hunch. Aeven voiced his thoughts. "I'm taking a gamble, ladies. I am betting that our key to the next level is this stone trapdoor resting right over there. None spoke, they only nodded. So far it was the best lead that they had. Grabbing the iron rung that was attached to the stone door, Aeven pulled as hard as he could.

It was very slow going but eventually he was able to lift the trapdoor high enough that it hit its peak and toppled over in the other direction, a resounding boom ensuing. At his feet, where the trapdoor had been, was now a hollow, boxed shape hole in the floor, a shallow hole that had a single, small wooden chest resting in its depths. This wooden chest's lid was open, and the chest was empty save for a simple purple pillow.

"This is one of the oldest tricks in the book." Aeven couldn't help but murmur to himself. Grabbing the purple pillow, he tossed it over his shoulder and discovered the true secret of the chest. Eight orb sized holes punctured the bottom of the chest, with words neatly written in the center of the circle *"One choice, one future."* Each hole had several pockmarks in it, as if whatever was supposed to fit in each hole was supposed to infuse something else.

I knew that it was going to come down to something like this! It was no accident that both colors I was seeing for this mural were the same colors as the sky'un'grael that I possess. Which means that I do, in fact, have two of the sky'un'grael. Two of eight. This begs the question, however, if there are eight slots in this chest, how many versions of this mural am I not seeing? What would a person see if they had all eight of the orbs on hand? Is this secret chest only one of several? No time to think on this, I need to act now with the information that I have on hand. This is a puzzle that I can eventually come back to. Maybe.

So, I am supposed to place a sky'un'grael here, no? Aeven's mind was a whirlwind of questions, and yet he couldn't stop and sort them out now. He just had to press on. *No one is forcing me to do this, these sky'un'grael* are *invaluable. Do I dare relinquish one? But I want to know what happens. I must know.* His fingers tapped on the green orb, moved over to the azure one and curled around it, paused for just a second, and then settled once more on the emerald orb.

Carefully placing the sky'un'grael in one of the chest's indentations, he heard the orb click into place. It was subtle, he almost didn't feel it, but as soon as the orb settled into it's slot, Aeven felt as if his soul shifted slightly within him. It was the barest of twinges, but his mind felt... different.

Closing the lid, Aeven took a deep breath and waited for something miraculous or life changing to happen. They needed a miracle at this point.

CHAPTER SIXTEEN

Cherry Blossoms

Cherry blossom willows towered over Scaldala like hands with dozens of spindly fingers, the thick roots of the trees slithering across the large room and down through the ground like eels in the water. The stone walls were cracked on all sides, the fissures snaking from the ceiling down to the deepest parts of the room. Scaldala stumbled across the uneven ground, walking slowly across the simple stone bridge that connected one side of the room with the other. Scaldala was showered with countless waterdrops as he tried to navigate between two thundering waterfalls that were cascading down on either side of him.

Scaldala started breathing in short, sharp gasps as he tried to pass through the center of the two deluges of water without being swept away to the abyss. Mere minutes felt like hours as one foot carefully stepped in front of the other, the rough stones beneath his feet slippery and slimy. Hunching over, Scaldala rushed forward the rest of the way and leapt through the final wave of water, breaking through to the other side.

"Finally," Scaldala huffed, hunched over and leaning on his javelin. "I don't know who the architect was of this castle, but he was a *lunatic*. Just... *why?*" Scaldala took a moment to appreciate the next section of room that lay before him. It was beautiful. He was standing on a ledge that had great magenta walls towering on all side of him. Great cherry blossom trees grew from countless terraces built into the walls, some with white pedals and others with a pinkish hue. The terraces themselves were overgrown with lush green grass and fragrant lavender.

Scaldala laid eyes on something that completely stole his breath away. *Are those prisons?* The terraces weren't just for looks. Each had a rectangular prison built into the center of each platform. The stone prison were constructed of bars that were comprised of ivy and stone. The ivy had completely overgrown most of the prisons, and yet Scaldala could still make out slumped figures that were resting against the prison bars. From what he could see, Scaldala surmised that they were very tall, perhaps reaching seven feet, with skin as pale as snow and long hair that resembled the same color as their tarnished wings. *Wings? I...I don't understand. It cannot be.*

Scaldala couldn't believe it. No, he refused to believe it. The aor'sii were dead, every tome ever written by man declared that well known fact. And yet here they were, sleeping as soundly as nourished babies. Scooting to the closest terrace that he could manage to get to, Scaldala sneaked to the edge of the rail-less bridge and tried his hardest to peer through the ivy and between the stone bars so that he could see the legend that rested only mere feet from where Scaldala stood.

He did not have a perfect view, but it was good enough; the aor'sii was almost perfect for lack of any better word. Her hair was long and deep red, cascading down her shoulders and over her voluptuous chest, finally coming to rest on the cold, wet stone floor of her prison. Her nose was dainty and spattered with countless freckles, her lips both full and alluring. Even with this aor'sii wearing just simple leather armor, she was breathtaking.

Her wings were the only flaw that Scaldala could see. Most of the feathers were ruffled and broken, and there were some patches on her wings where there were no feathers at all. Despite how large her wings were, they still managed to stay within the confines of the stone prison, somehow. Scaldala studied her face, it was quite contradictory to the rest of her body. It held a nasty sneer, and she kept shaking her head side to side as if she was trapped in a nightmare that she just couldn't wake up from.

Scaldala took a few steps back and inspected as many others as he possibly could from his vantage point. *Blast my height! I can hardly see anything!* Of the few others that he could see, most wore simple leather armor, while others wore pious blue robes or majestic plated armor; all, however, looked as if they were trapped in that same dreamlike state, trapped in a nightmare that would not subside. Taking as many mental notes as he could, Scaldala scurried onwards, black cloak fluttering behind him as if trying to bid this ill-omened and legendary room a proper farewell.

The walk alongside the stone fortress seemed to last an eternity. There were no apparent doors back into the castle, and the rolling plains around it were rough and broken, which made the walk even more deliberate and slow. Putting one heavy-plated boot in front of the other, Thrush was forced to face the internal battle that she was having within. She was starting to feel a slow change within herself, a change that scared her.

Thrush felt as if she had an overabundance of vitality and a great deal more of muscle strength, but she also started hearing whispers in the back of her mind. At times the voice was powerful and commanding, other times it was merely a whisper that babbled incoherently. It was like a voice you could hear but was just distant enough that the words they spoke disappeared before they could make it to your ears. It was very disconcerting, all the more so because Thrush didn't know if it was merely a figment of her imagination or something more.

Thrush wanted nothing so much as to strip off her armor and leave it for some other fool to find, but that would just be complete stupidity. She didn't even know if her armor was the *cause* of these voices, she was just assuming. *Maybe I just hit my head too hard on the way down. When I find the man that pushed me out the window, I'm going to have his head.* Thrush didn't fancy fighting in nothing but her underwear, though Keegan might get a kick out of that.

Thrush's black plated armor and her raven black swords were another matter altogether. Walking in the dead of night while trying to be as discreet as possible was one of Thrush's least favorable circumstances; sneaking was even that much harder to do while wearing as cumbersome of armor as she was wearing, and that excluded the faint rosy light that had started emanating from her like a wavering star.

Sometimes while walking, her armor would glow so bright that Thrush was sure that anyone within a league would be able to spot them, and other times her armor shone with no light at all. The whole situation confounded her, and as much as she thought about it, the more bothered she became.

She was certain that it was only a matter of time before soldiers assailed them from the broken hillsides. Despite her best efforts to contain her irrationality, Thrush voiced her fear to the stoic young man marching beside her.

Keegan's answer was simple. "No, I will not abandon you. I realize that we stick out like a sore thumb, but that cannot be helped." After a moment of silence, the man continued. "You realize that we could walk the entire length of this fortress wall and not find a single entrance, right?" His voice held venom now and Thrush knew that that venom stemmed from his anger at their situation and not at Thrush herself. At least, she hoped that was the case. The young knight continued his rant.

"Fortress walls are meant to keep intruders out, and by all that is good, we are wanting to intrude! You know it is only a matter of time before our whole group is slain, right? There were only seven of us to start out with in the first place and now our group is broken and scattered like rose petals in a river. We might all be heading in the same direction, but by god, we aren't together."

Thrush fumed on the inside. Fate never said that life was fair or that it would always deal out perfect situations to make life sweet and easy. Thrush had learned the hard way that you made the best of what you had because at some point in time you might not have those favorable circumstances that you once took for granted. Thrush grabbed Keegan by the collar and yanked him around, much to his dismay. Thrush stared him down. "Do I look like a bloody aor'sii, Keegan? Do I look like I have majestic wings that can fly us over these rotten walls?" Thrush spat in his face, "I am in this just as much as you are and don't you forget that fact. I realize how screwed our whole team is."

Instead of retorting with a snappy comeback, the man only stated, "your armor is starting to glow again." And it was, so much so in fact that she was half-blinded by the vibrant light. The smell of blood was heavy in the air, as was the violent screams of what sounded like a young woman. Both warriors whipped around, eyes searching but to no avail. The fog was still heavy in the air. "Do we just let it be this one time? We are supposed to be finding Scaldala, and I am worried about my sister. For all we knew it could be a trap."

"What kind of knight are you?!" Thrush sputtered, "Isn't your creed to protect and serve? Scaldala can at least fight for himself! Who knows what's happening to that poor woman!"

Thrush didn't need to think on it. She started sprinting in the approximate direction of the screaming. Scaldala could be anywhere by now and this woman was in immediate danger; Scaldala could fend for himself. Cresting the closest hill, Thrush barreled her way through rubble and rocks, and leapt over the ravines that had formed when the castle emerged from the planet. She just concentrated on putting one foot in front of the other.

Keegan sprinted swiftly behind her, his sword out and shield at the ready. The screaming was getting louder, and more frantic. Leaping over another gulch, Thrush landed heavily on both feet, breathing hard. She could finally make out who was shrieking, she was hunched at the base of the hill. She was a young, blonde woman that wore polished bronze armor and sported a majestic golden cloak, the patch of the Goldenfist was emblazoned on her shoulder.

She stood up with sword at the ready in one swift motion, the specialist wearing the slimiest of smirks on her face. Raising her thumb and forefinger to her mouth, the woman whistled twice, the sound shattering the silence akin to an arrow piercing the air. A sullen silence descended on the surprised duo as they watched eight more specialists creep out of the surrounding ravines and gulches. Each had weapons out and shields at the ready. These soldiers meant business, and not the pleasant kind. "Damn" was the only word that Thrush could think to say.

—⁂—

The entire fortress started to tremble as soon as the chest's lid slammed shut, only it wasn't the chaotic, random tremors from before. These quivers were more like the pulses of a heart. The throbs came fast and hard, hard enough to throw both Lidarian and Lucia to the floor like a child discarding an old ragdoll. Fre'ja managed to keep her balance, but just barely. Aeven fell forwards himself, crashing into the adjacent stone wall.

The panorama that surrounded them lit up in a bright, green light. Continents and ancient scripture both jumped out at Aeven and hung in the air of their own accord, flickering and fading as the fortress regained one of its sources of power. Before Aeven could make heads or tails out of the strange phenomenon, the entire section of hallway jerked upwards as if it were being pulled with ropes. The hallway ascended upwards with increasing speed, pinning all four of them in place.

Gravity wrestled Aeven to the ground as a deafening siren started to wail throughout the moving chamber, its piercing cry as shrill and persistent as a wailing baby. Faster and faster the room ascended, the three stone walls shifting from gray stone to thick glass as the chamber started to reach the upper levels of the stronghold. *So, it wasn't the entire hallway that was moving, just the floor and the ceiling. Interesting.*

Purple, dazzling light and lazy clouds enveloped the glass chamber, surrounding the team in a surreal, foggy box of illusions and shadows. All eyes latched onto the ceiling of their room as a very distinct 'clicking' sound reverberated throughout the chamber. It was the gnarled trapdoor directly above them, something was opening it. Aeven was forced to dive out of the way as something tumbled through, crashing down where Aeven had been laying only moments before.

Putting his back to the wall, Aeven unsheathed his bastard sword, Qualvalion, and tried to analyze this creature. *I don't believe it. A creature of legends is standing directly in front of me. The aor'sii never left Pry'ama? Have they been sleeping underground this whole time?! This creature looks like an aor'sii, and yet it is...different.*

This creature had flowing, cobalt blue hair, and matching azure wings that were tarnished and beaten. Its feathers were torn away in some areas, and the wing's bones looked as if they had been shattered in some spots and crudely healed. This creature's skin was sickly pale, its delicate nose and thin lips cracked and transparent. On its wrists and ankles were thick bracelets that shone with the same vibrant green that Aeven's orb had been. The rest of this creature's armor was comprised of sleek, silver armor that was pieced together by worn leather straps and small iron rings. Its boots were stout and silver plated.

This creature towered over Aeven, bathing him in its stretching shadow. Its sword was thick and rough, and was almost as tall as Aeven himself was, the black leather hilt itself was a good five hand spans long. The creature sniggered at Aeven, raising its sword slightly as if to taunt him. Aeven glanced at his three friends, each of them cowering in different corners of the platform.

I have little to no choice here, really. Am I really going to pit myself against a creature such as this, though?! Am I really going to duel an aor'sii? I can't think about it, just have to do it. I need to surprise it. Losing himself in adrenaline, Aeven ran forwards and jumped into the air. Leaning backwards, he kicked his boots out in front of him and kicked the creature square in the chest. The creature was heavy, abnormally so; stumbling backwards, it smashed into the glass wall, but did not crash through as Aeven had hoped it would.

The aor'sii smashed the back of its head against the glass wall and roared in pain, hand grasping the back of its head. Gasping in surprise, Aeven watched in incredulity as Lucia shouldered her way across the room and into the heaving stomach of the beast. Crashing into the creature's stomach, the aor'sii rebounded into the wall once more, the force creating thousands of fissures to bloom in the glass. Though fractured, the wall still did not shatter.

Grasping Lucia by the collar of her crimson cloak, the beast whipped her around and into the same glass panel that the aor'sii itself had just rebounded into. The glass finally shattered, thousands of ceramic shards floating out into the empty abyss. Blood spatters showered the air and flooring alike as the shrapnel ripped through Lucia's thin layer of clothing and sliced her skin, the chef now unconscious from the blow.

The aor'sii waved her out into the open air, chuckled, and then flung her into the corner of the room. *I just need to get up and under it. Even an aor'sii can't survive that far of a fall. Can it?* Aeven inched his way between the three women and the beast, his mind trying to tune out the persistent siren of the fortress. He could do this.

Lidarian held her own sword at the ready, the freckled redheaded woman assuming her own fighter's stance. She spread her feet unevenly apart, her sword pointed at the beast's feet instead of at his heart. *That stance is Drunken Willow Whistles in the Wind!* Aeven thought elatedly, *I know that form well, and I think she is on the right track. This creature's feet will be the most vulnerable of its whole body; if I keep it busy with traditional attacks then perhaps Lidarian can swoop in and put an end to this nightmare! I didn't know that Lidarian was trained as an Ailassa, that's simply amazing. And frightening.*

Ailassas are far and few between anymore, the cautious fighters having almost died out when the aor'sii disappeared from Pry'ama. A fighter trained in ailassa is able to utilize small sparks of nyvah and lyvah to deliver powerful, precise blows. Lidarian slithered behind the beast, Aeven in front, both swords at the ready.

The aor'sii lunged forward and roared in Aeven's face, its thick, monstrous sword crashing down towards Aeven's head. Aeven met the sword in the air, steel clashing against steel. The two weapons crashed into one another akin to a tidal wave slamming against a chasm wall. Stumbling backwards, Aeven gave the beast a roar of his own and pushed back with the remainder of his strength.

It was like pushing against the front of a ship that had set sail; no matter how hard Aeven pushed against it, this beast pushed harder and with more momentum. Its sword slowly inched downwards towards Aeven's head, the rusted blade almost resting atop the center of Aeven's forehead. Aeven watched Lidarian rush towards the creature's back with her sword still angled downwards, his breath coming to a standstill as her sword swiped outwards and delivered a deep slice on one of its legs. The beast roared, spittle showering Aeven's face. Finally tearing its weapon away, the creature spun around and pointed something at Lidarian's chest. Something the aor'sii had been grasping in its other hand.

The room reverberated with a colossal 'boom', the entire platform reverberating in shocking waves. To Aeven's horror, Lidarian plummeted backwards, rolling end over end until she came to a breathtaking stop at the edge of the broken glass panel, her body just as still as Lucia's was. The beast whipped back around and rushed Aeven, the aor'sii upon him before he even had a chance to think.

Fre'ja finally broke out of her stupor. Back against the wall, she snuck around the beast and leaned over her two fallen comrades. The aor'sii ignored her, instead focusing on Aeven. Its thick sword came around in a tempestuous arc above its head, green sparks emanating from the blade. Aeven felt very much outmatched; in the space of only a handful of minutes, this creature had managed to cripple two of his comrades, and all that Aeven had left going for him was his master wrought sword and his friend that was scared spitless. *No, no that's not true. I have some time fragments, a sky'un'grael, and that armlet that I'd found with Golbart. I have choices. But all are useless in such close proximity with this beast! Not to mention what's left of my energy. I'm just so tired.*

No! No. I have something else that I can use. Something that I shouldn't use, but I will. No, I have to. I know I promised myself that I would never utilize that vile energy again that courses within me, yet what choice do I have? My muscles are spent, my adrenaline is waning, and I cannot use the tools that I carry on me, neither. I'll have to do this, just this one time. Grimacing, Aeven sought out the power of the cosmos. The astral energy of lyvah, the energy source that protects the planet itself. An energy that is deadly for a single man to try and harness.

No matter how hard he tried to block out or forget his anomalous energy from within, it was to no avail. Aeven felt as if his skin was burning from the inside out. His mind screamed as he forced himself to open that lingering sea of energy that beckoned him. Aeven knew his sanity was in jeopardy, but he also knew that in only a few more moments, that aor'sii's sword was going to cleave him clean through. The pain from the exertion of opening his mind once more to new depths hit a point where Aeven thought he was going to pass out, the glass room glowing blurry and his mind going fuzzy.

Buckling to his knees, Aeven distantly felt his sword clatter to the floor, his hand grasping air. His vision darkened ever more, his hands moved of their own accord as lyvah flowed freely throughout Aeven's body. He felt his hands crawl up to his face, feeling as if they needed to know who, or what he was. Was he a human? Was he an aor'sii? Or was he *something more*? Or *something less*? He didn't know what he was.

A shrill pain crawled its way up his spine, through his neck, and nestled into the back of his mind. His head exploded in pain as a penetrating, sharp sound erupted from within. Aeven screamed, screamed at the tenacity of how sharp and shrill the sound was. Aeven couldn't see, couldn't hear; was he even capable of seeing or hearing? He didn't know. He faintly recalled being in the middle of a battle, but that could have been ages ago or minutes ago for all he knew.

His body jerked and then rose upwards so that he was hanging just below the glass ceiling, feet and arms spread eagle. Aeven tilted his head back and laughed, laughed at how wonderful it felt to be one with the caordin'torr once more. His body drew from nyvah and harnessed lyvah, combining both in what felt like ecstasy in the purest form. what was left of his self disappeared altogether as he opened himself up fully to the creature of the planet that was lending him aid. He allowed the chorr'gall to fully inhabit his mind.

The beast of old shrouded the mind that was once known as 'Aeven'. This is what he was created for, what the planet wanted him to do with his petty, insignificant soul. He is to become a vessel of servitude and survive to transform into the ultimate life form. The Goldenfist Corp? The Seven Devils? Knighthood? All seemed so small and irrelevant in comparison to what Aeven could truly ascend to. He was a key to unlocking what Pry'ama *should* be. He was one of *many* keys.

Wait, Aeven? Who is Aeven? He did not know. Aeven's vision snapped into focus and his laughs subsided, brief chuckles escaping his dry, chapped lips. His eyes fell on a creature that stood before him. A creature that deceived all so that their kind could trick death. It made Aeven sick. *What a disgusting species. Trapping us within temples that are bound in time. Locking us into an eternity of servitude. Pathetic. All so that they didn't have to confront death. They chose a fate for Pry'ama that will only end in mayhem and destruction. For them.* Aeven burst into another fit of laughter at the insignificance of such trivial historical events such as the aor'sii dying and humans destroying themselves with wars and strife.

All energy, all life forms, belonged with the caordin'torr and the planet. This pitiful creature was no exception. Aeven filled his entire body with the caordin'torr, so much so that he could feel it seeping out of its body in waves. Aeven summoned forth the vitality of the planet and focused it into the time spike that was on his person. The time shard lit up brighter than a bonfire, the azure color bathing everyone in its luminescent brilliance. Images flashed across Aeven's vision.

Kael'thalian wanted nothing more than to bring this creature standing before him to a bloody ruin. The aor'sii looked confused, its sword tip resting against the floor as the beast's dark eyes watched its adversary hang in midair of its own accord. Aeven, no, Kael'thalian, smiled in amusement. It was time to harvest this creature's energy that it has been selfishly hiding from the planet for so long.

Kael'thalian brought his hands up and shot them down towards the lone aor'sii. *No.* Kael'thalian thought grudgingly, a thought that was bitter and resentful. *This is no aor'sii. This is a breed that was created from the DNA of the aor'sii by humans. Not quite aor'sii, and yet not quite human.*

Sii'morth. So, the experimentation went further than even the humans anticipated, I see. Back to the planet with you, sii'morth.

The memory that Kael'thalian drew upon was one of an age not yet seen by this realm, an age that was ripped from the fabrics of time of what this realm would have seen if it had not been tampered with by the foolish aor'sii. *Such a fitting end for such an obtrusive life form.*

Kael'thalian's memory sprang forth and ruptured the small chamber as hundreds of small shards of energy and fire appeared from the depths of time and shot forth into the unsuspecting sii'morth. It did not even have time to scream as it was blown backwards, its body shredded into countless ribbons and then engulfed by roaring flames.

Its armor and weapons lay untouched; as for its body, however, all that remained were charred ashes and a putrid stink. Kael'thalian inhaled and laughed as he soaked in the vibrant energy. *This body is so weak!*

Kael'thalian thought sourly. *Aeven, I hope that you enjoyed your small taste of the caordin'torr; it has been a long time since you and I have met, years, I would say, though I have lost the concept of time. You will soon understand that you are nothing more than a key, and a catalyst. I will stay close by until you reach your decision. Decision? No, until you reach your destination. I release you!* Kael'thalian withdrew from Aeven's mind, and with it the currents of energy that creates the caordin'torr. Aeven fell to the floor in a crumpled heap.

Scaldala el'Connor came to a grudging halt. Slinking into the shadows of the oval room, he examined an extravagant dining hall that was overly lavish and a mite pretentious. The room itself was perhaps two hundred paces long, and just as wide. The flooring was painstakingly polished and sparkled with a silver hue. The walls were just as beautiful, slightly darker in color than the tiled floor. Dozens of dark, glass tables lined the center of the room, the chairs wrought of steel and copper. Marvelous glass chandeliers decorated the ceiling far above. The room was overwhelmingly big and made Scaldala feel just that much shorter.

Light from the morning sun shone down from skylights that were far above, the colorfully paned glass a crude map of Pry'ama. *Wait, light is shining down upon this room. I've made it to the uppermost floor of the castle! Aeven is here, somewhere.* The light spilled down atop a peculiarity that made Scaldala pause. He'd thought that he had intruded on someone having breakfast, but they sat at the table and did not move. He watched them for several minutes, hunkering down in the shadows with javelin at the ready, and yet they did not move.

They were three humanoid figures, slouched in the intricately wrought chairs. They were just sitting there, staring ahead, unmoving. Scaldala couldn't help himself. After watching them sit there for the better part of an hour, he finally snuck over to see what or who they were. The colored sunlight illuminated them akin to light spilling upon a circus performer. They resembled manikins, life-sized and intricately detailed dolls that were beyond lifelike. *No, not dolls. More like...puppets?*

They were constructed out of a type of glass and marble alloy, though Scaldala knew that was not quite right. The creature was soft to the touch, not quite as tough as glass and yet slightly harder than human skin. Not only was the alloy warm to the touch, as if the manikin was alive, but the 'skin' was only slightly opaque; Scaldala could see wisps of light dancing in each doll, each manikin possessing a different color of wisp.

When entering the room, it would have been impossible to not see the three dolls slouched over the table, for though they were unmoving, the dozens of wisps trapped within each manikin had the room exploding in radiant hues of greens, reds and purples, each color bursting forth from a different doll. *The energy from within them is alive enough.* Scaldala pondered to himself. *Though these manikins are not. Why is that I wonder? These puppets, or dolls, or* whatever *they are, seem so dainty, and yet they also seem incredibly resilient.*

Scaldala had to almost stand on his tippytoes to look into the doll's faces; they were taller than the average person. Almost double the height of what Scaldala himself was. That was something that Scaldala always seemed to notice anymore, how tall someone or something was when he was observing it. He just couldn't help himself.

Each manikin was only wearing the barest of clothes, as if they had been in the middle of getting changed before sitting down for some supper. His eyes latched onto their bare extremities, his mind racing. All three puppets were to covered from neck to ankle in tribal tattoos. Tattoos that Scaldala was well aware of what they signified. Scaldala remembered studying a tome in the Sa'thagrias athenaeum that focused on tattoos such as these.

This is sheer genius; to make sure that these tattoos were not lost to the mercy of time, an artist had scribed them onto manikins so that they could always be replicated. Simply incredible. Scaldala found no other oddities save for the manikins having a small black orb protruding at the base of each of their necks, half of the orb inside the manikin and half out. Smoky mist spilled out of these orbs and dissipated before it reached the ground.

These orbs tugged at an elusive memory, but for the life of him he couldn't remember what or why. *These orbs are bad news, I just can't remember why. The cosmos have mercy on us if someone were to accidently activate one of those. These three orbs seem to be acting as energy for these dolls, so I should be relatively sage. I hope.* And then it hit him like a slap on the back of the head; *these orbs are blood-links*! That's right.

When an artifact possesses a blood-link, it means that that item has within it a spiritual energy that needs human blood to function correctly. When a drop of blood is given to the orb, blood-link is said to harness a piece of that person's soul in exchange for the powers that the item is withholding. Scaldala had never seen it done before and thought that whole 'blood-link' thing was just a myth, or something that was forgotten.. *Well, blood on my biscuit.* Scaldala thought, *whoever had been the master of these three must have eventually died, lest he's hiding here somewhere. Which I doubt.* Drawing his dagger from its sheath, Scaldala sliced the tip of his left index finger and smiled in exhilaration. *I can't believe that I'm about to do this, but I can't just leave these artifacts here for someone else to steal! And I sure can't carry them.*

CHAPTER SEVENTEEN

Unlikely Savior

Thrush Balfourian's skin was tingling, and she knew that it had nothing to do with how crisp the morning was; she had just gotten Keegan and herself trapped, and she was livid with herself. Blood was pounding in her ears as if a war drum was being beaten inside of her head, and the vile woman that had tricked them was laughing as if she'd sprung the funniest of pranks on one of her friends. Goldenfist specialists crept towards them like spiders harrowing in on their prey, the morning sunlight dissipating the fog that swirled around them.

That hyena-like laugh was not helping Thrush's temper in the least bit. Of course, Keegan did not utter a single complaint, all he did was sidle up to Thrush so that they were back-to-back as the Goldenfist specialists encircled them. They were closing in for the kill. What Thrush really wanted to do was walk up and smash that laughing pig in the nose; Thrush's pride was hurt now beyond immediate repair, and that rankled her more than an itch that she couldn't scratch.

"So, your armor glows." Keegan hissed at her, "can it do anything useful to get us out of this bloody predicament?" His words held more than a little venom, and Thrush understood completely. In answer to his question, she drew both of her dark swords out of their sheaths and prepared to die at the hands of these rogues.

A heavyset, balding golden-cloaked soldier lunged at Thrush, and he too carried dual long swords of his own. Her black blades met his golden ones. Shifting from one fighter's stance to another, Thrush could distantly hear Keegan's sword crashing against other blades as he contended in his own heated battle. Before Thrush could think twice about lending her aid to her friend, stout soldier started hurling knives at Thrush, knives that were hidden all over his person. It seemed like dozens whirled past her, some coming very close to connecting with their mark.

Thrush ducked, she dodged, and even somersaulted as the knives were slung through the air at her. She knew that she was wearing heavy armor, and yet she wasn't protected in the places that he was aiming for. His hand went upwards one last time and then shot out, the knife sailing through the air akin to a yellowjacket homing in on its target. Thrush winced, knowing that her momentum of her armor was now working against her. She could almost *feel* the knife embedding itself in her head. She dropped sideways to the ground and the weapon flung past her by at least three feet.

"Good shot, Broderik!" the blonde woman cawed. She had not moved an inch since the fight broke out. *She has got to be the captain of this squad*, Thrush thought bitterly to herself, *she is calling too many of the shots for her to be anything else. I'm going to feel immense joy at taking her* out. Thrush stumbled to her feet, regaining her composure.

"I don't think I could have made that shot any better myself!" Thrush thought that the woman was just being sarcastic, until Thrush looked at her spotty face; it was full of approval. And then her words hit Thrush harder than any knife could have. Despite having an enemy at her back, Thrush tore around and found her partner crumpled to the ground with a knife sticking out from the upper part of his back. Keegan was unmoving, blood pooling out from his body like a flood.

Thrush did not know what to say or what to think; she sat there in stunned silence as the essence of her friend pooled out into the surrounding grass. Her emotions were caught between the intensity of a wicked, terrible squall and the sorrow of a loved one passing on.

Thrush soaked in the emotions, embracing the surge of adrenaline that threatened to drown her.

Leaping forward, she beheaded the smiling, bald man with as much passion as her muscles could muster. He did not move; he barely had time to even register that she had burst forth at all. Tears were streaming down her face, blinding her as he fell to her feet. If she could not see, then she did not have to acknowledge that her friend was lying dead not three feet away from herself. Her swords worked of their own accord and intuition, her sword strokes raining down on the weasels like lightning striking the unweary.

Her body had become a colossal ball of energetic light, crackling and spitting in all directions. The trained specialists came at her from all sides, some landing quick biting attacks, others swinging at her as a woodsman would have at a stubborn piece of wood. Thrush was a shadow amidst the night. She moved unexpectantly, almost like a dance, her footwork only superseded by her hasty sword work. No matter where she moved, her mind was always linked to Keegan and where he lay. She couldn't shake him off her mind no matter how hard she tried.

Thrush didn't know how she did it, or even why, but the longer that Thrush fought the Goldenfist specialists, the stronger that Keegan's presence felt to her. Like she could just reach out and touch him. As her arms and feet moved of their own accord, striking and defending, her soul was elseware. Her mind was trying to find Keegan, to tell him how sorry she was that she'd dragged him into a fight that they didn't belong in at all.

Keegan's voice burst into Thrush's head like someone suddenly clapping in a dead silent room. *Let me lend you my aid.* The voice spoke quietly, like two small rowboats briefly bumping into each other on a lake. Let me lend you my aid, *Harvester of Souls.* More tears streamed down her face, her own thoughts coalescing in her mind. *How can I miss someone so much that I imagine talking to them? I hardly knew him but a few days! And yet, I miss him gravely. Am I losing my mind? Am I going mad from a broken fighter's mentality? How can I possibly be hearing a dead man's voice in my own head?*

Be at peace Thrush, I am not completely lost yet. Keegan's voice seemed to say. *Just because my body is destroyed does not mean that my spirit cannot live on in tranquility.* Thrush's whole body was heaving and sweating from the exertion of fending off so many soldiers at once, and she could practically smell the lust for blood on these soldier's breaths. *Or is that my breath? Too hard to tell.*

Thrush didn't know how much longer she could possibly last, defending herself against so many blades coming at her at once. Her mind and body were disconnected right now, but she could tell that she was starting to reach her limits. She hoped that whatever Keegan was going to help with that he would do it quickly. She brought her blade up and struck the oncoming sword aside, immediately sidestepping another. In a whirlwind she spun around and brought her swords around in a diagonal arc, bringing two specialists to their knees. She stepped backwards and brought her swords up in a defensive stance.

Her body reached a tipping point; heaving as she tried to catch her breath, she felt better than she ever had in her life. In fact, she felt like her body and mind was going into an overdrive, her internal energy hitting a peak that she had never experienced before. *Use your mind, Thrush! Think! These specialists are tough, but they are rats and cowards. What do you think they will do when you threaten their captain? No need to waste this extra energy I am granting you! Use it wisely.*

Thrush nodded to the voice. He was right; she could end this brawl right now. She had slain many soldiers this morning, but many, many more lined the hill. They were toying with her. Putting her shoulder down, Thrush barreled her way into the blonde captain and grabbed a firm handhold of the woman's hair, yanking it hard and fast so that the vile rat could not react. Holding her sword up to the specialist's neck, Thrush smiled a wicked smile of her own.

The woman started shrieking, started to give an order, and then resorted to blubbering. Thrush smashed the top of her head with the pommel of her sword. Now, she was silent as the grave. "She is not yet dead, though I can certainly make that happen. Leave this hill. Now. You can come back for your *mistress* later when I am no longer here. Disappear away from the castle and we will have no more quarrel."

The wind and the soldiers both fell into silence, as if waiting for what was to happen next. A few moments passed and then the soldiers started to disappear into the fading mist and down the rolling hills. *That battle only cost me my body.* Keegan's voice murmured. *But it seems as if we have won. Somehow. Look here, I feel something emanating from that woman's coat pocket. A tool that we will both be able to utilize. Grab it for me.*

Thrush quickly rummaged through the captain's pockets and found two items of interest. One was a palm-sized, time helix, magenta in color, and the other a scarlet crystalized scale in the shape of a wedge; two forms of energy then. Keegan spoke again. *I am not able to transcend to the caordin'torr because of you, or, more specifically, your armor. For now, I will use that time helix for my spirit to inhabit until more permanent arrangements can be made. You take that time wedge and insert it into the Chronos Slot hiding there in your armor. Do not dawdle now, hurry! I only trust those specialists to keep their word for so long. The Chronos Slot is hidden behind a plate on your left uppermost part of your leg. I can sense it.*

It took her a few minutes, but Thrush indeed found it. *See the third slot down? That one is meant for a time wedge due to the shape of it. Insert it quickly now!* Thrush was hesitant, but did as she was told. Thrush had never heard of armor that could support the use of time fragments, and even more importantly she had always gotten on Aeven's case for using his as much as he did. *Time fragments just use too much internal energy! They're great for one battle, perhaps, but horrible when you needed to preserve your stamina.* The small, crystalized wedge was about the size of the palm of her hand and as smooth as butter, the scarlet artifact clicking into place as Thrush inserted it into the Chronos Slot. A small ball of energy immediately burst into her mind alongside the presence of Keegan.

"Okay Keegan, give me a quick rundown on how time fragments effect my armor and how that in turn affects me. What exactly do Chronos Slots *do*?"

Certainly. Keegan spoke. *Think of each time fragment as an artifact of emotion; ultimately, it is the caordin'torr that form these precious items of power. And powerful they are. We know that the caordin'torr is a river of energy that is comprised of both lyvah and nyvah; lyvah is the energy of the planet, nyvah the cosmos. This energy flows freely throughout Pry'ama, no, throughout the planet!*

Now try to keep up with me here. The temples that the chorr'gall are ensnared in were created by the aor'sii who used both lyvah and nyvah to create their prisons. The temples were created with caordin'torr, which means that the beasts of old are virtually bathing *in the most powerful form of energy known to man. And they've been bathing in it for* eons. *Well, when the aor'sii trapped those beasts within the temples, they didn't realize just what kind of an effect it would have on Pry'ama. Just as the chorr'gall have been warped by this pure energy, the energy, in turn, has been tainted by the chorr'gall.*

"I understand that." Thrush murmured, but you don't have to be so condescending about it. What does that have to do with these time fragments, though?"

I apologize, and I am getting to that. The caordin'torr sweeps through the chorr'gall temples and is touched by the beasts of old, creating two forms of energy that clash with one another. Feelings, emotions, thoughts, passions; all are trapped within those little crystals that make up time fragments. These fragments form on the outreaches of the caordin'torr, akin to rocks that a river pushes onto the riverbed. Time fragments are no mere rocks, however. They are sentient, living things that can evolve over time into very powerful tools, if used properly. Pour enough of your soul into one and you might be surprised at the outcome.

You can think of a time fragment as the essence of chorr'gall trapped within the essence of both lyvah and nyvah. All that the beasts of old have left are thoughts, dreams, and time. They are entwined in time just as securely as fate is. That is why when you use a time fragment and are able to bring forth a memory into existence, it is because that is the only weapon that the chorr'gall have left; memories, whether it be your own or drawn from one of the chorr'gall. Just keep in mind...hey, we have company!

A gauntlet came to rest on her shoulder. She'd been so tuned in to what Keegan was saying that all of her other senses had dulled. She was leaning down on one knee, both swords laying in the grass as she fiddled with her Chronos Slot and time fragment. She could try and utilize her new time fragment, yet she had absolutely no idea how it functioned. *That's a surefire way to get me killed! My best bet is the element of surprise. I hope.* Bounding upwards, Thrush elbowed the person behind her in the abdomen and spun around, her fist connecting with a nose. Looking down, she saw an ashen skinned man wearing golden armor laying in the grass, hand clasping a bloody nose.

"Golbart?! I don't know whether to laugh or cry at seeing you here!" Thrush spoke, her voice cracking, "But I don't think I've ever been so happy at seeing a friend. Even if it is you." Golbart didn't utter a single word. She had treated him horribly in the past. Finding his feet once more, Golbart glowered at her with his deep, dark eyes and finally spoke. "Rescuing you was not my first choice, but over the years I have learned not to let bitter rivalries come between life and death. If Aneiyrin had been caught already then you can bet that our swords would clash. In any case, follow me and hurry! We have a ride to catch."

Scaldala was speechless, his body quivering in place. His blood spattered across the blood-link of the first manikin, and his head exploded in so many different sensations that he couldn't distinguish his own consciousness from the sentience that settled in the back of his mind. He kneeled down on one knee and concentrated on the doll before him.

The first puppet that Scaldala had chosen to initiate the blood-link was the shortest of the three, and only by a hair, at that. He also needed to desperately find her some proper clothes. *I'm no prude, but did the artist of this manikin have to go into so much detail with her body? It's a puppet, for the elder's sake!* Her raven black hair was up in a short ponytail atop her head, and her skin was slightly darker than the other two, but still not so opaque that Scaldala couldn't see the flashing ruby red wisps dancing about inside of her. Her nose, lips, and chin were very dainty, and her body was lithe.

Her head jerked up, her navy-blue eyes locking onto Scaldala kneeling before her. He jumped in spite of himself and then immediately felt foolish. He knew that she was bound to move, he had just given her the spark of life, his blood. Her emotions awoke as well.

Oh, this is a woman alright! Trying to contain her emotions in my head is like trying to stop a wave from cresting. It cannot be done! This one is... irrational, bullheaded. But oh, so fierce. He worked up the courage to look into her face and then whistled softly. Her eyes were not eyes at all but orbs of crackling blue energy. She could still blink, it seemed. The manikin stumbled while trying to stand up, fell to the floor, and then caught herself with the palms of her hands.

Grabbing each of her hands, Scaldala helped her up and then helped her sit down properly on the bench of the table. She looked at him with surprise etched on her face, her features as vibrant and distinguished as a living human. She sat as still as stone as Scaldala moved to the next doll. The second manikin was the tallest of the three dolls, and just like what had happened with the previous manikin, when Scaldala released a drop of his blood onto its blood-link he could feel her presence settle down in the back of his mind. This sentience was the same, and yet completely different.

This puppet was emotionally steady and logical, akin to a beach where the ocean's waves were constant and steady. The emerald energy from within this manikin sparked and twirled as this manikin raised her head from its awkward position on the table and stretched her arms, her voluptuous body slithering to a standing position like a performer getting ready to dance for a large crowd. This doll's hair was stark black, just as the first's had been, and hung past her shoulders in hundreds of curls. This woman's face was sharp and strong, shining forth with confidence and intelligence. Her whole body was full and robust, her lips just as full as her breasts, and her eyes an emerald ocean that crackled with spirit and vigor.

This manikin also gazed at him, but not in contempt. No, she stared at him in wonderment. She sat next to the first and was just as still. *Am I sure that I can handle three of these creatures inside my mind? No, there really is no choice.* He initiated the final blood-link. This manikin had the palest of skin and was wearing purple lipstick. Her hair was just as black as the other dolls, and hers was held up by two sticks. Her emotional state was choppy at best, her emotions coming at him in short, sharp bursts. She awakened slowly, her dainty feet having a hard time finding stability. She was fairly muscular, and her eyes crackled with magenta energy as she studiously watched Scaldala with passion and curiosity.

He joined them at the table, pulling up a chair. Scaldala compared the three entities within his mind to the figures sitting across from him. I know that I need to be in a hurry to find Aeven, but to make a mistake with one of these dolls could mean my life, and that is something I should avoid. *These creations are mystifying,* Scaldala thought, *though those dolls were in a resting state, that energy had never stopped moving for a second. Which means that the energy is a separate entity from the dolls themselves? The energy is not there to support life for the manikins; that is what the blood-link is for, what my own blood is for.*

I am their master now, so I can name them, I suppose. Unless they already have names? Scaldala tried to probe each ball of energy within his mind, to interact with them, but it was to no avail. They were there, he could *feel* them, and yet he couldn't really communicate with them. He could *command* them, but not pull out any information that they might be holding. *They're like…clean slates. Tools that have never been used before, possibly? I could sit here all day and speculate, but my time is running out. Okay. Names.*

The first puppet, she is determined. Fierce. I'll call her Scarlet. His curiosity got the better of him, he just had to try one more time. Cautiously probing one of the many smaller essences that made up Scarlet's whole core of what she was, Scaldala was slowly pulled into a time and place that he'd never witnessed before. To thoughts and feelings that he'd never experienced. Into a memory that did not belong to him.

Jackson bolted from one corner of the room to the other, the stone chamber giving little to no light. He still couldn't believe that he'd been duped into this fiasco. Fletcher had always been a dreamer and a sweet talker. "Let's challenge the Manikin Master," *he said,* "the prize will be extravagant! We just have to complete a single battle against him." *What a fool.*

The three Kili'gul'mari Manikins surrounded him; their swords wet with blood from slaying his other two comrades. This arena was too small, and the darkness too thick. They called the Manikin Master the 'man with a hundred skills', and Jackson believed it. These dolls just couldn't be surprised, they anticipated his every move. All three moved in on him like a pack of wolves, swords unwavering.

Plunging behind a stone pillar, Jackson just narrowly the long edge of a blade, the edge slicing his ear. His own sword was clear across the fighter's pit, he'd dropped it in his haste of avoiding steel being plunged through his back. Jackson's eyes drifted over to the bodies of his comrades. His two friends were more than just lifeless, they looked…empty. As if their very essence had been drained. They looked like shells of what they once were. He closed his eyes and leaned back against the pillar; there was no use fighting now. He waited for the long piece of steel to inevitably sheath itself into his chest.

Scaldala's vision returned, his vision blurry. He was sweating and shaking, his heart resting in his throat. "Your memories are battles that you've partaken in? Interesting." Scaldala muttered quietly. "I didn't see him, but the one that controls you is called the Manikin Master? He was known as the 'man with a hundred skills.' I think I'm understanding you better now, and your purpose. You learn from your battles, you take away battle knowledge and are able to utilize it later.

"This might take a while but if I can have each of you focus on your best battle technique, I can create powerful battle paradigms where we work in perfect harmony with one another." Taking a deep breath and focusing his mind to the task ahead, Scaldala went to work on delving through the Kili'gul'mari memories. *I can do this, I just need patience. And I'm already late in finding the rest of my team. It's long since past me leaving this room.*

For his own piece of mind Scaldala created names for the remaining two puppets. The second Kili'gul'mari that he had awoken, the one with emerald eyes, he deemed as 'Radiant' because of her genuine personality.

The second puppet, the one with purple lipstick, she was full of curiosity and wonderment. Scaldala named her Azura. Crouching down once more in front of them, he beckoned them with his mind to follow. His mind was met with resistance. "I need to earn your trust, I see." He murmured aloud, "Like it or not, all four of us are linked now, for better or worst. Come, come, let us try again. No need for defiance. We're late already as it is.

CHAPTER EIGHTEEN

Questions and Quandaries

Aeven woke up, head in hands and back against a cold, rough wall. His vision was blurry, skin cold as ice. He was sweating and shivering, his insides alight with fire. His head felt as if someone had taken a mallet to it. Someone groaned next to him, a woman. A quick look showed him that it was Lucia. She too was waking up, and she looked just as miserable as he felt. A quick inspection of his other side showed him Lidarian sprawled out across the floor, head resting against the floor. She hadn't regained consciousness yet.

A sword clattered down next to him unceremoniously. His sword. And then an even bigger sword crashed next to Lucia, slowly followed by pieces of armor. Fre'ja was flitting from one corner of the room to the other, checking on her friends and then rummaging around for anything else that might be useful. Aeven was slowly starting to regain his self. The chilled wind was cold as it blew through the shattered pane, and the room that they lay in was slowly getting darker as dusk started to set. Fre'ja crouched down in front of him, piercing him with her sharp eyes. "You look okay," she murmured. "Aeven, I don't know what to say. You scared me. You weren't yourself." Her voice cracked at that last bit, and her eyes started swimming.

"I..." His train of thought wandered off, his head falling down into his hands once more. "I don't know what to say. Truly. I hardly remember what happened. I'm sorry. I remember proclaiming that creature as a sii'morth, and I remember incinerating him. But I don't know *how*." He stammered, "What are you doing with that sword and armor?"

Fre'ja regained her composure, the back of her hand wiping away the tears from her eyes. "Well, Lucia is the only one that doesn't have a way of defending herself. Most of the armor won't work, it's just too big. But his pauldrons could work. It isn't the most optimal, but its something. Oh, and that creature was carrying a short sword at its side; a short sword to it, a great sword to us. She can use that too!"

"I'm supposed to wear a scarlet chef's suit along with aor'sii armor?" A voice burst out suddenly, Aeven and Fre'ja jumping in place. "Do I look like a circus performer to you? An entertainer, maybe?"

"Hey!" Fre'ja sputtered, "I resent that! *I'm* a performer. And there's nothing wrong with being colorful. It would suit you, in my opinion."

"It's almost night again and we haven't caught Aneiyrin." Despair and angst filled Aeven's voice. "We were *so close*. He could be anywhere, at this point. He could be well on his way to the Spiral Rift, for all we know."

Fre'ja was silent for a time and then stood up, pacing over to the shattered glass wall. "No, I don't believe that," she stated solemnly. "Look how much trouble we've had navigating this place. Traps, puzzles. A battle. He might not be faring any better."

It took him a moment, but Aeven eventually nodded. Or tried too, at least. His head still hurt something fierce. She was right, they couldn't give up until they knew for sure. He took a more careful look around.

There was no apparent exit, save for the broken glass wall or one of the trapdoors on the ceiling. "Obviously I cannot go up and out one of trapdoors on the ceiling. I have neither the wings nor the height of an aor'sii, though I suppose someone could give me a boost up. I can't just dive out of that window either." Aeven muttered, his legs cracking as he tried to find his feet. "That platform couldn't have just brought us to a dead end. Well, one would *hope not* at least."

This room is just another puzzle. Or another trap. Use your intuition. Aeven hobbled over to the very same trapdoor that had held the wooden chest and peered downwards; Aeven's hunches were correct. The wooden chest had indeed disappeared, and in its place was an access way to what appeared to be a marble balcony. Dropping to his stomach, Aeven stuck his head through the trapdoor so that he could assess how high up he and his friends were.

Only about ten paces up, give or take. Not too bad. Once we drop through here there is no turning back, and yet we don't really have a choice.

He pulled himself back up and relayed the information to his friends, Lucia just finishing equipping herself. Lidarian was starting to stir as well. After a close examination, Lidarian was deemed to be fit to travel again, her confidence shaken just a little bit. Fre'ja pulled something out of her little pack that she wore; a loaf of Spider Eye bread. It was more than a little stale, but it felt like a feast as he broke it off into sizeable chunks and handed one to each of her friends. "We'll need to look for provisions, too," She mumbled to no one particularly. Sharing some water from his flask, Aeven nodded his agreement.

Aeven was the first to slither down the new exit. Grabbing the rim of the trapdoor, Aeven dropped himself down until his feet were dangling in midair. It was a short fall, Aeven tumbling forward as his feet hit the black balcony. The evening air was frigid and crisp, and Aeven admitted to himself that the cool wind against his face was refreshing. Leaning against the black and white marbled balcony, he took in the landscape below. Besides the newly formed ravines and chasms that the fortress had caused was moors and salt flats, weathered, pink pedaled cherry blossom trees vibrant against the otherwise dull terrain.

His eyes were drawn to a giant pit that had formed in the ground far below; a pit? No, it was more akin to a crater. A crater that competed with the fortress in size. As his three companions edged up to the railing next to Aeven, a soft-spoken voice floated down from a ledge behind them. "That new hole in the planet is called Sal'themar, or Internal Strife in common tongue." The voice stated. This castle didn't just emerge from the ground, it *moved* locations.

"'... And the serpent shall beckon forth the castle of old. Tearing open the fabrics of time to become reborn, he wears destiny like a cloak adorned. Armies will follow, and legions will fall, the trumpets blaring for the final call. He will rip asunder all ways of life, to bring forth Internal Strife.' That was a snippet from the Azure Augury, in case you were wondering. There are other versions, depending on what country you're from, but you get the gist of it. Tell me, do you know who it was that finally summoned this fortress from the great unknown? I'd surely like to meet them."

Aeven kept silent, his eyes settling over the carnage below in a new light. He had never put much faith in prophecies, let alone the Azure Augury. Not that the Azure Augury was any different than the rest of them, it was just much older and came from a time when the realm was shattered and then remade. Mere fragments of what was, what used to be.

"Are you the individuals that caused these phenomena? Phenomena or catastrophe, I cannot decide which. I personally cannot be too mad at you; if it weren't for you, I would still be resting in my eternal sleep. For waking me, I thank you!"

Aeven finally spun around, his head pounding and heart trying to pump out of his chest. The implications here were so vast. He fought against the glare of the falling sun as the waning daylight reflected off of the roof tiles and into the eyes of the viewers below. The young man hopped down from the ledge, and with him leapt down a beast that Aeven was very familiar with. In fact, Aeven had seen one last at the Silver Claw, when he had tried to compete in a race. The gentle creature looked like nothing more than a giant ferret, a ferret large enough for a full-grown man to easily ride. This beast's wiry fur was burgundy red with several yellow spots spackling its body. A metallic mask was strapped to the beast's muzzle, a mask that resembled a falcon's beak. On its hind legs were metallic talons that had several jewels embedded in them. A kor'zhul the beast was called.

The kor'zhul placed itself between Aeven and the boy; it seemed friendly enough, but Aeven wasn't going to take any chances. The young man captivated Aeven. He wore loose, cerulean trousers and a blue hooded jacket that had a single yellow pinstripe running down the length of his body. This boy was lanky, towering over Aeven by a good foot, and his silver hair was long and feathery, his facial features soft and refined. What had Aeven spooked was the things attacked to the young man's back, silver wings, wings that gently flapped with the constant wind.

Aeven's hand went immediately to his sword, his feet stepping back and taking a defensive stance. The young man's hands went up defensively. "Peace my friend. Don't you think that if I meant you harm, I wouldn't have let my presence be known?" Aeven was lost for words. Of course, this young man was right. Lidarian's hand came to rest on Aeven's shoulder, her voice soft and questioning.

"Let's hear him out, Aeven. We need answers for a change. Our solution to everything cannot be to rush in with swords swinging. Especially if you are what this boy is implying." Aeven glared at her for that last remark, but kept silent. *I'm a man that just wants to be left alone. That's it! The Azure Augury can burn,* Aeven thought bitterly.

"When I was buried in my crypt years ago, I was buried as a Drey'une of the Divine Heights. And I am still a drey'une, I suppose, though it seems to the naked eye that I have not aged a single day." the young man speculated. And then his voice started to quiver, his eyes looking at something that none but him could see. "They rounded us up like animals; those of us that could not escape or fight. They trapped us and then experimented. There were many of us trapped within the White Warren, and now there are just a bare handful. Something stopped them from experimenting on us, someone had intervened all those years ago. Those of us that are left were forgotten."

"The passion in his voice returned, his eyes reflecting the radiance of the heavens. This is what you need to hear, now." The young man continued, "your realm has yet to build this fortress in which we are standing on. It has yet to establish the sect of the drey'une and has yet to bury me alive. In actuality, I haven't even been born yet within Pry'ama."

Aeven was silent for a handful of minutes, his thoughts trying to make sense of such an absurd statement. *This boy has got to be yanking my chains. He does seem like a joker. I am no fool though; well, most of the time I'm not.* "And yet, here you are standing before us," Aeven stated indignantly. "And if you're going to stand there and make jokes, I'm going to hunt for the entire reason that were here. He's got to be close, if he's still here at all, that is."

The young man forestalled Aeven yet again by raising his hands in that same defensive stance, palms outwards and facing Aeven. "Just through that door is a vast library that holds books written ages ago as well as books that have yet to be written. You don't have to believe me. Go read for yourself of what happens once the Goldenfist Corp finally gets a handhold on the king's throne. Read of how the Sphere of Pry'ama is alit once again, and how the Gilgoben Sea swallow time. And if that still does not convince you, then maybe you should talk to the man that's just inside, the one with the orange orb. Him and I are from the same era if you'd believe it."

"What?!" Aeven snapped at the young man, "why didn't you say that he was here in the first place? I have the power to end this ridiculous adventure right now and I am going to do it. I don't have time to listen to your absurd stories. He went into the library you say?" The teenager nodded yes. "Good. This is your home, apparently, I will allow you to lead the way."

Lidarian laid a hand on Aeven's shoulder once more, whispering in his ear. "Take it easy on the boy. Do you forget so easily that you just summoned a castle out of thin air? Let's just keep in mind that anything might be possible, here."

"I *do* have an open mind." He whispered back, "But we all saw that castle rise out of the ground and create all of those chasms. How can it be buried underground and yet *not* have been built yet? *That* makes no sense."

The young man chimed in, whispering as well. "Actually, it makes complete sense. *When* this castle is built, it is done so *before* the prothesized serpent claimed his power. *Before he* shatters what is made and remakes the realm in *his* image. The serpent purges all that defy him and unites the rest. He will be able to level cities and rent chasms in the ground so deep that *entire castles* are swallowed by the planet.

Do you see where I'm going with this? You unearthed a castle that the serpent buried later in Pry'ama's timeline.

Aeven could stand here all day and argue with the boy, but instead he waved him on. Leaping atop his kor'zhul, the young man led them onwards. The balcony's single exit led to yet another tower, the spiral staircase within ascending upwards to the peak of the fortress. "Finally." Aeven breathed, feeling as if the weight of the entire heavens had just been lifted from his shoulders. "This was undoubtedly one of the hardest jobs that I've undertaken, and that speaks volumes. Never again."

Aeven could hear similar sighs escaping his comrade's lips. The young man spoke from the back of his beast, his head bobbing as he turned around. "By the way, my name is Sambsyne Maldraga. Do you realize that I am probably not the only one awakening from my eternal sleep? You bringing this fortress from the depths of time means that the eternal plague had never been cast technically, because the affliction happens in the future.

"I know that you saw the golems at each corner of the castle when making your way in; how could you possibly miss them? They aren't there just for decoration. In my realm's past and your realm's future, those golems were created to try and harness the energies of the chorr'gall; catalysts for the caordin'torr, if you will. I'll give you a single guess on who constructed those *machines*." He spit that last word out with disgust.

Aeven was of course bothered by this revelation. "Okay, the jokes over, bud. I get it, ha ha. Pulling a fast one over on me, real funny." Sambsyne looked down on him with a thoughtful look but said no more. *He sure looks serious for this being a practical joke. I still don't believe it though. It's nonsense.*

Rounding the last bend of the wide stairwell, they were confronted with a thick, aged wooden door. It was unlocked and he pushed it open. The room that they walked into was overflowing with thousands of books. Some were scattered across the jagged flooring, while others were stacked in precarious piles across the massive room. Bookcases lined every inch of the brick walls that spiraled upwards. Chandeliers hung down from high above, illuminating everything with dull, flickering light.

Stunning portraits also decorated the room, and Aeven couldn't help himself. Despite the prospect of finally catching Aneiyrin, his boots inched their way to the closest illustration. *This is just too much of a coincidence.* Each painting was of the exact same thing. Well, almost the same thing. The surroundings in each painting were different, and the colors used in each illustration were unique, but the theme was the same. *I've seen this before. But if what Sambsyne says is true, then technically these paintings haven't been painted yet. But if that's the case, how have I seen it before. No, no. I'm just going to go around in circles with this.*

It's that same type of pedestal that I saw in Koronin, at that shabby tavern. This pedestal has glowing runes on it just as the first had, as well as that colossal tome sitting atop it! And the roses. Blue roses are in this painting just as they were in the other. "Aletta, you weren't lying," he whispered aloud. "What truths was it that you'd found, I wonder." His eyes strayed up the ascending wall, to the other paintings. One of the portraits was painfully absent from the rest of the masterpieces, a dusty imprint left behind.

A confident voice boomed out; a haughty voice full of venom. "Welcome, Aeven, come and have a chat with me. we need to talk." The voice of poison floated from behind one of the many standalone bookcases, the man's boots echoing against the grimy floor as he paced back and forth. "I was about to leave, you sure know how to keep a man waiting. What kept you, I wonder?"

Aeven rounded the corner and came face to face with the very man who had given the orders to hang his father Athrim. He stood there in dumbfounded silence. "*You're* Aneiyrin?! Anger resounded within Aeven's very being. The middle aged man was tall; he towered over Aeven as they stared each other down. The dark-eyed, chiseled man wore the deepest of green mantles, his noble's clothes the darkest of silvers. His leather armor was simple but distinguished. At his side hung an ornate sword that had a curious attachment on the length of its blade.

This attachment acted as the sword's spine, and inserted into the 'spine' were a handful of time shards. "I see that you are admiring the newest addition to my weapon. It's a Chronos Keeper; if you try hard enough you could find one too for that behemoth of a sword that you carry there at your side," The man stated bluntly. "Technologies evolve, Aeven. Well, *eventually* they will. Chronos Slots are only the beginning, as I'm sure you'll find out, *serpent*. How does it feel to be both the savior of mankind *and* the one that will destroy them? That's quite the mantle to bear."

"I am *not* the serpent, I will *not* be the one to forsake my entire realm. *Never*. I am no eel." Aeven seethed, "and how *dare* you look me in the eyes after what you'd done to my family." The footsteps of Aeven's friends could be heard behind him, all coming to a standstill as the two men breathed into each other's faces, eyes locked and full of fury.

"I know you want to ram that sword of yours into my guts, Aeven, but look around you and tell me what you see. If you still revile me then, by all means kill me. You would be doing me a favor, to be completely honest." Aeven drew his sword and leveled it on Secledrin Gauge's neck. What could this rotten fool possibly show Aeven that would change his mind about killing him? Secledrin did not even attempt to arm himself; he stared at Aeven with a smirk on his face. All Aeven could see was his father dangling from a short length of rope, and anger erupted from within. His entire body quaked, the sword shaking in his hand. He couldn't think straight. "Why would you masquerade around Pry'ama as a thief when you hold almost as much prestige as a *king*?! Have you no shame?"

Secledrin did not speak, instead he pointed to a wooden table not five yards away that had a lone book open atop it. Aeven knew in his very soul that this had to be the evidence that Secledrin was counting on to change Aeven's mind; the look in Secledrin's eyes said it all. He *could* behead him here and then look at the book, but Aeven wanted to hear what the man had to say. Lucia and Lidarian stepped up beside Aeven and rose their swords up to his throat, nodding at Aeven to just go look at the book. Fre'ja followed him over, dagger in hand.

A lone candle was resting beside the book, flickering light dancing upon the open page. His name was neatly scribed at the top of the musty page. A very intricate and personal drawing of himself was sketched on the other open page, the sketch depicting himself as just slightly older than he was now with personal information scribed neatly underneath the drawing. Aeven's eyes blurred, his head growing woozy and heavy. All he could manage to croak out was "what trickery is this Secledrin?"

The man did not answer Aeven's question but instead said with that same stoic voice, "Flip to the next page." Aeven obeyed, and before his eyes appeared a detailed sketch of Secledrin, a Secledrin that was slightly older, just as Aeven had been depicted, and like his own page, this one had personal information about Secledrin scribed neatly at the bottom of the page.

"What is this?" Aeven breathed out, his entire mind now lost in this new book. Again, he flipped to the next page and just about collapsed in surprise. It was a very personal and detailed picture of his sister Arma, with a full page of information to follow. Aeven flipped through the rest of the tome but all he saw were pictures of men and women that he did not recognize, from dates and times that started from the foundation of Chraonos to far into the future of Pry'ama. His brother August was not in this text.

"I'll tell you why I stole the sky'un'grael from that incompetent general Kaosa. My reason is twofold. That relic that hangs at your belt, the orb that I stole, the sky'un'grael that you used to power this very fortress, Julian's Keep, these are artifacts as well as keys, or batteries of life some have taken to calling them. Others call them Waygates of Destruction. They are all *wrong*.

"After my own awakening years ago, I relentlessly researched about these artifacts that somehow seem to connect us all. I myself call the sky'un'grael 'time fissures.' I stole this from the warlord of the Seven Devils because he did not deserve it, nor did he know how to use it. No human does, it is useless for them to even try. Some that try to connect with a sky'un'grael experience a breaking of the mind, the knowledge revealed to them just too powerful for them to handle. Others start to change into beasts born of nightmares.

"There is one constant that always happens, however; the soul trapped within the sky'un'grael and the soul of the human trying to use the orb always end up switching spots. Kaosa was trying to evolve into something more. Something greater. The great caordin'torr is capable to much, but it should *never* be taken for granted."

"I don't understand. He was trying to evolve into *what* exactly?" Aeven interjected. In truth, Aeven did not understand most of the information that he had just heard, but that last bit that Secledrin had said pulled at Aeven's curiosity.

"You do not need to know what he was attempting to evolve into because you are already on your way there, my friend. You are, I am, and so is your sister for that matter. I am sure you have dozens of questions but wait until I am finished." Clearing his throat, the lord continued. "The second reason for me to steal that man's sky'un'grael was because I needed to see a certain leatherbound book with my own eyes that he had on his person. Yes, I am talking of Luxesma's Diary.

"After reading about the various experimentations, about what had been done to those poor babies from the women deemed as 'hosts'. All of these tomes you see lying scattered around told me only fragments that I had to piece together myself. I will reveal what I have learned to you. Do you know how much destruction a chorr'gall can cause if its temple is destroyed and its shackled shattered? The first king of Pry'ama did, unfortunately. Three quarters of the original Pry'ama was annihilated before the beast was finally slaughtered. The king had to do something, and so he ordered new machines to be constructed specifically for destroying chorr'gall, a process that took all of about five centuries to perfect.

"The king knew that he would *never* see the results of his decree, but he pressed onwards. Can you guess how many centuries ago that was? As of now, Pry'ama is in its fourth century. I'll spell it out plain to you; it's in the next century that these automatons known as 'golems' will be created. The first king was merciless, of course, and knew that his orders were not going to be able to be carried out in his lifetime, so he sent his toughest fighters to the one place where he knew that he could displace the aor'sii. He needed a weapon to defend himself in the meantime while the new weapons were being constructed. Sending Aelora Aegus to the very center of the planet, the king wanted them to slay the one that held dominion the aor'sii."

"What!?" Aeven gasped, "the aor'sii were answering to another entity?"

"Yes, if you can really call it a 'creature'. *It* is an entity created of energy and knowledge, a being that resides in its own temple created far beneath the planet's crust. This entity is known as the 'Father of Elders', and that's about all that is known about it. Only one warrior made it back out of the Father of Elder's temple alive, Aelora Aegus. Confiding to the king of what had happened, the king was furious at her failure and banished her from Pry'ama.

"This is what I've pieced together thus far. We are in the fourth century, no? Eventually the Goldenfist Corp will come to possess most of the sky'un'grael through deceit and mayhem. They will take it upon themselves to repower most of the lost realms that the aor'sii had built for mankind so long ago, which would then initiate events in time that cannot be undone. Under directions from one of the future kings, the Gi'ammune, or golems as you now know them, will finally reach completion and sent to battle against the chorr'gall themselves.

"This is where it all ties together, Aeven. Remember those babies that were born from the 'hosts' so long ago, those half breed infants? The Goldenfist Corp never stopped experimenting on them. The king needed a weapon to combat the chorr'gall, if one had ever gotten loose again, and those babies were the contingency plan. Who do you think was going to operate those golems once they reached completion? Their needs to be *some* form of pilot for the Gi'ammune."

"The king and the Goldenfist have been in bed with each other all along." Aeven whispered aloud, his eyes never leaving the tome spread out before him. "Say I believe you. What about this book, what does this book have to do with anything? Why is my picture in here, who could have possibly illustrated me?"

"Now I can't give away all of my secrets now, can I? Those stairs that lead up from this room to the top of this fortress will hold more answers for you, Aeven, answers that I am not able to give you now. You'll just have to see for yourself. What last little bit I do know is that by the Goldenfist combining so much energy in one location, this fortress, it created something that has been called a Time Shock. Or, should I say, it *will* create a Time Shock, since technically it hasn't happened yet. Aeven, by you summoning forth this castle from the shadows of time, you invariably ripped such a large hole in the design of destiny that you could probably march a legion through it.

"The half-breed babies from the 'hosts' had two forms of energy that they were drawing from, that was evolving them when they were being incubated. They had the energy of the aor'sii, of course because they were procreated from them. Can you guess the other form of energy that they were being instilled with? I'll give you a hint." Secledrin reached down and grabbed his coral sky'un'grael, throwing it up and down in his hand.

"What the Goldenfist, or the king, for that matter, did not count on was that both of those forms of energy were ultimately created by the Father of Elder, energy that he lived and breathed. You might think that when Aelora returned home from her perilous excursion that she had ultimately lost; not so. While she *had* lost her friends, and had *not* defeated the Father of Elders, it wasn't a complete loss. When the divine being learned that she had stolen his most precious artifact, the Azure Rose, he followed her back with a vengeance.

"It was a bloodbath. In his wake, the only ones he left alive were us, Aeven, the half-breeds that were being incubated and grown as weapons to defeat the chorr'gall. It was genius, actually, for him to leave us alive and to send Aelora up with the sky'un'grael. Why? Because we were absorbing the very energies that he lives and breathes. For years he was shaping us to be living weapons of *its creation*. We may have been created and grown by the Goldenfist, yet we were molded by the Father of Elders."

Aeven crashed down to his knees, hard. His fingers gripped the edge of the desk until they were white, his head resting against the back of his hands. "You know that I am right, you cannot refute me. How do you think you were able to summon an entire *castle* from the fingers of time and somehow *survive*? No mere human can even *attempt* that feat." Secledrin's hysterical laughter cackled throughout the room, "What path will you walk, *serpent*? Will you follow the will of the Father of Elder and become a living weapon? Or perhaps become a tool for the Goldenfist and pilot one of the renowned Gi'ammune? Or maybe, maybe you seek retribution for your heritage of the aor'sii and travel to each chorr'gall temple, earning their respect and trust so that you can later call upon them for battle? We are *brothers* Aeven, you'd better choose wisely."

CHAPTER NINETEEN

Anomaly

"You still have no idea what I'm talking about, do you, Aeven? You haven't figured out that last piece of the puzzle." Secledrin's voice screeched into the open room. "I will spell it out for you! You are an *anomaly!* You are even more different than the other half-breed children, different than the other *chegus!* At some point in your life, something happened to you, you were exposed to something that wasn't meant to be, and fate did not like that. How can I possibly know that, you ask? Because of that shard hanging around your neck! I can feel it like poison on the tongue, it *repels* me, *despises* me! It's a shard of corruption, and yet you wear it like a fashion accessory! It is like venom for the Father of Elder, venom to his children, to us! it should be impossible for you to wear that."

"Just shut up!" Aeven screamed, hurling the tome at him. It crashed into a shelf and papers exploded in all directions. "You took my father away from me, destroyed our family! It was *you* that whispered in the king's ear of what to do, who to assassinate. All political power moves. And now here you are again, trying to destroy the remainder of my life! Trying to take what little I have left; my identity." Aeven grabbed the desk with both hands and flung it against the wall, the resounding crash echoing through the entirety of the room. Fre'ja backed away from his, fear plain on her face.

Secledrin laughed at that. "Dear brother, you still do not understand what I am telling you, but that's okay. It's a little much for now. I will say it crystal clear, and you can make of it what you will. You *do not* have an identity, you never did. You are a *variance*, a *glitch*.."

"I promised myself once that if I ever saw you during my travels, I would make a point of ending your miserable existence. And here you are, standing right before me. I think I'm going to keep my promise, you deserve it." Dashing forwards, Aeven leapt over a pile of books with sword out and swinging downwards, his mouth twisted into a rictus sneer.

"You're too late, *brother*." Secledrin mocked, "I am going to see this through until the end! I will be the one to find *all of* the sky'un'graels, I will be the one to return them to our rightful father!" Aeven collided into an orange barrier midjump, the energy field crackling as he rebounded off of it and into a lofty bookshelf. Secledrin quickly kneed Lucia in the stomach, and then threw an elbow at Lidarian, catching her across the jaw. "Its been fun, and I'm sure that we'll meet again. He gave a mocking bow and then dashed through the aisles of books, quickly disappearing into the shadows.

Aeven stumbled to his feet and tried to give chase. "He raced towards the back of the library! I saw a staircase back their earlier, he's trying to escape!" Fre'ja screamed, "go, we'll catch up!" Aeven needed no more incentive. Dashing under the dancing candlelight, Aeven leapt over books and through the aisles until he found the secluded staircase. Taking the rough steps two at a time, Aeven burst through the large double oak doors and out onto the red slated rooftop of Julian's Fortress. It was deep into the night, but Aeven had the moon and starlight for guidance.

Well, were on the rooftop now, he couldn't have gone too far, one would think. "I know that you're out here, Secledrin! I can smell your stink! Come on out and let's end this. I have your head to deliver to a general, I wouldn't want to disappoint him, now would I?" Aeven took careful steps atop the red tiles, measuring each shadow as he searched the rooftop. Except for the exit of the library, there really was nowhere else to go. The roof was sloped and flat for the most part, but nowhere to really hide. Aeven checked and then doublechecked each crevice and shadow. "Wow, he really did disappear, somehow." He stated out into the open air. "He's really gone. We failed. I failed."

Aeven leaned back against the library entrance and took in a deep breath, his eyes studying the twinkling stars. *What does this mean for us? No, what does this mean for* me? He couldn't help but think about what Secledrin had said, what he had insinuated. Aeven's fingers wrapped around his time fragment that was around his neck, the one that his father had engraved for him with their family crest. *Is this really a time fragment, though? Maybe that had been Secledrin's whole purpose, just to fill me with doubt. Doubt is like poison for the mind. But why would he wait in that library for all that time just to tell me lies about myself. That doesn't make any sense either.*

Aeven didn't know what to make of any of this; what he did know was that he needed guidance in the worst way. Just this morning, Aeven had had a father and a sister that he could at least say that he was related to in blood, now he was a creation of both an experiment and the energies of the planet. *No! No. That's only true if I buy into what Secledrin was telling me. I...don't know what I believe.*

He usually appreciated his quiet time, but not this night. No, this night he needed the comfort of friends, lest his mind devour him with doubts and fear. He disappeared back down the dark stairwell, Aeven finding himself a seat at the same wooden table that held a new flickering candle, the chair that he crawled into high backed and rickety. Someone had gone to great length to fix the mess that he had made.

Lucia and Lidarian joined him as well with chairs of their own, their thoughts on the whole encounter thrown out into the open like a woman emptying a bucket of bilge water. Sambsyne opted to sit on the bottommost step of the stairs and keep mostly to himself, Fre'ja huddled up beside him petting his kor'zhul. The chef was the first one to speak up.

"Listen Aeven," the mature woman stated, "I know how confused you must feel, burn the depths of Sparodin, I am just as confused! We are sitting in a fortress that hasn't even been built yet, for Asher's sake! Or, that's what they say at least. Fear can twist people's words, though. My own input is that we need to remain focused. Obviously, our quest is now changed; is it even worth chasing Secledrin now? We know what he is attempting."

Aeven nodded, barely able to process her words. Lidarian spoke up next, her voice trembling and her hands shaking. "My thoughts are that we need to just lay out our problems and work from the ground up." She took a deep breath and then continued, "Secledrin is trying to initiate some type of ritual that has to do with the Father of Elders and those sky'un'grael, right? We just don't know what his time frame is. Aeven, you have one of those orbs, and you used one earlier when figuring out that puzzle. We need to retrieve that one. But if we keep those from his reach, that should buy us some time, right?

"Also, I think that it's worth being said that someone needs to alert each kingdom of what's going on. They have the right to defend themselves if worst comes to worst. Our country has been so focused on infighting and waging war against the Seven Devils and the Azure Skulls that our lords have developed a very cutthroat attitude. Getting them to help one another might be an even bigger battle than we can handle."

Lucia piped up again, arms crossed. "Okay but if we do that then we are alerting the king that we know that he is in bed with the Golden Fist, a secret that he probably wants taken to his grave. A lot of what Secledrin said didn't make sense to me, but what I do know is that creating colossal automatons to wage war against giant bestial creatures is a very good way to shatter the world back into what it once was."

"Okay, stop, stop!" Aeven finally interjected, hopping down from his chair and glaring at both of his friends in spite of himself. He couldn't sit down any longer; too many thoughts were causing him restlessness anxiety. Aeven opened and closed his mouth several times, arms crossed against his chest. "I'll be honest, I don't even know where to start. I don't even know if I *want* to know where to start. Lucia is right though; we start alerting the high lords of what's going on and the king will eventually catch on. Who knows what he'd do at that point? Fear can make people do very foolish things, and we already know that the king is pretty foolish as it is."

Lidarian stood up, chair crashing to the floor. "No, that's not right and you know it, Aeven!" She yelled, "I know that you aren't a knight anymore, but we cannot condemn the people to a fate that will end in annihilation! We'd be just as guilty of spilling their blood if we kept this secret to ourselves! No, we need to alert the high lords. We must."

Aeven sat in stunned silence finally said in a low voice "let us focus on and deal with just one problem at a time. Obviously, we cannot stop endless wars and infighting with one another, nobles will be nobles and there is no getting around that. You've both stated what problems you foresee, here is my opinion. Part of the reason that I am helping general Kaosa is because he was foolish enough to link himself with the sky'un'grael that he had, with the one that Secledrin now carries. If Secledrin keeps that sky'un'grael for himself, it means that lord Kaosa will eventually lose his soul to the orb, and a new soul will come to possess his body. It sounds outlandish, but that's how it is."

"That sounds like a mighty fine problem indeed." A solid voice boomed out. Scaldala rounded the closest bookcase, sniggering at the three surprised faces. Surprisingly, he wasn't alone, either. Trailing behind him were three women, or, at least, Aeven thought that they were women. A second glance had him guessing, there were just too many irregularities, the biggest being that each of them was dully alight in a different color, like they were glowing sporadically from the inside. These creatures also had dozens of tribal tattoos scribed across their bodies, tattoos so intricate that Aeven was impressed at the complexity of them. Aeven blushed and looked down at his boots. He knew that they weren't real women, but they could have been wearing more than the barest of clothes.

"Is this completely necessary?" Lucia spat, "Scaldala, I had thought higher of you before this. Why would you, of all people, allow three naked Scarrownian wenches follow you like some kind of perverse courtesan? You've got to be more than twice their age!" Scaldala's long, silver mustache turned ever downwards in anger as she belittled him in front of everyone else. Before he could open his mouth for his rebuttal, Sambsyne spoke up from the base of the stairwell, his voice soft and uncertain.

"Actually, those aren't women at all but kili'gul'mari. Those, like the Gi'Amune, were created shortly before the Eternal Plague was cast down upon the realm. Kili'gul'mari were just another tool created by the Goldenfist Corp."

"What is that even supposed to mean?" Lucia barked. "It is still disgusting that one such as Scaldala would allow those naked women to be at his beck and call. Isn't he supposed to be a renowned scholar? And a captain?"

"Just drop it!" Scaldala hissed at her, "They are not real, they are puppets. Yes, I will find them *clothes* and *armor* when we happen upon some. Excuse me that they are half naked, I was trying to hurry and find Aeven and didn't have time to search for a merchant." If Lucia's face was red before, it was purple now.

Scaldala swiftly turned to Aeven. "Explain to me everything that has happened since I left you. I want every detail. Hurry boy, hurry!" Aeven obliged. He desperately needed some advice, and Scaldala was probably the best choice right now. He did his best to recall all that Secledrin had said, his fight against the sii'morth, and even when Aeven had inserted his emerald colored sky'un'grael into the wooden chest. Scaldala was silent, nodding and making the appropriate sounds when Aeven reached critical pieces of his story, Lidarian and Lucia both piping up to give their own input and versions of what had happened.

Aeven finally fell silent, satisfied that his recollection was complete. After a few moments Scaldala spoke his thoughts. "Secledrin named you a chegus?" he asked quickly, his grey eyes both critical and inquisitive.

"Yes. He had said that he pieced together this information himself and with the help of all of these books, so he could be wrong, I suppose. I don't see how, though. He had a tome with my picture in it, and pictures of other people as well. They were very detailed." Heavy footfalls behind the subdued group interrupted Scaldala's reply as Thrush burst down the stairs, leaping over Sambsyne's hunched body, and straight into Aeven for a giant hug.

Golbart followed grudgingly behind, marching down the stairwell with a dark grimace on his face. Shaking hands with Aeven, he clapped him on the shoulder and found a seat nearby, eyes ogling the three puppets. Scaldala took an immediate disliking to him.

"How, under the moonlight, did you guys manage to make it to the *rooftop*, of all places?" Aeven sputtered, "And Golbart, I thought that you were headed for the Azaevia Mountains? What made you change your mind?"

"I'm almost afraid to ask this," another voice interrupted loudly, "but what kind of party are we having down here? I'm getting too old for this kind of thing!" It was one of the two men that Aeven had gambled with that fateful night, the night that those creatures had attacked. The dark skinned, gangly man held a certain poise as he marched down the stairs, like he was used to giving commands and being obeyed. His long hair was held back with a red bandana this time, and his slick attire was navy blue.

Smiles and cheers broke out as friends greeted friends and newcomers introduced themselves. Laughter and stories quickly followed as everyone found a chair and shared their part in the adventure, Aeven eventually having to retell what had happened and what they thought that meant for them. The levity quickly faded.

Eventually Lidarian's voice rose to cut everyone off short as the absence of her brother was brought to everyone's attention. Everyone fell silent, and with a pleading look at Aeven, she turned around and met Lidarian's searching eyes. Thrush's account of what had happened was choppy and short, and for a breadth of a second her armor radiated a pink glow that made the whole group stand up and shield their eyes. After the initial surprise, eventually it came out; Keegan had been slain by a Goldenfist Specialist.

Lidarian raised her fist and grabbed the front of Thrush's armor, laying several jabs into Thrush's face before Aeven could tear them apart. Golbart swooped in and contained Lidarian, grabbing hold of the young woman from behind as her incoherent yells echoed throughout the room. Thrush continued to lay on the floor, sobbing and yelling that she was sorry for her failure, tossing a glowing time fragment at Lidarian's feet. The woman cautiously picked it up and pocketed it, confusion marring her face. Faint patters on the rooftop announced it was raining. Lidarian disappeared from the room.

"We need to refocus!" Scaldala breathed, "let us break this down. A chegus seems to be a creature that is part human and part aor'sii; they are able to use both the planet's energy source as well as the Father of Elders. We also learned that if a normal human tries to use sky'un'grael for themselves, then they forfeit their soul and run the risk of experiencing a soul exchange with the soul that is trapped within the sky'un'grael. Aeven, do you see where I am going with this?"

"Yes." Aeven stated, "I believe this is exactly what we were talking about when you showed up. Eventually the souls that are trapped within the sky'un'grael will be released unto Pry'ama. Problem compounds onto problem. We will be living in a realm with souls that the Father of Elders trapped within the sky'un'grael, souls that he has been twisting and warping for *centuries*. I have a hunch that they no longer will be the brave, stoic warriors that once fought beside Aelora Aegus. They will be dark, bitter, and thirsty. Thirsty for the caordin'torr."

Aeven couldn't hold it in anymore, his mind was at the breaking point and his emotions a tempest of fear and anger. "How did this even happen? Why here, and why now? And why me?!"

"Now, those questions I am not able to answer, son." Scaldala said quietly. "At least, not yet. Alathreas Aelenburg had once written that 'oftentimes it is not fate that chooses a leader, but instead it is time that does. Time creates the only person with the right attitude and right tools to preserve the age in which the person was born into.' There have been a handful of other leaders like you, Aeven, born into an age where they seem to be the centerpiece of so much destruction. Unlike you, however, they sought a life of solitude instead of trying to fight to make a difference. That is what matters."

Aeven nodded his thanks, head swimming and legs heavy. "It all comes back to the same question. what do we do now? Secledrin still has the sky'un'grael, and we were already pushing our time limits with how long it's taken us to find him. General Kaosa was very sick when I last saw him, and that was months ago. We need to find him and ensure that he hasn't completed the soul exchange yet."

"And if he has?" Golbart rumbled, legs crossed and hands behind his head. "Do you have the guts to finish what you've started? Remember that he hired me as well. I'm just as disappointed as you that we will miss our big payday, but chances are that even if we *had* recovered the sky'un'grael, it'd still be too late."

"Then it's settled. It might not be the most looming problem, but it is certainly the most immediate." Aeven admitted, "Thrush, Golbart, and I will finish what we started and pay a visit to the general of the Seven Devils himself. And the rest of you? Let's devise a plan. We need to warn Pry'ama that devastation is just on the horizon."

The man with the outlandish clothes and red bandana finally spoke up, the cadence in his voice soothing yet commanding. "After all this time, I still don't think that I've introduced myself. My name is Johauna Beybridge and I have something that I can offer you; something that might make your journey just that much easier. He strode forwards and laid his own hand on Aeven's shoulder, his large smile spitting his head into two. "Aeven, let me introduce you to my greatest joy, a shuttle that can travel through the sky. Her name is FareHeart."

CHAPTER TWENTY

Wavering Reflections

Twilight shimmered overhead as Aeven leaned back against the frame of the library exit, his head resting against the doorframe. Though trying to stop general Kaosa from completing the soul exchange was certainly a pressing matter, it was just as important that his entire team rest and recuperate before such a big excursion took place. Some were headed to Kaosa, while others were dispatching to all corners of Pry'ama in the hopes of alerting the nations of what was going on. Scaldala el'Connor and Johauna Beybridge had hunted through the immediate surroundings of the castle and was able to scrounge enough food, clothes, and supplies to last them a good while. They ate well and most were sleeping now, save for Aeven.

His breath misted in front of his face as his fingers strummed an instrument that he'd found while pacing back and forth amidst the library; it was a harp, a small blue harp that was shaped like a wave. Each string was a different hue of blue. Though the sporadic melody calmed him, his restlessness just wouldn't subside. He stood up and wandered some more, disappearing down the stairs and through the archive. His boots were taking him somewhere unknown, and at this point he didn't much care. He just needed to be somewhere *different*.

Three hissing sets of eyes stared at him as he exited the library, Scaldala's puppets staring but unmoving. Aeven marched by them, and only one set of eyes followed him; a puppet that was leaning on a gleaming great ax. This one had purple orbs for eyes, and her attire was simple leather armor. Aeven smiled briefly at how excited Lucia had been that Scaldala had finally been able to equip his manikins properly. Aeven wouldn't admit it but he had been glad for that as well. They were pleasing on the eyes, but very distracting in such a perilous time. "You are called Azura, no?" Aeven asked it, "Well? Do you want to join me?" Aeven was halfway joking but the puppet stood up with ax in hand, awaiting its next command. "That shouldn't be possible, but I could use the extra company."

Aeven's mindlessness took them down several twisting corridors and through countless doors, both walking in complete silence. Aeven didn't know what he was looking for, or even if he *was* looking for anything specific. He just needed to *move*. He glanced over at Azura. She really was quite beautiful, in a rough way. Her skin was opaque, and yet purple and somewhat rough. At first glance her hair was raven black, but when she walked by a source of light it had streaks of dark purple in it. She had many piercings in both of her ears, and one small ring in her bottom lip.

Aeven stopped and grabbed her shoulder; something had caught his eye about her head. A reflection of light. Pulling her hair back with his hand, he saw that she had an enormous hole in the side of her skull that had been patched over with scoria, the scoria being more crystal than rock. It was *just* opaque enough that he could see something within her head, something that was about the size of a fist, and it glowed and hummed intermittently. "Now what could that possibly be?" *Azura is living proof that what Sambsyne and Secledrin say is most likely true. There is* no way *that the Goldenfist are even close to being able to produce something like this. Not now, not in this day and age.* "I bet all three of you have...this. Whatever this is."

"There are four of us." Azura spoke suddenly, Aeven shuddered in shock as his heart jumped.

"What...what did you just say?" Aeven croaked, "and you can talk?!" She repeated herself, her voice rough and monotone. "There are four kili'gul'mari. One of us is missing. Don't know how or why." She lifted her arm up and pointed straight ahead of them. "There is another one of your brothers."

Aeven whipped around, his eyes taking everything in at once. It was a laboratory of some sort, and it looked as if someone had gone on a rampage. Desks were overturned, chairs smashed into dozens of pieces. Aeven stepped forward slowly, his boots crunching against thick glass. Kneeling down, he looked at the shards more closely. The glass was abnormally thick. His reflection stared back at him.

He looked older, worn out. His face had hardened up some. He always assumed that he'd eventually look like his father, but that just wasn't so. Aeven had always known that he looked nothing like his father, and Aeven remembered once asking his dad why that was. Athrim's only response was, "because you take more after your mother's side, son." Aeven now knew how true that statement was. Aeven got his looks from his mother because she was human; his father had been an aor'sii.

Aeven closed his eyes and tried to envision what his mother possibly looked like. He'd always found it strange that his father had never been able to describe her to him, he always brushed the question aside and quickly changed the topic. Now he knew why. Aeven shook his head. He *did* have a mother, once. Or, at least, a woman that gave birth to him. Knowing how cruel the Goldenfist are, Aeven imagined that he was possibly held for a few minutes before being whisked away. Maybe.

He stood back up and beckoned Azura to follow him. The broken glass was a trail that led down the corridor and into a dusty old lab. Machinery that Aeven couldn't even begin to understand were set against the walls closest to him, and placated in the center of the rectangular lab was a great stone block, like what someone would lay on when undertaking medical needs. The glass crunched loudly underfoot as he inspected the stone slab. It was coated in dust, but speckles of dried blood could clearly be seen upon it, and looking down at it stirred something within Aeven. He couldn't place his finger on what, exactly, but this place felt familiar, somehow.

Against the furthest wall were nine cylindrical glass prisons, some shattered completely, while others were only slightly fractured. Some had a clear, smoky liquid within them, bubbles rising from the bottom and dissipating at the top. Most of the glass containers were empty, the broken glass blown outwards as if whatever had been contained within had broken free. Aeven completely ignored those, slowly striding to the one container that was still intact.

It was the last chegus to break free of Julian's Fortress. He floated in its prison of liquid, eyes closed and mouth turned downwards. The being was tall, it's arms crossed on its chest and the being's auburn hair flowing freely like thousands of long, red fingers trying to find freedom. He also possessed vibrant wings that crackled within the liquid; they weren't wings comprised of feathers, but instead of energy. Vibrant, ruby red energy. Its wings would sizzle and snap, grow larger, and then dissipate altogether before starting over again. At the base of this creature's feet was a small treasure chest the size of a melon, the metalwork copper and the wood somehow intact. "What could that possibly mean?" Aeven whispered to himself, "a gift from the future? But for who?"

Staring at his reflection in the glass prison, Aeven could feel the hatred start to build within him. The anger at his situation, at who had created him, at what he was supposedly destined for. He punched the glass, and then punched it again harder. *We were bred like some kind of animals! The king will get what he deserves. I'll see to it.* Unsheathing his bastard sword, Aeven made a choice as Azura looked on, emotionless. He slammed the pommel of his sword into the glass container. Again and again he struck it until the glass prison gave way. "You're on my team now, friend." Aeven whispered. "We will have our vengeance." Aeven raised his sword once again into the air, the pommel high above his head.

—ɷ—

Aeven's mind was shot, his muscles ached beyond belief, and his endurance was waning. Eying the slow rolling fog somewhat lazily,

Aeven halfheartedly shielded his face as another ocean wave breached the shadowed canyon walls above, showering him and his companions once again in all of its cold salted glory. With an ominous sigh, Aeven slowly turned in his saddle to gaze at his surroundings, several dark thoughts crossing his mind. It wasn't the eight leagues that they've had to travel that had him in such a foul mood, nor the thousands of stories he's had to endure from his aged companion, Golbart, but riding through bitter shadowed chasms while constantly having a deluge of frosty water dumped atop your head was never a wonderful experience in Aeven's book.

Aeven and his new team of sundry warriors had spent hours discussing and bickering about what the best strategy would be for trying to alert all nations for the oncoming onslaught of the Father of Elders. When it came right down to it, there was no easy approach; each warrior had decided to seek out a specific world leader, Johauna being the man that would deliver each soldier to their destination via his airborne shuttle.

Aeven, Thrush, and Golbart had decided to resume their journey back to the leader of the Seven Devils, to try and quell him before its soul was completely exchanged for lord Kaosa's. The shaded frigid valley walls where Johauna had dropped them off was very isolating, the precarious, uneven cliffs rising for miles above their heads. Balanced along the precipices, however, was another story altogether. With a partial smile, Aeven turned to the slow-moving rusty wagon plowing along beside him, its owner at the helm of the monstrosity.

Johauna had allowed Golbart to stow his wagon aboard his shuttle, though Aeven would have completely understood if the captain would have left the rusty garbage back at Julian's Fortress. "Golbart," Aeven inquired, edging his horse closer to the man's wagon, "to what point and purpose do those wolves serve at being carved atop the overhang as they are? And what's more, they seem to be sculpted out of—" Unable to finish his sentence Aeven could only gape at the marvel.

"That's right," Golbart spoke up, his eyes scanning the ridges above with knowledgeable insight. "Wolves carved out of black crystal. Servants, some call them, each one waiting for a worthy master to lay claim to their dormant hearts. It is said that until that point in time happens, however, those wolves lay in wait, guardians left to safeguard the past."

"Opel'sung, I believe that was the name of the village in which these crystal wolves were left to guard." Thrush butted in, "now just another remnant of the past, Opel'sung was once a prestigious city based across the very mountain in which we are trying to find passage. A tragedy is what you would call it, what befell that nation many ages ago. I guess you could say the wicked atrocities that broke the aor'sii could be laid at the feet of the very same man that laid waste to Opel'sung. It was, of course, Kordethion.

"Others are of the mind that it was King Randel II, the king that ruled over Pry'ama as a whole in 1303, who ordered Opel'sung razed because of political strife." Aeven frowned, his mood turning even darker.

"Kordethion again. The only thing that I know about him is that he had helped Aelora Aegus on her quest; and if that were the case, then he *should* be stuck in a sky'un'grael, no? King Randel II though, how was he able to demolish an entire realm? There should have been backlash from the populace. In the least he should have been dethroned, at the most, hung. I don't understand how he was able to convince his generals to commit such a crime against fellow Prymarians."

"It won't be so surprising after you hear what I have to say; it was because Opel 'sung possessed a special type of warrior. A type that the king *didn't* have. You know how petulant that king's lineage is. Opel'sung was one of the oldest citadels to have survived the last ages—each clan inhabiting the surrounding mountain range had secrets that you could only guess at. They were very powerful to say the least. It's only myth now but some say that most of these clans were able to scribe tattoos across the bodies of their brethren, instilling their ancestor's wisdom and supernatural traits to the next generation. It was surreal. In battle, these warriors were second to none—when they weren't debilitating their enemies with their spiritual powers, they were defending their households with swords that were almost as tall as they were.

"He dictated to the elders of Opel'sung that if they allowed some of his own soldiers to study with these mystique warriors, that, in turn, he would provide them with riches beyond measure. All the strength that they would ever need was resting in his hands, he said. Naturally, they wouldn't hear of it. Called him a gutless fool, they did." Resting the palm of her hand on the hilt of her sword, Thrush's voice became even more stiff. "Well, you can imagine the results of that declaration. Need I say more?"

Aeven let his horse fall back behind the unstable wagon, murky thoughts threatening to drown him in a torrent of questions. *Those wolves are just one more remnant of the past.* Shielding his head once again from the blitz of frigid seawater, Aeven's eyes took to roving the canyon walls, searching for more shadowed fragments that was lost to time. *What could the king have been thinking though, ordering an attack on his own country because he didn't get his way? And what was that that Thrush said? The soldiers of Opel'sung were able to scribe tattoos on their bodies? I wonder...*

Hours crept by as the trio slowly made their way from the spires of the mountains and down to the frigid valley below. Ringlets of fog gently meandered across the ribbed road, spilling over the side of the embankment, rolling over shattered tree stumps, volcanic rock, and loose debris akin to water spilling down a waterfall. It was tough to see more than ten yards ahead, and because of the fog, everything was damp and cast in a version of gray. One hillside looked much like another.

The deep canyon eventually transformed into a twisted island of boulders, flowers, and winding trails. The steep goat paths were treacherous, especially for Golbart and his horses, and the scattered patches of ruins was mystifying. Finally reaching an edge of the cliffside, the trio were able to see down below into the raging, perilous sea. The air was thick with mist and soaked their clothes. "More remnants of the past, perhaps?"

Aeven asked curiously, "I never realized how much history was established here on the outskirts of Calder."

Speckling the frosty sea beneath them were what looked to be shrines. Rising desperately out of the waves of the sea—as if in a plea to the heavens—rose multiple shrines scattered throughout the waters, temples that weren't in any particular pattern and yet spreading miles apart. Each shrine seemed to ascend about ten feet above the waves, built of solid stone. They were plain but durable. "I truly couldn't say why those were built here." Golbart finally admitted from the seat of his wagon. "Those are old enough that I doubt *anyone* would really know. Only a fool willingly travels the path that we are navigating, so I suspect not many people even realize that these shrines exist. There could be a tome, somewhere, stating what they are meant to symbolize. But that is neither here nor there."

Thrush waved in the direction of a goat trail angling down the side of the canyon, just wide enough for a horse to travel down. "Let's find shelter for the night. It's getting late." Thrush steered her borrowed horse, Oceandust, around in a sharp arc, horse and rider disappearing down a steep pathway that led to the lower banks overlooking the restless sea.

The descent down the wide trail was treacherous, with many awkward stumbles and abrupt plunges forward that was liable to break a horse's leg if the rider wasn't paying close attention. The trail was spackled with roots, snags, and crags, but miraculously none was hurt as they navigated downwards. Aeven's mount came to an abrupt halt on a sizeable ridge, the ledge protected by an old growth grove that could protect travelers from the onslaught of rain. Aeven couldn't help but turn around and watch Golbart navigate his prized wagon over and around the many snares and traps that the path had to offer.

The golden cladded mercenary snapped and tore at the reigns of his dusty horses, the animals wild eyed and lathering at the mouth. Aeven made a small wager with himself that at least one of the animals would break a leg or one of the groaning wheels on his wagon would shatter, but impressively, the mercenary was able to masterfully steer his animals to safety.

Aeven hopped out of his saddle and lead Cloud Chaser to a nearby tree, tying his lead rope to a branch that was near some healthy foliage. *For such a rugged landscape, this sure is a beautiful grove. Especially since its set against the side of the cliff.* Chraonos has some old growth timber that

Aeven has always admired, but these trees were simply majestic. The roots were thicker than a man's leg, and the red barked trees towered high into the sky, standing firm against the wind and storms. *The horses certainly aren't going to starve tonight.*

Crouching to one knee, Aeven snagged a barbed stem of one of the many colorful flowers swaying at his feet, the smell of sweet nectar filling his nose. "It's beautiful, isn't it?" Thrush breathed, her light laughter all but lost to the rolling waves of the sea. Chuckling himself, he presented his find to his companion. "For you, my lady." With a flourish, he gently put the rose in Thrush's hair, his eyes coming to rest on the most precious sight that he'd ever come to know.

Giggling softly, she grabbed Aeven by the shoulders and spun him around, the prized moment lost to the realization of what Thrush had keenly described as 'beautiful'. He'd been so enamored by the trees that he'd failed to look past them and further into the brush. There was a rotten, wooden railing that came up only about waist-high, evenly picketed to fence off part of the grove.

Beyond the fencing were stairs that were carved into the cliff itself, a natural stairway that ascended upwards and disappeared from view around the gorge's bend. A little wooden sign was picketed in the front yard beside the small gate, sloppily painted across it reading 'Heed thy Shadows, Heed thy Past.' "This," Aeven stated, "is very ominous, even for our standards."

"Thanks for stating the obvious." Thrush stated dryly, "it's getting late, and I think we'd be taking a fool's chance if we bombard our way up that stairwell. Who knows what's awaiting us up there? Calder is supposed to be where the majority of the Seven Devils' battalion is, chances are that's where general Kaosa is resting. If he hasn't gone completely feral, already, that is."

Aeven glanced behind him at the mercenary tending to his wagon and then spoke in a quiet voice. "Either way we need to finish off Kaosa. If he isn't a threat now, he soon will be. I also think that we need to keep an eye on Golbart from here on out. Don't forget that first and foremost, he is a mercenary. He will be looking for that big payday, and it might be at out expense. In any case, come on. Let's set up camp."

CHAPTER TWENTY-ONE

Mercenaries Divurge

No matter how he twisted and turned against the ground, he just couldn't find a comfortable spot to lay; roots and rocks jabbed him in his back and ribs, and he couldn't stop shivering from the rain, fog, and his soggy clothes. Normally he found enjoyment listening to the crashing waves and the trees rustling above, but not this night. All three of them had attempted to make a fire for warmth, but everything was just so damp that they had no success. Standing up, Aeven started pacing back and forth to try and warm up his body.

Thrush rolled over in place to watch him, and Golbart sat up. "This is useless. I say that we investigate where those stairs go, it might be somewhere at least warmer. At most it could be a means to finding Kaosa." Thrush stated bluntly, "perhaps we can finish this mission before daybreak and be well on our way back home. Maybe."

"And my wagon? My horses? My *wares*? Do I just leave my entire livelihood here for just any thief to have his way with?" Golbart barked, rising to his feet. "We had a plan to travel to Calder and finish off general Kaosa! Not to go meandering and exploring in whatever…" he waved his hand towards the fence, "…this is! How am I supposed to bring my stuff with me!?"

"We can't *not* explore this." Aeven stated, "we are close enough to Calder that this could very well be where Kaosa is hiding. If its not, then at least we know that he isn't here. How about you continue on to Calder and ensure that he is there, and we will be close behind you."

"And if you find him past those stairs?"

"Then the mission is over, and we can focus on more important matters. And you will be free to do whatever it is that you wish to do."

Golbart brightened up at that. "Freedom does sound nice." He disappeared into the darkness and began preparing for travel, carefully gathering up each of his horses and ensuring that they were strapped onto the wagon properly.

Nodding once at Thrush, they both gathered the few belongings that they had and strode over to the small gate. Unlatching the small clasp, they started the slow ascent up the winding stairway. The climb was very slow going, with every crash of a wave or stray sound bringing them both to a sudden halt. Shadows played games with him, his eyes not able to fully adjust to the light of the moon. Listening to Thrush's rushed breaths, Aeven came to a stop at the turning point of the bend. "Anything could be around this corner, are you ready?" Aeven whispered behind him, "this is it!"

The distinct sound of steel against leather filled the silence as thrush's long swords escaped their scabbards. His own sword wavering out in front of him at the ready, Aeven sprinted around the corner, his head rushing with heat and blood. He swung his sword down and around through shadows, mist, and darkness, a battle cry erupting from the back of his throat; his sword connected with something tough, rebounding back at him.

"Well," Thrush declared, "that was special."

Nodding his agreement, Aeven could only laugh. Of course, what the stairs would inevitably lead to is a door; it was only natural. Despite the mislead fear, Aeven noticed how simple the entrance was. It was a set of double doors, spanning at about five feet wide and eight feet tall, constructed out of honey-colored wood. Each door had a giant white stone ring with smaller metal studs lining the frame. The doorway was set into a large alcove that had lichen, slime, and corral growing around it.

"Here goes nothing," Aeven murmured to himself, rain pelting the back of his head. Stepping into the natural nook, Aeven lifted one of the stone rings and knocked against the wet wood. Silence, except for the door jarring open slightly. Stepping forward, Thrush brought her leather boot up and kicked the half-door the rest of the way open, her pale black armor reflecting the twinkling of the midnight sky.

Leveling her mirrored blades in front of her, Thrush stalked into the entryway, her whole demeanor reflecting vigilance and passion. Aeven slithered around the open door as well, his eyes and sword moving as one.

The inside was astounding. It was a knighting hall that looked very similar to the one in Chraonos. The floors were wrought out of stone tiles, running a good five hundred spans in either direction. Beautiful, gilded pillars ran the length of the hall, twelve on either side; each one was entwined with ivy carved out of blood-red stone, ivy that climbed from the base of each pillar to the wooden beams above, each vine encircling the room in its own creative way

Halfway down the antechamber were simple wooden benches, twelve on each side. There was a dais at the end of the room that was bathed in moonlight from high above. Aeven was dumbstruck. His eyes leaving the dais, Aeven studied a sizeable stained-glass window that was positioned directly above the podium, portraying a knight and an aor'sii kneeling as one. Aeven's heavy boots echoed across the antechamber as his feet made their way to the plain dais, his eyes never leaving the hallowed pane.

Memories threatened to crush him, aches and pains he'd long since buried quickly resurfacing. Calm images of Lacretia floated across his vision, the king's daughter's quiet laughter sparking warmth in Aeven's heart as he held her in his arms. Images of his father drifted through his mind as well, images of his dad at his knighting ceremony, his rigid demeanor displaying how proud he was to have a knight of Chraonos as his own son. Aeven pushed those thoughts away violently, effectively cutting himself off from his longing of the past; reminiscing was for the weak.

Bile rose into his throat. Coming to a halt beneath the large window, Aeven's raised his blade out in front of him, his ears catching the sound of steel abrading leather. Feeling a hand gently grasp his own, Aeven didn't need to look to know who was trying to solace him. Thrush's voice spoke out. "Sometimes, the past should stay exactly where it's meant to be—in the past. Time has a way of hardening our hearts to the wrongdoings wrought upon our souls, but it still hurts. The future, though, is only predestined by one person." Slightly squeezing Aeven's hand, Thrush tenderly brought the palm of her other hand up and placed it upon Aeven's heart. "You."

Nodding with understanding, Aeven sheathed his sword, his eyes lingering on the knight and aor'sii. "When I'd risen from my knee after I'd been knighted back then, only a single thought had come to my mind: It had been so simple. I thought, 'I'm going to protect those who can't defend themselves. I'm going to vanquish those who would wreak havoc and mayhem upon this kingdom, and I will unite each country in the process.' Peace. Prosperity. Look at the realm now; Chraonos is on the brink of ruin, warlords are altering this land into exactly what it shouldn't be—broken."

"You're right, Pry'ama is broken. But the question isn't 'what could you have done to stop it?' You can't change the past, nobody can. Events often spiral out of our control whether we like it or not. Such is life. No, what you should be asking yourself is 'What can you do to change this kingdom from what it is to what it should be?'"

Closing one eye, Aeven focused on Thrush with the other. "Can one man change the course of the future? With only his ideals and willingness to help others as his sovereignty?"

"That," Thrush affirmed, "depends on how hard you're willing to fight for your ideals. The only thing stronger than your principles should be your resolve. And remember this. It took the actions of a single man to plunge this realm into the sorry state it's in. It'll take another man with the best of hearts to rectify that man's selfish deed. Never waver from what you believe in, fight for it with your body's dying breath."

He could only nod; those words were exactly what a knight stood for. To hold steadfast in what you believed in, honoring your heart and the hearts of others. Laughing quietly, Aeven decidedly wrapped his arm around Thrush's armored hip and led her off of the dais, his frame of mind finding a much-needed sanctuary of peace.

"This hall, unless I'm mistaken, was once a gathering place for the drey'une." Aeven stated seriously, "that window depicts an aor'sii and a knight kneeling as one, a very ancient symbol dating back to even before Aelora and her team traveled to the Father of Elders."

"That's very interesting," Thrush countered, her hand brushing away Aeven's fingers. "But didn't Sambsyne say that technically the order of the drey'une haven't been created yet? That happens in the future."

Aeven was dumbstruck. "No, you're right. He is right. If we are buying into that whole theory, then this room shouldn't be here at all"

"I've stopped trying to figure out what is happening." Thrush admitted, "I'll tell you what I'm starting to believe. I think that this whole fiasco goes further back than you pulling that fortress out from the future. You doing that just showed us what has been *already* happening. It made us aware of it. I think that something happened *not that long ago* that created a disruption, if you will."

"A...disruption?" Aeven asked enquiringly. "What do you mean?"

"Like I said, I've stopped trying to put the pieces together. It's just... its almost as like this realm, the era that we live in, history. They're all confused. That's what I mean. Pieces of history are shifting together without any rhyme or reason. Take this room, for instance. It's a room that was created for the drey'une, and yet here it is, in the side of a cliff, on the outskirts of a forgotten city. The drey'une do not exist, and yet *someone* built this room for them."

"I understand." Aeven admitted, "and I think that you are right. How do we even begin to investigate that, though?"

"We don't. Not now, at least. But there is something else that we can look into, something more immediate. Look over there, and over here. Ashes on the floor. The lanterns hooked to the ceiling beams up there have been lit recently. We may not be alone."

Aeven had been so enamored with Thrush's theory that he'd completely missed the ash dust across the floor. "It could just be a lone refuge that is ducking in out of the rain, much like we are. But I agree that it does need investigating." Studying the hall with a more scrutinizing eye, the only constant factor of the antechamber seemed to be that everything built in or added on was replicated twelve times.

It was Thrush who solved the puzzle first. "There are only eleven wall hangings. If you'll notice, the omitted wall hanging isn't necessarily misplaced, but more conveniently built into the wall itself. The shadows residing in that particular area of the room are doing a phenomenal job of keeping the door hidden, almost too good of a job."

Thrush carefully picked her way to the far corner of the room, her body disappearing behind one of the twelve pillars. Aeven slowly followed his friend, several foreboding feelings clawing their way up his spine.

Rounding the engraved column, Aeven steeled himself and breached his way into the shifting shadows, his heart coming to a standstill when his eyes failed to locate Thrush and then calming down when he saw a nondescript door ajar.

Aeven poked his head through. The room was dark, cold, and was built for only a single purpose: to let the divine souls of the nobles find peace in death. It was a burial chamber. Dozens of stone coffins lined the room, each unique in their own way. Scrutinizing the closest crypt, Aeven could just distinguish a hood and wings emblem neatly engraved in the stone; an emblem that was unknown to him. Shivering, Aeven started to slither through the door when two pairs of voices caught the attention of his ears.

Cutting off an oath, Aeven slithered through the access and ducked behind the closest coffin. Sidling up next to Thrush, he listened to the heated argument. "It doesn't matter where that filthy bilge rat decided to hide, Denarius, nor does it much matter at this point. He is only one person, and you can see what the results are of your incompetence! Look at my body! I need that sky'un'grael back soon or I will unleash a power upon you and your own that even Sparodin will quake in fear at. Do you not understand? I provided you with the resources, the men! I am a high lord of Scarrow, I demand to be free of this *curse!*"

Aeven's ears caught the sound of steel being drawn, his own hands shaking violently from anger. *Aneiyrin stole this man's sky'un'grael as well?! Another high lord that will succumb to the soul exchange. His motives are starting to become clearer. Not only will Aneiyrin achieve his objective of finding and delivering all of the sky'un'grael, but in so doing, all of these high lords that have been keeping the sky'un'grael 'safe' will undergo the soul exchange and deliver to the Father of Elders his own personal army! I cannot even begin to imagine Pry'ama being directed by men that have been twisted and broken by the Father of Elders. Our realm really will be broken after that.*

"You can burn, Javin. I know you, I have informants that are closer to you than you think! I know that you've been playing both sides. If you wanted your precious orb back, you should have sent more trustworthy men to do your bidding!" The violent sound of steel clashing against steel reigned throughout the room, each stroke delivered and parried with precise movements. It wasn't a long duel and it ended quite violently with the man with the deeper voice bellowing in pain, the sound of steel clattering to the ground.

"Denarius, you scoundrel! I warned you. We'll do this the hard way, then. Give my regards to your sister. I am Tealginar, the Reviled!" The room exploded in a purple light, thousands upon thousands of sparkling wisps materializing around the dark room, revolving in a chaotic, random pattern. Raising his arm to shield his eyes, Aeven cringed as a vile, violent scream emitted from the man known as Denarius; the scream was so vicious and long that it shook Aeven to his very core. He tried to cover his ears to block out the inhuman scream and was unsuccessful.

Squeezing Thrush's hand, Aeven closed his eyes and hoped to the heavens that the afterlife would grant Denarius better luck than this harsh world ever did. A new voice spoke up, one that was deeper, rougher and more malicious. A voice that very much resembled that of Javin. Bellowing violently, it pitched its voice over the din of Denarius's screaming, its tone coming out rough and unclear, like it wasn't used to using common tongue.

"I told you, Denarius, you can't beat me. I'd had every intention of letting you go, but now that you know my secret, that can't happen. The man known as Javin has long since gone. Living in that vile darkness for eons, being twisted and toyed with by the Father of Elders. I can't even express how grateful this freedom feels. You should have taken the high road, Denarius. I *do* need that sky'un'grael back but now it is a moot point. I am bound to is as it is bound to me. Enough jabbering. Goodbye, fool."

A loud, wicked cackle filled the chamber, and then the sound of something being repeatedly beaten against the walls of the crypt. Shivering, Aeven grasped Thrush's hand all the harder, his eyes locking with hers. "This power, as you've so aptly described it, was a discovery that marks a new dawn for man—the era of knights and chivalry is over. Where honor and kindness had once reigned over this land, blood will now claim dominion. Blood will purge Pry'ama from all the weak-hearted men who feel virtue still holds sway. Denarius's incessant screaming and sharp shattering of his bones drilled a permanent hole in Aeven's memory.

Wrapping his arm around Thrush's shoulder, Aeven gently comforted her while desperately trying to weigh the odds of their escape. Denarius's screams seemed to last forever, Javin's mercy as forgiving as the heart of fire. Wrapping his fingers around the hilt of his bastard sword, Aeven could only wait for the onslaught to subside. The screaming stopped. A last guffaw escaping the beast's throat, the sound of his slow, dragging breaths faded into the dark depths of the ancient chamber, his heavy footfalls eventually disappearing.

Is that the true power of the sky'un'grael? Aeven thought direly, the ramifications overwhelming him. *It isn't just a soul exchange. Those orbs are portals for nightmares into Pry'ama. No, they're more than nightmares.* The sound of concrete grating against concrete rudely roused Aeven out of his trance. Carefully crouching on all fours, Aeven poked his head around the tomb, his eyes roving the area for the unfamiliar sound. It was indistinct at first and Aeven thought that the shadows might be playing games with his eyes, but when the stone cover of the farthest coffin moved a whole foot of its own accord, Aeven could only gape.

This night was full of surprises. Slowly, a head of dark hair rose out of the coffin, its eyes scanning the room with scrutiny. Locking eyes with Aeven, a gloved hand rose precariously out of the stone tomb and waved at the stunned duo. Without a word being spoken, the stranger hoisted himself out of the pit, his leather war boots and outlandish armor destroying what doubts Aeven had of this man being some sort of mercenary like he himself was.

He had the looks of a fellow mercenary at least, and Aeven had a hunch that if the man had truly meant Aeven or Thrush any type of harm he would not have waved at them. Standing up himself, Aeven made certain the stranger saw his bastard sword before striding over, his hand coming to rest on the handle of Qualvalion. Thrush followed in lockstep, swords clearly out and visible.

The stranger spoke, his voice holding a very thick accent. "The name's Rykin Denedrin, Crusader of Pry'ama."

"Aeven Lionrose." Aeven bit off curtly, thrusting his own hand out. "I don't suppose you'll let me in on how you came to be hiding amidst a hidden crypt of all places?"

Before Rykin could answer, another voice floated up from the bottom of the same stone tomb, this one more feminine and alluring. "Rykin, have you forgotten about me completely or what? I can't hold your sword for much longer you know. It's heavy." Twisting back around toward the tomb, Rykin's hand darted down and reappeared with a great sword, its spine adorned with great golden rings that ran the length of the blade.

Disappearing down into the crypt once more, he hoisted up the owner of the voice. Aeven gasped as the lady gracefully pulled herself the rest of the way out, her eyes catching Aeven's for a quick wink. The word beautiful didn't even begin to describe her. The first thing Aeven noticed was that her golden-red hair was pulled back into a very long braid, reaching to the small of her back. Her eyes were the deepest of green, like the color of a forest just after a storm. Her clothes were also outlandish, her greaves and wrist guards ebony in color. In short, Aeven could only stare. Thrush punched him in the shoulder.

Laughing lightly, she introduced herself, her voice reminding Aeven of the gentle rustling of the wind. "My name is Kindraya Wardlaw,

Sentinel of Chraonos. Pleasure to meet you too, stranger." Turning her attention to Thrush, Kindraya raised an eyebrow in question, the full lips of her mouth slowly turning upward.

"You can call me Thrush Balfourion, former scout for the nation of Ashenfelter." Her voice spitting venom, "And no, I don't trust you."

"It never occurred to me that you did." Brushing past Thrush, Kindraya glided over to where the corpse was, her body bent over the horrendously misshapen corpse. Rykin strode to her side, both quietly conversing with heads together. Aeven's misgivings started to grow.. Shaking his head, Aeven went to join them and immediately regretted it. He gazed upon the wrangled cadaver, his eyes lingering on the dozen of tombs surrounding him. The stone wall was coated red as well, almost as if an artist had tried to recreate a war scene from memory. Closing his eyes, he willed the images away.

"Rykin, I feel the resistance might be facing its last days of fame. They're picking us off one by one. Denarius may have been able to withhold the whereabouts of where we are hiding, but sooner or later I fear the high lords will find an informant who values his own life over that of us, his comrades." Wiping her hands across Denarius's cloak, Kindraya stood up and silently stowed something in her pocket; Aeven's eyes were too slow to discern exactly what the item was.

Crossing her arms, Kindraya posed her next question. "We have too valuable of information for it to be lost to treachery and fear, so what's our plan of action?"

"Our whereabouts may be in jeopardy, but that doesn't matter up here in these mountains. Our mission stays the same. If we can recover the lost item of power in the heart of Ashenfelter, then Denarius' death will have meant something. All we can do is hope that whatever we find in these mountains is enough to tip the odds in our favor."

"Then it is decided. For the sake of our final stand, I hope you're right. We'll hold true to our words, the outcome of the nation rest upon it." Waving her hand in Aeven's general direction, her voice rose in tone, her head turning just a fraction. So not all of the knights have fallen, I see. Is that not the Lionrose sigil embroidered on your cloak?

The Goldenfist Corp may have subdued the most vigilant of your order, but the Lionrose spirit never was one for being heedful."

Turning fully to face him, Kindraya slammed her fist down into her palm, lips turning slightly upward. "No, never heedful. Your family was one for defiance. Even now, at the face of extinction, you fight on. It was the same in the aftermath of the war. Your family hunted down us Azure Skulls with tenacity. And now here you are."

His order had been trampled under the hard boots of imperialism and change. It was all he could do to survive, protecting those that he could, and praying for those that he could not. No, the sacred rank of the knight has fallen far from where it had once stood; even Aeven could admit that much. Like the race of the aor'sii, the wings of the knights had been effectively crushed. Honor no longer held any value in this land; deceit and mayhem were the way of life now.

Biting his tongue, Aeven glanced at Thrush as her voice piped up, her hands held evenly out in front of her. "It seems that we have a common goal, then. We both need to delve further into the mountains then, and the odds that we'll make it through safe is a hard and dark gamble. I propose an alliance."

"An Alliance?" Kindraya tipped her head back and laughed, a wily laugh that echoed throughout the chamber. "Azure Skull rebels making an alliance with a knight and his *hound*? Come now, you've got to be joking."

Aeven crossed his arms, the idea of teaming up for the time being looking less favorable by the minute. "It'd be an alliance between four mercenaries, nothing more. I think it's a safe bet that all of us are hard up for company. Or are you forgetting your friend, here." Aeven waved down at the corpse strewn across the room.

Flipping her braid over her shoulder, Kindraya strode into the deepest recess of the room as Rykin stepped forward, his hand resting lazily upon his blade. "We can deal. For now." She said over her shoulder. "Lucky for us, before Javin made his appearance, Denarius had found a hidden passage. He was the shrewd one We will be travelling in the opposite direction of that *beast*, thankfully. Let us be off, we have a lot of distance to cover in such a short time."

CHAPTER TWENTY-TWO

Toil of the Tundra

*A*ivunall, *the broken nation of faith; what twisted, dark path of life has led us astray to this ungodly patch of land?* Taking a deep breath, August Castner let his eyes wander across the broken realm, his hand absentmindedly running through his filthy hair. Aivunall had been built more than two thousand years ago, the glorious realm covering almost the entire length of the frozen tundra. It was once said that no matter which nation was coming under fire or attack, the valiant soldiers of Aivunall would ride to their aid.

In those final days before the fall of the aor'sii, the Aivunallins took justice to heart, pledging their alliance to the holy winged creatures; they swore that they wanted to protect what was just, not what the king ordered out of sheer hate. The king, learning of this abomination, ordered three of his great realms, Scarrow, Galeshwyn, and Calder to march upon Aivunall and burn the audacious kingdom to the ground.

He shook his head. This was neither here nor there, and those kinds of dark thoughts would eat at him. Grasping his blue, fur lined cloak and pulling it tighter, August took a step back from the overhang and turned to his companions, all eyes drawing in on the splendor of the shattered nation; it was indeed a majestic sight to behold. A nation that fought for what they believed in and was rewarded with death. *King Wel'thaes Ahlstrom, so many deaths could be laid at his feet. But how can a lowly knight such as me even question his ambitions? In the game of war, I am but a pawn.*

Lacretia gurgled and laughed. Her faint laughter lifted the morose mood that had descended upon the group, Lacretia's smile growing bigger as her eyes lingered on a stray string that was blowing in the wind. Chuckling himself, August strode over to Keira and watched as his most elite soldier gently rocked Lacretia back and forth in her arms, August finding himself drowning in the newborn's lightly colored eyes.

It had been eight weeks ago when August had returned to his family's estates from a particularly ruthless assignment, the mission having been to hunt down and destroy a renegade group of knights, the infamous Azure Skulls. He'd found only blood and carnage. His secluded estate had been burned to the ground, his servants and squires slaughtered. August remembered bursting into the monastery that night, finding his bishop and Lacretia hiding behind August's trick door, and even more importantly, they were still alive and breathing.

Thrusting Lacretia into August's arms, the bishop Bemnian had told August to protect the baby with his life, for the last thing that Pry'ama needed as for the Azure Skulls to hold the infant princess hostage. If anything, the princess was in just as much danger from royalty as she was from renegade soldiers. King Que'thalias was a king that had no issues procreating; Lacretia has a handful of brothers and sisters that lived at Chraonos itself instead of here, on the outskirts of society. August could envision the king having no problem sacrificing Lacretia if worst came to worst. August had no choice but to gather what handful of soldiers he had left and disappear into the night, Bemnian's whisper that Lord Ossenius, the lord of Flayre'song, was still a strong ally for the household of Lionrose—perhaps the only ally left. August took those words to heart and left his livelihood behind him.

His voice clear and crisp, August spoke to the restless group, making sure to create eye contact at least once with each warrior. "We will make our way into the broken nation and create camp in the city's heart for a handful of nights. It's only a three-day trek from Aivunall to

Flayre'song, and if we're lucky, Lord Ossenius will grant us a safe haven. If we're not... well, just pray that we are." Slowly wrapping Lacretia in his own arms, August relieved Keira of her small burden so that she could prepare herself for the short journey downwards.

"Keira and Rennon, scout the perimeter of Aivunall then report back to me. It's better to be careful in these blasted lands than dead." Nodding their agreement at his decision, his two scouts bound silently down the iced goat trail, their shadowy forms soon lost to the impending night and raging winds.

"You can slaughter us," the renegade had whispered, her hand clutching her chest. "You can pretend you're dealing justice; pretend your protecting your king's honor. The Blades of the Moon, the Silent Songs, the Azure Skulls, no matter which renegade group we are, we won't stand down. In our hearts, we are one and the same. You may see us as rebels, miscreants even, but we're fighting for what we believe in—the right to live. What do you fight for, knight? Do you fight for what's right? What's just? You can kill me, you can kill every rebel you happen upon, but we won't give up until you nobles pay us what's do."

Shaking his head to purge those gruesome memories, August brought his gauntlet up and wiped away the beads of sweat that had started to form on his forehead. If it were possible to drown in your thoughts, August thought he'd never be able to breathe again. After their father had been hung, August and his siblings had each struck out on their own path. Aeven took to the mercenary life, and Arma swore allegiance to a lord in Amoriah. August, he remained in Chraonos, still serving as a knight. Still serving the king. He was never a Lionrose, only adopted into the family at a very young age. It was because of this that the king allowed him to stay.

Putting one boot in front of the other, August doggedly made his way down the trail, his silent entourage following in his wake. The stoic chasms howled violently with their ever-present screams as the fearful wind fled from one side of the canyon walls to the other. The trek downwards was onerous, but it went swiftly as his mind was encompassed in other thoughts. August slowly trudged his way across the grand, beautiful stone laced bridge, the gale and sleet defying him every step of the way.

August wearily watched his three comrades brave the storm ahead of him, each step taken with harsh, menacing emotions. Lacretia's chance for survival rested heavily upon each of their shoulders, and his comrade's worth in batter could make all the difference for her between life and death. August's attention came to rest on the soldier at point, Blair Kincaid, who was just a hair's breadth ahead of the others in the slow race across the stone bridge. Blair had been a commoner, much like he himself had once been, the two of them growing up in the slums of Chraonos together. At age twenty-three, standing at around six-four, with short dark red hair, Blair had the patience of a stone. Always deep in thought, he and Blair had spent many a day sharing thoughts on life, on what the meaning of it all was. Sparring was another common trait they both shared, a regular hobby they relinquished before August had been accepted into the Lionrose family.

Never losing touch with his closest friend, August had immediately raised Blair to his captain upon his acceptance into knighthood. Known as the tolerant behemoth, Blair now wore sturdy copper armor with a scarlet red cloak, the man's boots and gauntlets the darkest of leather. The man's weapon that he wore on his back was a silver glaive that he once won in a duel against a man of nobility, the weapon having several gems decorating its base.

His eyes sliding to the next soldier, August nodded absentmindedly to himself in approval. Valindria Granlund was every inch as tall as Blair, her dark blond hair pulled back into a long braid. At age twenty-five, Valindria was an astute combatant, her skills with knives and her great sword second to none. When it came to her temper, however, she was the opposite of her redheaded companion; her fury was much akin to that of a wildfire. August had first encountered Valindria at a questionable bar; her reputation at mercenary work was known to many, including the higher-class nobles. Despite her loyalties to herself, August couldn't turn a blind eye to her magnificent abilities on the battlefield. It had taken much bargaining, but eventually, she came around; gold always did the trick. She wore an olive-green coat and steel plated armor this day.

The last soldier August watched was Orvindrin Hallström. Only age sixteen, Orvindrin was much like himself, adopted into a noble family when his whole life had been rummaging through the slums of Chraonos. Orvindrin was only five-foot-five, with short brown hair and a scrawny frame, but where his skills lie, muscle wasn't the prerequisite. His mind was the talent that he was renowned for, that and his ability to sneak and infiltrate where needed. That was just as important as pure muscle, in August's opinion.

Like August's own estate that fateful night, the Hallström manor had faced arson as well, Orvindrin's entire family tried and executed with the whim of a thief's knife, all save for Orvindrin. Consoling the boy, August adopted him as one of his own. Orvindrin was a unique individual who chose to wear ragged cloaks and leather armor instead of the noble attire that he had grown up with. Orvindrin's explanation for this was that it was easier to blend in and gather intel when you looked like everyone else on the streets. That made perfect sense to August. The weapon that this boy used was a magnificent mahogany crossbow, the only item on his person that was worth anything of value.

Comparing one against the other, August didn't think that he could choose which warrior was the better in combat. Lacretia couldn't have asked for a more dangerous retinue for protection. Each of the warrior's duty was to ensure the baby's safety came first, a duty that each of them had come to relish and even sanctify. Everything else had to come second. Watching his men breach the great domed entrance of Aivunell, August's eyes slowly slid from his group of men to the broken city, the wind's ferocity blessedly cutting in half as he himself passed through the gate. Aivunell was a realm of ice. The toppled towers, the crumbling spires, the dozens of forgotten barracks, each was clothed in divine robes of snow and frost. Each building was enormous, dwarfing the group to a diminutive size. The great beautiful stonewall circling the city was half as tall as the buildings, the barrier glimmering with its jewelry of rime.

As his boots crunched down on the slippery stones of the paved streets, August's eyes couldn't help but pick at each shadowed boulevard, dozens of the lanes crisscrossing each other to the point of deception. Each avenue reeked of sedition. For miles his group marched, the heart of night descending upon them with a daunting passion. Every so often, the moon permitted August a glimpse of Keira loping along the great iced wall above, her shadowed figure stalking from shadow to shadow, trailing her comrades with a protector's zeal. Twice, August had caught her in just the right amount of moonlight to see Keira's hand clenched around her longbow, an arrow already knocked; he had faith in her.

"Halt!" August bellowed gruffly; his voice pitched just high enough to be heard over the howling winds. Sinking backward into the shadow of a building, August studied his immediate surroundings. He waited to speak until his soldiers were surrounding him. "We camp here this night. I trust these shifting shadows only so far, and I trust the night even less. Unless I am mistaken this building behind me is a 'warden's nest'; it should keep us safe enough. With a solid building keeping us shelter, defending it should be easy enough.

"Orvindrin," August spoke, "Go and inform Keira and Rennon where our camp is, then take first watch. I have a feeling that you'll need that crossbow tonight. I hope that I am wrong." Watching his esteemed scoundrel slip off into the night, August silently located the heavy wooden door to the nest and slowly tried to push it open. Caution was the key. It was locked. *Of course, the bleeding thing is locked. Why wouldn't it be?*

"This, sir," Valindria declared, making her way to the front of the group to stand beside August, "is my specialty. If I may?" Nodding his approval, August watched as his mercenary swung her long braid around her shoulder and set to work on the intricate lock, her fingers deftly handling the steel pick she'd dug up from amidst her belt. Despite the snow and sleet pelting her face, her deft fingers were a sight to behold as her hand carefully picked the stubborn rusted lock; August counted just under two minutes before the door swung ajar with a loud screech. A heroic smile plastered across her face, August couldn't help but chuckle at his comrade's finesse; Blair's laughter making the rest of the group jump in surprise. It was a silent trio, however, that guardedly walked through the doorway, each warrior clutching what they ultimately believed in, which was their weapons. Weapons that had seen many victories and few defeats.

Being the last one to enter the frigid building, August embraced Lacretia with one arm and his other hand coming to rest on his short sword hanging at his side. The Warden's Nest was exactly what he'd expected. From what August could tell, there seemed to be three large rooms, each room without a door. The room closest to them, to their immediate right, was the outfitting room. Racks upon racks of various weapons lined the walls, with outlandish helmets and brightly colored pieces of armor adding to the mixture.

Half a dozen battle flags adorned the stone walls. Flags of defeated nations or nations that had been in alliance with Aivunell, August didn't know or even cared to know. Glancing at his two comrades hunching over the oversized fire pit, no doubt trying to start a fire, August quietly inspected the next room. *It's a library, and yet I'm surprised. I shouldn't be, though. I know full well the power of knowledge, and it's most often the smallest tidbit of information that proves to be the most crucial key in the heat of war. It's something I'm sure the wardens embraced with open arms. Keeping the peace is no small task.*

In comparison to the armory, August thought that the library was magnificent. Rows upon rows of books crammed the large room, mantelpieces decorating every inch of the stone walls, with beautiful wooden shelves spread throughout the center of the room to add even more space to place the treasured tomes. Beautiful carpets adorned the cold flooring, brightly colored runners worked with the most complex of designs. Shaking his head in amazement August strolled through the hundreds of books, his fingers running across the spines of the sleeping volumes.

Reaching the other end of the room, a gorgeously wrought spiral staircase was there to greet him, each step polished to give off a dull shine. Curiosity getting the better of him, August found himself ascending the wooden stairs with searing apprehension, and at the same time his excitement building with each bold step. Aeven would cry if he could see this, then again, so might I. It was a loft. Spanning about thirty strides by thirty strides, the attic was roomy at best with even more tomes piled precariously around the floor and about half a dozen scooped in chairs placed haphazardly around the room.

Striding over to the edge, August couldn't help but beam as he placed his free hand on the small wooden railing, Lacretia gurgling in his arms. *I'd be a happy man if I could live here the rest of my days. Yet duty has a demanding voice.* "Keira!" He roared, catching his comrade skulking through one of the far rows. "Keira! What do you think?" Using his free arm, August encompassed the whole library with a sweep of his hand, the greatness of it all settling upon him like the finest of mantles. "Pretty exceptional, eh?"

"Yeah, sir, it's… grand. Listen, we need you in the center room, we think we've found something that might be of great value to us; something that might keep Lacretia alive." His comrade saluting him once, August watched as Keira disappeared into the adjoining room, her remark leaving him in silent stupefaction. Naturally, he had no choice but to follow. *Duties really starting to irritate me.* His men gathered in the only room he hadn't had a chance to inspect yet, August quietly slipping by the roaring fire.

All attention was focused on a giant table centered in the smallest of the three rooms. The smallest, and yet hands down the most important; it was the map room. What August had painstakingly mistaken as a giant table at first, was in fact a very enormous map encased in a giant glass container, the chart itself worked to the minutest of details. Lord Lionrose had once told me that to have a map is to have a key. Not a key to victory but a key to strategy. He had said that if you were to memorize that map, then you yourself were a key on that battlefield; you became a walking strategist that could direct multiple battalions and warriors without having to constantly consult those that do know the land.

And yet, to memorize a map such as this, it'd take months. The smallest of caves, the most shadowed of paths, even underground tunnels—all is marked here. This map seems to encompass almost the whole of Pry'ama itself. It's nothing short of bloody amazing. "Sir!" Rennon's voice boomed from behind, tearing into the thick silence like a man taking a knife to a sheet. August's blade bit into the doorframe before he'd even realized it'd left its sheath, his nerves and patience as frazzled as a Scarrownian Taskmaster. Swearing an oath, August sent splinters raining on the group as he tore his sword free of the aged wood.

Twisting fully around, August found Rennon, or at least Rennon's head, in the farthest corner of the room, his smile evident even among the deep shadows. "Sir, there's something I think you ought to see, a treasure of sorts. One I think you'll find… useful. Or at least interesting." And with that, the rest of the man disappeared, the trapdoor swallowing him whole.

Handing Lacretia over to Valindria, August left instructions for the group to find a way to secure the map from its glass home, his mood soaring just a little bit higher. *With a proper map at their disposal, finding an isolated route into Flayre'song shouldn't be too difficult, granted the map was drawn correctly of course.* Strolling over to the trapdoor, August guessed that it wasn't a long descent downwards from where he was standing, and the first thing that he noticed when his boots touched the stone flooring below was how cold the underground lair was.

By the time August had oriented his eyes to the deep darkness, Rennon had taken it upon himself to light one of the torches, which in turn caused August to become blind once more. Glaring at his scout, August finally found himself assessing the stone room. It was a finely constructed prison. There were only four prison cells on each side of the room, and the bars on each cell were constructed out of iced steel.

August strode over to stand beside Rennon, the man's treasure that he had been referring to becoming plain as day. "I found her like this, sir. Spooked me something fierce."

"Indeed." August murmured, finding himself crouching down beside his comrade. What he saw astounded him. The cell was very plain, with only a single chair and a pile of frozen blankets. And yet, it was what was sitting down, back against the cell's wall that had their attention. It was a manikin.

A life-size female manikin, if he were to give her a gender. Very slender looking, seemingly constructed out of some sort of glass alloy, her features very exquisite.

Her face was delicate, bright green paint shadowed around her eyes to give her a feral, wild look. Her lips were just a little too large—full and long—and her ears were dainty and slight. She even had dark hair that was cropped off at her shoulders. She was wearing a heavy black cloak, with the fur-lined cowl pulled up over her head. The armor that she was wearing was simple, leather armor and fur-lined gauntlets and boots. Her lip was pierced with a steel stud, and she had several rings pierced in her left ear. August's eyes lingered on her opaque face. If he looked hard enough, her face seemed to light up green for just the barest of moments.

She was clutching something within her arms. August felt a freezing knot settle in the pit of his stomach, something that had nothing to do with the snow and lingering chill in the air. It was a quiver, but it wasn't filled with arrows. Instead, half a dozen slender shards of crystal stuck out, each about the length of his forearm. Each splinter gave off a smoky colored aura, an aura that glowed and resonated from within the cell. Studying the shortest one, a slender shard that was giving off a dark purple radiance, August sudden felt inspiration plunge his heart, his insides bursting with enthusiasm and joy. *This is wrong. I'm in the depths of a frosty, dark dungeon with our very task in turmoil. It isn't inspiring in the slightest. And yet, I feel like I can achieve anything my heart desires.*

He shook his head and moved on. August's eyes carefully found the next shard, a slightly longer crystal that was a bloody, ruby red. *Pain! My liege it hurts, my failure as a protector for my family, the loss of lord Athrim and his beliefs. My heart is being shredded into a thousand broken pieces! I want nothing so much as to die right now.* Falling backward from his crouching position, August hurriedly scooted himself backwards until his back hit the stone wall, his breathing escaping his lips in ragged breaths.

It was Rennon's arm on his shoulder that awakened him from his stupor. "Sir, what's the matter? If it's this dungeon that you're worried about, I have the same feeling as you have. My insides are crawling with dread and bile. It's enough to spook a man, certainly!"

Rennon didn't feel a thing, and he was crouching right there beside me. What sort of vile trickery is this? And yet it intrigues me. To be able to give inspiration to your fellow man, to give despair. All qualities of a natural leader. Was it that puppet, or those shards that infiltrated my mind?

"Rennon." August interjected, shakily climbing to his feet. "Open the cell. I want a closer look." Nodding his agreement, Rennon hurried over to the bars and quietly fiddled with the lock, his attention riddled with cracks of frustration and anxiety. As his scout worked, August thought upon the man's past. He had been a guard for a merchant's wagon for more than two dozen years, his expeditions taking him throughout the whole of Pry'ama. Back when August was just a mere boy, his adoptive father Athrim had been out on a horse ride, riding along the borders of Amder'lael for treaty reasons when he had happened upon Rennon. Bloody. Tattered. The former merchants guard was on the brink of dying.

There are only rumors of how Athrim had managed to pull it off, yet Rennon had lived, his debt to the Lionrose family indefinite. A debt he carried proudly. "Careful, sir," the man said quietly, the cell door screeching open. "If there's any time to practice caution, it's now. Who knows what sort of treachery lies in that cell?" Rennon carefully stepped aside drew his thick knife.

Nodding his agreement, August's feet passed warily through the solid iced entrance, trying his hardest not to slip on the buildup of ice. Using the light from the torch that Rennon had lit, August stopped in the middle of the room and stared down at the manikin. Kneeling in front of the doll, his mind exploded in an avalanche of emotions. Valor. Cowardice. Pleasure. Pain. Wrath. Inspiration. Dozens of emotions gripped August's mind, each taking a hold on his soul, whispering the beautiful song for heroic deeds to take place and the murky chant of fury-wrought vengeance for his enemies.

Forcing himself to stand his ground, August sought to test his will, perspiration forming on his forehead as he defiantly took a hold on each passion, reining each one in with an iron resolve. "Enough!" August snarled savagely, his hand slamming vehemently into the doll's throat. Raising her to a standing position, August crushed her against the stone wall, his fury finally getting the better of him. He slowly started to feel like himself again, each passionate emotion dying in his heart.

Her eyes opened. They were beautiful orbs of crackling green energy inlaid into her gentle face. Something else caught his eye. Keeping her in place, his other hand brushed aside her cowl and scooped her hair back. She had a giant-sized hole near the back of her head that had been filled in with a combination of crystal and scoria. It was too dark to tell what lay underneath the barrier, but he could feel it vibrating and whirring from within. August couldn't bring himself to look away. She was enticing.

His breath catching in his throat, he watched as her mouth opened angrily, her beautiful voice sounding nothing so much as a striking ancient song. "You anger me, wretched man. I should smite you where you stand for treating a Kili'gul'mari such as myself the way you have. You should be bowing to me, accepting forgiveness. And yet, you have my deepest gratitude. I have my wings again. You've set this caged bird free."

Forcing himself to unwrap his fingers from her petite throat, August watched as her delicate body hit the ground, her momentum causing her to stumble awkwardly across the rough flooring. Regaining her composure, the creature strode up to August with a regal flourish, her head barely reaching his shoulders. "I think introductions are in order. They call me Elevia." Thrusting out her small porcelain hand, her voice wavered slightly as her light voice spoke up. "What might they call you?"

"They call him August Castner, knight of house Que'thalias, dedicated protector of the heir to the king, Lacretia Que'thalias." Rennon's voice boomed out, his shadowed form blocking the cell's entrance. "But most of all, they call him the Lion's Flame, a man who holds the Lionrose's spirit in the palm of his hand."

"A man of many names," Elevia breathed, her hand raising to slide a glass finger down August's arm. "And yet a man of many bloods. Destiny intertwines itself around you, and yet you force your way through the pages of time with naught a care."

Through the pages of time? "You got all that out of my name?" August spoke, his arm pulling away from her hand. Involuntarily, he took a step back.

"Yes," she whispered, "and no." Caressing her quiver of shards, the manikin locked eyes with August, her eyes changing to resonate a deep dark green. "You are a man of many names, that much is for certain. I can't help but notice, however, that your face displays a, shall we say, more dominant trait as to where your bloodline originated. Back then, back when man and aor'sii fought side by side, the aor'sii developed a remarkable system. Using their divine powers, the aor'sii marked each rank of their warriors with a specific scar.

"Their foot soldiers were blessed with a distinguished scar that ran from their right ear down to their chin; their scouts, a scar that garnished the very tips of their eyes. On and on, they marked their combatants, each class obtained certain gifts and blessings that all other ranks were denied. It was pure genius."

August refrained from reaching his fingers up to his face, but he could all but feel his own scar crawling across his features, the mark all but searing from the left of his forehead down to his chin. He could acknowledge that he had been adopted, he could even admit that where his true family originated, he had not a clue. He was a knight, pure and simple; any doubter would taste his sword. "What's your point?" he spat, his gaze towering over the Kili'gul'mari.

"Only this. I won't tell you what your scar represents. Not now, at least, but I will say this. These scars that I mentioned glowed with a vivid ardor, under the right circumstances. Your scar, however, doesn't glow in the slightest. In fact, it's kind of faint and boring. However, if what I believe is true, the cloak of fate will undoubtedly clasp around your very shoulders whether you accept it or not. We shall see." Opening his mouth to remind the doll who it was that set her free, August heard a fainter voice override his own, a voice that barely carried through the open trapdoor in the back of the chamber. A voice that rang like thunder.

"Sir, an enemy is breaching Aivunall. An enemy who vows that the snow of this city will be colored deep red in our blood!" The loud thud of heavy boots resonated throughout the chamber as Keira dropped from the trapdoor down to the stone flooring, her voice all but quaking in anger. "They swear on their own lives that they will have Lacretia's head tonight and end this pointless war. I fear they might even win. Orvindrin counted half of a squadron led by a leader that we had presumed dead for some time now, Horneld Kielmen.

"We haven't located the other half of this squadron yet, if they live at all, but I believe that they truly mean business." Keira appeared before August, eyes swiftly taking in the manikin and the slivers of crystal. Her knitted hat was crunched up in her hands.

"Horneld Kielmen." August spat, the name tasting like poison on the tongue. The Azure Skulls were a dying cause, but there was one man that continually sparked the flame for insurgence and rebellion. August had always suspected that it was Horneld that had burned his and Orvindrin's estate to the ground, though it could never be proven. This is one battle that he would gladly accept.

"I require armor and a weapon!" Elevia bellowed, her arm slinging her quiver of shards across her back. "If you are to win here today, you're going to need my help. You've set me free, the least I can do is repay you in your enemies' blood." August nodded his agreement, though said not a word. *Elevia is a mystery that I will have to investigate another day.* If they were indeed to make it to the next day alive, all available fighters would be sorely needed. Even if that meant slaying men that had had decent hearts at one point in time. The king's heir must live on.

"Rennon, show Aurlenelin to the armory and have her outfitted, but hurry. Time is not on our side. Keira, lead the way." Frost clawed at August's face as he slithered through the trapdoor, the distant din of steel clashing against steel just an afterthought as his eyes took in the violent scene of the Warden's den. Scarlet blood was spattered across the simple stone flooring as two of the Azure Skull's bodies lay sprawled haphazardly across the floor, a young boy with his head hanging askew and a feral looking female with eyes already glazed over. Both had deep-blue cloaks tangled around their bodies with a black skull clearly embroidered across their shoulders.

Bile rose in August's throat. Drawing his own weapon strapped to his side, August clutched the long handle of his longsword and slithered to the edge of the open doorway that led outside to the carnage of blood and snow. Keira's heavy breathing all but mimicked his own pounding heart. His head sneaking around the doorframe, August's boots carefully tread in the icy landscape as the cloak of darkness settled around his shoulders like a second skin.

The storm buffeted him, smacking into his body and trying to push him through the snow against his will. Keira's hand grasped his shoulder, her free hand pointing across the street to a derelict building. Or more appropriately, to a shadowed figure scaling the building. August nodded, no words needing to be said. Keira wanted to be the one to shoot him down. August watched his partner slowly stalk across the street, her graceful fingers deftly knocking an arrow to her bow.

Keira and August had been something of an item at one point, her dainty smile and fierce personality making her completely irresistible to him. The Chraonos laws were clear, however, stating that August must marry a woman of nobility since he was sworn to king Que'thalias now. Though August had grown up the same way that Keira did, he was now a noble and she was still a servant. August did the next best thing and accepted her into his honor guard once he himself had attained knighthood. Who knew what the future would hold?

He shook his head and brought himself back to the present. *Stay focused, fool!* Using the moonlight and his ears as his guide, the shadows proved to be August's greatest ally as his own senses intensified threefold, the dim silhouettes of his comrades barely discernable amidst the raging squall. *How do I distinguish friend from foe in this snowy gale?* Rushing forwards, he spotted them.

Orvindrin was crouched down behind the ruins of a building, his crossbow held in the crook of his arm as his fingers numbly tried to reload his weapon, his hood pulled back to show a strained face. Towering above him was Blair, fending off two harrowing soldiers that fought in lockstep. His glaive flashed and pierced through the darkness, the blade rarely missing its mark. August smiled; they were still alive. Feeling his blade and his heart throbbing with the same intense trance, August felt a daze descend upon him as his mind focused on the one thing he'd sworn to his king that he would do: protect one of his heirs to the throne.

Lurching forwards, August embraced the frosty wind as his boots crushed the snow in each careful step, his weapon ready to taste some warm blood with its icy tongue. He would slay any that tried to harm the future queen. August's pace increased. Ever so slowly the trance washed over him, bathing him in hostility and malice, partitioning his mind to fear no one and nothing, and to harness pain and death as his own sovereign. August was sprinting, the startled face of the first warrior just a distant blur as August's crisp blade pierced the man's head, blood soaking through the snow in a violent shower.

He leapt in the air, the pommel of his sword smashing down atop the second soldier's head, the man falling to his knees. His feet coming to rest in the snow, August brought the blade down across the back of the soldier's neck, the man's head flying up and then coming to a stop just a few paces from where the owner's body lay. All was still. Gazing up into the sky, August felt his breathing return to normal, his mind once more returning to the stillness akin to a frozen pond.

"It was perhaps for the best that these insurgent knights faced their end here. They would have harrowed us our entire journey if we'd tried to just escape instead." Valindria stated, hand coming to rest on his shoulder.

Raising his head slightly, August could just make out Lacretia nestled in Valindria's arms, her tiny hands grabbing for the dancing snowflakes. The sight inspired him. Good men may have been lost here tonight, yet hope still clung on August's heart. If only just. *These band of rebel soldiers, these are once men that we'd fought alongside not so long ago! And here we are this night, slaying them because we refused to pay them their dues after the war. I make myself sick.*

"If you'd just led an honorable life and fought for the glory of the king," August whispered to the broken corpses, his hands shaking from the bitter bite of the earth. "You'd have had a glorious end. Not the death of a traitor." Orvindrin spoke up, the slender boy appearing at his side. "Isn't that the problem though, sir? They *did* fight for the king. It was us that didn't honor our side of the bargain. We used them."

August ignored the boy, instead staring at the dead soldiers' faces that were forever burned behind his eyes. *That's the path we're all doomed to, the path of least resistance. You stray but a little, and you're met with destiny's vengeance. If there's anything I've learned, it's that you adhere to where you're supposed to go. There are no choices here. The crown has little patience for independent thoughts.*

Crunching in the snow. "Who's there?!" Orvindrin yelled savagely, bringing his crossbow around in a violent arc. A giant bellow escaping his lips, Blair leapt off the craggy boulder he'd been balanced on, crashing haphazardly beside his two comrades, his great braided beard billowing wildly amidst the crisp wind. August simply watched as two dim figures sauntered slowly into view, the chaos of the storm concealing their identity.

From what August could tell, both figures wore the same gilded armor, beautiful greaves constructed from gold and silver, with intricate designs carefully scribed into the alloy. Both soldiers also wore the same overlapping metal boots, both dyed deeper than the heart of night. Neither wore a chest plate, however, only deep blue tunics with elbow length gauntlets. What caught August's attention the most, however, was the headband each warrior had around their forehead; black circlets that looked forged from the murkiest of metals.

The circlet that the warrior wore on the right had a beautiful raven etched into the circlet; the other had a wolf. Both wore hoods. The one on the right raised his arm. Ever so slowly, faint and shadowed forms began to appear on the edges of August's vision. Concealed warriors were making their presence known but staying well enough back that August couldn't form a calculated, precise battle plan. These soldiers were no fools.

Raising his voice, August bellowed through the sleet. "If it's our lives you want, I suggest you lay down your arms. I outnumber you three to one." If weapons weren't any use, then bluffing would have to do. An invaluable tool when used properly. "I know you carry only a handful of men with you, August Castner. I also know what you carry. Or more appropriately, who you carry. Lay down your weapons, and we'll talk. We have a proposition for you."

Drawing his sword, a wicked-looking long blade, the man let the tip gently waver in the air, his gaze locking onto August's with a remorseless passion. "The alternative could mean the loss of a very young princess. The choice is yours." I hold too precious of a life to act reckless. A smart tactician knows when to withdraw as well. His fingers finding his frozen belt buckle, he numbly let it drop into the snow, his swords and pouch falling as well. He nodded his head. "We'll listen, then."

CHAPTER TWENTY-THREE

Pieces of the Past

"So? What's your story?" Aeven Kvalheim demanded, arms crossed and fire touching his eyes. The group had made it to a small cavern on the outskirts of Calder, but not without a heavy price. A group of Goldenfist specialists had gotten the drop on them, and now both Thrush and Kindraya were out cold. The modest fire broke the looming silence as it crackled. "It was you that they were after, not Thrush and me. I heard one of them call you out by name. Come on, man, speak up."

Rykin Denedrin was sitting cross-legged on the ground, across the fire from Aeven. He wouldn't divulge why the Goldenfist was chasing him. Instead, he poked around in the fire with a stick, staring down at something unseen. Aeven tried again. "I know that your with the Azure Skulls, does that have something to do with it? Did you steal something that was important from them?"

Finally, Rykin spoke up, his eyes alight with passion and hate. "Did *we* steal something from them? You mean like their entire livelihoods? Their *future*?" Rykin stood up, hand on the hilt of his weapon. "You're the last person that should be asking those kinds of questions. Tell me, how tasty were your *meals* that were *cooked for you* while you were out there in the dugouts? Because my can of beans was just simple *delicious*."

Aeven's head hurt from the constant barrage of hail and sleet, of the on-setting winter storms intent on making the trek as miserable as possible. His back, arms, and legs ached from carrying his best friend across his back until they could find a safe haven. Most of all, his heart hurt from the constant worry for his friend, her mind slipping in and out of consciousness.

Rykin and Aeven both had been applying salve to their friends' wounds, but with little to no success. No apparent progress was taking place.

Aeven realized that the only thing that was going to heal the pair of them was something that they just didn't have; time. It had been three days since that dire battle, three days of being hounded by agents of the Golden Fist Corp. The last of the h'arai had found her way to the bottom of the salty canyon only yesterday, Rykin's sword proving too much for the petite girl to match. It was only a matter of time before more agents appeared. Only a matter of time before both females of the party found a permanent sleep.

Taking a deep breath, Aeven shouldered Rykin out of the way and made his way to the back of the cavern, checking on his friend for the umpteenth time this night. Minutes past without another word being spoken, and then Aeven arrived at a decision. "I'm going to tell you a little bit about me, just so that we better understand each other."

Aeven's voice filled the small cavern; glad that the deep darkness was there to hide his twisted face. "I graduated from Fort Leign, the Chraonos Knighting academy only three years ago, obtaining knighthood and honor for my family, and soon after, glory. I proved my worth time and time again, reigning peace over destitute soldiers and conspirators, never giving myself pause. I wanted it all. When my adopted brother August, and soon after, my younger sister Arma, attained knighthood I strived even more to outshine everyone.

"My father, Athrim, was proud, but told me I was a loose cannon. Told me that I needed to slow down. I was cocky enough that I thought that he was jealous of me, of my skills. I had to prove myself. I thought it had been fate when a courier of the Goldenfist Corp darkened my doorstep one cold night, his light taps at my door a wakeup call. The Corp had a new program in development, he had told me, one that required the greatest of fighters. Naturally, word had spread of my finesse, my career as a seeker of peace. That wasn't good enough for me though. I had wanted more, and I got my wish.

"I'm ashamed to say this, but I didn't even give the academy a second thought. Not one hour later, I abandoned my knighthood, abandoned my family and my duty as the protector of the king's heirs to attain something even greater. I was to become a h'arai.

"The first step into Tai'drasial was a mistake. When I rode through those oval gates and dismounted in the depths of Region Eight, I had no idea how deep I was falling. The Goldenfist had gathered a handful of the most finesse, graceful soldiers that the Citadel could find. One was a descendant of the lost Kal'mara nation; another was a remnant of Aivunall. Each of us having something to prove, an inner fire that wouldn't burn out. Not two days later, we were put into training, each with our own instructor.

"If I described their methods they used as harsh, if I described the soldiering as cruel, unkind, or callous, then I wouldn't be doing the regiment justice. I can't describe the… onslaught… each of us went through to obtain what we wanted most. We were an anomaly in the city, something that should never have been allowed to walk under the light.

"The very first exam in obtaining h'arai status was none other than crippling that barrier in our mind that regulates our body's energy, infusing each point in our body with both lyvah and nyvah. It was ecstasy. It was ecstasy, and yet, each of us slowly started to realize a cold fact. We were an experiment. How would the human body function with surreal amounts of power coursing through its veins? So, when you see a soldier with its skin glowing slightly golden, or a soldier with eyes that absorb the light of day, just keep this in mind: your comrade, me, is one of the prototypes of those cursed, poor souls.

"I was second best, and that was a bigger blow to my ego than walking away from knighthood. We battled each other countless times, probably numbering in the hundreds. We fought in controlled battles, of course. In some fights, only nyvah was allowed, and in others, lyvah. Sometimes neither was allowed, and occasionally, *both* energies were required."

"Hold up, hold up." Rykin interrupted. "It's common knowledge that a person cannot use lyvah. It drives the mind insane, rots the body. So how did you manage it?"

"It only rots the body because it is pure astral energy. There is nothing wrong with it. In fact, it is probably the *purest* form of energy in existence." Aeven countered, "even more pure than nyvah, or the caordin'torr."

Rykin threw his hands up in the air, "now I know that you're lying to me. Do you think I'm a fool? The caordin'torr is the cleanest energy known to man. It's irrefutable."

"The caordin'torr is corrupted with the will of the chorr'gall, just as nyvah is poisoned by humanity. And nyvah is part of what makes up the caordin'torr, which makes it doubly dangerous. Will anyone handling nyvah become tainted by it, because it isn't pure? No, of course not. For eons mankind has used nyvah without a backlash. No, the reason that humans cannot harness lyvah is because we, ourselves, are not pure enough to handle something so *divine*."

Rykin splayed his hands out in front of himself. "Okay, then I give up. How did you do it?"

Aeven smiled in the shadows. "The solution to using lyvah is so simple, and yet none had thought to try it until recently. It was more of an accident than anything, really. Think of lyvah, nyvah, and the caordin'torr as a human body. Lyvah and nyvah are the arms of the body, each one always helping the other. The caordin'torr is the body itself, being a pillar for the other two forms of energy. When all three are combined, you have a *whole*."

Rykin stared at Aeven, puzzlement marring his face. "What does that even mean. Did you even answer my question? I cannot tell."

"I did, and I did not. Once I get to know you more, perhaps I will speak in a plainer tongue. For now though, let me continue my story. In any case, eventually we divided into factions. All of us were still friends, but immersed too deeply into training to take notice of every other trainee. H'arai may have been divided amongst themselves slightly, yet they were still whole in the eyes of others. The populace feared us. Peasants, soldiers, merchants, it didn't matter. We had free reign throughout Tai'drasial.

"Despite all that, we were ultimately still tools for the Goldenfist. We were assigned duties and missions just like any other soldier. And it was here that everything changed. Perhaps it was fate that landed me in that meeting, or perhaps I had someone watching over me that dark day, yet when the Goldenfist Corps head administrators held their annual assembly, I was one of two posted at the entrance to keep the peace. The other, naturally, was Curasi. Before that day I had never seen, much less met, the man known as Secledrin Gauge. Other known figures were there as well, such as Venegas—one of the last war heroes of the Barbrosion War—and so was Yoredrail Beign, one of the Goldenfist Corp head scientists.

"Perhaps it was an oversight on their part, or maybe it was a test to see where my loyalties truly resided. I'm a Lionrose, much as I'd lost sight of that small fact. For hours on end they discussed their plans for soldiers being deployed, which strategists to capitalize on and where to station them and so forth. And it all eventually came to the same result: Chraonos was going to burn and with it every city and citizen in alliance. The Goldenfist was finally finished with the king, he could offer them no more.

"My heart screamed at me to just get out of there, and I listened. As soon as darkness fell that night, I bolted like a rabbit towards its burrow. The Goldenfist Corp hates my family solely because of me. I was a turncoat, choosing family and honor over prestige and glory. I raised the alarms the moment I breached Chraonos, holding audiences with all manners of nobility. My father included."

"A former h'arai, I had guessed as much. Your precision in battle is too exact to be otherwise. Your skin and your eyes, however, proved my theory false. Your features look... normal." Adjusting his seating and taking a deep breath, Rykin continued. "I assume I'm missing part of this story?"

"Yes, but until you spill your guts about yourself and what you're up too, that part of the story will remain hidden. Now you know me just a little better."

Rykin nodded, his eyes not doing a good job of concealing his true feelings; the man showed fear. Inhaling deeply, the crusader ticked off each finger on his gloved hand, his voice remaining calm and even. His face said otherwise. "We have seven warlords tearing this land asunder, vying for power." He ticked another finger, "we were witness to the sky'un'grael releasing a beast upon the land," another finger came up, his voice strangled and rough. "lastly we have our two closest friends shaking hands with death while we're dancing in these mountains with those rotten Goldenfist agents. I fear we may be treading water by pushing further."

For a long moment all was silent, Rykin staring down at his boots in misery. Finally, he divulged a little bit of himself. "What I fight for isn't so easily answered. What do any of us fight for? I suppose that you can say that you and I are more alike than you realize. My reasons for fighting date back to long before I was born, to a time when history made a bit more sense. When justice and peace was something that one cherished. You've heard of the fortress of Aivunell? Of the shattered nation of faith? That's where my lineage lays, where my ancestry takes root. My great grandfather, my ancestor, was lord of Aivunell at that time, his son was the head warden, his daughter was the supreme scout of the citadel of Aivunell. My family was respected, and not without cause.

"We held peace in not only the city, but of the whole land itself. Like the knights, the wardens were upholders of justice. Baron Vradran, my great grandfather, foresaw a land of tranquility, his ambitions of the purest kind. Holding alliances with Flayre'song and Scarrow, Baron Vradran sent an emissary to the great city of Lillien'thel to start the treaty process of enacting an alliance with them as well so that they would be better equipped to defend the North. He held the ideal that with enough lords' fighting for what was right and true, the land might see an age where infighting ceased to exist.

"They were welcomed with open arms, and even more importantly, open to negotiate an alliance. A grand festival was held for all within the alliance; the Festival of Shards, it was called, for each shard of Pry'ama that was being united back together for a common purpose. The king was livid. Conspiring against the crown, he sent three armies against Aivunell. My great grandfather was still in Lillien'thel when word got to him of what was happening. Even riding the wind wouldn't have been fast enough. He rode his steed into the ground to try and save what he had staked that treaty on, but naturally, it was to no avail. My blood and those few poor souls that managed to make it out of that cursed slaughter alive are all that remain of us.

"That was my creed when I enlisted with Chraonos. I fought for them with my entire heart, envisioning a Pry'ama where we didn't have this infighting. The nobles had called on us when they needed us most, and we answered the call! We *won* our battles, brought victory to Chraonos, no, to Pry'ama, and you know what happened once the war was over? Us commoners were thrown out into the streets like dogs! You ask what I fight for? Here it is. I fight to right wrongs, and oppression is no exception.

"I'm telling you, Aeven, that we've found something that could very well turn the tide of this malicious war. Ashenfelter, that's where we are headed. Denarius was only in the middle of telling us what he'd found when Javin made his appearance. Bloody bad timing, that."

He must be talking about a sky'un'grael. It's too big of a coincidence to say otherwise. I must remember that above all things, I'm still a mercenary in all of this. Leading the life as a knight defending other people who would rather live a lie wasn't fulfilling in the least. Nobody cared about honor or trust. Living the life as a h'arai was just as bad, people dictating to you where to go, who to follow. Pushing you to your limits and not for the sake of achievements. No, pushing you so that you'd be better equipped to destroy people. No, not destroy—slaughter. *I may have breached that barrier in my mind, but in so doing, I'd torn myself apart. I dare not tap that reservoir ever again.*

My father had fought for the king. I'd fought for the king and was rewarded with spit in the face. No, my contract was to recover the sky'un'grael for Lord Kaosa, now its to destroy the very man that hired me in the first place. I signed that agreement in blood; his blood. *What would Rykin think if he knew that I was travelling to Calder to slay someone else that had taken the sky'un'grael for granted?* Can you be swayed from this, Rykin? I know what it is that you seek, and I can promise you that you will regret ever laying eyes on it. You remember the beast that slaughtered Denarius? That was a beast born of the sky'un'grael. That's the name of what you're looking for, right? A sky'un'grael?"

Rykin's face lit up in surprise and then immediately became subdued. "You're a very smart man, Aeven. Too clever. Just think what would happen if one of those beasts was on *our* side? We could change the tide of war. No, we could *fundamentally* change Pry'ama *from the ground up!*"

Aeven snagged his own orb from its harness on his belt and wedged it deep down into his pack. Rigidly standing up, Aeven gave his comrade a heavy pat on the shoulder. "I'm sorry for your losses, friend. And yet I'm sorry for your ideals even more. I apologize if this sounds harsh but abandon the sky'un'grael. You're trying to fight a war where you aren't even aware of which side you're on. Do you even know the sides? My advice, if you were to ask, would be to tread softly and go fight a fight where you have a chance at winning. Go fight a fight where you aren't trying to battle the planet itself. Remember that still waters run deep. Those sky'un'grael aren't to be taken lightly. I'll take first watch."

Leaving the brooding man in shadows, Aeven perched himself at the edge of the maw of the cave entrance, finding a slight crevice to protect himself from the deluge of the ever-present storm. Aeven had a sinking feeling of what he was to face in the morning, and he wanted to be as prepared as possible for any outcome. So, he would wait for everyone else to make their move before he made his.

CHAPTER TWENTY-FOUR

An Invitation

August Castner's boots crunched underfoot in the ever-present snow; this was a city where spring and summer ceased to exist, save for a couple short months of the year. Even the hardiest of trees dare not grow in the heart of this this icy tundra. Ruins of rime lay scattered before him, the moon no more than a hazy, frozen ball of ice in the shifting sky. The sounds of his comrades heavy breathing resonated all around him, and yet the soldiers that August was trying to pinpoint were akin to specters of the night.

"Give it up, August." One of the knights before him yelled over the din of the wind, his arms crossed and eyes speculating. "I know what you're trying to do. We can't all stand out here in this blasted wind, sleet, and snow. At this rate, that princess will freeze to death and you'll save me the trouble of having to be the one to assassinate an infant."

"How can you possibly live with yourself?!" August spat, taking an involuntarily step forward. "She's just a baby! Why her? The king has many heirs, some that I'm sure that I don't even know about. What is so fascinating about Lacretia?"

"You're a smart man, August. Shrewd, but lacking the capability to think for yourself, apparently. I used to admire house Kvalheim. In fact,

I still do, in a way. Despite what happened to your family, your brother and sister carved their own paths to walk. You're different, though. You are still the king's lapdog, even after he hung your father for all to watch. I should ask, how do *you* live with yourself?"

"I was adopted into the Kvalheim family, not born into it. Where was I to go after Athrim was hung? He should have made better choices in life. It's as simple as that."

"Wow. Woe be to the loved ones that cross you. After adopting you into their family, raising you and being there for you, you cut them off at the drop of a hat because of convenience? I thought that this tundra was cold, but it pales in comparison to your heart. No, you fit in with the king's circle perfectly."

"Enough!" August screamed, "what is it you want? Why are you here?"

"No!" Horneld Kielmen screamed back, sword now out before him.

"Don't you understand yet? How many generations of commoners are going to have to go through the strife that we did before someone finally steps up and makes a *change*? Despite the fact that we've been treated like animals for the last several generations, we still stepped up and helped the king when he asked for it.

"We *fought* for him, spilled blood for him while our own was being spilled. And our thanks for saving him from the king landing Pry'ama into yet another civil war? Our thanks for stepping up when he'd just driven a wedge amidst the knights? It was to throw us out into the mud, without food, without pay. Several families had lost their main provider, most of them starved to death. What was left of them turned into street rats, having to steal, cheat, and lie to just fill their bellies with food. Moldy food, inedible food at that."

Horneld Kielmen sat in silence for a moment, hand brushing his chin in thought. And then he spoke, just barely audible over the wind. "It's time for change, August. We've had enough. As long as the king keeps producing heirs, then there will be *no change*. History will invariably repeat itself and the commoners will continue to live a life of misery. That is why I am here, to finally change the future for the better."

August didn't know what to say. No, the king should have handled the war better, after all the commoners *were* a crucial piece of winning the war. King Que'thalias should have given a short speech in recognition, or perhaps handed out a few Scarrownian brass coins to appease them. But the glory and gold that they felt entitled too? "Come now, Horneld. Let's not get carried away here. Let's just call it what it was! The commoners fulfilled their duty to the king, and you guys impacted history. I'm sure the historians will pay you your dues in a blurb or excerpt in the Chronicles of Chraonos. But let's face the facts. You and your kind are *commoners*! The king barely respects the knights that are sworn to protect him, why would he go out of his way to help the likes of *you* and *your kind*? Of course you and your kind aren't animals, but you were surely bred to manage them!"

Horneld stood there dumbfounded, his mouth opening and closing as his face changed from scarlet red to a deep purple hue. "What?! How *dare* you mock us! All of you knights are the same! All cut from the same cloth!

Why does one's status have to determine what life they lead?! It's a system that only benefits you and your kind!"

"I'll ask one more time. Why Lacretia?" August breathed into the frigid air. For a moment, all August could see was the flurry of thousands of snowflakes dancing before his eyes, snowflakes that reminded August of all the lives that lived within Pry'ama; each different, and yet all the same. Horneld kept silent, but the second knight finally spoke up.

"We are neither servants of the king nor dogs for the rebel factions. Think of us as soldiers for a much higher force, and we'll leave it at that. The importance of Lacretia is much more important than you think, and not because she's the heir for a corrupt king. The fact that we sought you out and are telling you this should mean something to you. Lacretia's role in this story is not yet over."

Soldiers of a much higher force? Who can be more important than our king? I will not succumb to this fool's idle talk, nor will I break under his pressure. I cannot forget where my loyalty truly lies. I promised that I would protect Lacretia, and I will honor that vow. "I will protect anyone that was trusted to my guard. I will not allow the princess to fall into your hands as leverage to use against my kingdom or to be used as a trophy to be shown off. I'll only say this once. Forfeit now or die in anonymity!"

Ever so slowly the clicking of Orvindrin's crossbow being cranked back drifted to August's ears, and with it, the chaffing of steel against leather followed suit as his two warriors armed themselves. It was like a symphony of death with the howling of the wind and the smell of blood in the air. The man spoke once more, all traces of mirth absent from his voice. "You bend down to retrieve that sword of yours, August, and you embrace your own death. I will riddle you with arrows and leave your corpse here in this forsaken place you call Aivunall. You can believe me when I say that it'd mean absolutely nothing to my lord if I disposed of you now. Those are his words exactly. And yet, I wasn't ordered to kill you either, which is why I'm giving you this very last chance. Disarm yourselves and hand over the heir. Now!"

"Wait!" Elevia boomed out, the petite manikin strolling between the two men as a taskmaster would have intervened between two snarling dogs. Her black cloak billowed up in the wind, allowing all to see her new armor that Rennon had helped her adorn. Her chest plate was glossy silver, almost akin to a mirror. Her greaves were just as fine, the same stunning silver metal with matching boots that rose to her kneecaps. And atop her head sat an elegant circlet, blue gems embedded in the diadem. Woven into her hair were shards of crystal, whether they were the same compound as what she had slung across her back was yet to be seen.

Elevia started to speak again and Horneld interrupted her. "This is ridiculous. We obviously hold the higher hand here, knight, and it wouldn't mean a bleeding thing to me if I left you for dead. And yet, you still defy me. Your father said that this would happen, and I was a fool for questioning him. Pick your jaw up off the ground, boy. You think that us finding you way out here in the tundra was a mere coincidence? Who do you think told that priest who to give Lacretia too? And where to tell you where to go?

"Even from the grave, your father holds all the cards. Only now we play for keeps. I hold this letter for you from Athrim Lionrose to you. I'll give you ten minutes to read this, and if your mind isn't made up by then, then I slaughter you and your crew and take Lacretia anyways." Fishing a folded-up envelope from inside of his cloak, the man steadily trudged forward, his footfalls seeming to take a lifetime. Snatching the letter from his grasp, August turned a blind eye to the man and scrutinized the large drop of sealing wax holding the envelope shut. Not only was the imprint exact, but the sigil of the lion head was turned forty-five degrees to the right as well; it was his father's letter.

Crushing the wax with his thumb, August took a step back and shielded the parchment from the snow with his back. The ink was barely legible. *August, my son, you holding this letter can mean only one outcome has transpired, and I'm proud of you for holding your ground with the king's daughter. Lacretia means the world to us all, literally, and metaphorically. It breaks my heart to have to say this, but I have one last order for you before you let me rest in peace. I need you to leave Lacretia in Horneld's care. There is a lot more to this puzzle than meets the eye, and I can give only a few sketchy details for safety's sake. I hope you can forgive me.*

The reason that Gordeved, Bayenen, and I were hung wasn't because of deeds that our families had committed, that was a bald faced lie so that too many lords wouldn't ask questions. Quite the contrary. No, the three of us were part of the Kaulo'hul. Think of us as men of revolution. Initially, we performed research of our own amidst the Alenikor ruins. We discovered several underground studies. Half of them were caved in, and decay and nature had claimed a few more, yet the three of us were able to infiltrate the remaining catacomb. Secrets, August. I can't write this down for the sake of your safety, yet I hope that you understand when I say that Lacretia needs to go with the Kaulo'hul.

The hands that would slay her aren't the ones that you'd see coming, nor for the reasons that you'd expect. I've left a gift with Winlios for him to pass on to you, a gift that I think will change the tide of this war. I leave this last order with you and a blessing. I won't fracture your loyalties any longer; I know that you fight for the king with all of your heart. Make a decision, my son. Choose a side. Your father, Athrim Kvalheim

"I know this isn't how the stories turn out," Horneld spoke, his hand coming to rest on August's shoulder. "Yet if my words mean anything to you, your father was the most respected man amidst our ranks. The

Goddess Knight's blood truly did course through his veins. He was pure and true. A lot of him I see in you. This is the gift, which we were instructed to give to you." Reaching into his belt pouch, Horneld came to reveal a dark black metallic headband clutched in his grasp, a replica of the very ones that Horneld and his comrade, Winlios, sported. Bringing his hand up, the man let the piece of equipment fall into August's outstretched hand.

August gazed down at the craftsmanship and saw the etching of a hyena. His thoughts were muddled and confused. The king's orders for August and his adopted father Athrim's orders now clashing within him like oil and water. They did not mix. Lowering the circlet into his cloak's deep pocket, August spoke out to the man that was intent on reading August's actions. "Athrim and I have nothing in common. He may have adopted me, yet my own blood runs with my own heritage. He turned his back to my king, a deed I cannot forgive so easily. How could he call himself a Knight? You want Athrim's son? You want his blood? Look for Aeven. Look even for Arma, his daughter.

"Athrim's letter means nothing to me. Less than nothing. As for Lacretia, I will hand her over to you because I have no choice. If my squad dies here, then Lacretia will disappear without anyone being the wiser. I will persevere. Know this, however, if I ever see you again I won't obey your demands. We're not on the same side. I still fight for our king."

"Your king." Striding over to Valindria, the hooded man grasped Lacretia and secured her with the flailing blanket, the slicing wind only an afterthought to the overwhelmed group. "Even if Que'thalias found the darkest, most maggot-infested hole and starved to death there, it would still be too good for him. You want answers, knight? You want to know why your land is falling apart? Look in the ruins of the realms that once prospered. Scrutinize the Chraonos Chronicles for the inconsistencies and anomalies. Just don't look too closely in those you trust." And with his parting words, Horneld and Winlios lumbered darkly through the snow ridden gale, disappearing swiftly from sight, their squad following in their wake. August fell to his knees and punched the snow.

CHAPTER TWENTY-FIVE

Disgraced

A high-pitched voice bellowed loudly into the vociferous crowd, head crooked regally, and script held out before him. "Our great majesty, king Que'thalias of Chraonos, has endorsed the Goldenfist of a new program." The Chraonian was dressed in bright red attire, the feather in his hat bobbing this way and that as he read his spiel into the meandering crowd of people.

"His greatness is offering you this remarkable chance to serve our country proudly with nary a regret! Absolute strength. Beautiful endurance. The Goldenfist Corp is asking you to be a willing participant for these increased capabilities, and in return, you get to serve none other than our righteous sovereign in his overall plan to right this country's wrongs! Transformation is needed. Transformation!"

Stationed above the bustling throng, Aeven held his unyielding stance as his eyes prowled the local commoners, ignoring the internal bile and self-loathing threatening to drown him in remorse. Crooking his head to the side, Aeven encompassed his partner with a perturbed stare. Curasi Enlan was clad in his majestic purple h'arai uniform just as Aeven was. The uniform was standard now that the program was successful. The outfit was crisp, cunning. It had an edge to it that drew the eye. Both Curasi and himself wore a button up uniform that had a high collar, and black cloaks that spilled down to their feet.

Curasi was lean, with an edge to him that dulled even the finest of minds. Intelligent was another word used to describe his friend, and if anything, his friend was considered swifter than an arrow when loosed on the battlefield. The man had dark hair and even darker eyes. Returning Aeven's stare with one of his own, the man continued his own perusing of the crowd, his finger's sliding up and around the hilt of his long sword in an endless dance. Aeven surmised that restless could be another word used to describe his best friend. Shaking his head, Aeven kept vigilant.

"If you so desire a chance to embark on this wonderful, fulfilling experience, please step around me and line up next to those wagons stationed just over there. I will choose ten of you for each cart, fifty volunteers overall. Remember, this process for enhancing your body's capabilities method that take at least one year. If you have any good-byes to family members, any past dues or business you need to take care of, see to it now! And remember, the king thanks you." Majestically stepping down from the makeshift platform, the young lad nodded once at Aeven and Curasi and then disappeared into the milling crowd of people.

Thankfully, there were no uprisings from the commoners to arbitrate this time. Stepping forward, Aeven clutched the thick railing of the balcony, his attention focused on the shredding loss of humanity these poor souls were about to endure. Without having to glance over, Aeven knew his comrade was right beside him, and likely as not, his gaze was just as intense as his was, if not more so. Aeven tried to spark a conversation.

"Do you remember the first words that you'd spoken to me when we first enlisted in the academy? They were powerful, though I thought you'd been half-joking at the time. You said, 'If ever you doubt in what you're fighting for, don't interrogate your commander. Instead, interrogate that doubt, and then confide in your commander.' True enough words that I have tried to live by, Curasi, and yet I am at a loss. We, the Goldenfist Corp, are gathering and creating soldiers in mass, and yet we are lacking purpose, we're lacking direction, and most of all, our commander is sitting on the very throne of this country, leaving the decision making to corporate heads that have an overabundance of both money and ambition.

"I might have disregarded my title as a knight and embraced this more ruthless path to glory, yet my ideals haven't changed in the slightest. What do we do, Curasi? Who can we turn to if not our very king?" For a breadth of a second, there was complete silence from his friend, the rumbling from the crowd below drowning out all other sounds. And then spoke, his voice calm and direct, "The problem is that, well... you're seeing this situation as a problem. And it isn't. When the king's attention is so spread out that he is forced to focus on only a few choice problems, that leaves the rest of the issues completely wide open. Sure, we can't kneel before the king and ask him to interrogate these thieving specialists, we'd be hung before the next sunrise. I realize that we have an internal rot that needs cleansing.

"However, there are other forces moving in our country that hold power besides the Goldenfist Corp. I hear whispers on the wind that there are gathering warlords in the southeast of Chraonos, knights of a sort that are here for only one true purpose: to right specific wrongs. I don't know a lot right now, but I do know the name of the rogue that's supposed to set the cards in motion. He's already recovered his artifact that he'd been searching for, the last missing link to this puzzle. It's now just a matter of time before he acts."

The southeast of Chraonos he had said. "I see those cogs working in your head, friend, and I'm going to warn you now that if you bolt for those righteous zealots, you're going to have a dozen Goldenfist hounds on your heels. You and I know too much for us to just waltz out of this situation. We'd be a liability and you know it." Curasi's gaze hardened, his eyes scanning the entire crowd below. "It won't be long now before you and I are deployed across the country as these new soldiers are trained on the more basic assignments. Our abilities are starting to shine and are lighting a beacon for those in power. If you were to make a move, do it soon, Aeven because my doubts, such as yours, are in need of interrogating."

Nodding, Aeven's spine straightened just a little bit, his stance altering a fraction. Hearing his friend's advice was exactly what he needed, it came down to him making a choice. His mind made up, Aeven voiced a question that he knew he should have asked at the beginning of the conversation. "This infiltrator's name, Curasi, what is it? If I'm to locate these warlords, knowing this man's name might help me make the right connections."

"This is a name that you will want to keep to yourself for the time being. It could get you hung if said in the wrong place. Remember that he's an infiltrator, a spy that we don't know who is loyal to quite yet. His name, or alias I guess I could say, is Boru. I don't know much more than that, I'm afraid."

Skillfully crouching atop the cliff's precipice, Aeven breathed lightly and laughed loudly as the harsh, cutting wind-ripped at his hair. Large beads of sweat rolled down his face and body as his smile covered the beautiful site below, again laughing uncontrollably. Alenikor could be seen far below, the small town located on one of the three peninsulas that connected Pry'ama to the Moorlands. Alenikor was a sister city to two other towns, Ashenfelter and Theoden'shorb, all three nestled in the deep south of Pry'ama.

Aeven vaguely remembered visiting each city with his father when the knights were used mostly for diplomacy. Each of the sister cities were similar, and yet each had distinctions as well. Alenikor's roots were deeply rooted in hunting, fishing, and living off the land, whereas Theoden'shorb instead cherished books, sanctums, and thinking problems completely through before making a rash decision. Ashenfelter, surprisingly, was different yet still. Because Ashenfelter was bordered by the Krogvettian hills, and not far from there the Scarlet Churchyard, they focused mainly on military and keeping the peace. Aeven had always been amazed by the new recruits from Ashenfelter, they always turned out to be the hardiest of soldiers.

Desperate for a sanctuary for Thrush, any sanctuary for her to revive and recover, he'd taken the largest gamble of his life and abandoned finding Kaosa for the time being. Aeven had given his word that he would recover the sky'un'grael for him, and had practically signed his writ in blood. Now that Kaosa was doomed for his soul to become exchanged, there was nothing more that Aeven could do for the time being besides put him out of his misery. Thrush's life was at stake and that is what counted right now.

Straightening from his crouch, Aeven backed away from the crag's edge, his mind returning to his abandoned comrades. It had been days since that night with Rykin, the crusader having disappeared before the next dawn, and Aeven couldn't blame him in the least. In his heart, Rykin was fighting for the Azure Skulls and Aeven represented the very thing that he fought against. Rykin had his duties to his beliefs just as much as Aeven had his duties to his own motives.

Aeven studied Thrush, ensuring that she was not getting any worst. She was sprawled next to him in the dirt, her gentle breathing a very good sign. It meant that he still had time. The crunching of dirt behind him. "What's this I see?" A voice breathed, a chilling tune resonating from above Aeven's roost. "A mercenary and his hound, caught off their guard. Shame that." As quick as Aeven could hunch over Thrush in a protective stance, a shadow from above fell over them both. It took a moment for Aeven to realize that there was more than just a single soldier near them; there were half a dozen of them, all with skin that glowed slightly and all wearing their smart, h'arai uniforms. The Goldenfist had found him at last.

"Aeven Kvalheim, you are hereby named a heretic by the Gale Court itself. Give yourself over freely and the court promises you will have a good death, a knight's death. Show the least bit of resistance and you will be executed where you stand." Aeven had no great words to speak here, no practiced speeches or powerful quotes. In Aeven's book, it wasn't what a man said that spoke of who he truly was, but more along the lines of how the man said it. So, he let his whole demeanor say it all. Sliding his hand down to the hilt of his bastard sword, Aeven let his breath even out, his stance widen. Letting his gaze fall from the circle of men closing around him to Thrush's tarnished face, he made his choice. But then again, there had ever only been one choice from the beginning: to fight.

His bleary eyes rising to the blonde woman's venomous smile, the hooded lady's voice rang out. "So, you've chosen your fate."

"I am a Kvalheim. My outcome has already been chosen for me, as I'm sure you already know. 'A Kvalheim will weather the storm, and rise afterwards to shine forth his new light.' My father Athrim would quote that to me when I faltered at a challenge in life, so I tell this to you now: I am not scared. Death will be a blessing for this lone Knight of Chraonos." As if on cue, a raven started cawing from the crags above, its call echoing across the canyon walls and down to the city below.

"So be it," the h'arai spoke, her boots planting themselves a stride away from Aeven. "You are a relic of the past. *Knights* are no more." Her hand swept towards her comrades, soldiers that were keeping their distance from the pair of them. "Us, h'arai. *We* are the future. Passion." She spat. "Chivalry. Justice. All dead sentiments."

Despite his situation and his imminent death, Aeven tipped his head back and laughed, a laugh so loud that it startled the haughty agent. "I'm sorry but come challenge me when you've completed the Gauntlet of Sedethal. Come tell me how great you are when you've faced three h'arai who've completely opened themselves to lyvah and you have naught but your sword. I—"

Aeven's entire body started to quiver and shake, his insides feeling as if someone was taking a hammer to his bones. He started to scream, a fierce, inhumane scream that resounded through the far-reaches of the canyon.

Falling to his knees, Aeven's hands grasped his head, pulling at his hair. His nails scoring his cheeks with vivid bloody indentations. His vision darkened, a soft, sharp voice pierced Aeven's mind, a voice wanting to be heard. Aeven's inner voice, clinging on to his sanity before he lost his self again.

Opening his eyes to small slits, Aeven's vision took in a warm bask of calm blue light pulsating, enveloping Aeven with its calming, soft caress. His nerves, his muscles, his mind, all were dowsed in a cool frosty bath of hope. Coughing and spewing up his meager dinner from last night, Aeven's eyes sought out the cause of his azure radiance and found the source; his sky'un'grael was lit up just as brightly as he was.

Closing his eyes, Aeven stood up, lurching forward in the process. *Accept me, let me help you.* A voice whispered from within, *and in return, I will be your mentor, your master, even. Fuse with me.*

"No, you don't understand," Aeven spoke out loud, whether to the voice or to the h'arai, he was beyond his caring. "I bow down to no one! I am my own master!" Snarling, Aeven burst forward, ramming his shoulder into the woman, her face twisting into an ugly contortion of fear and pain. His fingers wrapping around her throat, Aeven kneed her twice in the stomach before she could react, her groans and yelling cut short; he tossed her to the ground. Backing up to his partner, Aeven scooped up Thrush in his arms and spun around to the cliff's edge, his boot catching a rather heavy man in the groins as he tried to make a grab for them. "I bow to no one, fools. You'd better get used to that." With one last look over his shoulder, Aeven sprinted to the cliffs edge, his eyes closing as he dove over.

CHAPTER TWENTY-SIX

Fugitive

You need to bond with me.

No! I will not. I don't understand who you are, but I have my own willpower, my own ambitions. My own love. It is mine, not yours. Do you understand?

It is natural for you to defy me. At first, every warrior does. But like the rest, you will come to realize you do not have your own free will, your own aspirations. Even who you choose to love is not your choice. Even now, plummeting to your death only leaves you with one ultimate choice. Am I correct?

Yes.

Then, you understand. You may smash yourself against the rocks, for your life is but your own. But your friend? You hold her in your arms and taking her life is not your choice. No, you are left with that single option, your past resurfacing yet again, to dictate what your so called free will of the present may or may not do. You agree with me, don't you, soldier?

Yes.

You are lucky; there is a shield around you, a barrier. It's as if I try to reach out and grab you and I cannot. It's like I...pass through you, as if you are a shadow. I will leave you be for now, but you will not always be so lucky. Your defiance will give way to reason. That I promise you. Soon, we will be one. Again.

Opening his eyes, the cold frigid rush of the wind beat at Aeven's whole body as if he were a cheap ragdoll that was thrown over the cliff's edge. The sharp, craggy rocks far below were rising toward him fast, too fast for Aeven to try and think of any other options except the obvious one. There was but one decision he could possibly make. His soul wracked with pain as Aeven forced his mind to open that sea of energy that he had closed so long ago, a path he had deterred from to save his own morality.

Inhaling, his senses told him to concentrate on the air around him, the sweet-salty taste of ocean strong in his mouth. Aeven smiled. Looking down on the top of Thrush's head, he watched as a shroud of flickering yellow energy whipped around them, harnessing them as a mother would a newborn child. Their descent slowed, the sharp crags taking their time on meeting the two warriors. His eyes widening, Aeven cut off an oath as his and Thrush's bodies caught what Aeven never saw coming.

The roof was rotten and the shingles mangled, but crashing through the wooden beams of the obscure building was almost too much pain for Aeven to endure. His last cognitive thought before darkness enveloped him was why someone would build a shack on the side of such a desolate cliff.

A soft hand touched Aeven's bare shoulder, a finger tracing his eyebrow slowly. "Your friend thinks that my lavenders are pretty. What's left of them, anyways." *Thrush has always loved plants. She loves them because her mom loved them. How could you know that though?* Aeven sat up in bed with a jolt, his mind and cognition snapping back into focus like the sharp crack of a whip. "Thrush is okay! She is awake?"

"Yes, she is fine. She recovered faster than you did, if you could believe it. You took most of the damage, your body sheltering hers as you toppled through my medical shelter and right through the floorboards. You landed in this poor building's catacombs, crushing my white roses. It's okay though."

Aeven couldn't speak; he was so happy. Thrush is alive and okay. His eyes settled on his caretaker, and he was positive that he felt something lurch from within him. She had curly, dark hair that had a streak of red from within. Her eyes were passionate, bright blue with such a sense of love and caring that Aeven couldn't pull his own eyes away. The young woman wore a flowing white robe with slashes of blue across the hem and sleeves. Aeven pulled himself to the side of his narrow bed and slowly sat up.

"My name's Aeven Kvalheim, and I suppose I owe you a thanks."

"Janelle Lloyd." She smiled, "and no, you don't owe me anything. Truth be told, I was in the middle of prayer when I asked for answers from my God. You were delivered and are no longer lost." The whole meaning of her comment not totally lost on Aeven, he broke his gaze from the beautiful young woman and wobbled to his feet.

"I might be lost physically, but you need to keep me out of your prayers. I don't mean to offend, but I've served this country passionately as a knight, I've crippled friends and rivals alike as h'arai, and I have scoured this land as a mercenary. I do not know which title I carry, but if there is a God, he closes his eyes to our world. All suffer, the way I see it." Very aware that he was walking around in front of Sadeline in nothing but his underwear, Aeven took to scavenging around the small room for his clothes and armor.

The room was simple, designed for recuperating patients, but a feminine touch had been added. Bright green draperies covered the windows, with deeper green comforters and pillows lining the handful of beds. Gentle light spilled in from the large oval window that was set far back against the wall, the weather outside calculating and brooding.

She spoke up, her voice unwavering. "I will pray for you anyways, Aeven Kvalheim. You've already been a blessing to me, and I want to return the favor. As for your friend, I saw her last walking back and forth on the bluffs, gazing at those temples rising out of the ocean. She seemed somewhat upset." Striding out of the room, she left Aeven to brood.

—∞—

The rocks were cold, hard, and wet. Climbing up the ragged rockface was tearing his gauntlets apart, yet it didn't matter to him. He just needed to see her. Hoisting himself over the last boulder, Aeven rolled onto his side and shielded his face from the wind's bite and the rain's rage. He smiled. "Thrush!" He bellowed against the roar of the storm, crawling to his feet. "Thrush, I've found you finally! I had to climb to God's doorstep, practically, but I found you."

Strolling to his best friend's side, Aeven laid his hand on her shoulder, his eyes gazing at what hers was so fixated on. Without looking over, she spoke. "I can't keep doing this, Aeven. I can't. You and I are fighting a battle that is trampling us to death. What happens when we recover the sky'un'grael? Who does it help? It doesn't help those destitute soldiers starving to death out there on the battlefield. Or those peasants? Each one of their farms is being raped with the ends justifying the means.

"Much as you hate to admit it, as much as you run from the truth, you are a knight. That's who you are. No, that is all you are. I was listening in earlier to you and Janelle, and I have to agree with her. You are lost. We both are." Drooping his head, Aeven knew what was coming before the words left her mouth, yet he knew this is the way it had to be. Fate was very compelling when it had to be, and despite how much you argued with it, and as much as you wanted fate to change, it still managed to sweep you under into a relentless current of unforgettable moments. Moments that always seemed to reshape what path you ended up walking.

"Kal'mara calls to me, Aeven. I know that we are partners and I love you dearly as a friend, yet I need to change for the better. I can become something more. If given the chance, I could liberate all of those imprisoned families that suffer from destitution. I could become… a knight… like you." Breaking off with a sob, Thrush threw her arms around Aeven and cried into his shoulder, garbled apologies and "I love you" breaking through. It was hard for Aeven to make anything else out because he was crying too. His throat constricted, Aeven let the distant beat of the ocean's waves speak for him, a constant reminder that though things may change from day to day, in the end a heart will never forget raw emotions.

The currents underneath is what really drives us. What is it that people see when they gaze upon me? I try and put forth a strong, vigilant demeanor because I'm the leader of our group, but people aren't interested in a leader's good, positive qualities. The public are drawn to your sins and downfalls. It irritates me to no end. I travel across the sea of Davalos to where this man Kordethion is supposed to be residing; word of mouth is that he has an artifact that is of the utmost importance. We will invite him on our quest. As I write this passage, I observe my fellow comrades lazing around this ship, and try to describe each of their fine, praiseworthy qualities to myself, yet I can't. Their own difficulties and sins stink too much. Yours truly, Aelora Aegus

"What an enlightening woman," Aeven mumbled, his thumb deftly flipping the wrinkled page. After Thrush's tearful departure, Aeven found the closest place to solitary peace he could think of in this undersized town, his own vision of his future now muddled and blurry. Perched in the drab lounge of the Gold in a Cup, Aeven added this dingy tavern to places he never wanted to visit again. Bad food. Horrible smell. And his mood was the worst of all, regret and longing washing over him like a lukewarm bath—he wanted Thrush back.

"If you see any of these six heretics, you will alert your town's official, you understand?" A voice thundered throughout the bar, several patrons making a point to ignore the man. Involuntarily, Aeven looked up from his book, dread quickly taking place of remorse. Goldenfist soldier. And he was hanging up some type of poster. Aeven never considered himself a coward, but by his standards he wasn't going to tempt fate by trying to leave right under this man's nose. Sliding further down in his rickety chair, Aeven waited until the soldier finished pinning up his shoddy artwork before making a move.

He knew it before he saw it; he'd be a fool to think otherwise. Aeven knew the dangers of being a mercenary, and now he is facing the repercussions. His face was the first of six lined up along the wall, and if one squinted hard enough, one could almost tell it was him. His eyes moving from left to right, Thrush's face was almost as ill drawn as his own—her head was way too big, and her eyes were drawn lopsided. Rykin was there too, along with Kindraya.

The last two drawings, however, took Aeven's breath away. Even if these final drawings were as shoddy as the first four, he could never mistake that beauty—Alletta Silversand, that beautiful lady he met when his voyage first began. The last illustration was of her co-owner of that inn, his name scribbled at the bottom of his face. Halaren McColllum, it looked like.

"You're a wanted fugitive, aren't you?" A voice whispered into his ear. Aeven knew the voice the moment she finished, yet it still made him jump out of his skin the way she could put so much resentment and accusation in such a simple statement. Women. Spinning around, Aeven would have laughed if the circumstances had been any different. Janelle had changed out of her magnificent robe, instead, adorning herself in green traveler's garbs with stout hiking boots and leather gauntlets. Her face was obscured, her jacket's deep cowl pulled way over her head, yet Aeven could still feel her baleful glare through the thick fabric.

Taking a moment to gather himself, Aeven adopted and disposed of a number of different ways of trying to explain his predicament. He finally settled on the truth, taking her hand and leading her out the door. "Here, take a walk with me." She was hesitant at first, and he could understand why. Not many girls would go out for a stroll with someone whose face was plastered on who knows how many tavern walls. He was a lot of things, but in his book Aeven was never the hopeless romantic.

Aeven's eyes scanned the nearby woods and decided on a patch of timber that looked somewhat secluded. Aeven finally let the truth spill out. "I am a mercenary, Janelle, pure and simple. I fight for money and for fame. I had prestige once and I had unlimited power before too; neither made me happy. I lost sight in what to believe in, and I even lost sight of who I was. I still don't know who I am.

"My partner Thrush and I were living the good life for about a year as mercenaries, raking in more money than we could spend. With every successful mission, our fame spread further, and our clientele got more dangerous. We wanted it that way. It was about six months ago that we got a request from someone that wanted a job done right and done discreetly, someone that is helping ravage Pry'ama. Thrush wanted to turn it down. It was stupid to even consider it. But, if we were successful, the man had promised he would deliver to this land what it desperately needed. Serenity. How can I say no to that? It was worth a chance.

"The object I was supposed to obtain is called a sky'un'grael. An artifact that should have remained in the depths of the planet. Apparently, there are eight of these items, each one tied to the mythical fighters that had travelled with Aelora Aegus to see the Father of Elders. I can't tell you the details on it, because frankly, I don't know myself."

Janelle finally spoke up. "I do."

Aeven was taken off guard. "You do what?"

"I know some of that story. We have some historical tomes here that talk about Aelora and her exploits. Her group, her squad; they were called the 'Harbingers of the Condor, and she called her fighters 'Condor Guards', or 'Alatheons' if were speaking in Vulganlung."

"Vulganlung?"

Janelle let out an exasperated sigh. "Yes, Vulganlung. We speak common tongue, right? A language that all can understand. But it didn't always used to be that way. Our language has evolved over this last era since the Great Shattering. Vulganlung then is what we now call common tongue."

"I see." Aeven stated solemnly, leaning back against a thick tree. "They were…Harbingers of the Condor? So, they *knew* the one from the Azure Augury? The one that is supposed to save mankind, and then turn around and scour them from the planet?"

"Well, actually the augury is somewhat hazy when it comes to that, specifically." Janelle admitted quietly, "The condor was very important to them, they named themselves after him, after all. It does state that 'A condor is born once more, to lay claim to the spoils of war', and it is well known that Pry'ama was being ravaged by many wars at that point in time. Between Aelora naming her squad after the condor and the quote I'd recited from the augury; one would *assume* that the condor had finally emerged."

Aeven nodded. *So, her group had a name. The Harbingers of the Condor. So that means that the ones that are trapped within the sky'un'grael are the Condor Guards, or the Alatheons.*

"How close were you and Thrush?" Sadeline asked quickly. Glancing over, Aeven saw her face turn bright red from deep inside her hood. *That's what she got out of that whole conversation? I don't think I will ever understand women.*

"We were close. We travelled together for more than three years. I don't think there was a secret about each other that we didn't know. We weren't lovers though if that's what you mean. Love makes things... complicated. When you follow the path of a mercenary, I've learned that the simpler life is the better."

"That isn't true. Life gets too simple, and it gets boring. You should know that one, Kvalheim." A voice hollered from somewhere deeper in the copse of woods. "Come now Aeven, don't look so surprised. These mountains are only so big, after all."

"I was wondering when you were going to show up again. How long have you been tracking me?" Putting himself between Janelle and the voice, Aeven clasped his bastard sword and slowly inched around. In Aeven's book, protecting the women was first on the list, even when it was from someone that you had come to trust. Sometimes you could never be overly sure.

"You can relax, I'm here as your ally and nothing more." Finally reaching the duo, Rykin sauntered over with hands up and away from his weapon. "Despite your harsh words Aeven, I hold nothing against you. I should thank you, to be honest. I took your words to heart and was traveling back to Chraonos as fast as possible so that I could try to save Kindraya. I had an epiphany. I spotted half a dozen black crystal wolves while exiting the Azaevia Mountains, all vigilantly protecting something dear to them, as you were doing for Thrush.

"I wanted to be stronger, to be faster, so I could do what you are doing now. I wanted to be more like you. I don't know how it happened, but I think the wolves... felt... my longing. Felt the ambitions of my heart. It spooked me, to be honest, but I felt the need to show these wolves that my blood was as good as theirs. That I meant what I felt. I sliced my palm open and laid it atop the first wolf I could reach. We became one."

Putting two fingers to his mouth, Rykin gave two sharp whistles. Watching the changing shadows of the grove, Aeven gawked as two barrel-chested wolves came slinking out of the trees, both as black and shiny as the clearest night. Shaking his head, Aeven addressed his friend.

"Rykin, you don't want to be more like me. That I promise you." Aeven shook the man's hand anyways, introducing Janelle to his former partner. "Where's Kindraya? I owe her a thank you."

"Indisposed still. I was at the harbor, thinking, when I saw your friend disappear on a ship that was heading back to the mainland; I had a suspicion that you were close, and sure enough I found a healer that could direct me to you. I left Kindraya at the same medical shelter that you had been at. They give her about a week to recover now that she has the correct medicine."

Sweeping his hand at the two wolves, Rykin introduced his new partners. "This larger one here is Riley, his fierceness and pride make up for his tendency to jump into the heat of battle without a second thought. Kojack is the smaller one. He has wits and guile. Both are a force to be reckoned with." Smiling broadly, Rykin watched as the two wolves tussled with each other. It was like watching two boulders continually collide "Until Kindraya feels like her old snap fire self, these two are my comrades."

Aeven crossed his arms. "I thought that you had pressing business that just couldn't wait? What changed?"

"The Seven Devils are swarming the base of the mountains, and you were right. Calder is their primary base. They are rebuilding the ruins into something more permanent. I couldn't even get close to what I was searching for, especially with Kindraya slung across my back."

"Is that a fact, Rykin? I don't know what scares me more. The fact that I find you here with Aeven Kvaldheim, or the fact that you are standing within a hairsbreadth of an experiment that was supposed to have been killed off long ago."

That voice! What are the odds of her finding me leagues from her inn?

On the outskirts of the Azaevia Mountains, no less. Interesting, that.

"Alleta Blackiston. If I could describe my surprise at seeing you, I would.

I have so many questions for you that I don't even know where to start. And, experiment?"

"Then by all means, let me start." Alleta refuted, striding the rest of the way up to the group. "It was no easy task trying to find you. You can rest assured of that. I had help, though. Halaren McColllum was an experienced tracker before settling down with me all those years ago. Right, Halaren?"

"Hmm" was all the sound that rumbled out of the thick man's throat, his stocky body strolling out of the brush not ten feet away. From what Aeven remembered of the man's soiled garbs from before, what he wore now was magnificent in comparison. Dark deep green trousers and boots, with a chain mail shirt and a fox skin hat to top it off. At his side hung two throwing axes and what looked like a dirk. Alleta was no different, her beautiful robe from before replaced by worn, polished silver armor that gave off a sparkling aura when amidst the sunlight. Her scaled boots and circlet atop her head made her seem majestic, both a bright golden color. Alletta sported a great sword that had vines sketched into the spine of the blade.

"Despite how I found you, mercenary, I made a proposition to you all those months ago. Do you remember? The night that you left our inn, it was raided by a squad of Goldenfist specialists. They were searching for what I assume is this." Alleta patted a slight bulge in her coat pocket. "The raiders torched our inn to the ground. I can't get into detail now, but I suspect that you are a very large piece of this puzzle, Aeven. Both you and that girl there."

Aeven of course laughed at that, and, by the look Alleta gave him, he knew that he was going to have to give a short explanation to appease all that were present. They deserved to know the truth. "Yes, Alleta, I am a large piece to this puzzle, and you were right in calling me for what I am. From what I've learned over these past few weeks, I am part aor'sii, though my body does not show it. There are several sky'un'grael scattered across Pry'ama that contain beasts from within. Oh yes, and I somehow was able to summon a castle from thin air, though I do not remember most of that." Grasping Aeven's hand, Alleta cut him off and led him further up the winding path, her other hand beckoning the others to follow. Aeven couldn't imagine what their group would look like if they happened upon a group of travelers. "We do not need unwanted ears to hear such important information, Aeven." She said quietly. "I have a gift for you."

A voice boomed out loudly. "There is another site I know you guys will sleep fitfully. Prison. Each of you are to throw down your weapons and come quietly. I don't have the patience for any more dog fights. I will riddle each of you with holes if I even smell foul play in the air." Stalking toward the ravaged group from the head of the trail was a man Aeven hadn't seen in more than seven years. *So, you're still alive, my friend. As am I. You know what the outcome of this encounter will cost for both of us.* Aeven thought bitterly. Forcing himself to the head of the group, Aeven drew his sword and stood face to face with the man that had mentored him in the worst of times.

"Curasi Enlan. Judging by your clothes, I see that you're still a h'arai hound, sniffing after whatever his majesty points at. You sicken me, friend." Spitting out his last words, Aeven chose a fighter's stance and brought his sword up. Pieces of his past were clicking together fast, and he was going to have to fight his way through to the very end.

"No, it wasn't his majesty that pointed at you, Aeven. Not this time." Drawing his own double-edged sword, Curasi took a step back and used his other hand to wave in the air. Not less than a dozen other soldiers slipped out of the trees surrounding the group, each bearing the offset eyes of the h'arai, their smart uniforms and black cloaks a complete contrast to the small, sleepy town. "You will come with us and preferably quietly. If that means killing you, I won't lose any sleep over it. I've lost fourteen soldiers between the four of you. Javin, take these prisoners into custody."

Javin. Vivid images flooded through Aeven's thoughts as he watched the man start to push his way towards him. Aeven was forced to back away from the malevolent soldier that had stepped forth, the man's wry smile destroying any doubts that Aeven might have had. One single h'arai would have been a handful for this entire group, Aeven knew that. But a dozen? Janelle's quiet sobs broke out into ragged screams when she realized what was about to happen.

"Javin, silence her first! We don't need her spooking our troops into a frenzy of mindless violence." *You realize that she is one of us?* That same mysterious voice spoke within Aeven's mind, *She is further along. She has accepted her fate and is protecting her priorities. Aeven, I will lend you my aid and you will witness my power. Have faith in your abilities to come!* It took a moment for Aeven to realize that the voice that was addressing him was internal, yet when it dawned on him that another offer of power was being made, his voice thundered out.

"No! Leave me alone!" Javin abruptly stopped, his eyes dropping to Aeven's waist and then back to his eyes. "You? You're...one of us?" Rushing forwards, the man grabbed the front of Aeven's armor and pushed him backwards into a thick tree. Rebounding backwards, Javin punched Aeven in the face and then kicked him in the stomach, once, twice, three times. Toppling to the ground, Aeven grunted, the wet soil tasting foul and rancid. He tried finding his feet and was met with a pommel into the side of the skull. His vision blurred. Resting his head in the dirt, Aeven watched as the ground around him began to bathe in a pulsating cerulean light.

I want to make a difference. Aeven thought quietly.

Then, so be it. The voice answered.

The commotion around him was all but a distant annoyance as Aeven's mind reeled with memories that weren't his own, from pain and pleasure that was all but foreign to him. Aeven's eyes fixating on his orb, he watched as the sky'un'grael didn't just glow, but instead burst out in a brilliant, blinding array of hues of blue that Aeven was temporarily blinded, as was Javin. Thousands of bright stars danced in Aeven's eyes, darting this way and that, forming a dome around the entire grove.

Staggering to his feet, Aeven sidestepped a thrust of Javin's blade and was thrown backward from the impact of another soldier being thrown into him. Tumbling across the ground, Aeven came to a rest with what he was sure was a broken arm. He didn't know how long he laid in that awkward position, but after a hand brushed his shoulder, it yanked Aeven back to the present. Aeven tried to shake the hand away until he saw that it was just Janelle, tear stains marring her face. She leaned in close.

"You're going to start to transform, Aeven. It's going to hurt at first, but there's no getting around that part. This is what we were created for." Aeven had so many questions to ask, yet he was sure that this was absolutely the wrong time to ask them. Glancing past Janelle, he saw that every one of his comrades was engaged in a valiant effort to stave off the imprisonment. Rykin was furthest from where Aeven laid, his great-ringed sword and two wolves keeping a small handful of the h'arai at bay.

Almost directly behind Rykin was Halaren and his partner, Alletta, the two fighting in such a smooth and careful circle that it seemed as if they were dancing instead of combating. Curasi and two other h'arai were at the center of this, and despite his friend's skill, he knew that it was only a matter of time before Curasi lost his temper and ordered his soldiers to use what force they were bred to harness. They were holding back.

It was obvious that Curasi didn't want his prisoners killed off yet. He still saw a purpose for needing them alive. Javin was the one that worried Aeven the most, for he knew what power that man harnessed. Aeven counted it a blessing that Javin was still a man at this point; it meant that maybe his team still had a chance of making it out of here alive.

"I am going to save us." Janelle breathed, her hood falling back from her face. Raising his hand to snatch her arm, Aeven's fingers grasped the air instead. He couldn't get up fast enough to stop her from striding up to Javin, her abrupt appearance causing him to falter in his careful steps. Her voice rang true. "We are done here!" She bellowed, her voice taking on a surreal tone, her command echoing throughout the trees.

Her gauntlet rose into the air, her glove swathed with dozens of wisps of radiance. Up into air the wisps rose, Javin's sword swinging wildly at the woman who confronted him. Janelle dodged, twisted, and turned, her boots bringing her slowly backward as Javin inched his way forward. Her arm never left the air, even more wisps ascending at a faster rate. Finding his own feet finally, Aeven grasped his sword and jumped into the fray, his sword drawing out in time to parry Javin's unpolished strikes.

Javin was too wild for Aeven to control in a fair fight, and he could feel the match start to spiral out of control, fast. With each thrust of Javin's blade came a delayed parry from Aeven's sword, and as much as he tried to fight at his best, Aeven was starting to feel the wear and tear of the past weeks. It wasn't long before Aeven's armor had a large gash down its abdomen. Aeven soon sported a clean slice near his left eye and a fractured shoulder that left his right side almost completely useless. *This man is too feral for me to contend with!* Aeven thought recklessly. Feeling his final blow was at hand, Aeven chose a stance that would give him the best opportunity for a counterattack and watched as Javin inched forward, his face grimaced in a frown.

Falling to a knee, Aeven couldn't keep his legs underneath him any longer. He watched as the thousands of wisps above the tree line started to move as a whole. Gradually they descended, moving in a vast circular motion, much akin to a colossal funnel. All movement on the battlefield came to a halt as the swirling mass picked up speed, torrents of wind and green light creating a spectacular but dizzying effect. Choosing his moment, Aeven came to his feet and dove at Javin, his hand grabbing the man's collar. Startled, Javin cursed as Aeven used what energy he had left and spun the man around and over his shoulder, slamming the soldier into the soil.

Positioning one leg into Javin's back, Aeven implemented a chokehold and held firm despite his screaming shoulder. When the man passed out, Aeven pushed him the rest of the way to the ground and hobbled up. The closest wisps were now only feet above the ground. All came to a stop. The wisps stopped moving, the fighting came to a standstill, and even the very wind seemed to hold its breath. The only movement was the bright, hazy illumination of the wisps. And just as soon as they arrived, the jaded wisps dissipated, leaving tens of thousands of glittering sparkles cascading to the dirt. And at the center of where the funnel of wisps had been now soared a very tall woman, her wings as green as the darkest of forests, and both beating in unison. Aeven was witness to a reincarnation of an aor'sii descendant.

CHAPTER TWENTY-SEVEN

Deception

Aeven's steps faltered, and his hopes soared. Beating her elegant wings below the tree line was a miracle of itself and a personal savior for Aeven and his friends. Her armor that she wore was constructed of light itself, her boots and horned helmet celestial masterpieces. She sang. She sang a song of hope, of love, of life, and of holiness. Her majestic voice carried throughout the grove, nature itself humming along with her, creating a beautiful melody that captured every combatant's attention.

Janelle spiraled downwards to the ground, singing a song that none but her could understand. She touched down upon the soft earth, the very grove seeming more vibrant, more alive. Stepping ever so slowly forward, her voice picked up its reverence and grew louder. Aeven couldn't breathe. His head pounded. Aeven sputtered and knelt to the ground. *I am released.* The voice stated bluntly.

Screaming, every pore of Aeven's body felt as if it was lit afire a hundredfold, his eyes burned with the passion of a wildfire, and his mouth felt charred and burnt to a searing crisp. Janelle's voice continued, her song reaching a new level of beauty and radiance, combining with the screams of Aeven to create a haunting tune of pain and passion.

"I am free." Aeven panted, his body slick with sweat and dirt. Leaning over him, he watched as her palm came to rest on his heaving chest, his body still wracking with spontaneous spasms. When she stood back up, his eyes never left his chest. Her handprint was imprinted right above his heart, a glowing tattoo that gave off a dull shine. Janelle smiled. Her song ebbing away, all eyes warily watched as she rang out true and strong.

Janelle grasped her sword, a foot-long blade of crystal imbued with light, the chegus stabbing the air in front of her and giving a momentous battle cry. "We need to finish this!" Aeven heard Curasi yell distantly, the sound of battle once again ringing throughout the grove.

"Do not let that *beast* alter your command! Heed my words and fight on, my brethren!" *You and I are one now, Aeven. Choose your identity as you see fit, yet just know that you are no longer who you once were. That man is shattered and dissipated. We are on a new path, one of righteousness and glory.*

I am not your plaything! I tread my own path and make my own choices! Clambering to his feet, Aeven knew that he was different the moment his body's momentum pitched him forward and onto his face. He felt sleeker, in a muscular way. His abdomen, his biceps, his body felt more definitive.

Aeven heaved himself off the ground yet again, frowning as he watched his breastplate crash down into the mashed mud. He tried to regain his balance and toppled forward himself, landing in the mud beside his armor. Aeven realized it was his back that was throwing off his momentum. He felt top heavy, as if he had sprouted…*No!* They were very faint behind him, small bursts of a hazy, blue outline of wings, but it was enough to throw him off.

"Easy, Aeven, I know what's going through your head and you need to calm down. Regain your composure! Help your friends." Feeling Janelle's hand grab his own, Aeven felt his anxiety recede slightly. He made it no more than three steps forward before the entire grove was blasted with light so intense that all had to drop their heads in their hands, weapons falling into the muck. Minutes crept by as his eyes burned from within, and a handful of minutes more before he could blearily see a few feet ahead of himself. All soldiers were forced to regain themselves. A sickly laugh erupted from deeper in the grove, something crashing towards them at a slow pace.

This beast was tall, easily topping out at seven feet. His skin was a sickly pale yellow, warts and stretch marks enveloping a good part of his body. The beast was fat, to put it lightly, with only a single loincloth to cover his exposed areas. His eyes were dull, small sockets peeping out of an overly prominent brow line. It had a flowing black beard, the facial hair cascading down his chest in an unruly manner. The beast plodded slowly up the trail. All fighting ceased. Almost as one, the scattered h'arai and Aeven's squad formed some silent agreement that this new beast was imminently more dangerous and worth battling than each other. Curasi and Aeven stood shoulder to shoulder with each other as Javin broke through the final tree line and into the grove.

"We need to right this wrong," Janelle stated, her eyes holding energy that sparked with anger and righteousness. Aeven glanced from side to side, watching as each of his team members took up the lined rank, the h'arai vigilant and ready. "God has dominion over this land, and we were meant to be here for a reason. We will show this beast what our divine God does to men that stray from the path of holy righteousness." Sadeline finished.

Aeven's thoughts were slightly different. *I don't know about divine Gods, but what I do know is that this creature is vastly different than the 'Condor Guard' that Janelle had mentioned. Are these what the Alatheons truly are? The Chronicles hint that when Pry'ama is under the most distress, the Condor will be born again and swoop in, intervening and saving what is left. The Condor Born of the Sea. One would assume that the Condor Guards would be at his side, and yet here one is before me, a revulsive, twisted nightmare of what it once was.*

Aeven's first footfall was for the first step it would take to cleanse Pry'ama of its blistering cysts of poison and subterfuge. Aeven's second step was for the bravery he would need in the upcoming months, for the valor and truth to confront his king and instill justice that was long overdue. The drawing of his sword, the pace Aeven's sprint took him was just an afterthought as his boots pounded forward, toward the very facet of evil that threatened the planet itself.

Javin all but came to a grudging halt as Aeven drove his knee into the heavy beast's gut. Gurgling in surprise, the beast stumbled backward, giving Aeven the chance to drive home yet another blow. Backtracking, Aeven ducked as the beast tried to slap the back of Aeven's head, his movements slow and uncoordinated. The Alatheon tilted its head back and laughed a deep, fiendish laugh. And then Javin was on him, the great beast darting forward and throwing too many jabs for Aeven to contend with.

It wasn't long before Javin landed a strike of his own, catching Aeven across his jaw. And before Aeven could get in a counterattack, Rykin was on Javin like a wasp. His sword strikes were so straight and true that it would have had a taskmaster nodding in approval. Not one of his blows landed home, however. For each strike Rykin threw, a chaotic wisp was there to take the hit, shooting off a shield of black energy.

Aeven added his own sword strikes to the impending tempest of blades, his own meeting the same resistance. For every sword swing that the duo threw, a handful of wisps were there to meet it. Again Javin laughed, his guffaws made all the more terrifying because of the screaming voices from beyond the grave that resonated throughout the grove. Javin's lust for violence and death intensified.

Grabbing Rykin by the top of his head, Javin whirled him in a haphazard semicircle, nonchalantly tossing him into the side of a shattered tree. Rykin went down hard, unmoving. Curasi and his team joined Aeven, the stupor of having to fight such a monstrosity slowly dissipating from the ragtag squad. The h'arai bombarded the beast from afar with crackling orbs of nyvah, the wisps becoming just as much of a deterrent for the energized weapons as they were for blades. The orbs of nyvah rebounded off of the smoky shields and crashed into the eldertrees, blowing them apart into wooden shrapnel.

The attacks only seemed to invigorate the twisted Condor Guardian. Alleta and Halaren appeared behind the lumbering beast like spirits from the grave, each of their weapons swinging with fanatical force. No longer did the wisps just defend; they started to retaliate. Aletta and

Halaran's swords both crashed down in unison at the Alatheon, and there was a sudden explosion of darkness as a wisp combusted in front of them. Aeven bit back a curse as they were both blown backwards, smashing into stumps and boulders.

It seemed like only a handful of moments before Aeven found himself alone against the beast, dozens of unconscious bodies sprawled all around the fighting pair. Raising both arms into the air, Aeven set his bastard sword in position to impale the beast, even if it meant leaving himself wide open to be gutted like a fish. *I have a plan! Obviously, I can't strike it with my sword, and I can't chance opening myself up to lyvah and nyvah; I cannot lose myself again. But I have one more tool at my disposal.*

A dazzling pit of light erupted from the ground directly below Javin. As if on cue, Aeven tumbled backward, hands coming up to guard his eyes as the pit of light sent tendrils of radiance to envelope Javin. The beast roared and bellowed, screaming for his deity to rescue him from persecution; none answered his call for Aeven knew that the Father of Elders was not forgiving of failure.

Ever so slowly the beast was pulled down into the pit, his shrieks hitting a whole new octave once his head slid downward. Raising his sword upwards in a yell for joy and triumph, Aeven's hand delved into his cloak pocket, squeezing the HALO that Golbart and him had found months ago. *Not too bad for a novice Trapsmith, eh?*

So much energy being consumed. Such a waste! Aeven couldn't help but think to himself. Javin's whole body started to quake as the beast stopped sinking into the pit of light, his head shaking back and forth as his body shone with a vivid smoky light. *Javin's energy is just so... tempting. How could that man waste so much potential power?*

Aeven found the situation humorous for some reason, chuckling at the Alatheon and what his greed had done to him. Before Aeven knew it, he was laughing, laughing at the man that was so determined on using the energy of the planet that he hadn't even considered watching out for the Father of Elder's faithful servants. Aeven buckled over and gripped his sides, his knees hitting the dirt and his palms splayed out in front of him.

Javin rose out of the hole of light, floating before Aeven, his beady eyes bouncing back and forth as his jowls quaked with obvious fear. Aeven's laughs were hysterical now as the beast hung before him, Javin's skin pulsing with that same smoky light, pulsing with the beat of Aeven's heart. Energy pushed against Aeven's mind, enticing him, calling him to taste once more the power that coursed through the veins of the planet.

I need that energy, I need to become one with the chorr'gall, I need to become one with the planet. No, I need to become one with the Father of Elders. The core of the planet beckons me, begging me to fuse with it and give it new life. Shall I answer it? Aeven distantly heard himself think, his body rising into the air to become parallel with the twisted Alatheon .

Energy crashed into Aeven's mind, whether it be energy from himself or the energy before him he knew not; he just knew that the euphoria of it felt so good. It felt good, and yet something niggled at the back of his mind. It was like an itch that he just couldn't scratch.

Aeven laughed harder, his head finally falling back as his laughs thundered into the sky above. His hair felt longer, felt sleeker and different. Wings of azure energy spanned out behind him, giving him flight. Smoky light spilled out from his pores, illuminating the decimated grove and those that were sprawled within it. *I am a chegus. I have come for my energy.* Grasping the tendrils, no, the very fabrics of what created Javin and his amnesty of a body, Aeven ripped the beast apart with his bare mind, fusing the excess energy with himself to create something more. Something the planet has yet to witness. The Alatheon exploded in a shower of sparks.

—⚝—

Sambsyne couldn't believe his eyes, no, he refused to believe his eyes. Clasping the small, metallic chest that Tyniathas had given him, Sambysne soaked in the carnage below. Tyniathas was still adjusting from being free from his glass prison, but he would be a valuable ally in the days to come. The cockpit of the shuttle was cramped as all aboard crowded around the grimy windows. For ten minutes now, the shuttle has been hovering just above the swaying tree line, the spectacle below just distinguishable through the damp foliage. There was not a breath of disturbance as all watch what was sure to be a five-hundred-pound creature float up from a hole of light in the ground and then explode into thousands of wisps of light.

Aeven was hovering in front of where the beast had been floating, his head tilted back and laughing at something unknown. As if the wisps were synchronized, thousands of them rose high above the tree lines and far above the shuttle, what sunlight there had been quickly vanishing. The embers of energy remained high above for only the barest of moments before they came crashing back down through the brush and directly into Aeven's chest.

Aeven seemed to take the force of the impact well, his body only pushed slightly back by the recoil. Aeven's body started to glow a divine white, his indigo wings growing even longer and more elegant, his very body growing taller and sleeker. Even Aeven's hair was changing from short brown to long and cerulean blue. *This is not coincidence.* Sambsyne thought bitterly to himself, *the last reason that Pry'ama had been cast with a plague was because of creatures like Aeven. Creatures that absorbed such momentous items of power like the sky'un'grael and the planets energy to become something so much more than a Chegus.*

Sambsyne remembered the dozens of nations were reduced to rubble in only a few days' time, nations that tried to fight back but were obliterated by an entity so powerful that it could blow a chorr'gall out of the sky with a few mere thoughts. Aeven's laughing grew louder, more boisterous, and deeper, his body turning around in midair and his eyes settling on what looked like an honest to goodness female chegus.

The woman stepped forwards as if pleading with Aeven about something, her hands waving desperately around and face bright red. All aboard the shuttle gasped at the same time as the woman turned to run and she suddenly exploded in a shower of yellow sparks. This time Aeven did not absorb the wisps, but instead he watched as the wisps blew through the ground towards a destination unknown.

All was still. Aeven hung in the air, his laughing seeming to have subsided, his eyes searching for something beneath his very feet. The rest of the warriors that had been involved in the battle lay still on the ground, whether unconscious or killed Sambsyne knew not. The ground began to grow darker, more rugged, and grey. The foliage, grass, and trees withered in place, and instead was replaced by dozens of glowing, iridescent eggs that had veins growing up and around them, veins that were reminiscent of tree roots. These eggs were about the size of a man's head, and the shells on them were opaque.

"He isn't just using nyvah and lyvah," Sambsyne gasped suddenly, realization hitting him like a rock in the side of the head. "He's *tainting* the very pool that the planet, no, that the Father of Elders draws from! These creatures that he's breeding are pockmarks on humanity! They are like the ca'or but...different. Corrupted. The ca'or are supposed to be creatures of the planet, born and bred to protect it from humanity overreaching. But now...Aeven could very well have confused them, changing their genetic structure into something more bestial. As long as these *things* live, the planet will slowly be dying of poison, and it will no longer have creatures to defend itself."

"Why would he do that though?" Scaldala asked, "he'd only be hurting himself, after all."

"I think it's because it is the one way to get back at the Father of Elders for trying to corrupt *him*. This way, Aeven has a legion of creatures at his disposal to ravage Pry'ama, and the other chegus, the aor'sii, the sii'morth, even the Father of Elders, will not be able to touch him due to nyvah and lyvah being infected. They can certainly try, but it will be of great detriment to themselves. What's worst is that the chorr'gall will be *bathing* in this tainted energy, they won't have a choice with being bound in their temples and all. If they are released...there won't be a Pry'ama left to speak of.

"The only good news here, if you can call it that, is that with Aeven corrupting the very energies that make up Pry'ama, he himself won't be able to use it much more either. I think here, what we are seeing with those larvae, is the beginning of the end, but it will take him awhile to build up enough of his legion to overwhelm Pry'ama. Pry'ama has *some* time, but not a lot. What he's done is leveled the playing field."

"So as of now, he is untouchable." Scaldala breathed, fingers grasping his temples. "And tell me, when are you ever going to open that blasted chest? You've only been holding onto it for weeks now."

"This chest is not for me. I am only its keeper. And are you okay? Why are you grasping your head like that?" Sambsyne asked, concern touching his eyes.

"Yes, yes, its just…I just got a terrible headache. I'm sure it's nothing, however. Tell me, what do you mean that chest isn't for you? How do you even know what is in it? It hasn't even been opened yet!"

"Because this chest is something that I *do* remember, this chest is from the future from when I was supposed to be born. It is for the Condor when he is proclaimed. It is for him, and him alone. I am the caretaker of this chest until the time is right and the Condor is born."

"So Aeven never was the Condor." Scaldala breathed, "you could have fooled me. Does this happen in the future? With Aeven, I mean."

"No." Sambsyne stated solemnly, "this is unprecedented. Aeven never was in the future, far as I can tell. And if he was in the future, in *this* state of being, I would definitely know. He…he *shouldn't be here at all*. He is going to devastate all manner of life."

"Then it is time to go alert the high lords of Pry'ama. It is time to unite."

www.ingramcontent.com/pod-product-compliance
Lightning Source LLC
LaVergne TN
LVHW091718070526
838199LV00050B/2448